RESOUNDING PRAISE FOR
THE AWARD-WINNING NOVELS OF
ROBIN BURCELL

D0958600

By Robin Burcell

ROBIN BURCELL

THE BLACK LIST

HARPER

An Imprint of HarperCollinsPublishers

This is a work of fiction. Names, characters, places, and incidents are products of the author's imagination or are used fictitiously and are not to be construed as real. Any resemblance to actual events, locales, organizations, or persons, living or dead, is entirely coincidental.

HARPER

An Imprint of HarperCollins*Publishers*
10 East 53rd Street
New York, New York 10022-5299

Copyright © 2013 by Robin Burcell
ISBN 978-0-06-213354-0

First Harper mass market printing: January 2013

HarperCollins® and Harper® are registered trademarks of Harper-Collins Publishers.

Printed in the United States of America

Visit Harper paperbacks on the World Wide Web at
www.harpercollins.com

10 9 8 7 6 5 4 3 2 1

To Susan E. Crosby.
May you always find your Pansy Pot.

Acknowledgments

For Their Expertise and Guidance

I owe a debt of gratitude to the many people who helped me with details, advice, research, and support. If any errors are made, the fault is mine, and I ask you only to remember that it's fiction.

To Susan E. Crosby, who always has such good advice. I can't thank you enough.

To the wonderful women in my book club, for being my beta readers and offering great insight: Cindy Brink, Sharon Flemmer, Wendy Grupe, Liz Hittle, Wendy Johnson, Penny Lawley, and Michele Silva.

To FBI Special Agent George Fong (ret.), for taking the time to answer all things FBI.

To Colin Campbell, West Yorkshire police officer (ret.), for help with police procedure and traveling in London.

To Sergeant Dale Miller, Lodi Police Department (ret.), for assisting with information on bombs and explosives.

To Rhys Bowen, *New York Times* bestselling author, for vetting some of my British phrases.

To Twist Phelan, attorney, writer, and friend, for answering questions pertaining to law.

To DP "Doug" Lyle, MD, for taking time from his writing to answer medical questions when my various characters found themselves injured in the line of duty.

To my mother, Francesca, who reminded me of the wonderful places we'd visited in London and helped with a few key scenes there.

To my agent, Jane Chelius, always my champion.

And, of course, to everyone at HarperCollins who put in their time to make this book wonderful, and especially to my editor, Lyssa Keusch, who brings out the best in me.

For a Worthy Cause

To Thomas. A. Sanchez, "Thom" to those who know him well, for his generous donation to the Lodi Library. I hope you enjoy your cameo role.

THE
BLACK
LIST

1

FBI Special Agent Tony Carillo tossed his keys on the table in the entryway of his condo, dropped his coat over the back of the sofa, then walked into the kitchen. It had been one of those days, the sort where whatever could go wrong, did go wrong, starting with the arrest of the bank robbery suspect who decided to run at the last minute—right into an oncoming SUV.

Carillo opened the fridge, anticipating the leftover Christmas turkey dinner that his neighbor Mrs. Williams sent over, which reminded him that he needed to put a new bulb in her porch light. She was too old to be climbing up that stepladder, he thought, when he heard a rustling noise coming from the spare bedroom he used as his office. He quietly closed the refrigerator door, drew his gun, then stepped into the hallway, careful to avoid the one spot in the hardwood floor that creaked as he made his way to the back of the house. He paused just outside the office door to listen.

There it was again. The sound of rustling papers.

Finger against the trigger guard, he swung into the room.

His wife looked up, saw the gun, her eyes going wide as she dropped a book. "Tony . . ."

Hell if his heart wasn't beating out of his chest. He quickly lowered his weapon, holstered it. "What are you doing here, Sheila?"

"I—I was just looking for something to read."

He glanced at the papers on his desk, saw the envelope addressed to his former partner, Sydney Fitzpatrick, still sealed, thank God. Sheila wasn't exactly known for keeping out of things that didn't belong to her, and he casually straightened the papers, making sure the envelope was covered. "I mean what are you doing here? In my house."

"It's *our* house."

Not the conversation he wanted to have right now. "Until your lawyer finishes sucking me dry. You need anything else to help him accomplish that? Blood type? DNA sample?"

"This isn't easy for me, Tony." She tucked a long strand of blond hair behind her ear, her hand still shaking, probably from seeing him pull a gun on her. "I'd like to speed things along, especially now that I'm getting married."

"Word to the wise, Sheila," Carillo said, walking out of the room, trying to keep his temper in check as she followed him out. "Wait for the divorce to be final before you tie the knot. Less problems that way."

"You're such an ass."

"What are you really doing here?" He entered the kitchen, then looked back at her.

She turned away, unable to meet his gaze. "I need a place to stay until Trip gets out of jail." Jefferson Colby III—or Trip, as Sheila called him—was her current boyfriend. A real piece of work, this one, Carillo thought, arrested for allegedly embezzling money from his employer, a charity no less.

Carillo opened the fridge, eyed the six-pack of Sierra Nevada on the shelf, figuring it wasn't nearly enough. He grabbed a bottle, closed the door, then faced her. "No."

"Aren't you going to offer me a beer?"

"No, because you're leaving."

"I can't. There are people after Trip. They might come after me."

"So Trip *is* guilty of stealing money from his employer?"

"No. Of course not. But you don't understand."

"You're right. So fill me in."

"The charity he works for. He thinks it might be a front for some criminal thing."

"A criminal thing? Really, Sheila? Something beyond the fact Trip was skimming money from it?"

"It's like I'm talking to a brick wall! Why do I even bother? They set him up."

"Of course they did."

"At least talk to his friend in Washington, D.C., Dorian Rose."

"What is that? The name of a ship?"

"His friend who got him the job."

Carillo took a long drink, wondering where she was going with this.

"I'm serious."

"Dorian Rose. Washington, D.C. Anything else?"

Sheila narrowed her gaze, took a frustrated breath and said, "Dorian Rose works for a sister charity in Washington. One of his and Trip's friends was killed in a car accident after he found some discrepancy in the books and reported it. I mean, it was a real accident, so they don't know, but before he died, he told Dorian to have Trip call his brother-in-law in London and have him see if the same thing was going on there."

"What thing?"

"I have no idea. Whatever it was, Trip thinks it's going on here. And now Trip's brother-in-law won't call him back, and then Trip was arrested and I think I'm being followed."

Carillo stared at her a full second as what she was saying sunk in. "And you, of course, decided to keep all this from me because . . . ?"

"Trip told me I couldn't tell anyone. He said it was too dangerous."

"What the hell do I look like? A Boy Scout? That's my job, Sheila. And it helps when people tell us *exactly* what is going on so we don't *goddamned get ourselves killed.*"

"You're yelling at me."

"Yes, I'm yelling at you! What the hell were you thinking?"

"That maybe Trip would tell you?"

"Jesus," he said. "He's in friggin' jail, so I think the likelihood of him mentioning it to me is about nil. Which is not to say I believe you."

"Does that mean I can stay?"

He took a deep breath, then looked at his wife, wondering how it was he'd stayed married to her as long as he had. He'd loved her once. Hell, he still loved her, even though she'd slept her way through half of his friends over the years and, after the most recent round of counseling failed, he knew when it was time to let go. Past time. "You can sleep on the couch."

She rushed forward and hugged him. "Thank you, Tony."

"Yeah," he said, holding his beer away to keep it from spilling, and wishing he'd had the foresight to bring home a case of the stuff. "Write down everything you know about this charity, this Dorian Rose guy, how we can get ahold of him, and anything else you can think of."

Sheila took a pad of paper from the drawer, then started writing, and he tried to ignore the occasional tear running down her cheek, since each one made him want to drive out to the jail and strangle Trip until he confessed to exactly whatever the hell was going on. One thing was certain. He knew when Sheila was keeping secrets, and he was sure she hadn't yet told him everything—a fact confirmed the following morning when he discovered that not only was Sheila gone, but so was his ATM card.

2

Sydney Fitzpatrick tossed the newspaper on the coffee table, disgusted at the California State Legislature's latest efforts to balance the budget—the early release of prisoners into the parole system, because the jails were too full. Apparently someone forgot to mention to the lawmakers that they'd already laid off hundreds of parole agents earlier in the year due to lack of money. Never-ending circle, she thought, as her eleven-year-old half sister Angie rolled a tennis ball across the floor near the Christmas tree, hoping to teach her shepherd-mix puppy to fetch. But try as she might, Sydney couldn't stop thinking about the news article. The same thing was happening on the federal level, too, even at the FBI where she worked. They'd frozen all hiring, and she'd heard rumors that they were canceling the next recruit class for new agents.

"Watch, Syd," Angie said.

"I'm watching."

Sarge scrambled after the ball, stopped when his tail hit an ornament, turned, eyed the shiny orb swinging from the lowest branch, then jumped up, trying to nip it. Angie dove forward, catching the pup, shaking her finger at him. "No, Sarge. No!"

"Angela!" her mother said, walking into the room just in time to see her precious collection of decorations threatened by the dog's antics. "Be careful. Those are older than you are."

"Everything's older than I am, Mom. Maybe you should be more specific."

"Is playing with your dog outside specific enough?" she asked, constantly challenged by her youngest daughter, a change-of-life baby who was far too intelligent for her age. "Do *not* play near that tree again, or the dog goes out," she said on her way up the stairs.

Any retort her sister had planned died at the sound of a sharp rap at the front door, and Angie jumped to answer it, Sarge bounding after her. She threw open the door before Sydney could remind her to check out the peephole. All Sydney could see was a dark suit as her sister hugged the man, saying, "I was hoping you'd come."

"Hey, squirt."

The voice belonged to Tony Carillo, her former partner before she'd transferred from San Francisco to the FBI Academy at Quantico to teach forensic art. Angie opened the door wider and dragged him in by his hand. "Look who came by to see *me*."

"I was in the neighborhood. Bank robbery in Marin yesterday. A couple houses I want to check on a tip we received."

Sydney glanced out the window. His blue Crown Victoria was parked in the drive, the front seat empty. "You're by yourself?"

"I was thinking maybe you'd like to go with me."

"Hard as it is to believe, I did not fly all the way out from the East Coast so I could work a bank robbery with you."

"I'll go if she won't!" Angie said.

Carillo grinned at Angie's enthusiasm. Her dream was to

be a cop, and he loved to encourage it. "Let's talk your sister into coming first, eh, Angie. We wouldn't want those skills of hers diminishing now that she's sitting behind a desk in a classroom all day."

"If anything," Sydney replied, "my skills have been sharpened these last few months. Besides, it's Christmas."

"Last I checked, it was the twenty-seventh."

"And I'm off until New Year's."

Angie's mouth dropped open as she looked at Sydney. "You *can't* let him go alone! What if something happens?"

"Yeah," Carillo said. "You don't want something to happen to me."

"I am doing nothing today and enjoying every second—"

Her mother came down the stairs carrying a basket of dirty clothes. "Hi, Tony. Are you staying for lunch?"

"Sorry, Mrs. Hughes. Working a case. But thanks."

She hefted the basket on her hip, then pinned her gaze on Sydney. "How about running Angela down to her ballet lesson, then basketball practice? It'll give you two some good quality time together and I can get some laundry done."

Vegetating between ballet *and* basketball? *Definitely* not on her list of how to spend the rare day off. "Geez, Mom," Sydney said, standing. "I'd love to, but they're running shorthanded at work, and Tony needs my help."

"Bank robbery," Angie said solemnly. "FBI stuff."

Her mother gave a sigh, then continued on through the hall into the laundry room just off the kitchen. If she'd had her way, Sydney would be teaching kindergarten at some secluded private school where nothing bad ever happened.

Carillo turned a triumphant smile Sydney's way. "Get your gun, Fitzpatrick. We've got a bad guy to catch."

"This is for you," Carillo said once they were in his car. He handed Sydney a thick envelope.

"Gee, and here I was hoping for coffee and a doughnut. What is it?"

"The BICTT numbers. Figured it was safer to give it to you in person, what with Sheila snooping around."

Sydney fingered the envelope. The acronym stood for Bank of International Commerce Trade and Trust but was better known in their world as the Bank of International Crooks, Terrorists, and Thieves. Even the CIA had used the bank, which had caused a major government scandal a couple decades ago, before it was shut down. Sydney had stumbled across several players in the BICTT cover-up while investigating her father's murder and found the original set of numbers, which the government confiscated. Carillo, being a firm believer in governmental conspiracies, made a photocopy of the numbers, feeling that somewhere, sometime, they might come in handy. Now all they had to do was figure out what they meant. "Any idea what I'm supposed to do with these?" she asked.

"Well, I sure as hell wouldn't flash them around. And for God's sake, don't start running them on any computers. Doc figures if you do, you might as well hold up a sign asking the CIA to come knocking on your door," he said, referring to his current partner, Michael "Doc" Schermer.

"Lovely." She tucked the envelope beneath the seat. "So why'd you really want me to come with you?" she asked as they drove south on the freeway toward San Francisco. "You caught that bank robber yesterday. I read about it in the paper."

"Doc's out of town," he said. "Wasn't anyone else I could ask. It's about Sheila."

Carillo and Sheila were in the midst of a contentious divorce battle over the "custody" of Carillo's modest condo. It was, as far as she knew, the big holdup in why they hadn't finalized the divorce.

"What'd she do this time?"

He glanced in his rearview mirror, then changed lanes. "You remember that boyfriend she had back when we were working your father's murder?"

"The guy with the mansion?"

"Not him. The other one. The guy from England."

"Must have missed that update."

"Yeah, you might've been in Mexico dodging a few bullets at the time." He signaled for a right turn, glanced over his shoulder to check for traffic, then gave her a pointed look before turning his attention to the road. "She's talking marriage with this one."

"Bigger checkbook?"

"Bigger something," he said. "And as much as I'd like to move on, get Sheila out of my hair, the guy bugs me."

"He's not you?"

"Aren't you the funny one. He's being investigated by the locals for skimming money from the charity he works for, and Sheila's insisting I look into it and clear his name."

"Only a minor conflict of interest, eh?"

"I called the detective investigating it. Clear-cut case. Not a lot I can do, even if I was so inclined—which I'm not."

"So she's involved with a dirtbag. That can't be the only reason."

"She took off last night. Said she was scared, wanted to spend the night at my place because she thinks someone's trying to kill Trip."

"The boyfriend who's in jail?"

"Right. So, I let her. Only she took off with my ATM card. Guess I probably should have changed the PIN when she moved out."

"I'm assuming you called the bank?"

"I did. She used it for cash at the market about a block from her house."

They drove across the Golden Gate Bridge, through San Francisco, then on to San Mateo, and he pulled into a subdivision of houses that had to be worth a small fortune, parking at the end of the street. Carillo pointed to the last house on the block.

"*That's* Sheila's house?" Sydney asked.

"It is."

"What is this guy? The CEO for the charity?"

"No. Apparently the charity owns the property. Isn't it nice to know when you donate money, it's being spent wisely? They lent it out to him."

"Nice. And here we thought working for the Feds was cush, because we got paid holidays. So what are you planning to do?"

"Find Sheila and talk some sense into her head. She doesn't have to save every stray that wanders into her fold."

"That what you were? One of her strays?"

"Except I couldn't be saved." Carillo cruised up the hill, stopped in front of her house. A white BMW convertible was parked in the driveway. "Well, her car's there," he said. "Can't wait to hear what she has to say."

The two walked up to the door and Carillo rang the bell. No answer. He looked in the leaded decorative glass of the door, then pulled out his cell phone and called her. "Still not answering. Something's up. This is too weird, even for Sheila." He headed to the side gate, opening it to allow Sydney to enter first. "I think we could jimmy one of the dining room windows back here. These are nice and low. Easy to climb in."

"How sure are you about this?"

"I'm not sure about anything. Sheila's a ditz, no doubt about it, but she seemed genuinely upset last night." He took a pocketknife and slid it into the window, popping it open. "I told her these windows were crap and that she should secure them better. But no. She didn't want to waste the money when they were only going to be here until the divorce was final and she got her claws on my condo."

"So what are you trying to say? She's a gold-digging stray saver? Which is going to sound so good when we get picked up for felony breaking and entering."

"Nothing's going to happen." Carillo drew his gun, sat, then straddled the window ledge, one foot inside, one outside. "Besides. I hear the water running upstairs. She's probably in the shower."

"That'll go over good in divorce court," she said, drawing her own weapon, then following him in. "We're the FBI, your honor. Breaking into estranged wives' houses while they shower is what we do."

Everything looked neat and tidy, she thought, as they walked through the kitchen toward the living room. No sign of a struggle or any trouble.

Carillo stopped. Listened. "Definitely coming from the second floor. Which maybe explains why she didn't answer her phone." He holstered his weapon, appearing much more relaxed now that they knew she wasn't lying dead somewhere with a knife-wielding suspect standing over her.

They started toward the stairs. Carillo stopped when he saw Sheila's purse on a table in the hall. He reached in, pulled out her wallet, found his ATM card, and shoved it in his pocket. She was surprised he didn't take the two hundred bucks Sheila had withdrawn from his account along with it.

The upper story consisted of four rooms—two unfurnished bedrooms, an empty bathroom, and the master bedroom, where the sound of running water seemed to originate. He and Sydney stood on either side of the closed double doors that led inside. Carillo, his free hand on the doorknob, looked at Sydney. She nodded and he unlatched it, then used his foot to push it open. They peeked in. The room appeared unoccupied, the bed neatly made. Two doors on the far wall, both closed, faced them as they entered. A thin strip of light reflected beneath the door on the left, undoubtedly the bathroom. The other, she assumed, was the closet.

"Time to find out what's going on," he said.

"Sure you don't want to wait until she's done?"

"If I thought she wouldn't run off, yeah." He crossed the room, his footfall silent on the off-white carpet.

Sydney hung back, fairly certain that Sheila was not going to like that her soon-to-be-ex was about to burst in while she was showering, especially with a spectator in the room.

He opened the door, then pointed for Sydney to enter.

"Me?" she whispered.

"You think *I'm* going in there?"

"You're married."

"By a technicality."

"You are *so* going to owe me." She gave him a look, then pushed the door open the rest of the way, the hot, moist air hitting her face as she stepped in. She stared at the steamed-up glass enclosure. Empty.

"What's wrong?" he asked.

"There's no one here."

"What?"

He pushed past her, moved inside, opened the glass door. "Where is she?"

Sydney glanced out into the bedroom. "A better question is why is she hiding from you?"

"Because she stole my ATM card."

At which time they both looked over at the closet, still closed.

He and Sydney flanked it. "Sheila?" he called out.

Sheila, however, was not in the closet. She was under the bed, poking her head out from beneath the bed skirt and looking imminently relieved when she saw Sydney and Carillo standing there.

"What the hell?" he said.

"I'm sorry!" she said, crawling out. "I thought you were them."

"Them who?"

"I told you last night. The ones after Trip."

"Isn't he in jail?" Sydney asked.

Sheila sat on the bed, her hand to her chest as she took a deep breath. "He got out this morning."

"And what?" Carillo asked. "You needed my ATM card to welcome him home?"

"No," she said, turning an angry glance his way. "I needed it so they couldn't trace my movements and find me, thereby finding him. Don't you think it's odd that they dropped the charges right *after* they learned I asked you to look into it? Like they *knew* you'd find out they were setting him up?"

"Great. He's out. So where is he, then?"

"In hiding."

"Hiding? Under the bed with you?"

"My God, Tony. What part of this don't you get?"

"The part where you go sneaking off and don't answer your goddamned phone so I think you're lying dead somewhere."

"You mean you actually care what happens to me?"

"Finish your goddamned story so I can figure out what's going on."

"Fine. I heard a car pull up and looked out my bedroom window, expecting to see the maid's car, but saw yours instead. I freaked."

"Because you saw *my* car, the same one I've been driving every day for the past year?"

"No. Because, A, my maid has been coming here for six months at seven-thirty in the morning and has *never* been late until today, and, B, I wasn't expecting you. Naturally I thought you were the guys after Trip, so I hid. Happy?"

"Ecstatic. So what now?"

"Now I pack a few days of clothes and go to meet him. And then we need to get a hotel or something so they don't find us. I don't suppose you'd let me use your credit card?"

Sydney, trying to ease Carillo's frustration, asked, "What makes you think someone's after you?"

"Trip. He told me."

"Why does he think this?" she asked.

"I have no idea. I only know that he's too scared to come to the house."

"And yet," Carillo said, "he had no problem sending you here?"

"He'd be furious if he thought I was here. He thinks I'm at your house."

"He just went up a few notches in my book."

"So I *can* use your credit card?"

"Tell you what, Sheila. Assuming any of this is true, I'll follow you to your hotel, pay the bill, then sit down with Trip and get to the bottom of it."

"You'd do that for me?"

"If it will bring me peace for an afternoon, yes."

She got up off the bed, put her arms around him. "Thank you, Tony."

"Yeah, yeah," he said. "Get your things together. Sydney and I will wait for you downstairs."

He and Sydney walked out, and he closed the door behind him.

"You buying that?" Sydney asked.

"I think she watches too much TV."

"At least Trip's off the hook for embezzlement."

"What more could a prospective wife ask for?" Carillo said as he and Sydney started down the stairs.

The doorbell rang and they heard Sheila call out, "It's probably the maid. She's got a key."

"She gets a maid, I get the bill," Carillo muttered as someone turned a key in the lock, then opened the door.

A small woman in dark clothing stood there, shoving something in her pocket before turning around to pick up a caddy filled with cleaning supplies. She straightened and looked right at them, her eyebrows shooting up, not in fear, but in inquiry. "Are you Trip?" she asked, focusing on Carillo.

Carillo froze. "How long did Sheila say her maid worked here?"

"Six months," Sydney answered.

No sooner had the words left her mouth than Sydney saw the woman reach into the caddy, pulling out a black semi-auto.

Before the woman's gun cleared the bucket, Sydney drew and fired. She heard Carillo's almost simultaneous shots. The woman fell back, looking surprised as the bucket and gun clattered to the floor. The two agents approached, keeping their weapons trained on her. Carillo opened the door, looked outside, checking for more suspects. Sydney kicked the woman's gun away and it went sliding.

Sheila, hearing the gunshots, ran out of her bedroom, stood at the top of the stairs, then screamed.

She sank to her knees. "Oh my God . . ."

"I take it that's not your maid?" Carillo asked.

She shook her head. And when she recovered, said, "Now do you believe me?"

Sydney took out her phone to call 911. As she punched in the numbers then put the phone to her ear, Carillo said, "Guess we better find out what happened to the real maid."

She looked at Carillo. "This is *not* how I wanted to spend my Christmas vacation."

3

Sydney walked up the driveway after Carillo dropped her off that evening, and she stared at the two-story gray and white house of her childhood, with the ivy growing up the side, its twisting trunk as thick as a tree. An ancient oak stood on either side of the yard, moonlight filtering through the branches. Tiny white Christmas lights twinkled in the bushes that bordered the front porch as though fireflies hovered over them. She loved this house, the one constant in her life that didn't change. It didn't matter where she lived or where her job took her. This was home, and she walked up to the steps and sat, not yet ready to go inside.

Although the curtains were closed, she knew her mother, stepfather, and Angie were sitting inside, laughing, being a family. It was what she thought of when feeling overwhelmed. It brought her comfort and gave her strength.

Why then was it having the opposite effect as she sat there now?

She glanced at the envelope Carillo had given her in the car and knew why. She'd left California partly because of these numbers, moved all the way across the country so her work wouldn't bleed over into her personal life. And here she was, letting it happen again. Sure it was Carillo's wife this time, but she'd interrupted her holiday visit with her family, and suddenly become embroiled in a murder investigation that meant she and Carillo were now on administrative leave until the facts were sorted through. Worse was that any chance of a simple, peaceful vacation was now going to be ruined because of the constant phone calls from the investigators who would undoubtedly find one more question to ask, one more detail that needed to be outlined. That was the primary reason she cut short her trip, deciding to return back to Washington, D.C., tomorrow. She didn't want to subject her family to having to hear any of it.

"Hey."

She looked over, saw Carillo standing in the driveway. "I thought you'd left."

"You were looking a little lost. And I guess my conscience got to me. Like you said, not how you pictured your Christmas vacation."

She shrugged, then let out a sigh. "Not so much that as my mother is going to be . . . disappointed. It's bad enough that I'm late, but I'm trying to figure out how to even tell her. Sorry I missed dinner, but had to knock off an assassin who mistook Carillo for his wife's boyfriend."

"I dunno. Sounds good to me."

"Yeah, if you're describing the plot to a movie, maybe. Not when you hate everything about your daughter's job."

"Angie would like it."

Sydney smiled at the thought. "Definitely."

They sat there in silence for several minutes, just staring out at the moon-dappled lawn. After a moment Carillo said, "I've been thinking."

"Not good."

"Sheila mentioned that some guy in Washington, D.C., could back up Trip's story. Maybe shed a little light on what's going on—" He stopped, pulled his phone from his belt, looked at the screen. "Text from Doc. They found the real maid in a Dumpster behind her apartment complex."

"You think Trip's innocent?"

"I have no friggin' idea. But I can sure as hell tell you that if I have to spend the next several days on administrative leave because of something he did, I want to know exactly what I'm suffering for."

"If I had to guess, someone's pissed about Trip stealing a bunch of money. Maybe it'll be a lesson for Sheila to quit taking in strays."

"I wish that's all it was," Carillo said. "I get the feeling that Sheila's so besotted with this idiot, she's going to get dragged down with him. And since it involves my wife, I'm not about to trust just anybody looking into the case. I don't think they realize how squirrelly she can be."

"You know they're not going to let you investigate your own wife's case."

"Exactly. Which is why I've been thinking, you know, maybe you could give Griffin or Tex a call. Ask them to check out this Dorian Rose guy Sheila was talking about. She says he can verify Trip's story."

"Why them?"

"One, because they're in D.C. Two, because I'd like to get the opinion of someone I trust, not some poor schmuck who was low man on the totem pole and got stuck on-call over Christmas vacation. Three, I'd like it kept below the radar."

If anyone had the means to interview someone and keep it below the radar, ensuring that Carillo's name never came to light—especially if something went awry—Zachary Griffin and James "Tex" Dalton could. The pair worked black ops for a covert government agency called ATLAS, based in Washington, D.C. "I don't know. This is not exactly their thing."

The front door opened and Sydney's mom poked her head out. "You're home. I thought I heard someone out here."

"Hi, Mom," Sydney said, tucking the envelope with the BICTT numbers beneath her arms. Her mother, unfortunately, was overly inquisitive when it came to her professional life. "Yeah. We're, uh, just going over a few things."

"Well, hurry. We're holding dinner for you."

She closed the door, and Sydney waited a few moments, making sure that her mom wasn't about to pop back out again before she started talking about Carillo's case. "They're pretty strict over there, Carillo. It's got to be a national security threat before they get involved. I know they're going to say let the locals handle it."

"Just a call, Syd. What can it hurt?"

What could it hurt? The fact that she was here in California, and Zachary Griffin, the man she wanted a relationship with, was in Washington, D.C. After the last operation they'd worked, she thought for sure there was something more there. She'd even called and left a voice mail, wishing him a merry Christmas, and yet, he hadn't called back.

As much as she wanted to call again, she didn't want to seem desperate, and now Carillo *wanted* her to call . . .

Sydney took a breath, realized she was being selfish. Maybe it was Carillo's wife and not him, but if anyone owed Carillo, she knew that she did. She eyed the envelope in her hand. Back when she was looking into her father's murder, when she'd found these numbers, Carillo had been the one person in her life who stood by her, helped her when she needed him.

She wasn't about to forget that.

"I'll call in the morning before I leave for the airport. They're likely to be in a better mood if I don't wake them from a sound sleep."

4

Zachary Griffin tossed his bag onto the floor, then placed the tiny white box on the desk, eyeing the mountain of paperwork that had piled up in his absence. He'd been in Mexico over Christmas, had just gotten back, in fact.

Tex walked in just then, saw the box. "What'd you get me?"

"Same thing as I did last year," Griffin said. "Nothing."

"How was the mission?"

"I've had better."

"No success?"

"If there are any terrorists entering through the route that informant laid out for us, good luck to them. Marco and I spent Christmas night hiding beneath a bridge while a couple drug cartels battled it out above us. The only thing traveling on that route is drugs and guns. Unfortunately there a dozen routes we weren't able to check out, so we have to hope the border agents are on their toes. We know they're coming in that way. What would be nice is to know the names they're using to enter the country with."

"Let's hope the next team is more successful."

"I see you're not volunteering."

"Blond," Tex said, tugging at his hair. "Sticks out like a sore thumb. If you're not too jet-lagged to go out, I could use you for a quick contact."

"I've got a week's worth of reports to get through. Sure it can't wait?"

"Sydney called. *Reader's Digest* version, someone tried to kill Carillo, because they thought he was Sheila's boyfriend. Seems she's gotten herself involved with a two-bit hustler caught skimming money from a charity."

"Carillo's okay?"

"Fine. He and Syd ten-exed the hit man. Woman, actually. So how about it?"

Griffin leaned back in his chair, shrugged. "Sure. I'll meet you downstairs."

Tex started to leave then looked at the box. "Is that for Sydney?"

"Just something I picked up."

Tex eyed the gift and then him, raising one eyebrow. "You want my advice?"

"No."

"Well, I'm gonna give it anyway, because that's what friends do."

"Butt in where they shouldn't?"

"If she finds out from some other source that she was on our radar when she was looking into her father's case, that our agency was in any way—"

"I get it."

"Yeah? Well maybe think about mentioning the fact *before* you give her whatever's in there." Tex turned and left, and Griffin stared at the little gift box, trying to get it out of his head that Sydney had called Tex and not him.

It shouldn't matter. They'd never officially gone out, after all. Merely worked a couple ops together. And sure, shared a

kiss here and there, as opportunity would have it. The necklace he'd picked up for her in Mexico? A trifle. The fiery
opal pendant had caught his eye, a thank-you gift was all, for
her help on his last mission in France.

They were not, however, a couple, even if the thought was
one he'd entertained while hiding beneath that bridge in
Mexico. It was merely something that had helped pass the
time while bullets were flying.

So it shouldn't really matter that she'd called Tex and not
him.

It didn't, he convinced himself, then opened his drawer,
shoved the gift box inside, and took out his gun to follow
Tex.

Griffin and Tex pulled up in front of a red brick two-story
structure, its painted green trim peeling from the wood
around those windows that weren't boarded over. A chain-
link fence in front of one of the buildings leaned precari-
ously from its post, a plastic trash bin the only thing holding
it up. The melting snow flooded the gutter and puddled on
the sidewalk, reflecting the bare gray branches of the trees
above.

A black man stood out front of the apartment building, his
hands shoved in his jacket pockets, his shoulders hunched,
looking as defeated as the neighborhood. He was not watching them, however; his gaze seemed to be fixed off in the
distance, as though eyeing the bright white capitol dome visible against the clear blue sky, perhaps wondering what his
leaders were doing for him. Griffin and Tex exited the vehicle, their doors closing almost simultaneously, and the man
finally turned in their direction, eyeing them suspiciously as
they walked up.

"You wouldn't happen to know Dorian Rose?" Tex asked.

"Who are you?"

"A friend of a friend."

He seemed to think about answering, then said, "Second building, apartment one. Office."

His accent reminded Griffin of one of their contacts who had emigrated from Kenya. "Thanks."

He and Tex continued past him, then on up the walkway, just as a blond-haired man about his height was exiting the building. He looked up, saw them, his blue eyes widening as he backed in, slamming the door shut.

The man on the sidewalk said, "That would be Dorian."

Griffin and Tex ran to the door, Tex pulling it open. Dorian was nearly down the hallway, and in the moment it took them to survey the premises and determine if they were rushing into some sort of an ambush, Dorian darted around the corner. They pursued, the floorboards bending beneath their weight. They heard a door slam. When they reached the corner, the stench of backed-up sewage assaulted them. The hallway was empty, the single tenement bulb barely throwing enough light to cast a shadow. There were several apartment doors on either side, and Griffin had no idea which one Dorian had disappeared into.

They walked down the dim passage, its once white walls mostly gray from the waist level down. He listened at each apartment, hearing the ambient noises of general living, TV, laughing, talking, arguing, all coming from behind various doors. There were two, however, that seemed to be quiet, whether because no one was home or because someone was hiding within and the residents were covering for him, Griffin couldn't tell. At the end of the hall was the stairwell, and he signaled Tex over, then pointed to it, saying loudly, "He must have gone upstairs. Let's check."

He and Tex entered the stairwell, Griffin indicating that Tex should continue, and he pressed himself against the wall while Tex stomped his way to the top. About twenty seconds into it, Griffin heard the slight creak of a door opening. He waited, waited, then popped out just as Dorian emerged. Dorian jumped back in but couldn't push the door shut in time as Griffin darted forward, grabbed it. He shoved his foot between it and the frame and Tex rushed over, put his shoulder to the door. They almost landed on top of Dorian as he let go, dropped to the worn, stained carpet, putting his hands over his face.

"Don't kill me! Don't kill me! I didn't tell anyone."

Griffin scanned the room, saw about fifteen men, women, and children, a few in African dress, some cowering on a threadbare sofa of indeterminate color, others on the floor, their dark eyes staring in fright at the two of them. The only things moving, in fact, were the huge cockroaches scurrying behind a large American flag draped across one wall and the wooden African carvings on the other wall. Not a weapon in sight.

"Told anyone what?" Griffin asked, returning his attention to Dorian.

"Anything. I swear!"

"Jesus," Tex said. "Can't we move this outside? Smells like a broken sewer line in here."

Griffin reached down, grabbed Dorian's arm and dragged him to his feet. "Let's go."

A woman on the couch clasped her hands together, her black eyes pleading. She would have stood, but the man next to her held her back. "Don't hurt him."

Griffin looked at her, then at Dorian. "We're not going to hurt him. We just want to talk."

Her hands covered her mouth, and if anything she looked even more frightened.

Keeping a firm grip on Dorian, he backed from the room, Tex covering them, then following. Tex pulled the door shut and they marched Dorian toward the front, not stopping until they were outside the building.

"Mind telling us who you're running from?" Griffin asked, placing him so his back was against the brick facade.

Dorian looked from Griffin to Tex. "This isn't the best neighborhood in the world. Lot of bad people out there."

Tex took a business card from his wallet. "We're investigative reporters from the *Washington Recorder*," he said, handing the card to Dorian. "And since we're not in the business of killing news sources, you're going to have to trust us."

He stared at the card, looking even paler. "Who sent you?"

"Trip."

"But . . . *why*?"

"Something about clearing up an embezzlement case."

"Embezzlement . . . ? *That's* what this is about?" Dorian took a deep breath, and almost collapsed against the bricks. "Oh my God. I thought—"

Griffin exchanged glances with Tex before saying, "Thought what?"

"Nothing. Just that I've known Trip for a lot of years. He's—He's screwed up before, made accounting mistakes, and I think he's grasping at anything that will get him out of the hole he's dug."

"What sort of accounting mistakes?"

"Look. I haven't seen him in maybe two years, so if he actually stole over a million bucks, I doubt he'd call me to confess."

"A million?" Griffin asked. "We were told this was some small-time thing."

"This *is* about that money from San Francisco's showing of *From Sticks to Bricks,* right?"

"*Sticks to Bricks*?"

"The documentary fund-raiser. They're having one here in D.C. on New Year's eve. At twenty-five hundred bucks a pop and over five hundred tickets sold, that's, well, a lot."

Enough to get someone killed, Griffin thought.

5

"What do you mean someone tried to kill Carillo?"
Ron Nicholas McNiel III, Griffin's boss, asked from the
doorway, his overcoat draped over one arm. Apparently he
was on his way out. Griffin was at his desk, Tex seated in
one of the mismatched chairs, his boots propped up on the
other.

"Mistaken identity," Tex said, then gave him the rundown
on what happened. "They thought he was Trip."

"The guy you told me was shacking up with Carillo's
wife?"

"The same."

"If," Griffin said, "we believe this Dorian we just ran
down, Trip made off with a lot of money, which would piss
off some powerful people. It would explain why someone
placed a hit on him."

"How much money?"

"Maybe a million or more."

"When I agreed to let you two go out on this, I was under
the impression it was a small-time embezzlement case. If I

recall your words, Tex, it was 'in and out.' As in it *wouldn't* take up much time."

"It didn't," Tex replied. "Couldn't have been in that dump longer than, what? Five minutes?"

"Why do I get the feeling you're going to qualify that with: And yet . . . ?"

"Because," Griffin said, "we think Dorian was lying. That guy was afraid of something, and I don't think it was about Trip being a suspect. There is way more to this than some simple embezzlement case."

McNiel eyed the clock on Griffin's wall. "While I appreciate that we owe Carillo, this sounds like something he needs to step away from, and you need to be done with."

"It's his wife," Tex said.

"Soon to be ex, if I'm not mistaken," McNiel clarified as he put on his coat. "And it's not her, it's her boyfriend, or did I misinterpret? Carillo's walking a thin line if he's involving himself with this."

"He's not really," Tex said. "He just wants a little extra intel. And it is Carillo. We can't just leave him hanging."

"You have to throw this at me when I'm on my way out the door to a Senate intelligence meeting?"

"You'd rather we didn't tell you?"

"Sometimes, yes," McNiel said, digging his keys from his pocket. "Do me a favor. Wrap it up so that Carillo can turn it over to the locals and you can get back to what the government is really paying you to do." McNiel started out the door but stopped, looked back at them. "Pearson's going to be at that meeting," he said, referring to the head of the FBI's foreign counterintelligence squad. "Please tell me Carillo called the police about the woman he shot in his wife's house?"

"Sure he did," Tex said. "Home invasion."

"And they bought it?"

"No reason not to at this point."

"Some days I love my job. This isn't one of them." McNiel gave an exasperated sigh. "I'm serious. Wrap it up and get out."

McNiel slid into the room as the meeting was called to order. Senator Dorothea Burgess eyed him, saying, "So nice of you to join us, Director McNiel."

"Apologies. Conflict in schedules."

"More important than something that's been on your calendar for three months?"

"The vice president thought so."

That shut her up, and he looked for a seat. There were two vacant. One next to CIA's Ian Thorndike, and the other next to Pearson from the FBI. He chose Pearson, since Thorndike still had issues about Griffin and Tex leaving the CIA to join ATLAS.

There wasn't enough coffee to get past the first hour's budget reports, and Pearson elbowed him twice when he nearly dozed off during Thorndike's dissertation on why his budget needed to be increased when everyone else was being asked to make cuts.

"There's such a thing as overdoing it," McNiel said under his breath.

To which Senator Burgess asked, "Did you have something you wished to share, Mr. McNiel?"

"No, ma'am."

"Because if there is, I'm sure Mr. Thorndike wouldn't mind turning over the floor?"

"Actually," Thorndike said, "I would mind. I'd like to discuss the way money is allocated in the refugee resettlement program. Over ten billion dollars that could—"

"I believe," Burgess said, "the figure is closer to *one* billion. Not ten. That's quite a difference."

"Unless," Thorndike said, "you include what's coming from the welfare budgets."

"We're not. You're talking about a completely different budget, one in which we have no oversight."

"Feel free to point that out to the taxpayers, who aren't differentiating which pocket they're paying it from."

"Did you have a point, Mr. Thorndike?"

"Yes. If you're going to continue dumping that kind of money into the program, some of it needs to be diverted into *who* you're letting into the country—especially considering the mass emigration from East Africa and the lack of resources and funding to ensure that those coming in are who they say they are."

The senator's expression turned icy. "Heaven forbid we allow nonwhites into the country?"

It was Pearson who answered. "No, Madam Senator. Terrorists, unfortunately, come in all colors. If you would take the time to read the FBI and CIA's joint analysis of the areas we feel are the weak links in—"

"So everyone from East Africa is a terrorist now?"

Pearson took a deep breath. "Of course not. But it only takes one."

McNiel had to appreciate the man's position and the effort it took for him to maintain his temper.

Senator Burgess, however, appeared unmoved. "When you get evidence that any of these terrorists are getting past the gatekeepers that the UN *and* the U.S. have put in place, *do* let me know. Until then, I'm more interested in how to address our real concerns, going over the reports from each of your departments on where you're going to make the cuts necessary without compromising the integrity of your programs."

"More cuts?" McNiel said.

"Mr. McNiel? You have something you'd like to address before the committee?"

He wanted to address a lot, but Pearson gave a slight shake of his head, warning him to back down. That meant one thing. Pearson needed the meeting to end and fast, so he responded with, "No, ma'am."

"Thank you, then. For the record, I believe the proper screening measures are in place, and unless you can show me otherwise, we'll move on."

"Remind me why we're kissing her ass?" McNiel asked as he and Pearson walked out of the building. The question was rhetorical. They were kissing her ass in hopes she wouldn't recommend slashing their budgets all to hell. Burgess, like every other senator out there, was swayed by the lobbyists. In Burgess's case, since she happened to be heading the refugee committees, her lobbyists were paid by the so-called charities, who wanted to keep the refugee resettlement system exactly as it was, security flaws and all, because it worked for them.

Pearson shook his head. "Don't get me started . . ."

"So why was it you stopped me from taking her on head-to-head?"

"Because I got a call from MI6 about five minutes before the meeting started that one of their agents in Somalia has verified intel that Yusuf's *definitely* heading for Mexico."

Yusuf, a Somalian terrorist, had recently escaped from a prison in Mogadishu, and according to intel reports was considered a threat to the United States. "Where?"

"We're not sure. I was hoping that maybe Griffin's trip to Mexico was successful. Better to stop him before he crosses the border."

"The lead didn't pan out. But we've sent another team down. Too big an area, unfortunately . . . Thorndike knows?"

"Yeah."

"Some reason he didn't bring that up to her royal highness and the rest of her court?"

"One. CIA is working a delicate undercover op. After the

recent debacle in the Mideast involving the loss of most of their assets, they're not about to lay any cards on the table."

And no wonder, McNiel thought. Thorndike, Pearson, and he could shout national security until they were blue in the face, and Burgess and every other politician would still be racing to the first TV camera they saw. "What's the other reason?"

"We heard the way Yusuf's arranging to get into the country is the golden passport."

"The refugee resettlement program?" There were mile-wide holes in the program that put out a welcome mat for any terrorist with half a brain to circumvent the system. And that, of course, meant the last thing they wanted to do was alert the one senator whose darling it was. It wasn't that they didn't trust Burgess, more that they had serious doubts she'd be cooperative when it came to the cold hard facts that put her and that program in a bad light. "I take it that has something to do with Thorndike's op?"

"Not quite sure," Pearson said. When they reached the street, he hailed a taxi, then said, "All I can say is, if the intel is true, we need to get on it fast."

He was right, McNiel thought. If any man had an agenda, it was Yusuf. And they definitely didn't want him in this country.

6

The creaking hulk of a truck rumbled across the rutted Mexican road, kicking up gravel and dust, the early morning air slightly chilly. Yusuf heard one of the drivers say that they were a few nights from the American border. He was glad to hear it, as it had been a long and arduous trip from that hellhole of a refugee camp in Dadaab. Unlike the others on this truck with him, migrants who hoped to cross illegally under cover of night or be smuggled over the border hidden in cargo, Yusuf actually possessed an American passport, showing he was a twenty-three-year-old from Burundi, not Somalia. He'd need to find a place to wash the streaks of sweat and dust from his skin and don a set of clean clothes, then walk across once he got there.

If stopped, he'd show his passport, and if questioned, answer in perfect English. He hadn't yet shared that he even knew the language. There had been no need, and wouldn't be until he reached the border. He did not, however, know any Spanish, and had managed this far not understanding a word of the language by pretending to be deaf. If someone spoke, he pointed to his ears. They nodded in understanding, then pantomimed in exaggerated movements and spoke louder, gladly helping him past any obstacles, getting him food, water, whatever it was he needed.

Playing deaf was how he'd learned to get by in the orphanage, a place where he'd spent most of his childhood, a place where the sound of American bombing was a constant reminder of the explosions that had killed his family. Although he'd been surrounded by other orphaned children, he always felt alone. They were not his sister and brothers, who had died beneath the rubble of what was once his house. These children had each other.

He had no one.

Until the insurgents arrived. That night, they dragged all the boys, screaming, crying, from their beds, herded them into a truck, and took them to a camp where they taught them to fight, hold a gun, rig a bomb. They gave them purpose, a reason for living, at least in Yusuf's mind. And one of the men had discovered his ability to mimic sounds he heard, changing his voice to match that of whoever he was around.

This was a particularly useful skill in one so youthful, one of the leaders said, and so they taught him English and had him watch movies until his accent was no different than that of the Americans who'd invaded their country. The other boys, those who had sense, were envious at his newfound status. While they huddled around fires at night, trying to stay warm, he was taken into the leader's tent to show off what he had learned.

Even then he found that he did not belong. The other boys shunned him. And when he tried to make friends with the older fighters, they pushed him away. Only the leader talked to him, made him practice his English. According to him, Yusuf would change the world. He would change history and be able to reach Paradise.

And so it was that when the insurgents came once again

in the middle of the night, this time tearing down the walls of the prison, Yusuf was the first to volunteer for the assignment that would take him to America for the supreme sacrifice.

The old truck bounced along the dusty road, and as the American border drew closer, he knew without a doubt that this was what he had been trained for.

What he'd waited for his entire life.

7

Griffin scanned the reports one by one, searching for anything that might lead them not only to where Yusuf might gain entry into the country, but also where this cell he was allegedly activating might be located. McNiel had, rightly, redirected every operation to the location and capture of the man they considered to be a major threat to U.S. security. CIA had warned that ever since he'd been kidnapped from the orphanage in Somalia by a terrorist group looking to enhance the numbers of their army, he blamed the U.S. for the deaths of his family, and had nursed that grudge into hatred.

Tex walked in with a new stack of paperwork. "Not a lot here, but the FBI forwarded a theft report from National Nuclear Security Administration. Some hospital in California that closed down after an earthquake is now missing a radiotherapy unit. They're not sure if it was stolen, or maybe moved to another facility. Still trying to track down the records, which were lost in the earthquake."

"Where in California?"

"North of Los Angeles. And according to the report, it was a couple months ago. Nothing's been seen or heard since."

"Let's hope it's not related. The thought of Yusuf with nuclear anything isn't one I want to entertain."

Tex dropped the reports in Griffin's In basket. "Here you go. More of the same. Like looking for a needle in a haystack."

He left, and Griffin glanced over at the photograph of his late wife. She'd always excelled at this sort of thing. Looking for the missing puzzle piece, the bit of information gleaned from seemingly random reports that clinched a case. She'd loved the work more than him, which had doomed their marriage from the beginning. That still didn't take away the pain when she died, and he kept her photo as a reminder of the good times, not the bad. Hers was a senseless death that made little difference, because the world would never know her sacrifice. How could they, when the government would never acknowledge that she even worked for them . . . ?

"Zachary . . . ?"

He looked up, saw one of the secretaries from downstairs, watching him from the doorway. "Sorry. A little lost in thought."

She glanced at the photo as she walked in, and he could tell it made her uncomfortable, probably because she didn't know what to say. She handed him an envelope. "This came by courier."

"Thanks."

It was addressed to the editor of the *Washington Recorder*. He opened it, finding two tickets to the documentary fund-raiser Dorian had talked about, *From Sticks to Bricks*. There was a typewritten note, stating that they were extending press passes to a few select newspapers. Scrawled in blue ink below it was a message reading: "Thought you could use these." It was signed, "Dorian."

Griffin set it aside, since McNiel had made it clear he'd rather they didn't involve themselves, their priority now being the hunt for Yusuf. So be it. An hour later his phone rang and he was surprised to see it was dark out.

It was Tex.

"I just got a call from Dorian Rose. He says he's changed his mind. He wants to talk now, but only if I come alone."

Griffin glanced at the envelope. "He sent you tickets."

"He mentioned it. Thing is, there was something off about his call. The cadence. Like maybe someone was telling him what to say."

"Where are you?"

"A couple blocks from his apartment building."

"I can be there in fifteen minutes."

Dorian Rose lived in a middle-class neighborhood filled with brick-fronted elegant apartments worlds apart from the slums they'd found him in that first day. His window faced the front, and Tex had already driven past. "There's a central lobby with an elevator," he told Griffin when they met up. "Dorian lives on the second floor. It looks like there's a fire escape on the side that you might be able to use to access his unit and see in."

They split up, Tex driving to the front, Griffin driving around to the back of the unit, then walking to the side. As soon as he got there, he realized the futility of trying to get up on the fire escape and called Tex. "Too high. I'm going to have to get—"

A gunshot pierced the night, echoed off the brick wall.

"Tex?" he said, running toward the front of the building.

"Hell. Tell me that wasn't Dorian's place?"

Momentary relief flooded through Griffin on hearing Tex's voice as he pushed open the lobby door. "Sounded like it. Where are you?"

"Just up the street. No goddamned parking out front."

The elevator pinged as the door opened, and Griffin saw

a woman standing within, digging through her purse, seemingly oblivious to his presence as he entered and she exited, pulling her keys out as she walked toward the lobby door. Griffin hit the stop switch on the elevator, then ran to the stairs, taking them two at a time.

"Elevator's waiting," Griffin said into the phone. He'd made it to the first landing when Tex announced he'd arrived. By the time Griffin made it to the third floor, Tex was stepping off the elevator.

"Stairs were clear," Griffin said.

They moved to either side of Dorian's apartment door, their guns drawn, just as the door across the hall opened and a woman, gray hair, her face a network of wrinkles, poked her head out, eyeing them and the weapons they held. "My you're fast. I only just called 911!"

"Might want to close that door, ma'am," Tex said. The moment she did, he nodded, and Griffin reached out, turned the knob. It was unlocked and Griffin pushed the door with his foot, peered in, smelling the sharp scent of tobacco from a recently burned cigarette. He entered, followed by Tex.

They found Dorian lying in a pool of blood on the kitchen floor just beside the dinette table, a gun nearby, and a note on the table next to an ashtray filled with cigarette butts. Cold air swept in through the kitchen window, probably cracked open because of the smoking. It was undoubtedly the reason for the clarity of the gunshot when Griffin was standing outside.

He and Tex searched the rest of the apartment to make sure no one else was present. Something about the place bothered Griffin, but he couldn't put his finger on it. They returned to the kitchen, both men standing over the body, as sirens sounded in the distance.

"You better get out of here before the cops come," Tex said, peering out the window.

"What are you going to do?"

"Talk to the old lady across the hall and find out what she saw."

Griffin took one last look around, noticing the distinct demarcation of dust on the bookshelves in the front room . . . "They were looking for something."

Tex was snapping photos of the suicide note with his cell phone. "Will you get out of here?"

He left, rushing down the three flights of stairs, guilt weighing heavily on him, even though he knew better than to think that Dorian's death was his fault.

Taking the last few stairs two at a time, Griffin skidded around the corner into the lobby, then stopped cold at the sight of several uniformed officers blocking his way, weapons pointed at his chest.

"Police!" one of them shouted.

Griffin raised his hands. "I'm a cop," he said. "I have a gun."

"That right?" one of the officers replied. "You got any ID saying so?"

Which is when he realized he'd left his Department of Justice ID in his desk, because he'd been on a mission in Mexico. There was no ID for ATLAS; it didn't exist on paper. "No. I'm working undercover with the FBI."

"You and every other crook. Meantime, lock your hands behind your neck and *don't* make any moves." The officer nodded to his partner, who stepped up behind Griffin, gripped his hands as he searched him, removed his weapon, then cuffed him.

"And who is it at the FBI you want us to contact?"

"Special Agent Sydney Fitzpatrick. Quantico."

They led him to a waiting patrol car, put him in the back, then slammed the door closed.

Back less than a day and things were already starting to go wrong.

8

Tex heard the heavy steps of the police in the stair-well, then knocked harder on the neighbor's door. "C'mon, c'mon," he urged.

Finally, the sound of a lock being turned, and the door opened slightly, a chain still securing it from the inside as the white-haired woman peered through the crack. "Oh, hello."

"I was hoping to ask you a few questions about what happened."

"Is everything okay with Dorian? He's such a nice young man."

The footsteps grew louder, and he eyed the small placard on her door beneath the apartment number where her name was printed out: Edna Davis. "Mind if I come in, Mrs. Davis?"

"Oh, of course. Here. Just let me undo the chain." She fumbled with it for a few seconds. "My fingers don't work as well as they used to."

Tex attempted a patient smile, all the while silently willing her to move faster. If the cops rounded that corner and saw him . . .

"Here we go," she said as the chain fell, rattling against the frame, and she pulled the door open. Tex stepped in, and he heard the footsteps slowing as they reached the top of the stairwell, preparing for the entry onto Dorian's floor.

Timing was everything, he thought as she closed the door. Outside in the hallway, he heard the commotion of the police across the hall, and he hoped she wasn't paying attention.

"Is Dorian okay?" she asked again. "I couldn't tell if it was a gunshot or a firecracker."

He had a feeling she'd be too upset to talk if she knew the truth, and so decided a partial truth was best. "We believe it was a gunshot."

"Oh my. I hope no one was hurt."

"We're checking into it. I'm just wondering what you can tell me about him."

"Very polite, that boy. Would you like something to drink? I was just about to make a cup of chamomile tea."

"No, thank you, ma'am," he said, following her into the kitchen, taking in the layout of the apartment, cookie cutter to Dorian's. Peering out the window, he saw no sign of the police on this side of the building. "You were saying about Dorian?"

"Was I? Oh, yes, nice young man. Worked at that charity that everyone's so keen about these days. The one on the news?"

"Sticks for Bricks?"

"Something like that. He talked about it a lot, but he *wasn't* extolling its virtues." She opened the cupboard and sighed. "My daughter-in-law is six inches taller than me, and when she visits, she always puts my favorite mug on the top shelf. I think she does it on purpose. Would you mind?"

Tex walked over, saw the upper shelf filled with assorted mugs. "Which one?"

"The one that says, 'Queen of Everything.'" He handed it to her and she proceeded to fill it with water from the sink, saying, "Ironic, since I don't have anyone to lord it over, but my husband gave it to me before he passed. Are you sure you don't want some tea?"

"No ma'am. You were saying Dorian was unhappy at the charity?"

She put the cup in the microwave, pressed a button, and while it heated up the water, she tore open a bag of tea, saying, "Maybe unhappy wasn't the right word. But when I suggested leaving my money to it instead of my no-good son, Dorian made me promise to leave it to the Red Cross instead. Odd, don't you think?"

"They're a good organization."

"Yes, but they don't have Micah Goodwin, do they? Very handsome, that one." The microwave dinged, and she removed the cup, then dropped the tea bag in, saying, "Dorian was always going on about Micah. At first saying how wonderful he was, but these last few weeks, well, I gathered that something was wrong. That's when he told me to leave my money to the Red Cross."

"Any idea what caused his change of heart?"

"He said they weren't spending the money they were given. All very confusing. And then tonight, when he helped me carry up my groceries, he asked what I would do if I knew something bad was going on that was hurting a lot of people. Before I could even ask him what he meant, that tall black man showed up at his apartment again. He's from Africa, you know. I heard them arguing, and the man told Dorian that he would pay for breaking his promise and not talking to the landlord. He said they were all going to protest, and Dorian begged him not to do anything foolish. That was it. Scared me half to death, they were yelling so loud, and I ran in here straightaway and bolted my door."

"Do you think that's who fired the shot?"

"I don't believe so. I saw him drive off when I went back down to get my mail."

He heard the police radios outside in the hall. "I don't suppose Dorian or this man mentioned any names?"

"No, but I gathered the man might have worked for Dorian at the charity," she said, just as there was a knock at the door. "More officers?"

"Probably. May I use your bathroom, Mrs. Davis?"

"Of course. Just down the hall, to the right."

"Thank you. Don't forget to look out the peephole."

"Who's there?" she called out.

"Police."

He heard the sound of the door opening, then Mrs. Davis saying, "I was just talking to one of your detectives."

"What detective? We haven't called them yet."

"The one in the bathroom," she said. "I'm sure he'll be out in a moment."

9

It was well after ten P.M. by the time Sydney made it to the police department and asked to see the watch commander. Tired from her flight out from California, she wasn't sure that she was the best person to try to pull this off. First, she was technically still on administrative leave for the shooting in California, and would be until the Bureau's psychiatrist cleared her for duty. Second, she had no way to explain why a covert agent that didn't exist on paper was allegedly on the FBI payroll. She only hoped the ID Tex had provided her, once he made his way out the neighbor's fire escape, would pass muster, since she really didn't have time to look at it. Her only saving grace was that she knew a number of MPDC personnel from her years working in the capital.

When she saw Lieutenant Thomas Sanchez standing at the counter, it was one of those Thank God moments, and she searched her memory banks for a thread of something pleasant to break the ice. He owned a pristine 1960 Cadillac, last she recalled. She smiled and held out her hand. "Lieutenant Sanchez. Good to see you. How's that pink Cadillac of yours?"

"*Champagne* pink."

"Right. How could I forget?"

"Running like a dream," he said, shaking her hand. "What brings you to my humble digs?"

"Heard you've got one of my people in custody."

"He'd be the guy they caught running from the building? The one working undercover?"

"Correct on both counts."

"Interview room down the hall. Don't suppose you have ID for him?"

"Of course," she said, figuring he wasn't going to simply let Griffin walk out of there without an explanation. Now all she had to do was think of one, and she slid the packet Tex had given her across the counter.

He opened it, pulled out the FBI credential and badge. Looked like the real thing. Hell, it probably was, knowing ATLAS. "So," he said, examining the ID. "Why didn't he have this on him?"

"Deep undercover. So we'd appreciate it if his name didn't pop up in your report. Or mine, either, for that matter."

Lieutenant Sanchez took a drawn-out breath, as though weighing his options, then handed the packet back to her. "We're running a homicide investigation. You realize that?"

"You did talk to the witness across the hall, the old woman who verified that they came *after* the sound of the gunshot?"

"They?"

"We had another agent. Also undercover."

"You're killing me here, Sydney. Anything else you want to spring on my investigators?"

"No. I think that should do it. About the neighbor . . . ?"

"Yes, we did talk to her, and yes, she mentioned *two cops* were at the door, with guns out, so thanks for clearing up that inconsistency. Then again she also said Veronica Lake was there, so I'm not sure we can put much store in her testimony."

"Veronica Lake?"

"Yeah. Apparently the woman's an old movie buff. Everybody took on a description of a character to her. I think your guys were from *L.A. Confidential.* The corrupt cops, if I remember correctly. But back to this second officer she *allegedly* saw. Let's say he was your agent. I don't suppose you have a reason as to why he didn't come forth while we've got his partner downstairs at gunpoint?"

"Like I said, *deep* undercover."

"What sort of operation you running here?"

No goddamned idea, she wanted to say. What came out was, "Huge embezzlement case. You know what a cluster these things can be."

"Next time, maybe have one of your guys waiting in the wings, give us some warning, so we don't shoot the hell out of each other."

"Will do. Thanks, Lieutenant." A moment later she saw Griffin walking down the hallway. And though it hadn't been that long since she'd last seen him, a couple weeks, maybe, she found herself looking forward to the contact. Silly, she thought. She had a high school crush on someone who did *not* return the feeling. He was, however, easy on the eyes, tanner, and if anything leaner, and she justified her crush as merely having good taste. Perhaps because they were in the midst of the police department, neither spoke. Outside, though, when etiquette suggested that she should have asked how he'd been, or mentioned that it was good to see him again, what came out of her mouth was, "FBI? Really?"

"I was facing down the barrel of two large-caliber weapons. You're not flattered I thought of you?"

"Not when it's *my* job on the line."

"You're not going to lose your job over this. I might, but yours is pretty safe."

"Where to?"

He gave her the address of Dorian's building, then leaned back in his seat, a vacant look about him as he stared out the window. They were stopped at a red light. A man and a woman stood on the street corner, laughing, both having just emerged from a nearby bar where a red neon light advertised beer on tap.

"How was your Christmas?" he asked out of the blue.

"It was nice. How about yours?"

He didn't respond, and she heard the low hum of his cell phone vibrating.

Griffin answered it, listening, then told Tex, "She's dropping me off now."

She parked in front of his black SUV, and he opened the door, waved at her, his attention fixed on whatever it was Tex had to say.

She sat there in the dark a few moments, waiting until he started his vehicle before she drove off. And as she headed in the opposite direction toward home, she wondered if she and Griffin were ever going to be on the same page. Maybe if she had the guts to tell him exactly how she felt?

That'd be the day . . .

10

The following afternoon, Sydney looked up from her desk in the basement of the FBI Academy at Quantico, surprised to see Carillo standing there, since he was also still on administrative leave because of the shooting, and hadn't mentioned he was flying out. And then she thought of the envelope he'd given her, the BICTT numbers she had locked in her file at home. "Has Doc found anything on the—"

"Look who's with me," he said, pulling both Sheila and Trip into her office.

Definitely not here because of the numbers. She waited for him to fill her in.

"Cafeteria?" he said. "Sheila and Trip haven't eaten lunch yet. Sort of a whirlwind flight out, once we found him."

"Perfect," Sydney replied. "I was just about to take a break."

They walked down the hallway to the elevator, then rode it up, Carillo silent, his hands shoved in his pockets. Sydney had a million questions, but it was clear he wasn't willing to talk in front of the other two.

"So," Sydney said, once the elevator started its ascent. "How was the flight?"

Trip answered, his English accent not as heavy as she expected. "A bit rocky."

And Sheila said, "A bit? I've got a bruise on the top of my head from the luggage that fell out."

The cafeteria was nearly deserted, since most FBI recruits were home for Christmas break. A few command staff lingered at some tables in the corner but basically ignored them as they walked in. Carillo dropped two twenties at the register, telling the cashier, "I'll pick up the change on my way out. Cover whatever they're having." He looked at Trip. "You two good with that? Pick a table, have a seat. I need to talk to Sydney for a few minutes, go over the details."

"Very good," Trip said, and he and Sheila each took a tray, sliding them along the buffet counter.

Sydney and Carillo got their coffee, then took a seat near the windows. Outside, large soft flakes swirled down onto a vast white countryside. "I *thought* you were trying to keep this below the radar," she said.

"Not like there's anyone around here to see," he replied. "This place is like a graveyard over the holidays."

"So what gives?"

"Griffin didn't call you, I take it?"

"No."

"He and Tex want to interview Trip. I figured I'd bring them here to burn some time. One thing I did learn was that Trip apparently went so far as to ask the jailer to tell his attorney that he was being released two hours *after* his actual release time, all so he could avoid him when he got booted. He thinks his attorney is part of the plot."

"And do we know exactly *what* this plot is?"

"Not yet. But I asked Doc to do some digging. Apparently his attorney is from some high-powered international law firm, which makes me wonder why they'd be interested in defending a sleazy embezzler like Trip, guilt or innocence notwithstanding. Which means the guy's either really big on the pro bono stuff, or someone with the funds is taking a very deep interest in Trip's extracurricular activities. Which is why I need to ask a big, big favor. I need you to put the lovebirds up for a few nights."

Sydney, about to take a sip of coffee, lowered her cup to the table. "What happened to putting her up at a hotel?"

"Hey, it was Griffin's idea, not mine. He didn't want to risk a paper trail."

"Scotty, then."

Carillo raised his brows and simply looked at her.

"Okay, bad idea," she said, knowing that once her ex-fiancé, Mr. By-the-book-Scotty, found out some crime was involved, he'd never let them stay—at least not without notifying his superiors. "If it was Griffin's idea, why not at his apartment?"

"Maybe it's not big enough. Besides, it's just for a few days," he said. "Until we find out what's going on. And, hey, look at it this way. He's thinking about you."

Not quite what she had in mind, she thought, trying for a semblance of a smile. "Fine. They can stay."

She and Carillo finished their coffee, then walked over to where Sheila and Trip sat eating their soup and salad.

"Good news," Carillo said. "We can all stay at Sydney's place."

Sheila reached out and squeezed Sydney's hand.

"Brilliant," Trip added.

"Anytime," she replied. Her cell phone vibrated. She pulled it from her belt. "I need to get this," she said, grateful for the interruption, which gave her a few moments to get past the idea that someone else was running her life. "Fitzpatrick."

It was Earl, who worked security in the lobby. "You have a couple visitors here to see you. From the *Recorder*, apparently."

"Thanks, Earl. I'll be right there." To Carillo, she said, "Tex and Griffin are here."

"I told them I was heading over from the airport. I think they want to talk to Trippy, here."

Sheila frowned. "*Quit* calling him that."

"So eat up. It's not polite to keep them waiting," he told them. He gave Sydney an apologetic look, adding, "Hope you don't mind. I volunteered your office."

"Anything else you forgot to mention?"

"Hard to say. I was a bit jet-lagged."

"Bring them down when you finish your lunch," she said, then left to meet with Tex and Griffin.

Tex gave her a welcoming smile when she walked into the lobby. "Hello, darlin'."

"Always nice to see you." She looked over at Griffin, not even sure what to say to him. His poker face gave her no clue as to how he felt about this turn of circumstances. She decided, however, that it was high time to set things straight with him. In the elevator, she said, "Carillo's bringing Trip and Sheila down once they finish lunch, so that should give us plenty of time to go over the details."

"Details?" Griffin said. "We just want a drawing."

The elevator door opened and the three stepped out into the basement hallway. She looked over at Griffin. "A drawing? Why am I the only one who doesn't know what's going on?"

Tex looked from her to Griffin, saying, "I'll, uh, wander down to Sydney's office and let you two hash it out." He hesitated, then added, "Which would be where?"

"Third door to the right." She waited until he disappeared into her office before turning her attention to Griffin. "Every time you guys walk in here looking for me, something bad happens. And now you want me to put up one of your witnesses in my apartment?"

"First off, they're really *Carillo's* witnesses. Second, all we're asking is a few days. Until this blows over."

"They tried to kill Carillo because they thought *he* was Trip. They killed someone last night, almost beneath your nose," she said, making an effort to keep her voice low.

He looked at her for a full second. "We're helping Carillo and you're mad at me? What's this really about?"

"You could have called and asked me, not Carillo."

"I'm sorry. But for God's sake, it's just a drawing."

"It's *never* just a drawing with you, Griffin. Or I'd still be sitting in my office blissfully unaware that ATLAS even existed."

She turned away, feeling like a fool, not even sure why she was blowing up at him, and she walked down the hall and stopped in front of her door, only to find Tex sitting on the edge of her desk, pretending exorbitant interest in an out-dated copy of the vehicle code that a previous agent had left behind. "How much did you hear?"

"Pretty much all of it, darlin'. But I'm on your side. He should have called you. Not nice. He does, however, need your help."

"The problem is, when it comes to Griffin, 'help' is a four-letter word."

11

Carillo sat in the back of the room while Tex inter-
rogated Trip. Sheila sat in a chair off to one side, her attention on a *Better Homes and Gardens* magazine that
Sydney dug up to keep her occupied during the process.
Carillo had not questioned Trip on the plane trip over. He
was a smart enough investigator to realize that something
bigger than embezzlement was going on, and not just
because Trip wasn't exactly forthcoming with the entire
truth.

"I told you," Trip said to Tex. "I didn't call that attorney,
Ferris Gerard. He just showed up at my arraignment, saying
he was representing me. It's not like I was in any position to
turn down a lawyer."

"Had you ever met him or anyone else from his firm?"
Tex asked.

"No. Frankly, I thought maybe it was a perk of the job.
They were paying my salary, housing, and transportation, so
why not an attorney? I think that's when I started realizing

that maybe this was all too good to be true. All I did was keep the books."

"That was your job? A bookkeeper?" Tex said.

"Yes. Apprentice, actually."

"So you had no experience at it?"

"Only a bit. I came from an accounting company. I was let go in the downturn. I wasn't very good," he admitted. "Which was why I was so amazed. But they said they were all about second chances, and someone from my old firm recommended me."

Sheila rolled her eyes, before focusing on the magazine once more. "A patsy, you mean."

His cheeks reddened, and Carillo, feeling sorry for him, said, "You don't know that."

"No," Trip said. "She's right. I think deep down I've known for quite some time. I just didn't want to admit it."

"Okay," Tex said. "Clearly you were brighter than they thought, or they wouldn't be after you. What'd you do that got their interest?"

"I'm not sure. There was the time when I first noticed that there was an error in the bookkeeping. The figure that was totaled for the deposit was much lower than the figure I thought was brought in by the last fund-raiser. It was off by at least a couple of hundred thousand if not more. Normally I don't know how many tickets are sold to these high-priced formal events. That's handled by Marsha and Shirley in the office down the hall, but I remember passing by their office and hearing one of the women mention that she'd sold two hundred tickets."

"How much were the tickets?" Tex asked.

"Twenty-five hundred dollars. Each. I remember doing the math in my head, thinking there were a lot of rich people in San Francisco who care more about bringing in refugees than helping the poor people in their own backyards. We're talking five hundred thousand dollars, and that doesn't include the items sold in the silent and live auction at the dinner. But when I got the deposit the next week, there was less than two hundred thousand dollars accounted for. I brought it to my supervisor's attention, and he told me he'd look into it. When I asked him about it again, he said he'd taken care of it, that someone had transposed a figure and he'd fixed it. But the thing is, when I checked the bank statements, they deposited less than three hundred thousand."

"So two hundred K is missing?" Carillo asked.

"Of ticket money. It's possible there's silent auction money missing as well."

"So that's when they started riding you?"

"They weren't riding me at all. They moved me to another building, telling me it was a promotion, gave me more money, less hours, and left me alone."

"What sort of promotion?"

Trip started tapping his fingers on the tabletop, realized what he was doing and clasped his hands together in his lap. "Phone solicitations. I was in charge of the phone bank. Thirty people in a basement all assigned to cold-call for donations to the refugee program. We'd take it all. Cars, clothes, anything they had lying around, and the stuff didn't even have to work. We just needed it so that the government would match it with cash. That's when I called Dorian here in D.C. with my suspicions, asking him what he thought."

Tex leaned back in his chair. "Remind me how you and Dorian knew each other?"

"We both worked for the same volag."

"Volag?"

"Short for volunteer agency. He still does, or, did, until . . ." He took a deep breath, looking uncomfortable.

"So you called him," Tex said, guiding him back.

"Right. He said he'd take a look. As I said, he works—

worked for A.D.E. Affinity Data Enterprises. They're sort of an umbrella over all these refugee charities. Handled all our accounting. A few days later he said he found the same thing with some other charities."

"What other charities?"

"He didn't say specifically, but they'd have to be under the A.D.E. umbrella. They're all geared toward refugee resettlement. But he said he wanted to talk to Vince to go over what he found, and then he told me to be careful, that something wasn't right. I just figured I'd hear from him, but a few weeks went by, Vince was killed in that car accident, and then I was arrested for the theft of the money I pointed out as missing. And that's when this attorney showed up. And as I explained earlier, I thought it was a perk of the job until Dorian got a message to me at the jail through Sheila and told her to tell me not to mention anything to anyone, especially not my attorney. He didn't trust him."

"This . . . volag you worked for, A.D.E.?" Tex asked. "Based in London?"

"No. Here in the States. They have offices in London. Hell, they have offices all over the place. Any country that's moving refugees, there's an A.D.E. office."

Interesting, Carillo thought, and he slipped from the room to call Doc in San Francisco. "You busy?" he asked. "I was wondering if you've found anything on this charitable organization called A.D.E. Something's up with this group."

"As in they're not doing any of this out of the goodness of their hearts? You realize I was already one up on you? I started digging into them after you shot your wife's maid. Well, the fake one."

"Find anything?"

"Beyond the obvious? Sending an assassin out on an embezzlement case? I've tried a dozen ways to see how it connects to this charitable organization and I'm finding nothing.

Zilch. Like their haloes are glowing so brightly, you can't see past all the warm and fuzzy. It's sending the hairs on the back of my neck prickling."

If there was one thing Doc was good at, it was sensing things on a deeper level, an uncanny ability to know when something wasn't right. And even without the hit on Trip, clearly something wasn't right. "I'll be careful. Keep me informed."

12

"Let's start off with a basic description," Sydney said, angling her pencil to the topmost corner of the paper. She decided that she needed to put all her conflict with Griffin aside. Clearly he didn't feel the same way about her as she did him, and it was now getting in the way of their working relationship. "The woman you saw in the elevator."

Griffin looked up and to the right as though picturing the subject in his mind. "Five-seven, thin build, shoulder-length, reddish brown hair."

"Eyes?"

"Brown."

Sydney jotted the information down. "The thing you remember the most about her."

"The woman's hair. Sort of a film noir look."

Sydney looked at him over the top of her sketchbook, tempted to ask him if he pictured Veronica Lake. But one of the cardinal rules in doing a witness sketch was that you didn't put words in a witness's mouth. Every question needed to be open-ended. "Any particular style?"

"Wavy, side part. What else do you need?"

"What were you doing during the hour before?"

"I have no idea. Why do you need to know?"

"Cognitive interview techniques." She didn't need to explain it to him. It was something he was familiar with, though probably not when it came to doing a drawing. When used, it could help someone recall the smaller salient details that might be overlooked.

"The hour before? Paperwork."

"The *entire* hour. Actions, thoughts, weather. I'm sure you can summarize without leaking secrets of national security. Very simple, even for super spies."

Griffin looked mildly annoyed. "I was looking at a picture of my wife," he said, which made her wish she hadn't asked. But then he added, "The secretary delivered a packet allegedly from Dorian, and then Tex called, saying Dorian changed his mind and wanted to meet. Pissed about the short window to recon the new area. No daylight. Cold out. Heard the gunshot, ran in, the elevator opened—" He stopped mid-sentence, his gaze again moving to the side as though seeing something in his mind's eye. "I remember seeing dangling earrings. Distinctive shape. Like an upside-down question mark."

As much as Sydney wanted to quip I-told-you-so, she held her tongue about his remembering this tiny yet significant detail. What she did ask was the shape of the woman's face.

"Heart-shaped."

She drew, then turned the paper so he could see it.

"A little wider in the forehead."

Sydney made the correction, turned it back to him.

"That's it."

And so it went. Back and forth for the next two hours, with only a short break between for coffee. Unlike other drawings, with other witnesses, there was no small talk to make the witness more comfortable, nothing to fill in the seemingly endless minutes while she sketched and shaded. And as she worked in silence, she wondered what he was thinking as he sat there.

She felt his eyes on her but didn't look up, and she decided she needed to settle this thing between them. Whatever it was, because hell if she even knew. Her pencil moving across the paper, she finally came out with it. "The truth is that I was upset partly that you consulted Carillo instead of me."

"Why?"

She put down her pencil and looked right at him. "I *called* you over Christmas."

"I know."

"I just thought . . ."

"I was in Mexico. On a mission with Marco. I didn't get the message until yesterday."

Which made her feel every bit the idiot. "Doing what?"

"Trying to find the route they're using to smuggle terrorists into the U.S. via Mexico. Unfortunately, not successful."

"Oh."

And the rest of the sketch was done in silence, because Sydney had no idea where to go next, and it was clear that neither did Griffin. By the time she finished shading in the hair, he appeared more than ready for this to be over. She showed him the final version.

He reached out. "May I?"

She handed it to him, and their fingers brushed as he took it from her. His attention, however, was on the drawing.

He studied it. "Something's off . . ."

"What would you do to change this? Make it look more like her?"

He held up his hand, blocking out part of the drawing, probably to see if he could isolate what was bothering him. "Her cheekbones," he said after a few moments. "They were higher. Sharp, but nice. She was pretty."

In that deadly sort of way, she told herself as she erased the area, resketched, then showed him.

He nodded. "Definitely her."

Once he decided there were no further changes, she gave him the final drawing, and was glad when Carillo knocked on the door, saying Tex was done interviewing Trip.

All she could think about was that she still had no idea where she or Griffin stood. She told herself it didn't bother her at all.

Sometimes the lies came easily.

13

New Year's eve dawned bright and cold, and when Griffin entered his office that morning, he tossed his keys on his desk, his gaze catching on the envelope that Dorian had sent.

"I was about to go get coffee," Tex said, stopping in the doorway.

"Already had some." He picked up the envelope. "These are the passes that came for you yesterday."

"The From Sticks to Bricks charity fund-raiser?"

"The same. I was wondering if Dorian sent them on his own, or was he forced? Of course, the bigger question is, why?"

"Since he thinks we're reporters, maybe it was to talk us *out* of doing an investigative article. I think we should go."

"*You* should go. Someone needs to work surveillance."

"Two-man team's not going to cut it," Tex said. "Who are you planning for a third person?"

"It's New Year's eve. Not like there's anyone around."

Tex sat in one of the chairs and leaned back, propping

his boots up on the edge of Griffin's desk. "There's always Fitzpatrick."

"She's on administrative leave."

"Like red tape has ever stopped us? Or are you trying to avoid her?"

"Why would I do that?"

Tex gave a cynical laugh. "Talk about stepping around the elephant in the room."

"Any two-ton behemoths present are wearing cowboy boots. And for the record, *she's* the one who asked not to be included. *I'm* merely respecting her wishes."

"You need to tell her, Griff. Before you do anything stupid."

"Stupid?"

"Like sleep with her."

"Weren't you on your way to get coffee?"

Tex stood. "Don't say I didn't warn you."

"Close the door on the way out . . . and take your elephant with you."

Syd had just returned from the grocery store when Tex called, asking, "Any chance you're free tonight, starting around five?"

"Depends," she said. "If you have a better offer, I'm there."

"Stakeout. Dress warm and bring a gun." He told her what was going on. Not what she had in mind for New Year's eve. Still, it beat sitting at home with Carillo and company.

Sydney walked into the *Washington Recorder* right at closing, and one of the staff looked up, saw her, then made a phone call. Apparently her presence around here was old hat. A minute later the elevator door opened and Tex emerged in a tuxedo. "A little overdressed, aren't you?" Sydney asked once the elevator started its ascent.

"Did I mention you'd be in the surveillance van with Griffin?"

"You sort of glossed over that part."

"Guess we could always ask Carillo, and you could have the night off."

"So I can sit home drinking cider with his wife *and* her lover? Hmmm . . . Let me think about it . . ."

"So how is Carillo?"

"A little stir crazy, being cooped up."

"Beats going to their funeral," he said, leading her into the conference room, where their equipment for the night was laid out on the long table.

He was sorting through the earpieces when Griffin walked in.

"I need the keys—" Griffin stopped short at the sight of Sydney. "You're definitely not Marco."

"Dang." Sydney reached up and felt her face. "I *knew* something was off when I looked in the mirror this morning."

"Marco couldn't make it," Tex said. "Last-minute replacement." He inserted the earpiece, then turned to Sydney. "Does this receiver make me look fat?"

"Do I have to answer that?"

"Where're the keys?" Griffin asked, looking slightly perturbed.

"My desk."

Griffin left, and Sydney eyed Tex. "Glossed over me being here, too?"

"Might've slipped my mind."

"Should be an interesting evening."

"Hey. I'm the one facing danger."

"From Griffin, maybe."

An hour later Griffin and Sydney were seated in the surveillance van, watching the front of the hotel as Tex parked, then walked across the lot into the lobby. There was an awkward silence between the two, and Sydney looked over at Griffin as he stared straight ahead.

She laughed. "I don't bite, you know."

Griffin didn't quite smile, but it was close to one as he handed her a set of binoculars. "Sorry. I've had my mind on other things."

"Tex isn't trying to set us up, is he?"

"Not exactly. There *is* something I need to talk—"

Tex's voice sounded in her earpiece. "I'm walking in."

Griffin keyed his radio. "Copy." He lifted his binoculars for a view.

"There's a sign directing all press members to check in at the silent auction table," Tex told them.

And Griffin said, "How much you want to bet that wasn't there until *after* they sent us those tickets."

"Don't want to lose track of your special invitees."

Music played in the background, and then she heard Tex introducing himself to someone. "James Dalton. I'm with the *Washington Recorder.*"

"Welcome, Mr. Dalton," came the man's voice. "Let me just get you checked off. Are you here with anyone?"

"Unfortunately my wife wasn't feeling well," Tex said.

"Sorry to hear that. Looks like we don't have your home address on file . . . One of the raffle prizes is an all expenses paid trip to Hawaii if you want to provide it. Might cheer your wife up if you win."

"Business address won't do?"

"I think they're hoping to add to their mailing list," the man said. "Every little bit helps, you know. Your ticket stub."

"Thank you," Tex replied.

Sydney lowered her binoculars as two men from the hotel exited the lobby, one leaning heavily on the other, staggering as they crossed into the parking lot in their direction. They stopped one row up, the man on the left bending down, probably puking his guts.

"Little early to be drunk," Griffin said, then adjusted the volume on their receiver. "Music's louder. Tex is probably moving deeper into the ballroom." He keyed the mike. "Anything interesting yet?"

"Besides a half-full room of overdressed patrons and enough champagne to get a third-world country inebriated? I'd rather be in the van."

"That's what happens when you lose the coin toss," Griffin radioed back.

About a minute of nothing but music followed, then Tex making the rounds, slipping into and out of social groups, and being introduced to one politician after the other. "They could hold a Senate meeting here," he said to one bystander, who laughed. A moment later the man was introducing him to yet another person, saying, "Senator Burgess, this is James Dalton, *Washington Recorder*."

"Mr. Dalton . . ." came a woman's voice; Sydney assumed the senator's. "I'm sorry to say I don't subscribe to your paper."

"Imagine it's a bit conservative for your tastes, ma'am," Tex said.

Griffin reached over, turned up the radio, saying, "What the hell is she doing there?"

"You know her?" Sydney asked.

"More importantly, *she* knows Tex, and they're not exactly buddies."

Someone laughed in the background, and then the senator asked, "Is it a coincidence you're here, Mr. Dalton, or am I somehow supposed to believe you're supporting the cause?"

"The world is full of coincidences, Senator."

"Isn't it. I—"

"Ah, Senator Burgess," came another man's voice, this

one filled with enthusiasm and admiration. "So good of you to come to my documentary." Apparently Micah Goodwin, the man behind the fund-raiser.

Sure enough, the senator replied with, "Micah. How *very* lovely to see you again."

"And who have you brought with you?" Micah asked.

There was a hesitation, and then Tex saying, "I'm one of the reporters covering your event. James Dalton from the *Washington Recorder.*"

"Always glad to meet the press," came his reply. "Especially for a cause as worthy as this one. Have you seen the documentary?"

"Unfortunately not all of it," Tex said.

"Well, at least the senator has."

"A *wonderful* cause," she said, the perfect politician. "Ah. But I see my husband waving to me across the room. You'll excuse me?"

"So tell me, Mr. Dalton," Micah said. "Anything about the documentary you'd like to know?"

"What can you give me in a line or two?"

"This . . . For every person present tonight, we're able to relocate one refugee from the overburdened camps to this country to start a new life. Moving them from a hovel of sticks and tarps to a real brick building."

"Every person present?"

"Twenty-five hundred dollars. You have no idea what it feels like to walk into a village, war-torn, poverty-stricken, feeling helpless and insignificant, because all the money won't make a difference to these people. But when we bring them here, they have a chance. I can't tell you what a sense of fulfillment this has all brought me. Having a place in this world, knowing that my little documentary has helped pave the way for so many underprivileged refugees who had nothing."

And so it went for several minutes, small talk, people discussing the film and what a good cause it was. Apparently Tex had moved off by himself, because a moment later he said, "You two might want to get in here. I found her."

"Found who?" Griffin radioed back.

"The woman Sydney sketched. Only they were wrong about her looking like Veronica Lake. I'd say she's more like Jessica Rabbit."

"How the hell do you know it's even the same woman?"

"She's wearing the earrings Sydney drew."

Veronica Lake . . . Jessica Rabbit. Whoever she was, Tex was all for getting a closer look, because what he saw was intoxicating. She wore a silver lamé dress that hugged every curve, the discreet slit up the side hinting at silken legs that went on forever, and he pictured her bloodred stiletto heels being kicked off in the middle of his bed. "I think I'm in love, Griff."

"Down, boy. We're on our way in."

Tex glanced toward the main entrance, where all the doors stood wide-open to the lobby beyond, but didn't see Griffin yet. Unfortunately the auburn-headed bombshell turned and started walking in the opposite direction, her silky hair cascading down her back, her dress shimmering with every step.

Love, lust, who was counting? He quickened his pace, gaining ground, then almost ran into her when she suddenly stopped next to a table piled with books.

"Oh my God!" She jumped, her hand going to her chest.

"Sorry about that," he said. "I wasn't watching."

She looked around her, then turned back to him. "No, no. It's probably my fault. There were these guys— Never mind. It's like I'm running in fifteen different directions and I have no idea what I'm doing."

"Have you read it? The book?" he asked, picking up a copy and opening the front cover.

"I'm sorry. I didn't catch your name," she said.

"James Dalton, with the *Washington Recorder*."

"Eve Sanders." Her mouth parted slightly, showing a line of even white teeth. Then, lowering her voice, she said, "The *Recorder*? As in the same reporter who talked to Dorian Rose?"

"I am."

"I realize this is awkward, but when he told me you had contacted him, I—I just had a feeling something bad was going on. I guess I just never expected that he'd kill himself. It was all very surreal. I mean, I'd just left his apartment."

"You were there?"

"I was, but he didn't answer his door, so I left. I just—I knew he was in there. And now I have to wonder if there's something I could have done differently. Maybe knocked louder, stopped him from taking his own life—"

"Is something wrong?" he asked when her attention was suddenly diverted toward the front doors.

She pulled her gaze back to him. "Sorry. I thought I saw— I'm just tired." She reached out, grasped his arm. "You *aren't* going to write about this, are you? Dorian's suicide?"

"No, ma'am," he said.

A moment later he heard Griffin announcing, "We're here."

Tex looked in that direction, saw Griffin and Sydney to the left of the doors, each with a camera hanging around their necks, their attention on Tex, undoubtedly waiting to find out what to do next.

"Friends of yours?" Eve asked, apparently noticing his interest.

"My photographers," he told Eve.

A moment later Tex watched as two men moved to either side of Sydney and Griffin, stepping in close. Too close. Unfortunately, Micah Goodwin walked up to the podium to begin his speech, and the applause drowned out whatever the two men were saying to Griffin.

A third man walked up behind Tex and Eve, and in a voice just loud enough for the two of them to hear, said, "Don't move, Mr. Dalton. I have a gun pointed right at you."

And to prove his point, he pressed the weapon into Tex's side.

14

Nothing like the sobering feel of hard steel against your rib cage, Tex thought, as the sound of applause finally died, and Micah Goodwin stood at the podium on the dais.

"Thank you," Micah said into the microphone. "But I won't bore you with a long speech, other than to say I appreciate your support tonight, your generosity in growing my dream of bringing refugees from war-torn Africa to a better life here in the U.S. As one man I was powerless. Together we're building dreams."

More applause, and then he continued with, "And while it goes to show what we can achieve when joined by others of a like mind, there *is* one person here who deserves special thanks. Eve Sanders, the lovely young volunteer worker who managed to put my otherwise unknown documentary in the hands of the great people at A.D.E. *Without* her, I wouldn't be an international phenomenon. More importantly, we wouldn't have all of you wonderful people coming together to ensure the success of From Sticks to Bricks. Eve? Where are you?"

Scattered clapping, then Micah saying, "Ah, there she

is near the book table with a group of ardent admirers."
Micah glanced to his side, where a man was working what
appeared to be a sound and lighting system. "Terry, shine
that spotlight over there. See her? Silver dress. Come come,
gentlemen. Don't let her walk out without the acknowledg-
ment she deserves."

Eve stilled as the light hit them. "What should I do?"

The gunman shoved his weapon deeper into Tex's side,
using his body to shield it from view, as he quietly said, "Ex-
tricate yourself, Ms. Sanders."

She glanced at Tex, then down at the weapon, before turning a bright smile toward the podium. "They'd rather see
you, Micah."

"Not the men," Micah replied, to some scattered laughter.

Now or never, Tex thought, then called out, "Would you
like me to bring her up?"

"How about it, folks?" Micah said into the microphone.
A thunderous round of applause, then he waved them to the
podium.

The gunman leaned over and said into Tex's ear, "Be *very*
careful, Mr. Dalton. We *still* have your friends."

Not for long, Tex thought, placing his hand at the small of
Eve's back, ushering her away from their would-be captor.
As they neared the stage, he glanced back, saw the two men
walking Sydney and Griffin toward the side door.

He grabbed Eve's hand, doubled their pace.

"What are you doing?" Eve whispered.

"Improvising."

He hurried her up the few steps to the podium, then leaned
over to speak into the microphone. "Mr. Goodwin, you're
going to have to forgive me here. If we could swing that
spotlight over by the front door . . . where my photographer and his assistant are *trying* to make a getaway . . ." He
waited and the man working the lights did as asked. The two
thugs on either side of Sydney and Griffin froze like deer in

headlights as Tex continued, "Before they rush off, I was hoping you'd allow my photographers to snap a few photos of you mingling with the crowd. We're talking some good front page material, courtesy of the *Washington Recorder*."

"That ought to make the politicians happy," Micah said to laughter from the audience. "Let's get those cameras up here and sign some books!"

And like magic the crowd herded Griffin and Sydney toward the stage, and the two gunmen fell back.

"You did it," Eve said.

"For the moment. We still have to get out of here."

Sydney stood in the midst of the flashing red and blue lights that lit up the front of the hotel, reflecting off the plate-glass windows and those of every car parked in the lot. She'd called MPDC to make sure they had a clear route out to prevent anything from happening to the other guests, should the kidnappers attempt to take them by force. Once the cops showed up, their alleged kidnappers fled and the threat was averted. "Sometimes," Sydney said, "you have to do things the old-fashioned way."

"Effective," Griffin replied. "Unless you want to preserve your cover."

"*Your* cover. I never had one," Sydney countered as Lieutenant Sanchez walked up, eyeing her with a mixture of frustration, annoyance, and curiosity.

She put on her best smile, since maintaining a good working relationship with the local cops was always a plus. "Lieutenant Sanchez. Thanks so much for getting everyone here so quickly."

"You mind telling me what's going on?" Sanchez asked.

She drew him away from the others, conscious of where Eve was standing, even though Tex was doing a good job of keeping her out of earshot. "You recall the suicide related to the big embezzlement case we discussed last night?"

"Or didn't discuss, if I remember correctly."

"Right. That one. This is a follow-up to that."

"Let me guess. You wanted us to come charging in, save the day, then pretend like it didn't happen?"

"Not exactly. After all, we had five hundred witnesses in that ballroom, and one of them's bound to question why you're here. I figured you could spin it as a robbery attempt."

"A robbery?"

"The men who tried to force us from the ballroom had guns."

"And who was it they tried to rob?"

"The reporter, photographer, his assistant, which would be, uh, me, and that woman in the silver dress. Any chance I can use one of your interview rooms to take a statement from her?"

"You want my damned car keys to drive her to the station, too?"

"I think we have the transportation covered."

"You know what, Fitzpatrick? When you finish digging out of this can of worms, you are going to owe me. Big-time."

"You're with the FBI?" Eve, her silver lamé gown at odds with the scarred and battered police interrogation room, stared at Sydney as though seeing her for the first time. "James Dalton and his photographer? Are they FBI, too?"

"No, ma'am," Sydney said. "They're with the *Recorder*. They were doing an investigative piece involving the embezzlement from a San Francisco charity. I asked to accompany them in hopes of getting to the bottom of whatever is going on. And a good thing, it turns out."

Eve wrapped her bare arms around herself. "I can't believe this is happening to me." She closed her eyes, rocking back and forth. "I thought he was going to kill us. When he pointed that gun at James—" She looked at Sydney. "Is he here? This is all my fault. I should have called the police when I first saw them."

"I can bring him in if you like."

She looked relieved. "Please . . ."

"I'll be right back." Sydney left her, walked down the hall to where Tex and Griffin waited in a small seating area. "One damsel in distress asking for a mild-mannered reporter."

Tex jumped up, a boyish smile lighting his face.

Griffin gave an exaggerated sigh. "Try not to drool, Tex."

"Ah," Sydney said. "New lust. It's kinda cute, don't you think?"

Griffin leaned back in his chair and closed his eyes. "Wake me when you're done."

Syd and Tex returned to the interview room. Eve stood the moment Tex entered, and with only a moment's hesitation, threw herself into his arms.

"Easy there," he said, patting her back, keeping his expression suitably concerned. "You okay?"

"I—I think so. I thought we were going to die. What if you hadn't gotten us up to the stage? How did you even think to do that?"

"Just lucky, I guess."

Sydney pulled her chair out, clearing her throat. "We should really get started. It's been a long night. Eve, why do you think they came after you?"

"It's rather obvious, don't you think? They want to know if I know where Dorian Rose hid this book they're looking for."

"What book?" Sydney asked, since this was the first any of them had heard about it.

"Accounting book? Bank book? The book that tells them where all the missing money is?"

"Had you seen these men before?"

"Not until yesterday. Right before Dorian—" She looked down, clasped her hands in her lap. "He called to say that his friend Trip had talked to some reporters and he was worried, because they—you, I assume," she said, looking at Tex, "wanted him to talk about Trip. We all sign nondisclosure agreements. We're not to talk to the press unless it's a designated script. Micah's very particular about his program's image. That's why he likes to get to his venues a few days early for prepublicity interviews, that sort of thing. Handle it himself."

"Dorian called me," Tex said. "Around seven last night. Any idea why?"

"To give you the book. I mean, that's the only reason I can think of. Which was why I was so spooked when I saw the two men at the fund-raiser tonight. I think I saw the same men at Dorian's apartment right after I got there. They were just driving off. They have to be after it, too."

"This book?"

"I can only surmise. After all, I don't know for a fact. What I do know is that when this much money changes hands, charity or not, people's priorities shift and not always for the better. Back when Micah began, when I first started helping him, no one cared about him, his documentary, or his program. He'd get the occasional donation check, if he was lucky. But I'd seen what A.D.E. had done with some other similar ideas and I knew that they could turn things around for him with the proper backing. And I was right. Micah's Sticks and Bricks fund-raisers are hugely popular since the release of his most recent documentary. He's so personable, he makes people feel as if they're actually making a difference. Pack a ballroom full of donors, and suddenly everyone wants to help the refugees. Who doesn't want to be part of that?"

Tex nodded, saying, "I can see your point. But how does he get the funding to where it needs to go?"

"By running the money through A.D.E. They specialize in refugee-related charitable funds, which is how they're able to keep their overhead down. "

"How many of these signings have you done?" Sydney asked.

"Twenty-three, so far."

Tex whistled. "You're talking over a million bucks a pop."

"Micah is big money."

Huge money, Sydney thought. "Any idea why these men would target us at this fund-raiser?" she asked.

"None," Eve said. "It doesn't make sense. Unless they thought you were carrying a lot of cash? That's the only thing I can think of." She took a breath, looking at her watch. "Look, I know this is important, but I really have to get back. Micah will be expecting me, we have an early flight out, and frankly, I'd like to be off the road before the New Year's revelers hit the streets."

"Of course," Sydney said. "I can't think of anything else to ask."

She glanced at Tex, wondering if he wanted to add anything, but all he said was, "I'll walk you to your car, Miss Sanders." He stood, and Eve followed suit, and as he walked out, he winked at Sydney.

Great. She only hoped he remembered they were working a case, not running a dating service.

15

"Something is off," Sydney said to Tex and Griffin.
Eve had returned to the hotel, where she was staying in a
donated suite with Micah, certain that his personal security would suffice for protection. She, Griffin, and Tex had
returned to ATLAS headquarters. "I'm still trying to figure
out that interview."

"What do you mean something is off?" Griffin asked.

"With Eve. What? I'm not sure. We were in that room a
half hour interviewing her. Did she really tell us anything?
Don't you think she should have been more upset? Her
friend committed suicide or was murdered, and someone
pulls a weapon and tries to kidnap the both of you . . ."

"Seemed appropriate to me," Tex said.

Griffin raised a brow.

Sydney continued with, "And what about the fact Griffin
saw her seconds after Dorian shot himself?"

"True," Griffin said. "We only have her word that Dorian
didn't answer the door."

Tex looked aghast. "Are you saying she pulled the trigger
and set up the suicide?"

"I'm just laying out the facts," Griffin said.

Tex shoved his chair back, obviously miffed at the direction the conversation was moving. "It's late and I want to go home. What's your point, Sydney?"

"There's more to her than meets the eye."

"Damned straight there is."

"All I am suggesting is look past her cleavage."

"I *like* her cleavage," he shot back, then left the room.

Sydney turned to Griffin, who shrugged, saying, "What do you want from a guy who thinks she looks like Jessica Rabbit?"

"Jessica Rabbit? A frigging *cartoon* character?"

"A *hot* cartoon character. Never mind the movie she's in is his favorite."

Sydney stood, glanced at the clock. Almost midnight. "I'm going home."

"I'll walk you out."

The parking lot was deserted, theirs being the only two cars present. A light dusting of snow covered the ground, having fallen while they were inside, marred by a set of footprints, Tex's undoubtedly, since his car was pulling out of the lot at that moment. A few snowflakes drifted down, and everything seemed quiet and peaceful.

Sydney waited while Griffin double-checked the door, making sure it was locked. When he turned toward her, he stopped, listened to the rat-a-tat-tat of fireworks popping in the distance. "I think someone jumped the gun by a couple minutes."

They walked side by side, their footprints joining Tex's, the snow quickly melting beneath their feet. When they reached the cars, Griffin said, "Thanks for helping out tonight."

"I'd say any time, but I'm not sure if that's true."

He laughed, and they stopped, stood there for an awkward

moment, and then he leaned forward, saying, "Happy New Year." He gave her a quick kiss.

It took her by surprise, and before she could say anything, he kissed her again, this time wrapping his arms around her. It took her a moment to right herself, to realize that this kiss was the real deal, and when he stopped to look at her, it was because he was waiting, wanting to know if she was okay with this. She reached up, pulled him closer, and lost herself. Before she knew it, they were leaning against her car, the icy metal against her back, bits of snow melting against her jeans and Griffin's warm, lean body pressing into hers.

He kissed her ear, and she heard him taking a deep breath, letting it out, and then another. "Stay with me," he said.

She hesitated, and she could feel his heart beating, or maybe it was hers, she didn't know, but it seemed like everything hinged on her answer. If they were going to be together, this was the time. She tried to say yes, and found her throat suddenly dry. Instead, she nodded, and when the tension suddenly left his shoulders, she realized he'd been waiting in anticipation for her answer, not sure of the outcome at all.

"At your place?" she finally said, when she found her voice.

"Yours might be a little crowded for what I had in mind."

She smiled. "Let me pick up a couple things from my apartment and warn Carillo he'll be babysitting by himself?"

"How about I follow you?"

"You afraid I might skip out?"

He laughed, then looked at her with a dead serious expression. "You wouldn't, would you?"

"Not a chance. But I'd rather not parade you in front of my houseguests, should they not be asleep."

He pulled a pen from his pocket and took her hand, writing his address on it. "This way you won't lose it. Don't take too long."

"I won't," she said, and he kissed her once more, then opened her car door for her. It was everything she could do not to break every speed law getting home. The drive was fairly smooth. Not a lot of revelers on the road at this hour. Several minutes into the drive, she noticed a set of headlights in her rearview mirror, the vehicle hanging back just far enough to make her wonder if it was on purpose. After a minute she signaled and made a right. The car followed, and just when she figured she was being tailed, it sped past. Cop, she realized, probably trying to decide if she was some drunk driver before moving on to the next vehicle. And sure enough, she saw it up ahead, lights flashing as it followed a weaving Ford Focus down the street.

The rest of her drive was uneventful, and before she knew it she was pulling into the parking lot of her apartment complex, as a limo taxi pulled out. Smart person, since this was *not* the night to be out driving after drinking. She parked in the underground garage and walked to the elevator, her footsteps echoing across the pavement, hoping that Carillo and company would all be asleep, because she wasn't sure she wanted to explain to him what she was doing heading out. She'd leave Carillo a note saying where she was. Easy enough.

A quick ride up to her floor, she walked down the carpeted hallway, hearing laughter and music behind several doors as she passed. Hers, thankfully, was quiet, and she carefully inserted her key, not wanting to wake anyone.

She pulled the door open, saw the kitchen light on, heard the TV. Stepping inside, she turned the dead bolt, then walked into the living room, glad to see no one was awake. Carillo was passed out on the chair in front of the TV, his head dropped back, mouth open. Sheila was splayed across the couch, one hand hanging over the edge, a bowl of popcorn spilled across the carpet as though it slipped from her grasp as she passed out. A medicine bottle was knocked beneath the couch, and she picked it up, glanced at it. Sheila's sleeping pills. At least she wouldn't have to worry about Sheila waking up as she slipped out. Sydney walked over, scooped the contents back into the bowl, and set it on the table, then eyed the rest of the room.

Apparently Trip was the only one who had the sense to go to bed.

She gave one last look at Carillo, surprised, if truth be told, that he'd drink that much, and she picked up the half-full champagne bottle from the coffee table, worried that Sheila might knock it over when she stirred. She set it on the counter, then headed for the bathroom, trying to decide what she needed to take, passing the darkened spare room on her way.

She flicked on the light, took a deep breath, eyed herself in the mirror, then froze. Sleeping pills. Only *half* the champagne was missing. Not near enough for anyone to pass out, least of all Carillo, who had said he was going to drink apple cider. "Shit."

She backtracked to the spare bedroom. Pushed open the door, turned on the light. The bed was empty. She checked her room. Empty.

She ran into the living room, shook Carillo, willing there to be some logical explanation. Not tonight, she thought, seeing Griffin's address written on the palm of her hand. She shook Carillo harder. "Wake up, damn it!"

He stirred slightly and she checked his pulse. Slow, steady.

The same with Sheila. She grabbed the pill bottle, dumped them out, saw only four were missing. Enough to put them to sleep, not enough to kill them.

Sydney ran to the kitchen, reached for her cell phone, wanting to scream, cry, something, and it was everything she could do to keep her voice calm when Griffin answered the phone. "We have a big, *big* problem."

16

San Ysidro Border Crossing

"What was the point of your trip to Mexico?"

"Shopping." Yusuf opened a bag to show the Border Patrol agent a black leather coat. "Cheap." There were a number of agents at desks, interviewing various persons who were trying to get into America, those they'd pulled aside for extra screening. Yusuf had been prepared, told this was likely, due to his appearance. Thus he'd waited for a busy holiday, where due to the higher numbers of people walking across the border, agents were likely to be in more of a hurry and not so thorough.

"Are you a U.S. citizen?"

"No." He handed the passport over, worried as the agent typed something into his computer. The cost to get his student visa from the United States had used up most of his funds. "I go to college here. UCLA."

"When do you graduate?"

"At the end of this year."

"Shouldn't you be wearing a Lakers sweatshirt?"

"Lakers sweatshirt?"

The man pointed to Yusuf's thick shirt, and the San Francisco Giants emblem on the front, which he was assured was a popular thing to wear in the U.S.

Yusuf held his ball cap in his hand, running his fingers across the brim, trying to figure out the nuances of a Lakers sweatshirt. Did that mean he'd sweated on it? There was something wrong, he could tell. And then it struck him. Sports teams. He wasn't sure what it had to do with sweat in his shirt. "Yes. I like the Giants." He smiled.

The agent's fingers flew across the keyboard, then paused as he read whatever was on the screen. Yusuf couldn't see what was there. But he saw the man's eyes seem to focus in on something a moment before he pushed his chair back and said, "Wait here."

He stood, then walked across the room to speak to another agent, this one with hash marks on his sleeves. That man looked over at Yusuf while the first agent discussed what it was he found or saw . . . Yusuf's heart started beating, and he forced himself to remain calm, look unconcerned. Someone who had a valid reason to be in the country would not worry. Not be scared.

"Hey!"

The shout startled him. A dark-skinned man was making a dash for the door. The agent ran after him, grabbed him by the shoulders, and then the fight was on. A mass of green uniforms coming from every direction tackled the man. As they fought, Yusuf eyed the door, wondered if he picked up his things, casually walked that way, would they notice.

His agent, the one who'd seemed suspicious, or curious—he couldn't tell—was at the bottom of that pile, having been one of the first to help. Who would notice?

No one, he decided. Certain he wasn't being watched, he

reached over, slipped his passport off the desk and then took his plastic bag with the jacket inside, stood, then waited. Someone took out pepper spray, and he felt a sting as the agent sprayed it in the man's face. It hit another agent, his, and he knew this was a sign and backed toward the door. He opened it, looked out, saw a few uniformed men standing just outside. Would they stop him?

Not if they were busy.

"There's a fight in here," he said. "A big fight."

The agents all ran past him, and he let the door fall shut, then started walking among the other pedestrians into America.

It was all coming together.

Very soon now. Very soon.

Border Patrol immigrant inspector Daniel Balthazar rinsed the residual pepper spray from his eyes, feeling grateful it wasn't too large a dose, then returned to his desk after they'd finally managed to get the suspect into a holding cell. A typical case. The man had been working illegally in the United States for over two decades. This was his second attempt to reenter the country, to rejoin the family he'd been forced to leave behind.

Daniel felt for him, but their hands were tied. And now, unfortunately, he had an assault charge on top of the immigration charge.

He pulled out his chair, sat, then stared at his computer, the screen he'd started typing the name on. "Oh shit."

Gil, sitting at the desk next to him, glanced over. "Oh shit, what?"

"The guy who was sitting here. Don't suppose you've seen him?"

Gil scoffed. "I was on the bottom of the dog pile beneath you. Not like I was taking note."

Daniel stood, a sense of panic arising in him as he looked around the office, not seeing the guy. He walked to the door, ran out, looked around, then hurried through the building out to the footbridge, trying to find him among the pedestrians walking across to California.

Gone.

"What's wrong?" Gil asked when he returned to his desk out of breath. Daniel sat and stared at the computer screen, not moving. "You get a little too much pepper spray in the face?"

"The guy who was sitting here when the fight happened. I think he got through."

"You were going to dump him?"

"I was thinking about it."

"He show up on any lists? Any lookouts?"

"No. But something was off." He went over the conversation in his mind. "The guy said he was in college, but his conversation was stilted. I was asking him about his sweatshirt. Wearing a Giants logo in UCLA. It was like he didn't know what I was talking about."

"Foreign student. What'd ya want?"

Daniel wasn't the sort to get worked up over an illegal alien, certainly not someone who was just trying to go to college, get an education, but the guy who'd slipped from his desk during the fight got to him. That whole conversation about the Lakers. A real college student, or at least a college student from UCLA, was going to know who the Lakers were, but the way the guy looked at him when he'd mentioned the sweatshirt . . . Daniel rewound the video surveillance, watched the fight going on, then saw the man reach over, slip his passport from the desk and casually walk to the door, informing the agents outside about the fight.

Gil walked over, watched with him. "You sure you want to put it out there? It's not like they're gonna find the guy. Damned needle in a haystack once he crosses over. And you'll get razzed for weeks, never mind written up for letting him go."

"What if he's someone?"

"Chances are he's just a schmuck like the poor guy we tackled earlier, but if you want to make something of it, send out a teletype, call the agents working the Greyhound station, and move on. We've only got about twenty thousand more pedestrians to screen before the day's out, and the line ain't growing any shorter."

Daniel typed up a BOLO, then sent it out.

Possible illegal border crossing, suspicious person. Name used may be Abdoul Hassad, reporting to be student at UCLA wearing San Francisco Giants sweatshirt. If contacting individual, notify US Border Patrol Immigration Inspector Daniel Balthazar. Advise on possible routes of travel.

That done, he got back to work. Gil asked him about it when they were changing in the locker room at the end of their shift. "They check the Greyhound for you?"

"Yeah. A few times. Nothing."

"Bet he took the very first bus. I wouldn't worry about it. Probably nothing."

Yusuf paid the taxi, then got out at the storage facility. He had memorized the unit number, 314, and found it near the back. A man was unloading boxes out of his truck into a nearby storage unit. He wiped a sheen of sweat from his forehead, then drank from a can of Red Bull, nodding at Yusuf as he finished it off, then tossed the empty can into the back of his truck. Some of the UN workers drank it back at the refugee camp, and he'd heard one say it was a stimulant, laughing that they weren't allowed to chew khat, or *qaad* as his countrymen called it, so they drank Red Bull instead. Yusuf had never partaken in chewing the plant, nor could he see drinking the manufactured substitute.

He nodded back at the man who continued unloading his boxes, then turned the corner and found 314. The padlock hung there, taunting him. It was supposed to be a combination lock. He'd memorized it before he left.

Now what? He had no key, and someone seeing him with bolt cutters, even if he had a pair, would rouse suspicion.

And then the long-ago memory came to him of one of the boys at the orphanage showing another boy how to pick the padlock . . .

A soda can. He retraced his steps, saw the man struggling with a heavy box that seemed off balance, and he ran up. "Let me help."

"Thanks, bud."

Yusuf took hold of one side and together they walked it into the unit, which was filled with dozens of boxes, all marked.

"Right here near the door's fine."

They lowered it to the ground, and Yusuf said, "Do you need help with anything else?"

"I got it from here. The rest are light. But thanks."

Yusuf walked out, eyed the Red Bull can lying in the pickup. He couldn't just reach into the back of the truck. "Would you mind if I take that?"

"You one of them recyclers? Feel free."

Yusuf hesitated, trying to determine if that meant yes.

"Go ahead. You can have it."

"Thank you." He reached in, took the can, then walked back to the locked storage unit, fishing his small folding knife from his pocket. He sliced off the end of the can, then cut out two squares, slicing each, then folding them into shimmies, which he inserted into the lock on each side of the shackle, allowing it to pop open.

He tossed the pieces of the can and the lock on the ground, then slid open the door, just as he heard the sound of a vehicle driving around the corner. Before he could slide the door shut again, he heard, "What the *hell* is that?"

Yusuf turned around and saw the man he'd helped staring through his open driver's window into the storage unit. Yusuf had been taught that to remain calm was the key, even when he saw the man look down at the open lock and the pieces of aluminum can used to pick it. Any show of surprise or anger would draw attention. Just like what happened at the border crossing with the man they'd tackled. "It's used for cancer therapy," he said about the machine.

The man stared at it. "Huh. Never seen one up close. Looks like it belongs on the Starship Enterprise. Laser beams or something, right?" He laughed.

Yusuf pretended to laugh as well. Starship Enterprise. He thought back. Space movie. "Right."

"You a doctor?"

"No. I fix the machines. This one's broken."

"Ah. Well, thanks for your help and all."

He drove off, and Yusuf immediately turned on the light, closed the door so no one else would see him, then set about dismantling the machine, removing a lead capsule the size of his fist from the protective rotating head. He hurried out of there and was walking down the street when he saw a patrol car arriving at the storage facility. There were no lights, and the officer didn't even seem to notice him as he drove on past, turning into the gate.

The man with the boxes would have called the police, Yusuf thought, probably because of the lock picking. It hadn't occurred to him before. But apparently it didn't matter. Perhaps the police had too much violent crime to tend to and so couldn't send someone out right away to investigate.

A good thing, he thought, holding tight to the small metal

tube a couple inches in diameter. It contained cesium 137, a water-soluble radioactive powder, something he was aware could make him very sick the longer he had it with him. He walked a couple blocks to a grocery store, then used his phone to call the taxi company again, this time for a ride to the Greyhound station. He smiled at the man working the ticket counter. "Hi. One ticket to Washington, D.C., please."

17

McNiel walked into Griffin's office late that after-
noon. "It's New Year's. Why are you here?"

"Same reason as you," Griffin said. "Catching up on reports."

"I forgot my tickets to the symphony."

"Okay, maybe not the same reason."

McNiel narrowed his gaze, approached Griffin's desk and
peered at the computer screen. "What about this don't I want
to know?"

"We've had a few complications."

Tex rushed in the door. "Just got this photo from Homeland Security—" He stopped short at the sight of McNiel.
"Hey, boss. Just . . . working away . . ."

"I always find that when you do the work you're *paid* to
do, life is a *lot* easier. For me, at least, since I'm the one who
has to sit in front of the Senate intelligence committee and
justify our dollars spent."

And Tex asked, "How exactly does that occur if we don't
exist?"

McNiel started for the door, saying, "I don't suppose either of you have bothered to take a look at the intelligence report I put on your desks before I left yesterday . . . ?"

Neither answered, because they hadn't. They'd been too wrapped up in Carillo's case.

"Try your In basket. The folder with the big 'Priority' stamp across the face of it." He paused in the doorway, looking back at them. "Marked for a reason, I might add."

He left, and Griffin found the folder in question and opened it. "So what did Homeland Security have to say?"

"If Trip flew out anywhere, it wasn't under any name we have."

"Maybe he's still here, then," Griffin said, scanning the report.

"Not likely." Tex waved the sheet of paper he'd brought in. "This sort of—"

"Hold up." Griffin reread the paragraph just to make sure he hadn't misunderstood. "This might explain a few things about Dorian's death and the armed intruders at the charity last night."

"You gonna share?"

"They traced some money that was funneled to a Somalian terrorist group they think was helping facilitate Yusuf's movement into the country."

"Does it tell us where Yusuf is?"

"No."

"Then how did that earn a big fat Priority stamp?"

"The money comes from a charity."

"Like *that's* a new source?"

Griffin shook his head then turned the page. "Maybe it's not the charities. It's the umbrella organization that disburses the money." He looked up at Tex, still trying to wrap his head around what he just read. "A.D.E."

"The group that Eve works for?"

"The same."

"Please tell me she's one of the good guys . . ."

"She's raking in a million bucks a day for A.D.E. So far it's not looking good."

"But she was my Jessica Rabbit . . ."

"Sorry, bud."

"Yeah, it gets worse." Tex took a deep breath, letting it out in frustration as he laid the photocopy from the airport security camera on Griffin's desk.

A limo, undoubtedly from the service that picked up Trip from Sydney's complex, was parked at the passenger drop-off zone in front of Virgin Atlantic. Three people were standing by the limo, waiting for their luggage as the driver removed it from the trunk. Trip, Micah, and Eve.

Sheila sat in a chair at Sydney's kitchen table, her shoulders slumped, a look of disbelief on her face as she faced her interrogators, Griffin and Tex, while Sydney and Carillo stood in the background. Carillo nursed a large cup of coffee, and a killer headache to boot. Sydney didn't feel the least bit of sympathy for him. He wasn't the one whose night was ruined by Sheila's idiot boyfriend. His headache would go away. She, on the other hand, had every reason to hold a grudge, even if she couldn't exactly announce why, she thought, as Sheila listened to what Tex was telling her.

"What are you trying to say?" Sheila asked. "That Trip set me up? He wouldn't do that." She looked at Carillo. "Tell them, Tony."

"What can I say, Sheila? The guy drugged us."

"Then he had a good reason."

"Ya think?"

Sydney gave Carillo a surreptitious kick, whispering, "*Not* helping . . ."

Carillo crossed his arms, leaned against the wall. "Sheila. Just answer their questions."

She wiped at a tear, then waited for Tex to continue.

He slid the photocopy of the airport security footage, asking, "Have you ever seen any of these people before?"

She looked at it. "Sure. Trip, Micah, and his assistant Eve."

"Where did you last see them?"

"Last night. Trip, I mean. Micah and Eve in San Francisco, where they finished up their West Coast tour."

"Ever overhear any conversations between them?"

"No." She eyed the photo, then looked up at Tex, her eyes glistening. "You don't think that he and her are . . . you know . . ."

"I'm not sure what to think."

Griffin asked, "How did you and Trip meet?"

"At coffee around the corner from my house. I heard him ordering with that English accent. I just love to hear him talk."

Sydney could hardly blame Carillo when he shifted on his feet, whispering, "Seriously?"

Tex, however, gave a sympathetic nod. "Any idea what other names he might have been using?"

Sheila glanced down at the photo, shaking her head, her voice low, disbelieving. "Are you sure his name isn't real?"

"Pretty sure, ma'am," Tex said.

"But he was taking me to meet his family."

"Any idea where they live?"

"Somewhere in England . . . ?"

"Letters from anyone? Return address from anything we might be able to trace him to?"

She shook her head, looking around the room. "Do you think he made that up, too?"

When no one answered, her face crumpled. "But he said he loved me!" She covered her eyes with her hands, sobbing.

"Ah, geez," Carillo said on an exhale. He walked over, put his arm around her shoulder. "How about you go lie down. Take a nap, okay?"

She nodded, allowing him to help her from the chair, then

walk her into the spare bedroom. "I can't believe . . . what an idiot I am . . ."

"Nah, trust me. There's way bigger idiots out there."

Sydney, glad to see Carillo finally coming round, waited until they disappeared into the room before asking, "Wouldn't he have had a visa when he flew out here with Carillo?"

"We already checked. His ID was American. Driver's license only with his aka. So whoever facilitated his U.S. stay did a damned good job of getting him some good old-fashioned American ID to get into the country and out of it."

"He wasn't on the same flight as Micah and Eve?"

"The only one we can even place on a flight is Micah," Tex said. "And yet we have all three passing through airport security around the same time. Since they couldn't get past there without a ticket, we have to assume the worst. They're gone. Right along with our lead to wherever this money is disappearing to."

Carillo returned, picking up his coffee cup.

"How is she?" Sydney asked.

"A mess. And here I thought Trip was *the* one." He sipped his coffee, made a face, then walked over to the sink and dumped it. "My impending alimony aside, what now?"

Griffin leaned back in his chair, sliding the photo back into the folder. "Donovan's meeting up with a local MI6 agent as we speak."

"Donovan?" Carillo asked.

"Donovan Archer. Another ATLAS agent," he replied, and Sydney recalled the man from the last operation she worked with Griffin in France.

"So what does this mean?" Carillo said. "They think Micah's in on it with Eve and Trip?"

Griffin shook his head. "According to what we can find, he's clueless, not only about the high volume of money being funneled out, but that any of it is making its way into terrorist hands. Right now, finding Trip and Eve are our best leads. We can use your help."

Carillo poured a fresh cup of coffee. "As much as I'd love to put one between Trip's eyes on the government's dime, someone's gotta babysit Sheila until we're sure no one's coming after her. Take Sydney. She's better at that international stuff."

"I think she's better off here," Griffin said.

She wanted to ask why, but the bedroom door suddenly opened and Sheila came out. Her eyes were bloodshot, her nose red and running. Her expression was one of hope as she stood there, focusing on Carillo. "If you thought I was in danger, you'd do everything you could to protect me, right?"

"Sheila—"

"I think Trip would, too. Protect me. Even if it meant leaving me behind. That means his heart's in the right place."

Carillo's chest expanded as he inhaled deeply, probably trying to keep his temper in check. "Yeah. Sure it is."

"If you heard him talking to his niece Emmie, wishing her a happy New Year, you'd see what I see. He's a good man. That's why he left me. To protect me."

"You think he would have said something," Carillo muttered under his breath.

"He probably didn't because he was worried I'd follow him. And for all your FBI intelligence, you think you'd ask the person he called from my phone *right* before he took off. Maybe I should go look for him myself. God knows you're not doing any good."

"*What* person?" Carillo asked.

"How the hell should I know? His phone was dead, so he borrowed mine."

"You have the number?"

"Of course I do. How do you think I found out he was flying to England?"

18

Carillo was about ready to slam his fist into a wall as the meaning of the term "stir crazy" became abundantly clear. The moment Griffin and Tex copied every number from Sheila's phone, they left. Sydney, tired from apparently having to stay up to make sure he and Sheila didn't die in their sleep by aspirating on vomit, had napped all day, leaving him alone with Sheila, who spent the remainder of the day *and* night watching a Dr. Who marathon, crying at the English accents because they reminded her of Trip.

When Sydney finally emerged from her room, Sheila was demanding that Carillo take her home.

"I'd love to," he said, "but you know damned well I've got my psych evaluation tomorrow afternoon. I can't go back to work until they release me, and I'm sure as hell *not* going back home until that happens."

"So what am I supposed to do in the meantime?" Sheila asked. "Sit here and twiddle my thumbs? I doubt whoever's after Trip even knew I existed. Trip was a *very* private person."

"Yeah. Kept a few secrets, didn't he?"

"I want to go home, and you can't stop me."

"Be reasonable, Sheila."

"I *am* being reasonable. And besides, we're imposing on Sydney. It's not fair to her."

Carillo looked to Sydney, silently willing her to talk some reason into his wife's head. "Tell her it's not an imposition."

"If she thinks it is," Sydney replied, "you can both check into a hotel."

"See?" Carillo said. "No imposition."

"That's not what she means, Tony, and you know it."

To which Sydney said, "Maybe she could stay with Doc until you get back."

"*That's* your way of helping?" Carillo said.

Sydney ignored him, and Sheila said, "Can't you at least call Doc? I could stay at the condo. Whoever was after Trip wouldn't know to look for me there—if they were even looking for me at all."

Knowing she wasn't going to let up until he attempted, he called. Doc agreed, and Carillo made the flight arrangements.

Early the next morning he and Sydney personally escorted Sheila into Dulles International Airport and up to the security gate to stand in the long line of passengers waiting to be screened before being allowed into the terminal. Sydney moved off a few feet, giving them the illusion of privacy.

"Doc will be waiting for you when the plane lands," Carillo said.

"I'll be fine. They weren't after me," Sheila pointed out. "They were after Trip, and he's gone."

"Yeah, well, just in case, I'll feel a lot better knowing that Doc's with you."

"I really don't think he needs to stay with me at the condo, Tony. It's not like they know where you live."

"Just until this blows over, okay, Sheila?"

"Fine." She leaned over and kissed him on his cheek. "If I

didn't say it before, I really do appreciate what you're doing for Trip."

"I'm not doing it for him."

"I know." She offered a smile, then handed her ticket to the guard, and Sydney and Carillo left her as she made her way through the lineup to the X ray and screening.

Carillo watched her until she slipped her shoes on, gathered her belongings, then walked off toward her gate.

"I think Sheila's right," Sydney said. "I don't think she was ever a blip on their radar."

"Surprising, considering the stupid moves she's made since this whole thing started. Doc, at least, will keep her in tow."

"Breakfast?"

"Definitely. Gotta gear up for that psych eval. This whole forced-leave-after-a-shooting-to-make-sure-you're-mentally-fit sucks. I feel like going in and telling them exactly what I think."

"That'll get you a fit-for-duty. Not. They already think you're stressed, Carillo. Don't push it."

"I know how to play the game, Sydney. I'll be released and I can get back to San Francisco and my nice boring life."

"And sign those divorce papers?"

"I can practically smell the ink drying."

Carillo held the door for Sydney, then followed her into the building and to the elevator. The shrink on retainer for their fit-for-duty interview was on the sixth floor. "You know why they make us come here, right?"

"I'm sure you'll tell me."

"Throw us off our game," he said. "They do it on purpose. Home court advantage. Just like we do when we're interviewing some dirtbag suspect."

"Or maybe they just like being in their own comfortable office instead of one of our sterile interview rooms?"

"I just want to get back to work. I don't like all this sitting around doing nothing. You know they're out to get us."

"Then don't give them a reason to."

His phone rang, and he pulled it from his belt. "Carillo here."

It was Doc. "You did say your wife was set to arrive this afternoon?"

"Yeah. Why?"

"She wasn't on the flight. I checked. She canceled at the gate and took the next flight to London."

Carillo stopped in his tracks. "Please tell me you're kidding."

"With everything that's happened? I wouldn't kid about something like that."

"Son of a bitch . . ."

"You want me to do anything?" Doc asked.

"I'll get back to you. Thanks." He disconnected, then hit the number for Sheila, wishing he could reach through the phone and strangle her. "Call me as soon as you land. Do *not* leave that airport."

"What's wrong?" Sydney asked.

"That idiot wife of mine made a slight detour on her way to San Francisco. By way of London."

Sydney's mouth dropped open. "What the hell are you going to do?" she asked when she finally recovered. "You haven't even told them what's really going on. It's not like they're going to let you go chasing after her."

"First step, get through the damned psych eval."

Carillo was *not* a fan of psychiatrists, psychologists, or any other medical professional who purported to know when an agent should or should not be allowed to return to duty, especially when *he* was the focus of that diagnosis.

"How are you today, Tony?"

And he especially hated it when they called him by name as if they personally knew him.

"Hunky-dory."

The woman checked her notes, lifting up a sheet inside the manila folder. "I'm curious, since we don't seem to have discussed it. Why is it you flew all the way out here instead of seeing the doctor they have on retainer in San Francisco?"

"Seemed like the prudent thing to do."

She gave a neutral smile, as though waiting for him to enumerate.

He was good at waiting games.

"Why?" she finally asked.

"Couldn't say."

"Can't or won't?"

"Is there some magic phrase you need me to use so I can get back to work?" he asked, fast losing patience. "I've got a full caseload, and the way budgets are being cut right and left, the taxpayers will appreciate if they're getting their money's worth."

"You seem a little stressed."

"Seriously?" She didn't know the half of it. And unfortunately it wasn't like he could tell her. "Every day I'm kept from my job is another day these dirtbags get away with crimes because some misguided psychoanalyst feels like she knows what's best for me. When she's only met me twice, I might add. You can call it whatever the hell you want. Just get me back to work."

She closed the folder and stood. "I think we're done here, Mr. Carillo."

So it was *Mister* Carillo now. "Then how am I supposed to go back to work?"

"I was going to suggest a couple more days. I'll have to rethink that."

"To something shorter?"

"When's the last time you took a vacation?"

"I dunno. Couple years, why?"

She walked over, pulled open the door. "I'm recommending you don't come back until you've had at *least* a week off."

"A week? What the hell am I supposed to do in the meantime?"

"Take up knitting, for all I care. You have seven days. Use it."

He grabbed his coat, headed out, then stopped in the doorway. "Do I stay home? Go somewhere?"

"I'll leave that up to you."

"I've never been to London. You think seven days is enough time to visit there and maybe some of the surrounding areas?"

"You want more time, call. Getting away from work is *exactly* what you need."

"Thanks, Doctor. I'm feeling better about this already."

19

Since Sydney's agenda was quite the opposite of Carillo's, she had no trouble getting her return to duty from the psychologist, and as soon as she walked out, she picked up Carillo from the lobby downstairs, then drove straight to HQ.

While Carillo was in getting his "vacation" approved from the powers that be, Sydney tried several times to get through to Griffin to let him know this latest turn of events. For whatever reason, he wasn't answering.

Frustrated when she couldn't even get Tex to answer his phone, she called Griffin back and left a voice mail. "Sheila took off to England. Can you call when you get a chance?"

"Maybe you should text him," Carillo offered.

"If he's in his office, the signal won't go through. Besides, politeness dictates he should return my call. It's not like this isn't important."

"Except he has a stubborn streak almost as wide as yours."

"Wider."

Carillo checked his watch. "You could always drive over there."

"And how will you get to the airport?"

"I'm a big boy, Fitzpatrick. I can fend for myself."

When she hesitated, he said, "Go already. We're talking about my wife, and if anyone at ATLAS can find out what the hell she's involved in or heading into, I'd like a heads-up before my plane lands in Heathrow."

"All right. I'm going."

She drove to ATLAS headquarters, telling herself that she was doing this for Carillo's case, *not* because she wanted to see Griffin. What she didn't expect was to be thwarted by the reception staff, who wouldn't let her past the first floor of the *Washington Recorder*. It didn't matter that they recognized her from past visits. Unless Griffin, Tex, or someone from the "editorial staff" floor gave permission, she was not getting on that elevator. They would, however, be more than happy to pass on the message that she stopped by.

Lovely.

If only she could remember exactly how to get in the secret back entrance, through the subway tunnels below, not that she'd have any better luck in that direction. The massive vaultlike steel doors that led into ATLAS headquarters via the underground could only be accessed by fingerprint and code. As she walked through the parking lot, she called Griffin one more time, got his voice mail, informed him that she was there at his office, then stopped short when she saw his black SUV. Turning, she looked up at the fifth floor, about where she thought his office was situated, knowing damn well he was up there. Maybe even watching her.

Why the sudden noncommunication thing?

She returned to the lobby and walked up to the receptionist. "Can you relay *one* more message to Mr. Griffin?"

It was about that point she realized that the man was looking at someone behind her. She turned, saw Griffin standing in the elevator, holding the door open. She didn't even want to decipher the look on his face.

"You needed to see me?" he said, moving aside so she could step on.

"You didn't return my phone calls," she told him once the elevator door shut.

"I was in a meeting all morning. Did you think about calling the secretary to have her interrupt me?"

"You have a secretary?"

The elevator stopped on his floor, and he allowed her to disembark first. "Someone has to screen the calls from impatient FBI agents. What were you planning on telling him downstairs to get me there any faster?"

"That I'd follow you to England to investigate this myself."

"England?" He gave her an amused look as he escorted her into his office. It was pieced together from a surplus warehouse of castoffs: scratched and scarred gray metal desk; one guest chair, also gray, with attached slate blue vinyl seat back and cushion, circa 1960s; another chair, dark wood with burgundy upholstery, looking like it hailed from the mid-1980s. The only luxury in these days of budget cuts was his ergonomic desk chair. "Quite a ways to travel just to get me a message."

"I followed you to Rome, didn't I?"

"Good thing I showed up when I did. Saved you from embarrassing yourself."

"Why?"

"I'm not going to England. So what was so important you couldn't wait for me to finish my meeting, check my voice mail, and get back to you?"

"Carillo's wife took off to London after Trip."

"How?"

"I'm guessing she walked up to a ticket counter, plunked down her credit card and said, 'One flight to England, please.' I'm pretty sure it didn't occur to Carillo that she would do something that stupid."

"Apparently he's not the only one who underestimates the opposite sex."

"I wasn't *really* planning on taking off."

He gave her a look that said he only half believed her as he took a seat, typing in his password to access his computer. She glanced across the room to a photo of Griffin and his late wife, Becca, both in ski gear on the slopes of some mountain.

"Looks like her flight's already landed. We could have stopped her if we'd known earlier. Carillo's going after her, I take it?"

"Yes. His plane leaves in about an hour."

"Have Carillo call me on the landline before he leaves. I'll fill him in on a few things."

"What things?"

"There's a bit of overlap on Trip's charity and a case we're working. I'll call Donovan. He can put Carillo up at the safe house MI6 is letting us use."

"What sort of overlap?" she asked.

"You're going to have to trust me on this," he said, getting up and walking her to the door. "We have a lot of things going on right now, and it would take way too long to go into it. Do you need an escort to the lobby?"

He was teasing her, and she was glad to see that his mood was improving. "No. I think I can manage. Assuming you can trust me to get from here to the elevator on my own." She started to walk out but then stopped, realizing there was a big unanswered question. "Back in my apartment when we first learned Trip flew to England. Why were you so adamant that I shouldn't go?"

He drew her in, closed the door, then kissed her, just like he had on New Year's eve. "Does that answer your question?"

A knock on the other side of the door startled her.

"Griff?"

He took a deep breath, stepped back and allowed Sydney to move away before he opened the door. "Yeah?" he said.

Tex looked up from some piece of paperwork. "Here's the—" And then he saw Sydney standing a few feet away. "I'll, uh, come back later."

"I was just leaving," Sydney told him. She walked out, Tex moving aside to let her pass.

"Syd?"

She stopped at the sound of Griffin's voice, turned, hoped she looked more composed than she felt.

"Call Carillo and tell him that one of us will fly out with him to help." He was pointing toward Tex.

She smiled. "Thank you. I'll do that."

20

Eve unwrapped her scarf, then sat at the table, across from Lou, the one man in England she could trust. He was the one who had helped her arrange the last-minute ticket for Trip. "Sorry I'm late," she said.

"Do you think he suspected you?"

"Trip? Not a chance. All he wanted to do was get out of the U.S. and away from his girlfriend. Fool that he is, I think he's more worried about Sheila's FBI husband stirring things up than any threat that might come on this side of the Atlantic." She leaned back in her seat, grateful to have a moment to relax, no matter how brief. "I have Sheila's husband to thank for being brought in for questioning at the D.C. event, something that was *not* on my agenda. Apparently he or his wife called in a couple reporters to look into Trip's embezzlement charges."

"And Micah?"

"I've got to finalize a few arrangements later this afternoon at the hotel where his event is taking place. But I can tell you this. If Micah ever comes up for air and notices anything he shouldn't, they'll probably kill him. Right now, he's so busy patting himself on the back, he hasn't a clue what I'm doing. He sure as hell didn't notice when three gunmen—" Her gaze caught on Lou's watch as he lifted his cup to take a drink. "Oh, crap. Is it really that late? I have to go." She pushed her chair back and stood. "I'll call you the moment I hear anything."

Eve rushed out the door, then down the street, weaving through the pedestrians who had just disembarked from a double-decker bus, all of whom seemed to be going in the opposite direction. She pushed through them, reached the corner. The light was red and she looked to her left, saw no cars, then stepped from the curb, only to be pulled short when the man next to her grabbed her by her arm.

"Careful, miss. Traffic comes from that direction," he said, nodding to her right just as a black taxicab zipped around the corner, proving his point.

"Thanks."

This time she looked to the right, saw it was clear, then darted across the street and on around the corner toward the Tube. She rushed down the stairs, slapped her fare card against the reader, pushed through the turnstile, then hurried to the platform, breathing a sigh of relief that she made the train. She walked toward the front, took a seat by the door so that she could exit the moment it stopped. As long as there were no unexpected delays, she should only be a minute or two late.

Hardly enough to warrant a second look. She hoped.

The train stopped and she let herself be carried by the forward momentum of the exiting crowd, then hurried up the steps, dodging passengers descending from the street above. In less than five minutes she arrived at the A.D.E. building in the financial center of London. Clayton Barclay, CEO of A.D.E., maintained an office here, as well as in the United States. American by birth, he'd lived in Great Britain these past three years but traveled extensively between the two countries to run the worldwide organization that collected, accounted for, and disbursed the money from a number of different charities beneath the A.D.E. umbrella.

The warm air from the lobby washed over her as she pushed through the rotating glass door, and once inside, she removed her gloves, grateful to be out of the cold. Barclay's office was located on the third floor of the four-story building, a quick elevator ride up. She entered the offices, greeted the receptionist, then walked back to the meeting room, where she saw him seated at the conference table through the open door. She entered and smiled at him, even though inside she had nothing to smile about. The entire operation was bungled from start to finish.

"Eve. Good of you to make it." Barclay gave her a cold look as she sat down, and all she could do was take it. He was the man in charge of the money. The man in charge of them all. "Now that everyone is present," he said, "we can get started on the progress report." He looked right at her. "Eve?"

She hadn't expected to go first and wasn't prepared. "The book's still missing."

"Where is it?"

"I can't say, primarily because the person I was *supposed* to get it from is dead."

"Dorian Rose?" Barclay said. "He was talking to reporters."

"You were supposed to give me a chance to talk to him. What'd you think he was going to do? Just hand the thing over to a couple thugs who show up at his door?" she said, nodding to Willis, one of the gunmen seated across the table from her.

Willis smiled. "You seem on edge."

"Could it be because you and your idiot partners almost ruined the fund-raiser and all the work I've done so far?"

Barclay slammed his hand on the table and she nearly jumped from her seat. "A couple reporters showed up asking questions after talking to Dorian Rose. What did you think I was going to do? Let them have free rein?"

Two reporters and an FBI agent, she amended silently. Not that she was about to correct him. The last thing she needed was to end up dead because he mistakenly believed the FBI involvement was *her* fault. Trip was the one to blame for that, and she knew his life wasn't worth a whit once Barclay learned the FBI was snooping around and he had anything to do with it.

That wasn't her concern at the moment, and she took a calming breath as she wracked her brain, trying to think of a way to spin this. Somehow she needed to smooth it over before Barclay lost his temper and decided she was more of a liability than an asset. She had no intention of ending up dead like the others. "I can understand your concern about the reporters showing up. But sending someone to the hotel after them was a mistake. Do you have any idea what Micah would have done if he'd learned that a few reporters were kidnapped from his event and later killed?"

"Shed a few tears and order you to send flowers?"

"The man lives and breathes his charity, *as long* as he feels it is doing more good than harm. I've worked with him on a daily basis these last six months. I know him, his mental fragility. If you send him into an emotional roller coaster over a few reporters who don't have a clue what's going on, you're going to shut down your biggest cash cow."

"And how would you know they have no idea what's going on?"

"Because they think this is one big giant embezzlement case stemming from money Trip allegedly stole. Every question that they asked was directed to that. And since their star witness, Trip, has fled the country, I seriously doubt a two-bit paper like the *Washington Recorder* has the resources to track him down."

Barclay stared at her for several seconds, and she was certain her heart was beating loud enough for him to hear. Finally he relaxed, sat back in his chair, offered something akin to a smile. He turned his gaze to Willis. "Tell me more about Dorian Rose. You were the one following him before his unfortunate demise. Surely you have some idea about what he told the reporters."

"Don't think he said much at all. They weren't together long enough on the first contact, and since we were listening in on the phone for the second, we know nothing was said."

"Then where the hell is this missing book? Why hasn't anyone found that for me yet?"

The man shrugged, and Barclay turned his gaze back to Eve.

As much as she'd hoped to hold this card close, she realized she had no choice but to state what now seemed obvious.

"I don't think it ever left the country, as we were led to believe. I think it's right here in London. Why else would Trip return, except to retrieve it?"

21

Tex sat down at the table inside the tavern near May-
fair, monitoring the numbers they'd copied from Sheila's
phone back in the States, while his partner in the case, Donovan Archer, ordered their lunch. The number Trip called
about twenty minutes before Sydney had seen the limo pulling out of her apartment complex belonged to a cell phone
with a U.S. number, registered to a name and address they
determined were fraudulent. That, however, wasn't what in-
trigued him. What made it the number to watch was that it
was currently here in London. Tex was tracking it in real
time, which is why they settled in the pub about a block from
the phone's location.

Donovan walked up a moment later with two mugs of
beer. "Any luck?" he asked, sliding one of the mugs Tex's
way.

"Still sitting in the same place. You get ahold of Carillo?"

"Yeah. He says Sheila's number still hasn't shown up on
the monitor. He's sitting tight."

"Good thing Trip isn't the brightest bulb, using Sheila's
cell phone to make his getaway . . ."

"Unless he did it on purpose . . ."

"I like my theory better."

Tex set the phone on the center of the table and they watched the small screen while waiting for their order. The phone hadn't moved for the last twenty minutes, showing a steady signal coming from the same area. The moment the waiter appeared with their lunch, it changed. "We might want to get that to go. It's finally moving."

"Which direction?"

"South."

Unfortunately, the signal ended somewhere in the vicinity of Claridge's Hotel, when its owner apparently decided to shut it off, or the signal was lost due to the building's infrastructure. They walked up and down the block, hoping to pick it up again, but no such luck.

"It would be nice to know *whose* phone it is," Donovan said.

"Have you tried Sheila's cell again?"

"Voice mail. And to quote Carillo, 'Knowing her, she probably let the battery die.'"

And suddenly Tex's phone pinged, as the signal came back to life. "It's here," he said. And they looked into the glass-fronted lobby area of Claridge's Hotel, only to see Eve Sanders standing just inside.

They entered, and she looked over, saw Tex and froze, her expression moving swiftly from confusion to something Tex thought might have been a mix between shock and anger. And then, recovering quickly, she walked over, her brows raised as she said, "Why are you here?"

"Told you," Tex said. "I'm writing a story on Micah."

Donovan added, "Are you staying at this hotel? Pretty posh place."

"And who are you?"

"Sorry," Tex said. "My new photographer. Donovan Archer."

"Seriously?" She crossed her arms. "You followed us to London just for a story?"

"You know editors," Tex said. "They're sticklers when they want something done."

"A five-page *nothing* paper like the *Recorder* can afford to send two guys to London to follow up on some *fluff* piece, when every other paper in the U.S. is going bankrupt?"

"I'd think the answer is obvious," Tex said. "Rich owner."

"*Very* rich," Donovan added. "And he's taken a liking to your boss. Must be all that charity work he does. So here we are, doing what we get paid for."

"What the hell did you guys do? Call every hotel until you found me?"

"We're tenacious when it comes to following up a story," Donovan said. "In fact, we have a lead on some guy whose wife ran off to find Trip. You know anything about that?"

She looked away, clearly upset by this turn of events. But then she turned back to them, her face the epitome of calm as she said, "His girlfriend, I expect. They're quite the pair. I haven't seen him since we got here. And I definitely haven't seen her. I'll call you if I hear anything. Where are you staying?"

"Haven't decided yet," Tex replied. "It was sort of a spur of the moment assignment when our boss found out Micah's next tour stop was in London."

"I suppose if you've gone to this much trouble, you might as well stay here."

Tex looked around. "Thanks, but no thanks. Our boss might be rich, but I'm pretty sure he'd draw the line at a five-star hotel. What we *would* like is an interview with Micah, then we're out of your hair."

She seemed to think about it for a moment. "Fine. I'll set it up for tomorrow morning. But rule number one, no more showing up at his events. Not after what happened the last time."

"Not like we invited the robbers."

"No. But apparently they zoned in on you over this thing with Trip's friend, Dorian, and my duty is to protect Micah. Whatever Dorian and Trip were involved in, I don't want anything to do with that. Are we clear?"

"Perfectly," Tex said, then tipped his finger to his forehead. "Appreciate your offer, ma'am."

"I'll call the Dorchester to let them know you'll be by tomorrow, say ten?"

"You're not staying here?"

"No. This is where Micah's event is tomorrow night." She took out her cell phone. "It *is* just the two of you, right? Your FBI agent friend isn't here with you? What was her name?"

"Sydney Fitzpatrick. And no, she's apparently done with the case."

Eve moved off to make a call, and Donovan leaned toward Tex, asking, "You think she's really calling the hotel?"

"Don't know and don't care," he said, his gaze firmly planted on her backside as she walked toward the front desk.

Donovan eyed Tex in disbelief. "You talk about Griffin with Fitzpatrick? You're scaring me."

"No harm in looking, Donnie boy. Besides. What's not to like?"

Tex's phone rang and he answered the call.

It was Griffin, saying, "I have some intel."

Eve walked up at that moment, so Tex said, "Can I get back to you? Reception's a bit spotty."

"Call me when you're in a secure location."

Eve smiled at them. "Everything's set for tomorrow at ten. I don't suppose the two of you have a couple business cards? I'll make sure they get to Micah so he knows who to expect. And if I hear anything on Trip's girlfriend, I'll call."

Donovan and Tex both pulled a card from their breast pockets and handed them over, and Tex followed it with, "Looking forward to tomorrow."

Carillo glanced up from the computer monitor, a look of hope on his face, when Tex and Donovan returned to the safe house.

"Eve hasn't seen them," Tex said. "Or so she says."

"Now what?"

"Do what you're doing. Watch for Sheila's cell phone to pop up on the screen, or Trip's if he happens to ever turn his on. Start calling hotels she might stay at. In the meantime, we'll keep looking."

"She'll be fine," Donovan added.

Tex returned Griffin's call. "You rang?"

"Two things. Lisette's flying into London to help. I want her to connect with you first in case you're able to find any other threads we might have missed."

"You said there was something else?"

"Confirmation that Fitzpatrick's assessment of Eve was spot on. There's more to her than meets the eye. We've got visual intel showing Eve talking to known arms dealers outside of the capitol. On more than one occasion. Just want you to know what you're dealing with. I'm faxing the photos to you now."

22

Eve stood at the corner waiting for traffic to clear,
this time making sure she looked to the right before she
rushed across the street. Lou was inside the pub when she
got there, at a table in the corner near the window overlook-
ing the quiet street near Paddington Station.

"You're not going to believe who showed up here," she
said when he handed her a beer. "The two reporters."

"I thought you weren't worried about them."

She slipped out of her coat and hung it on the back of the
chair. "Not when I thought they were on the other side of
the Atlantic."

"Any idea what they're doing here?"

"If they're to be believed, chasing after Micah for a story."

"You don't believe them?"

Eve sat back, eyed the thin head of foam at the top of her
beer, then took a long sip. The slight bitterness was refresh-
ing after her hurried trip out here. "This has turned into a
goddamned nightmare, I'm not sure what to believe. They're
staying here in London."

"Where?"

"I don't know. Trip swears he told them next to nothing, and since he knew next to nothing, I believe him. But the fact they're even here is scaring the crap out of me. I do *not* want to end up in a body bag because two Clark Kent wannabes are searching for clues to a Pulitzer pipe dream—assuming they really are reporters. There's something about them that's not quite right." She reached into her coat pocket, pulling out their business cards. "See what you can find on them."

He read the names, then slid the cards into his pocket. "Have you heard anything on where this book might be?"

"No. But like I told Barclay this morning, I don't think it ever left the country."

"So now what?"

"Divide and conquer. I have a feeling that Trip is going after it. Which is why you need to follow him tonight. Failing that, he trusts me. I think I've convinced him to hand it over once he gets it."

"Are you sure you want to do this?"

"I think it's a little late to be asking that, don't you?"

It was almost five, the streets around Trip dark. He watched the building until he saw Byron coming outside into the gated courtyard to light up a cigarette. Thank God for bad habits, he thought as Byron flicked his lighter, cupping the tip of his cigarette against the cold wind, the tip glowing as he inhaled. Trip pulled his hood over his head, shoved his hands in his pockets, then walked to the locked wrought-iron fence, saying, "Spare a cigarette?"

"Sure." Byron reached into his pocket, then looked at Trip for the first time, really seeing him. "Are you *mad,* coming here?"

Trip pulled his hood down lower in case anyone might be

looking out the windows. "I need to know what you know about this book."

Byron glanced behind him, then motioned Trip to one side of the gate, where a tall hedge in the courtyard blocked the view from the office. "That depends. Why?"

"You're all in danger," Trip said. "You need to get rid of it."

"As much as it's worth? Besides, it's our only insurance. I have a wife and a kid—"

"Dorian is dead."

"Exactly," Byron said. "So I'll be damned if I give up the only thing that's probably keeping me and my family alive right now."

"The only reason you're alive right now is that they think *I* took it with me to the States. They killed Dorian when they thought he had it, and since they didn't find it there, they either think I brought it back or it never left. And which do you think the logical conclusion will be?"

Byron stared at him in disbelief. "You don't think I'd be stupid enough to keep it?"

A feeling of dread swept over Trip as he envisioned any number of things happening to the book. "What on earth did you do with it?"

"Don't worry. It's safe."

" 'Don't worry'?" He reached through the wrought-iron fence, grabbed Byron by the front of his jacket and pulled him so that Byron's face was wedged against the cold iron bars. Byron's eyes widened as Trip demanded, *"Where is it?"*

"Good God, man. Calm down. Marty has it. He's always had it."

Trip let go of Byron, took a step back, his knees almost giving out at the thought that his ex-brother-in-law was behind this. "Marty . . . ? Why?"

"Because he's a money-hungry sod, that's why. I'm not sure, but I half suspect he's the one who pointed the finger at Dorian."

Trip tried to wrap his head around the thought. *Nothing* made sense. "Marty wouldn't do that."

"Wouldn't he? Who do you think set you up to take the fall for those accounting errors?"

Trip refused to believe it. And yet it all started making sense. "They tried to kill me . . . Ever since I called Dorian about my suspicions of embezzlement . . ." He should have listened when Dorian tried to warn him about Marty. "This is crazy. Does Marty even know what it's about?"

"See, that's your mistake. Blowing it all out of proportion. Marty and Vince made the thing to protect us. And it has—"

"You bloody idiot! They're trying to kill everyone who knows about it! You think Vince's car accident was really an accident? Probably the only reason *you're* still alive is that they're waiting to see what your next move is." Trip leaned against the wall in defeat, feeling as if the world was crashing down around him. He was too small against such a big power, and to hear he was being betrayed by his own brother-in-law . . . "I have to get that book from Marty. They'll kill him the moment they suspect he's got it."

"They're watching me, too, which is why I don't dare walk out with the thing, even if I knew where Marty hid it. They're watching all of us."

"You have to convince him, then. Warn him. It's our only hope."

"What if I found a way to get him to bring it to you without anyone knowing?"

Trip hesitated. He didn't necessarily like Marty, even if at one time Marty had been married to his sister, but that didn't mean he wanted anything to happen to the man. Still, what choice did they have? Any of them? "Tell him I think it's too dangerous for him to carry anywhere. But I have someone who can help. Someone I trust." Trip pulled a card from his pocket and handed it to Byron. "This is a long shot, but if Marty can get it to this person, we might have a chance."

Byron took the card, glanced at it. "A chance for what?"

"To stay alive."

Byron flicked his cigarette to the ground, the glowing ember shattering into tiny sparks as it hit the brick walk. "I'll see what I can do."

"Byron. Back when this started, Dorian told me we're pieces of the puzzle, and they don't want anyone putting it together. Tell that to Marty. Tell him to be careful."

"We'll be fine," Byron said, then turned and walked back through the gated courtyard to the door of his building. He opened it, the light from inside spilling out, silhouetting him for a sharp, clear moment before the door sliced the air with a snap, taking all the light with it.

Dread swept over Trip as he stood in the dark. He'd been a fool to ignore what had been so obvious. How had he not seen that this would all fall apart? He only hoped Marty would do the right thing before it was too late.

Hands shoved in his coat pockets, he started toward the street and walked maybe half a block when a black sedan pulled up alongside him. The back tinted window rolled down and a man he'd never seen before said, "You're Trip?"

Trip's heart started beating double time. "Don't know anyone by that name." He kept walking. The car followed at the same pace.

"You have a sister named Beatrice? A niece named Emmie? Cute thing. Blonde. Turns five in a couple days?"

Trip froze. His tongue turned leaden in his mouth.

"Get in," the man said, and he opened the car door. "You and I are going to have a little chat."

23

MURDER-SUICIDE IN QUEEN'S PARK HOME

Martin Branford saw the headline out of the corner of his eye, while reaching for one of the teddy bears tucked in with the travel mugs at the cash register. He put the bear on the counter, then handed the cashier his money.

"Cappuccino extra dry!" she called out to the barista as she placed the bear in a green gift bag, its brown velveteen head visible over the top. "Sorry I didn't have a larger bag. Must be for Emmie, then? She started school yet?"

"Next year. I'm picking her up after work today. My ex is finally letting her spend the weekend," he said.

"Bring her by in the morning. We'll make something special."

"I will . . ." Marty lifted the paper from the rack, shoving his briefcase to the side to read while he waited for his coffee, wondering how any bloke could feel so overwhelmed to take his family's life. Deciding the article was too depressing, he intended to skip over it, except the company name jumped out at him.

Affinity Data Enterprises.

Marty worked for A.D.E. . . . A wave of nausea swept through him. Suddenly the gift, coffee, and the dreaded contact with his ex tonight were quickly forgotten, and he had to read the entire thing again to make sure he wasn't imagining it.

An accountant from Affinity Data Enterprises shot and killed his wife and 13-year-old son at their home, and fatally shot himself, police said.

The bodies of Byron Nicholas, 38, his wife, Judith, 34, and their son, Byron Jr., were found Tuesday night in their bedrooms. Police were called after a neighbor heard the couple arguing and then later heard gunshots. The neighbor stated that the couple had been arguing for quite some time over finances. A Metropolitan Police Service spokesperson said it appears to be a murder-suicide, and a note from Byron was found in the home. The deaths remain under investigation.

"Oh my God . . ." He stared at the article, his stomach twisting. The words turned incomprehensible as he frantically tried to reread it. There had to be a mistake. Byron and his family dead?

The names in the paper refused to change, and he dropped it on the newsstand, grabbed his briefcase, then turned toward the exit, nearly running into the man and woman standing behind him.

"Marty!"

He stopped, looked at the cashier in confusion.

"Emmie's gift?" She held the bag, the teddy bear tucked inside a sea of white tissue. "And don't forget your coffee," she said when he came back for the bag.

"I—of course. Thanks."

He left the coffee, but took the bag, fumbling with the handles as he slipped it over his arm to dig his mobile from his pocket. He pushed the door open with his hip as he called work. The sidewalk was crowded with pedestrians clothed in heavy coats, hats, and scarves, their heads down against the cold wind, and he stood against the building out of their way. "It's Marty. Is Clarence there . . . ? Yes. I'll hold . . ."

Clarence came on the line. "Marty? You've heard?"

"In the paper. What happened?"

"Just like it said. The police think it was murder-suicide."

"I—I can't believe that."

"It happens. Heaven knows he was under a lot of pressure with the new contract. I heard they were having financial difficulties."

"But he was fine last night. He didn't say anything about finances."

"You were with him?"

"He popped into my office before he left for the day." He went over the conversation in his head. It was cryptic, yes, but under the circumstances, understandable. Certainly nothing that led him to think Byron would murder his wife and son, or take his own life, he thought, glancing into the shop window. He saw the auburn-haired woman who'd been standing behind him pick up one of the bears and show it to her companion. The man, Marty didn't recognize. The woman . . . seemed familiar.

"Did he give you anything?"

Marty drew his gaze from the pair inside. "Sorry. I lost my train of thought."

"Byron's papers. Documents? Books? He didn't give you any, did he?"

His heart skipped a beat. Someone had to have gotten to Clarence for him to be asking about the book. "No. Of course not. Did you look in his office?"

"Not there. Would he have taken anything home?"

"Byron? Never." Marty started down the sidewalk, then stopped, wondering if he'd truly been blind. "Clarence. You don't think . . . ?"

"Think what?"

"What if it wasn't suicide?"

"Of course it was. Financial difficulties. His wife was threatening to leave him. Boyfriend, so I'm told. That'd put anyone over the edge."

"I hadn't heard about the boyfriend . . ."

"Are you coming in?"

"I—I'm almost to the Tube."

"See me when you get here."

Marty dropped the phone in his pocket, going over his conversation with Byron last night. He'd been prattling on about Trip and that damned book. No. It was something else. Something Byron said in his attempt to get him to turn over the book . . . Something Trip had told Byron. Jigsaw puzzles . . . ? That was it. Someone wanted to make sure the pieces didn't fit. That no one ever put them together. They were all pieces. Every one of them.

Sure Byron's conversation was strange, but murder-suicide strange?

Marty walked toward the Underground on autopilot, thinking about the book. Byron almost had him convinced to tell him where he'd hidden it. Marty, however, knew the value of the thing, even if Byron and Trip didn't. It was worth millions. He'd never have to work again.

Murder-suicide . . .

He couldn't wrap his head around the idea. Byron loved his son. Yes, he was under pressure, but not enough to take his or anyone else's life. Certainly not his family's?

Puzzle pieces . . .

Marty followed the other commuters down the stairs, dug out his wallet, touched it to the reader to deduct his fare from his Oyster card, then pushed through the turnstile to catch the next train. The woman he'd seen in the coffee shop walked up a minute later, sipping her coffee as she took her place beside him on the platform. She eyed the teddy bear and smiled. "Someone's going to like that," she said.

"My daughter," he replied, trying to be polite. He was glad when the train arrived, and quickly boarded. Several empty seats were available, and he took one on the opposite side of the car, wondering how he or anyone else at work was going to get anything done. First Vince Stern's car accident, and now Byron Nicholas and his family.

Someone wanted to make sure the pieces didn't fit . . .

Byron's face flashed in his mind, his curiosity over what the book looked like, the probing questions. It was another reason he'd decided against showing it to Byron. Almost as if Byron had hoped to take the book for himself.

Just as he had.

Marty opened his briefcase, but looked up just as the woman from the shop turned quickly away. He had the distinct feeling that she didn't want him to know she'd been watching him. Or was he being paranoid, overthinking what was surely a simple matter with a simple explanation? She was *not* watching him. People killing their spouses and committing suicide wasn't that rare. One merely need open the paper to see it happened. Byron was no different, he decided. Besides, it wasn't any business of his.

Puzzle pieces . . .

He held the briefcase tighter, and his heart started pounding.

Someone wanted to make sure the pieces didn't fit . . .

Marty thought about the contract they'd been working on. Each of them assigned something different, always secluded . . .

Murder-suicide . . .

The air grew hot, stale, the passenger compartment claustrophobic. Suddenly it seemed *everyone* was watching him, including the auburn-haired woman.

Three more stops until his office. At the next, several passengers poured on and he gave up his seat to a woman holding a baby. He moved near the door and stood facing inward, briefcase in one hand, Emmie's gift in the other. Just go to the office. No need to mention the business card Byron had given him.

He fixed his gaze on the floor as the warning came over the loudspeaker.

"*Mind the gap . . . Mind the gap . . . Mind the gap . . .*" On the third and final announcement he pivoted on his foot and slipped through the doors. They whooshed shut behind him, and he heard the train pull away as he rushed toward the exit, not even bothering to fish out his wallet to touch the Oyster card as he passed through the gate, then rode the escalator up.

He was *not* paranoid. That woman *had* been staring at him. He went to that coffee shop all the time and had never seen her there. Nor on this train. Why today?

When he stepped out into the street, he started shaking, not from the cold, but the rock-solid belief that Byron would never have committed such a crime. He would never have killed his wife or son no matter how upset. And with that realization, all his paranoia returned, and he looked back, saw the woman emerging from the Underground, her silver-haired companion behind her.

He hurried around the corner, then ducked into a restaurant, the first open business he found. The hostess, a young brunette woman, greeted him as he walked in. "One for breakfast?"

"Yes. Can you point me to the washroom first?"

"To the left through the double doors."

"Thank you."

He walked quickly, trying not to bring attention to himself. The scent of bacon and roasted tomatoes filled the air as he passed the kitchen on the way to the restroom. Once inside, he closed and locked the door, then leaned against it while he tried to gather his thoughts, calm his breathing. Vince had warned him about keeping the book before he was killed in that car accident. But he had needed the money. He owed more than his house was worth and Bea was demanding child support that he couldn't pay.

A pipe dream. A foolish, deadly pipe dream to think he could extort money, sell the book, and get the easy life. They'd killed Byron and his family, and they were now following him. Which meant one thing. They'd gotten to Byron through his family. Probably tried to get him to tell them where the book was. And Byron had given him up.

Emmie.

His breath caught.

What he wanted to do was hide in this stale bathroom and never come out, but all he could think of was his daughter and keeping her safe. Feeling his heart pounding in his chest, he set the gift bag and his briefcase on the ground, then turned to the mirror over the rusty sink, the faucet dripping away. The man who stared back at him was anything but brave, but he tried to see himself as Emmie might see him. She didn't care that her father was slightly overweight or had a receding hairline. She believed he could do anything, and when she put her small hand in his, *he* believed it.

He had to make it right for her. Protect her. After a steadying breath, he took out his phone to make two calls. The first was to his ex-wife. Her voice mail picked up, and he said, "Bea, it's Marty . . . Something's come up. I—I'm in trouble. I think someone got to Byron and his family. They're dead . . . Oh, God. Bea. I need you to take Emmie to your mother's in Cornwall. Don't tell anyone. Stay there until you hear from me or the police. I'm sorry . . . I—Can you please tell Emmie that Daddy loves her? That I'll always love her?"

He wanted to say so much more, but he disconnected, glad now that he was divorced, that fate had stepped in and taken Emmie from him, out of harm's way.

Now, the only thing left was to make sure that these people who were after him did not follow him *anywhere* near Emmie's home. He pulled out the business card Byron had left for this reporter, the one Trip had given him, knowing in his gut that Trip must want him to contact the man for a reason. A good reason. He called the number, and as the line to the *Washington Recorder* rang, he eyed the teddy bear, then brushed his finger against the brown velveteen. It was nearly as soft as little Emmie's blond curls . . .

24

Tex waited near a bench on the riverbank, a stone's throw from where the red arches of the Blackfriars Bridge crossed the grayish green water of the River Thames. Even the rays of the early morning sun couldn't penetrate it, and he shivered in the cold. He was still trying to get past the photos that Griffin had sent showing Eve talking to those arms dealers. He wasn't sure why, because she was pretty, maybe—a sorry excuse—but he wanted her to be innocent. Hard to dispute what he'd seen, especially now that there was a connection to possible terrorist activities.

"Someone coming your way." The voice was Donovan's. He stood on the bridge, watching from above. "That him?"

"Not sure," Tex said, adjusting the volume of the Bluetooth in his ear. The man in question, wearing a heavy black overcoat against the crisp December air, descended the stairs at the end of the bridge down to the pedestrian walkway alongside the riverbank, but instead of approaching Tex, he turned, and walked the other way. More importantly, he wasn't carrying the green shopping bag with a teddy bear, which their contact had mentioned as a way of identifying him. "Negative."

"You think whoever was following him got to him? He should have been here an hour ago."

"Let's hope not." He could be three hours late and Tex wasn't about to leave. Not after hearing the fear in their contact's voice.

A few minutes later he saw a man walking toward him from under the bridge, not via the stairs as he'd anticipated. He was carrying something in each hand but was too far away to tell for sure. "Donovan. You have a visual?"

"Looks like . . . you ask . . ." The high-low siren from an ambulance passing over the bridge covered his transmission.

"Repeat?"

"Looking over his shoulder. Worried."

"You have a view of the walkway on the other side of the bridge?"

"Not enough to see if he's being followed. You sure that's him? He was supposed to get off on the bus stop here."

"Maybe he's being cautious." And well he should if it involved Trip and this elusive book. "I think he's the one." Black overcoat, blue scarf, briefcase, and the telltale green shopping bag. Tex put him in his mid-thirties, his receding brown hair windblown, his face tense with a sheen of sweat on his forehead and upper lip.

The man hurried his pace when he noticed Tex watching. He gave one last look behind him before stopping at the bench, his breaths coming out in short gasps. "You're the friend of Trip's? The man I talked to on the phone?"

"Yes. You're Marty?"

"Marty. Yes. S-Sorry I'm late. I was followed by a couple, and I hid out. Tried to lose them. I—I'm not used to this sort of thing. Do you mind?" His hand shook as he handed Tex his briefcase, then set the paper-handled bag on the bench. A gust of wind blasted across the river, rattling the bag and blowing the nest of tissue that cradled the head of the teddy bear within. Sunlight glinted off its black-bead eyes as it stared out, impervious to the threatening weather. "Before I tell you what this is all about, I need you to promise one thing. That you'll find my daughter and wife and keep them safe. I don't want what happened to Byron to happen to them."

"We'll do our best," Tex said, having no idea who Byron was.

"Well, then. Just so you know," he said, removing his gloves. "It's well hidden in that Kipling story."

"Kipling?"

"I couldn't think of where else to hide—" His eyes widened. He grabbed the scarf at the side of his neck, his mouth opening as though dumbstruck. A dark stain appeared on the blue wool beneath his fingers.

Tex pulled him to the ground behind the bench, the briefcase flying from his grasp.

"What the—" Donovan said. "Where'd it come from?"

Tex saw someone dart into the shadows beneath the bridge. "Under the stairs behind the column."

"I see him!" Donovan's transmission came out in a rush as he jumped over the rail and into the greenery, after the suspect. Tex made a quick visual, looking for a second shooter, recalling that their informant said he'd been followed by two people. No one stood out. He turned to the injured man, whose face looked ashen and who was losing blood fast. The dark stain grew wider on the scarf with each pulse, undoubtedly because an artery had been nicked. Tex gathered up the length of blue wool, pressed it against the man's neck trying to stanch the flow of blood.

His pulse was slowing, growing weaker. He'd be dead before they ever got him to the hospital. Sooner, Tex thought, if he let go. "What about this Kipling story?" he asked, hoping the man wasn't too far gone to answer.

He made a gargling noise, followed by ". . . take the bear . . . to Emmie. Promise."

"I will," he said, figuring Emmie must be his daughter.

A shadow fell over them. Tex looked up, the morning sun obscuring his vision of all but the silhouette of a woman looking down at them, the light behind her creating an aura of bright auburn around her head, then a glimmer of silver at her ears when she kneeled.

"Eve?"

"I can help."

The man reached out to Tex. "Don't—"

"Tex!" came Donovan's voice in his ear.

He glanced over, saw Donovan and a dark-haired man struggling over a gun. Pedestrians fled up the stairs, from under the bridge.

"He needs you," Eve said, slipping her hand beneath his. "Go."

The moment he felt her hand put pressure on the artery, he ran toward Donovan. He was almost at his side when the shooter saw him approaching and suddenly let go of the gun. Donovan faltered back, catching himself just short of the river wall, then chased after the man up the stairs. Tex stopped in his tracks. Turned toward Eve. And that was when he realized what the informant had said about being followed . . . Not by two people. By a *couple*.

A man *and* a woman.

He raced back, his feet flying over the brick pavers. She stood, Marty's briefcase in her hand as she looked right at Tex, her dark red hair blowing about. He felt like he was moving in slow motion. She hopped over the low retainer wall, then up the embankment, through the shrubs toward the street. Even before he had a chance to think about following, she jumped into a waiting car and took off.

"I lost him." Donovan's voice sounded tinny, and Tex glanced up, saw Donovan standing on the top of the bridge.

Figuring he had a few seconds before the police arrived, Tex kneeled beside the victim, who stared unseeing into the sky. He checked his pulse. There was none. The man never had a chance, even if Eve had stayed, but Tex hadn't wanted to leave him alone. Not like that.

Sirens sounded in the distance. He'd rather avoid interacting with the local law enforcement, too much that couldn't be explained, and started toward the bridge, figuring they had about a minute to get out of there, maybe less.

But the wind rustled the tissue of the teddy bear that sat on that bench, its black eyes watching Tex, and he thought of the promise he'd made to a dying man for someone named Emmie.

The sirens grew louder.

"Time to move, Tex."

"Meet you back at the safe house." He opened the man's coat, saw an ID card for A.D.E. hanging from a lanyard on his belt and pulled it free. He stood, grabbed the bag as the first patrol car, its light flashing, sped across the bridge, skidding to a stop near the stairway. Tex strode off in the opposite direction, trying to lose himself in the handful of pedestrians walking near the river.

He had no idea what was going on, but one thing was clear. That hit was too well-orchestrated to be anything but professional.

25

Eve hugged the briefcase against her chest as she glanced in the side mirror and saw the multitude of emergency lights converging on the bridge all growing smaller as Lou sped off. "We weren't the only ones there," she said when she caught her breath.

"I gathered that."

"Marty must have called them after he slipped us outside of the Tube. They were waiting for him under the bridge."

"Who was it?"

"The reporters from the *Recorder*."

He looked over at her, saw the blood on her hand, then nearly slammed on the brakes. "Jesus—"

"It's not mine."

He took a deep breath, turned back to the road. "I thought you said they wouldn't be a problem."

"I'll take care of them."

"You'd better. They're becoming a liability." He stopped at a red light, then nodded toward the briefcase. "You gonna open that?"

She held it fast for a moment, then finally lowered it.

When she opened it, her heart skipped a beat then thudded against her rib cage as panic gripped her. She couldn't move, couldn't speak, and her brain seemed to trip over her memories as she tried to recall if there was any way she'd made a mistake.

"What's wrong?"

"It's not here."

Lou checked his mirrors, turned down a street, and parked. "What do you mean, it's not there?"

"Exactly that." She held the briefcase wide, allowing him to see in.

"Did you drop it?"

"No."

"Then he had to have had it in his hands."

"No. When we got to the bridge, he handed the briefcase directly to the reporter. I saw him. Why would he do that if it wasn't in here?" She leaned back against the headrest, feeling faint, nauseous even. "I can't believe this . . ."

"We'll find it," Lou promised. "It probably fell out in the bushes when you were running up to the street."

"A book? I would have noticed that. What are you doing?" she said when he pulled out. "I can't go back. The place is probably swarming with cops, someone's bound to have noticed me, and I'm covered in blood."

"You drop me off. I'll look, then meet you later."

She reluctantly agreed, even though in her gut she knew nothing had fallen out of that briefcase. About two blocks away he got out and she took the car and watched him walk off.

Somewhere between the Tube and the bridge Marty had done something with that book. It didn't even matter at this point. All that did matter was that *she* didn't have it, and in that one moment she felt completely alone.

It had been a long time since she'd cried, and if she had the time, she might consider it, but right now she had about ten minutes to think of a way to spin this.

She'd failed.

More importantly, she truly feared what the outcome would be.

"Are you people insane?" Eve said, storming into the room. "You can't kill every A.D.E. employee under the sun. Byron? Now Marty? People are going to start suspecting something is up."

Barclay, the head of A.D.E., narrowed his gaze at her, a flash of anger at the interruption. "And you have a better way to deal with those who want to defy me?"

"I was this close to getting the book you want, and you kill the only person who may have an inkling where it is."

"It wasn't in the briefcase, was it?"

"You *knew* it wasn't there, and you let me go anyway?"

"Trip informed us."

She stopped cold in her tracks. Lou had tried following Trip but lost him. "Where is he?"

"We picked him up last night outside the A.D.E. office. Apparently he thought it would be a good night to reconnect with an old friend."

"That's why you killed Byron and his family? Because of Trip?"

"We had to make sure he was telling the truth. Byron, of course, said Marty had it, and here we have Trip saying Marty absolutely does not have it."

Eve tried to reconcile what she saw beneath the bridge, Marty meeting with the reporter, handing him the briefcase. Why, if not to hand over the book? "Trip said Marty did not have the book?"

"Precisely."

"Then why kill Marty?"

"As I explained, Byron assured us right before he died that Marty did, indeed, have the book. And was the man not trying to pass the briefcase along to this . . . person moments before he was shot?"

Eve stared at the men sitting around the table. "So just kill everyone?"

"Are you growing soft, Eve?"

"No. I'm concerned you're not thinking things through. Someone's bound to start wondering at the short life-expectancy of A.D.E. employees and their families."

"Random acts. They happen."

"Not to people working in the same company."

"Your concern is touching, but you'll find that once we recover the book, poor distraught Trip, who was fired not once but twice from the same company, will end up taking his own life out of guilt for killing his brother-in-law."

She couldn't believe what she was hearing. "You're insane. The police will never believe that."

"They already do. A few well-placed witnesses were *very* helpful to the police investigation, and the shooter certainly matches his description."

"And what if Trip doesn't produce the book?"

"He has two days or we kill his sister and niece once we find them. So you see, Miss Sanders, he's going to die anyway. The question is who he intends to take with him?"

Eve wasn't sure what she could possibly say to that. What might cement her position or make it worse. She opted for the positive. "It seems you've thought of everything."

"Oh. We have. I only hope no one got too good a look at the woman who stole his briefcase."

His smile left a sick feeling in the pit of her stomach. He'd serve her up to the police in a heartbeat just as easily as kill her and toss her out with the trash. She knew, however, that any sign of weakness would be a grave misstep, and so she smiled right back at him. "We can only hope."

26

Tex's phone rang about five minutes after he got back to the safe house. The number on his caller ID showed the phone they'd followed to the hotel on their arrival to London. Eve. "Hello?"

"You may believe you know what you saw. It's not what you think."

"Then what is it?" Tex asked.

"I can't talk right now, I'm being watched. But if you'll meet with me after Micah's program tonight, I can explain everything."

"I've already had one person shove a gun in my side in your presence, and a man killed right in front of me. Not sure if I'm liking those odds."

"I didn't do it. Please . . . just meet with me."

"Tell you what. I'll think about it."

He hung up on her, picturing that moment in his mind's eye when she'd looked at him, Marty's briefcase in her bloody hand right before she fled . . .

Donovan walked in then, and Tex told him about the call.

"And what? We hallucinated the whole thing?"

"I'm still trying to figure her out."

"I take it the book was in the briefcase she took?" Donovan asked. He was rolling up his sleeve to examine his elbow.

"I can't believe I let her get it. When it hit me what I'd done . . ."

"The guy had a gun. On me. You did the right thing."

Tex grinned. "Some might say that was debatable."

"So what's with the teddy bear?"

"I sort of promised the guy I'd take it to his daughter, Emmie."

"You know where he lives?"

"Not yet," he said. "Found his ID. We can arrange to have one of the locals drop it off. Maybe after the notification's made." Because he sure as hell didn't want to have to tell some little girl her father was dead. Or the wife, either.

Donovan craned his neck trying to see his elbow. "What do ya think? Bandage or not?"

"Butch up. It's barely a scrape."

"It's bleeding."

"A mosquito would starve on that. Air it out."

Donovan rolled his sleeve down. "The guy tell you anything else before he was shot?"

"Not a lot. He said he was being followed, but before he told me what that was about, he said I had to protect his wife and daughter, then something about something happening to someone named Byron. Oh, and something about it was well-hidden in a Kipling story. I'm guessing this is the book everyone's after."

"Kipling?"

"Special annotated version or something."

"That's it?"

"That's it," Tex said, taking a seat at the table and picking up the newspaper he hadn't had a chance to read yet. "And then he was shot. Hence the promise to get the teddy bear to his daughter."

Donovan eyed the bag.

"Trust me," Tex said. "Nothing's in there. I already looked. It's just a kid's toy."

"Which makes you wonder what the hell's hidden in this book."

"Got me," he said, unfolding the paper and shaking it out on the table, eyeing the front page.

"Sandwich?"

"Shit."

"I was thinking more like roast beef."

"No. This. Look."

He pointed to the headline that read MURDER-SUICIDE IN QUEEN'S PARK HOME. "We were wondering what prompted this guy to call us? Here you go."

Donovan leaned over the table, read the article. "Byron? That's the name Marty mentioned?"

"That's it. Entire family. Murder-suicide. I'm guessing Marty thought otherwise."

They both turned, eyed the teddy bear.

"Shit, is right," Donovan said. "If Eve just called wanting to meet, I'm guessing the book *isn't* in the briefcase, and they're *still* looking for it. We've got to find his kid and his wife before they do."

Trip lay on the floor in a dark room, his hands tied behind his back, his feet bound together. He wasn't sure what time of day it was. He'd drifted to sleep during the night off and on, startling awake whenever someone entered the room. The door opened and bright light spilled in, blinding him, and he didn't see the boot coming at him until it struck his gut.

"Get up!"

The blow knocked the breath out of him, but he attempted to pull his knees to his chest, trying to sit. It took a few tries but he did it.

"On your feet, you idiot."

"I can't."

And the man reached down, yanked him by his arm to his feet, then shoved him in a chair. It was Willis, he realized. One of Barclay's men. Trip shifted so his wrists weren't pressing against the wooden back. "Where am I?"

"Shut up. Now where's the bloody book?"

They hadn't found it . . . Was it possible Byron hadn't given Marty up? "I told you it's safe. Hidden. And if anything happens to me, it goes public."

"That right? Funny, seeing as how Byron said otherwise, right before we killed him. Said you were lying, and your brother-in-law? The one you blame for getting you fired? Byron said he's got it."

"I told you, Marty doesn't have it!"

"Yeah. We figured that out when we killed him, dumbass."

"Marty's dead?"

"Just like your sister and her kid are gonna be if you don't cooperate."

Trip's throat closed. It was several seconds before he could even breathe, move. And then an anger like he'd never known surged through him. "You bloody well better leave them alone!"

"Didn't think we cared about them, did ya? Tell ya what. You cooperate, they live." He reached out, grabbed Trip by the scruff of his collar and put his face so close that Trip could smell the tobacco on his breath. "So I'm gonna ask you again, and listen real careful like. Where's . . . the . . . book?"

Trip stared at the man's mouth, saw it moving as he spoke, tried to think. What had Marty done? Was it possible they'd all been pawns? All because of Marty? Or was this Byron's doing? He tried to go over the conversation with Byron last night. Had he missed something? Byron said Marty had it. Where the hell was it?

"Well?" He shook Trip until his head jerked back.

"I'll take it from here."

Trip looked over. *Eve?* How long had she been standing there? "What's going on?"

"Leave us!" she ordered.

Willis stood fast, holding Trip's collar.

"I said leave!"

He hesitated a second, let go, then stalked out the door, the light temporarily blinding Trip as he tried to look out, see where he was.

The door slammed closed and he turned his attention to Eve. "I don't understand. What's going on?"

She walked up to him, leaned over, put her face close to his, whispering, "You need to listen *very* carefully. I don't think they have your sister or niece yet, but it's only a matter of time. You heard what happened to Byron and his family? To your brother-in-law? It's important I find them first. Do you have *any* idea where your sister might be?"

He shook his head.

"Trip, you have to trust me. I can't help you or them if you don't cooperate. Where's the book?"

"I swear, I don't know," he said, not believing her for an instant.

She sighed, then stood up straight. "Trip, you know if they find that book first, your life, their lives, aren't worth a damn. The sooner you get me that book, the sooner I can help you."

"I—I just need time."

"How long?"

"Two days, three days, maybe?"

"I'll try to hold them off." She pulled a knife from her pocket, opened it, and sliced the rope at Trip's wrists. "You have my number."

She walked out, slammed the door, leaving Trip alone in the dark once more. It took him about two seconds to come to his senses. He bent down, loosened the knot at his feet, then stood, walked to the door and put his ear to it, listening. Hearing nothing that sounded threatening, he opened it, looking out into a dank alley in a part of town where it wouldn't have mattered if he had screamed all night. No one would care. No one would come.

And how was that different from now? From this illusion of freedom he had as he hurried down the narrow alley to the street beyond? He ignored the stares from the few individuals who lingered in the shadows, as though they were sizing him up as a potential victim. But if any of the rat-faced men who stood in the dark corners thought about moving in his direction, they backed off with one look from him. He would fight to the death rather than jeopardize his sister and niece, and it must have shown on his face.

Now all he had to do was figure out where Marty hid the damned book.

27

"Are you busy?"

Sydney was surprised to hear Griffin's voice on the other end of her phone. She expected that once Tex and Carillo had left for England, Griffin would have little official reason to contact her—which is not to say she didn't want him to. "Not at the moment. Why?"

"I need to talk. I'd rather not relay it over the phone."

"It's not—"

"Carillo's fine. With Tex." She breathed a sigh of relief as he added, "Where can we meet?"

"Your office is fine. I'm just leaving my apartment."

"See you in a few."

Traffic was the usual stop and go at the morning hour, and it took Sydney about a half hour. Unlike her last visit, the man who'd barred her way yesterday greeted her, saying, "Mr. Griffin's expecting you upstairs."

"Thank you."

Griffin was waiting for her in his office, along with Director McNiel.

McNiel stood, shook her hand, saying, "Good to see you again."

"Likewise."

But instead of taking a seat when she did, he said, "I'll leave you two at it," then left the room.

She found herself staring at the closed door, before forcing her gaze back to Griffin, when she realized he was speaking.

"I need someone with clearance and law enforcement powers to work some reconnaissance with me on the local level. We don't currently have an ATLAS member with those qualifications."

"Clearly a government oversight."

"Since the current administration is not going to fix it anytime soon . . ."

"This is that overlapping investigation you were telling me about last night?"

"It is. We received word that a terrorist might be trying to come into the country, possibly through the refugee resettlement program."

"Trip's program? This Sticks and Bricks thing?"

"We don't know. It could be a completely separate criminal enterprise taking advantage of an inherently flawed system. Whatever this hornet's nest is that Sheila's boyfriend stirred up may or may not be part of it. But we'd be foolish not to investigate further."

"Does Carillo know?"

"He does now."

"Pearson, or someone from foreign counterintelligence?"

"Pearson's the one who informed us of the terrorist connection. He's forwarded a number of suspicious circumstances reports from your office that we're going to need to follow up on, which made me realize you would be an asset to the investigation. He suggested your name, but I wanted to ask you before I finalized anything."

"There's a first."

He gave a half smile, as though to acknowledge that his agency had circumvented the normal channels in the past. He did not, however, comment, apparently waiting for her response on whether she was willing to work alongside him.

And that was a big question. They seemed to finally be at the beginning of an actual two-way relationship. Sure, it was more expedient to bring an agent on board who already knew ATLAS existed and what most of their protocols were, but what if they actually ended up sleeping together? "Are you okay with this?" she asked.

"I've worked with you before."

"Not that part . . ." She let it hang there, since the door was still wide-open.

He glanced toward the doorway, then back at her. "You mean the part we almost but haven't *quite* made it to?"

"Yes."

"If we ever *get* to that part, I'll let you know. So how about it? I need to call Pearson."

"Forget Pearson. Why wouldn't we get to that part? And if we do, is there some reason it would change your mind about working with me?"

He picked up a pen from his desk, clicking it open, closed, over and over, seemingly unaware he was even doing it. "I feel protective toward you. I don't want the same thing that happened to Becca—"

Of course. His late wife. "I'm not her. And the feeling of wanting to protect the people you care about? It's never going to go away."

"I know that. Now. So I learn to work with it instead of against it."

Sydney made a show of looking at her watch. "I have a few errands to run. Let me know what Pearson says."

She started toward the door when he called out to her. She stopped, looked back at him.

He returned the pen to his desk. "The whole thing with Becca didn't come out right."

"Baby steps, Griffin. But let me warn you. I am *so* not waiting until next New Year's eve."

He followed her to the elevator. "What about a date?"

She looked at him, amused at the hopeful expression on his face. "A *real* date? Like dinner, that sort of thing?"

"Tomorrow night?"

"I'll mark it on my calendar. But you better not stand me up."

Griffin watched from his office window, saw Sydney crossing the parking lot to her car, very much aware of how close he'd been to mangling his peace offering. Comparing her to his late wife was not what he'd been trying to do, even though it seemed to have the desired effect. They were officially going out tomorrow night.

That was what he wanted, wasn't it?

It was, except for one tiny detail, and he could almost hear Tex's voice in his ear saying that he better tell Sydney about ATLAS's involvement in her father's case before their relationship went any further. A part of him knew Tex was right, but he also knew that Sydney would not take the news well. She'd shut down and any chance they had of making a go of it would be gone. He wasn't sure he wanted to risk that.

He'd tell her.

But not yet . . . One day.

"How'd it go?"

Griffin looked over and saw McNiel in the doorway, and it took him a moment to switch gears, realize McNiel wanted to know if Sydney had agreed to work with him, not go out with him. "Fine. Fitzpatrick's on board with it as long as Pearson agrees."

"I'll get started on her security clearance."

Griffin called Pearson, got his approval, then phoned Sydney to let her know she was now on loan to ATLAS. She arrived after lunch, and he met her in the lobby, escorted her to the floor above his. "IT works up here. We need to get your fingerprint into the system."

He opened the door to an office where three men and one woman sat at mismatched government surplus desks, surrounded by computers. One of the men looked up, saw Griffin, waved them over. "You're Sydney Fitzpatrick?"

"Yes."

"I'm Pete. I just need your right index finger . . ."

She held her hand out, and he guided it to a small glass box on his desk, pressed it to the surface, and her print appeared on his computer monitor. He then held out a small keypad, attached to his computer with a USB cable.

"Punch in a code and you're done," he said.

"Code . . . ?"

Pete turned away, giving her privacy, and Griffin said, "So you can get upstairs without an escort."

She took the keypad from Pete, pressed the numbers, then handed it back, saying, "You mean I'm a member of the club now?"

Pete typed something into the computer. "That and a buck will get you a bag of chips from the break room, but that's about it."

She thanked him and they returned to Griffin's office, where he gave her a file folder. "These are the reports on the theft of a radiation therapy machine from a hospital in California."

"It relates how?"

"Because after the original theft north of Los Angeles, another report came in from San Diego PD saying they found the machine in a storage unit, dismantled, with the capsule containing the cesium 137 missing. That could be used to make a very effective smoky bomb."

"Is that like a dirty bomb?"

"Similar principle, smaller scale, with the threat being from breathing in the smoke from the explosion. A whiff of cesium 137 will kill you in about four days, and it won't be a pretty death," he said as he handed her another folder. "More importantly, the description of the man last seen near the machine matches that of Yusuf. If it is him, that means he got into the country by taking on a new identity. So we now have several tasks on our hands. Find out where he is, what identity he's using, and who issued the identity so we can close that loophole."

She examined the photo inside, saw a pleasant-looking man with dark hair and eyes staring back at her. "Find the identity broker, maybe find Yusuf?"

"Find the *right* identity broker," Griffin said. "Too many of them out there all looking to make a buck off the many refugees who have never had any form of ID, and find themselves in a Catch-22, unable to get into the country without identification."

"And the refugee programs somehow facilitate this?"

"By helping the refugees obtain sometimes fraudulent documents that give them that much needed ID. Unfortunately it's the same method used by the criminals and terrorists, who have a distinct advantage in a completely screwed-up system that is fueled on both ends by vast sums of money and a proliferation of corruption."

"And what's our role?" Sydney asked, sorting through the paperwork.

"Take a closer look at some of the local charities to see if any of them are involved. Considering what's gone on with

A.D.E. and From Sticks to Bricks, it seems like a logical place to start."

"We're just going to march up there? Tell them who we are?"

"Actually, no. I wanted to start with the refugees themselves. Tex and I chased Dorian Rose at one of the apartment complexes out near the naval yard. Dorian knew someone was after him then, so it stands to reason that someone there might know something."

28

"Where to start?" Sydney asked Griffin once they ar-
rived at the row of apartments.

"Somehow I doubt it matters."

And he was right. They entered the first building, over-
powered by the musty smell of mildew and mold. The hallway floor was uneven and soft in places, as though if one
stepped too hard, the boards might cave in. Sydney knocked
on the first door, and no one answered. A woman peered
out of the second door they knocked on, smiled and shook
her head, apparently not understanding English, and the
language Sydney heard from behind the next door wasn't
one she recognized. At the third door, a young black child
peered through the two-inch crack. "Is your mom home?"
Sydney asked.

He cocked his head to one side.

She showed her badge, saying, "FBI."

"Police?"

"Yes," she said.

He opened the door wider, pointing toward the door leading outside, saying, "Offees."

"Can you show us?"

The office, it turned out, was another apartment in the building next door. The boy ran off before they could thank him, and Sydney and Griffin walked in, finding the office was the first door on the left.

Before they even had a chance to knock, the door opened and a dark-skinned man standing about an inch taller than Griffin looked at the two of them, saying in a deep and melodious voice, "You must be the police. No one else comes here."

"FBI, Special Agent Fitzpatrick," Sydney said, and handed him her card. "And you are?"

"I am Ito Abasi. What can I do for you?"

His English was clear, but his accent strong, and Sydney couldn't place it. "We're looking for someone who might have known Dorian Rose."

He eyed the two of them, as though contemplating his next move. "Why?"

"He was killed several nights ago."

The man's mouth opened, then closed. He stepped to one side, saying, "Come in. Please."

The apartment was cleaner than expected. Sure, the carpet was stained, worn in spots, the walls in need of one or two more coats of paint, but Sydney had seen worse. "Did you know Dorian?"

"I did. He was our liaison with the refugee program."

"When did you last see him?"

"Less than a week ago. Around five I met with him at his apartment. I was waiting for him, to apologize, actually, for the article that came out in the paper about the state of the buildings and evictions. He had promised to speak with Mr. Redfern, the landlord, about the evictions, but did not, and so I felt our only recourse was to go to the press. Unfortunately I lost my temper. But we only argued, and then I left after he promised to address our concerns."

"With Mr. Redfern."

"Yes. I cannot say who is responsible for killing Mr. Dorian, but if anyone should be brought in for questioning, it is Mr. Redfern. He slowly murders people every day by allowing these buildings to stand in disrepair. They might not die violently, but if they stay here they will surely die."

"We'll make sure the police and Social Services look into the matter. Thank you for your time."

"Are you not going to see for yourself, at least?"

She and Griffin both made a show of appearing interested in the apartment.

"Not here," he said. "The new paint hides much. This way, please. The people who live in these buildings, they are all refugees from Africa." He led them out, then down the hall, and the farther they walked, the heavier the stench. He knocked on a door that was opened by an older woman, a bright multicolored scarf wrapped around her head. Sydney couldn't understand what was spoken between the two, but the woman allowed them entry into a living room, where at least ten people sat, mainly women and children. "There are two families who live in this apartment," he said. "From Somalia. The charity Dorian works for, A.D.E., brought them in. They live here until the A.D.E. assistance runs out in the first month and hope the welfare kicks in. It is not enough to allow the families to find better housing or separate housing."

Griffin remained by the door, while Sydney looked around. What they were seeing wasn't anything they hadn't seen before, an apartment not fit for humans to live in. "We can call Human Services."

"For what? They have nowhere to put these people. The

shelters are full and it is more than the mold in the ceiling from the water pipes above stairs and the stench of sewage because he will not fix the toilets. Do you know what the landlord, Mr. Redfern, said to me when I asked for them to be fixed?"

"No," Sydney said.

"That they are used to crapping in a hole in the ground. This is a luxury to them. The same with the roaches and rats. What are a few bugs and rodents to someone who lived beneath a tarp held up by sticks? Why replace the carpet when it is better than the dirt floors they left behind in Africa? Do you see why I have an anger deep within? And *this, this*, is one of the better apartments."

Sydney looked around at the faces of the children, watching her with large brown eyes, and the women holding them in their laps. "I understand your concern. But I'm looking into a murder."

"And I am showing you *why* he was murdered."

"You know who killed him?"

"No. But I believe it is why he was killed." He turned to the woman who had let them in, saying, *"Asante,"* in a quick show of thanks, then directing Sydney and Griffin out and back to his office. He did not, however, invite them in. Instead, he walked them outside and pointed down the street to the capitol dome off in the distance, its grandeur in stark contrast to the neighborhood they currently stood in.

"It's not just here in your capital where this is happening. It is everywhere in this country. Places just like Mr. Redfern's buildings, a few better, many worse, and the charities and parasites that feed off the revolving door of refugees. These people, they come to America looking for shelter, a place away from war and death and unspeakable crimes, and this is where they are brought. It is as you say, big business. *Very* big. Without the refugees, there is no money to be made. And money is made every step of the way. These people have no hope, no chance of succeeding. They have left one hell only to land in another. And *that* is why Dorian is dead."

He looked Sydney in the eye, adding, "To put it succinctly, there is far too much money at stake, and Dorian was a threat."

29

"Carillo has way more experience working homicide than I do," Sydney told Griffin after they returned to ATLAS to further investigate the buildings owned by Redfern.

"Which, when compared to my experience, makes you the resident expert."

"Assuming that Dorian did not commit suicide—"

"A safe assumption."

"Then we want to look at who had motive and opportunity. Your password . . ."

When he moved to her side, leaned forward, and typed a series of letters and numbers in, she was acutely aware of his proximity. Tonight was their official date, and try as she might, it wasn't likely to fade to the back of her mind. "Since everyone involved in this mess seems to be tied to Trip somehow, I'm guessing the motive has something to do with A.D.E. and their refugee programs."

"We need everything we can find on them," she said. "Property, finances, you name it. I think we should also do the same to the landlord, Larry Redfern." When Griffin didn't move, Sydney added, "How about you call Doc, while

I do some digging around here. Between the two of us, we may have something we can work with."

That did the trick, and he walked around to the other side of the desk to make the call. She felt as if she could breathe again, then chided herself.

Apparently she'd need to work on ignoring his presence, or this was going to be a *long* investigation.

Doc found the information before Sydney had even finished running the man's name. Griffin put him on speakerphone.

"Your landlord owns about half of the slums surrounding the area you were visiting," Doc said. "A few past minor health code violations, but other than that, nothing."

"That's it?" Sydney asked.

"Actually it says a lot. If the places are as bad as you say they are, someone is either blind as a friggin' bat or there's some money changing hands for them to look the other way."

"No one can be that blind," Griffin said.

Even this far removed, it wasn't easy to forget what she'd seen, never mind what she'd smelled. "Anything else?" she asked.

"I'm thinking the property owner isn't an individual. RWW Property Management. Too many layers between the name here and trying to find someone who belongs to it. But we can definitely pinpoint who represented him, her, them, on the health code violations. The Redfern Group. I'm e-mailing the link to his firm . . . Pretty upscale. K Street. In fact, it looks like Redfern is very involved in Washington's lobbyist industry."

Which explained the upscale offices, Sydney decided. Anyone in the business of persuading Washington to pass laws that favored their respective clients needed to keep up appearances. "Any connection to A.D.E., besides Dorian's?"

"That one's gonna take a bit more time. A.D.E. has a lot of fingers in the pie. Little itty bitty charities spread all over the map. Quite possibly these properties are slices from the same pie. I'll call you back when I get something."

"Thanks."

Sydney brought up the Web site for Redfern's law office. Definitely upscale.

"Feel like taking a drive?" she asked Griffin.

"Nothing else on my schedule."

"How do we want to do this? FBI? Social Services? *Washington Recorder*? Or would having two reporters walk in send him into a panic?"

Griffin smiled as though amused. "Safer to use the identity he would expect to see. The one he'd be the most relaxed with. I'll call upstairs and get a couple Social Services IDs."

"You can do that?" she asked, then recalled the very legitimate-looking FBI credentials Tex had provided for Griffin the other night. "Better question is *how* do you do that?"

"Beauty of modern technology. That and having all the requisite blank documents that merely need a photo added. Mine's on file. You'll need to go up and have one taken."

The Redfern Group was on the top floor of a building filled with several lobbying firms, and Sydney wondered if Redfern's office retained any of them to make sure his client's interests continued to be met.

A receptionist sat at a half-circle desk in the spacious lobby. An unimaginative logo of a red-colored fern leaf in a brass circle adorned the wall behind her. "May I help you?"

"We need to speak with Mr. Redfern."

"Do you have an appointment?"

"No. We're with Social Services. It's about a few buildings his clients own."

"Hold on, please." She picked up a phone, called a number,

then passed on the information. "Yes, sir." She covered the phone, saying, "He's in a meeting."

"We'll wait," Sydney said.

"They'll wait," she said into the receiver. "How long?" She looked at Sydney.

"As long as it takes. We're on salary."

She repeated the information, listened, then hung up the phone, saying, "He'll be with you at his first opportunity." She directed them to the chairs near a shimmering silver wall-mounted waterfall.

"Quite the knack for getting past the gatekeepers," Griffin said after they took a seat. "A technique you've used at my office?"

"Once or twice."

They waited thirty minutes. At first Sydney wondered if Redfern was testing their mettle, but then a door opened and a woman emerged, followed by a man Sydney assumed was Redfern, judging from the way he shook the woman's hand, then thanked her for dropping by as though it were some casual visit.

"Plan B," Griffin said quietly. "That's Senator Burgess, who unfortunately knows me."

"What's she doing here?"

"Good question," he said as the senator looked their way, made a comment to Redfern, as though Sydney and Griffin were the topic, then walked directly toward them.

"Mr. Griffin. Not a place I would expect to run into you," Senator Burgess said.

"Likewise."

"Funny," Larry Redfern said as he walked up. "The receptionist announced you as someone from Social Services?"

"Probably my fault," Sydney said with her best ingenue smile. "Miscommunication is all. I was *referred* by Social Services."

"And you are?"

"Sydney Fitzpatrick, FBI." She held out her hand. He shook it and she smiled at the senator. "And you are?"

"Oh, sorry," Griffin said. "This is Senator Burgess."

"Nice to meet you," Sydney replied.

"And you." The woman looked from Sydney to Griffin. "What on earth—"

Griffin held up his hands. "Don't want you to get the wrong idea. I'm not here."

"Well," Sydney said. "Not in any official capacity. We're just friends from way back. Going to lunch as soon as I finish interviewing Mr. Redfern."

"I'm surprised that the FBI would be here at all," Burgess said, making Sydney wonder who was running the show.

Sydney turned to Redfern. "I'm sorry. It's not really a big deal—the interview, I mean. Anonymous calls or not, the law says we have to look into it. Is there someplace you and I can talk?"

Redfern gave her a skeptical look. "My office."

Sydney smiled at the senator. "A pleasure." Then, to Griffin, she said, "I shouldn't be more than a few minutes."

"I'll catch up on the latest issue of *People*." He picked up a copy from the glass table, then sat back. "Pleasure to see you again, Senator."

Sydney followed Redfern across the lobby to the doorway that led down a long hall. His office took up a large corner space, the floor-to-ceiling windows giving an unparalleled view of the street below and the capital skyline. Inside, the accommodations reflected understated elegance and money, its modern black and burgundy leather and glass furniture a far cry from the mismatched surplus from Griffin's office, or the gray cubicles she herself was used to before she ended up in the basement at Quantico.

"Wouldn't mind having this to work in," Sydney said when he offered her a seat in a chair that was far more comfortable than it looked. "What sort of attorney are you?"

"I'm a real estate lawyer."

"And your firm?"

"General practice —litigation, corporate, white collar defense. You said you were here about an anonymous call from Social Services?"

"Something about the unfit living conditions of some property that seems to be associated with your firm down near the naval yard."

"Naval yard? One of my associates mentioned something about one of his client's properties in that area . . . the plumbing. The client who owns the property is having financial difficulties, and when a main sewer line broke, well, you can imagine the difficulties that caused."

"Especially for the residents, I'm sure. Who did you say the owner was?"

"One of the local charities . . . a shelter, church, honestly the name escapes me at the moment. I'd be glad to have my secretary look it up and get back to you."

"That would be great. In the meantime, if you or your associate, or whomever, could look into *addressing* some of those living conditions, then I can get back to the more pressing cases on my desk."

"Of course," he said, standing. "I'll see what I can do about getting them the help they need to move forward with those repairs. No need to trouble yourself any further."

"Thank you, Mr. Redfern. I had a feeling that this was something that could be dealt with on a very low-key level." She left a card on his desk, eyed the several files upon it, one labeled W2. Tax files, apparently. Disappointed she couldn't see anything that clued her in on what was going on, she said, "I may, however, check in again to see how your client is progressing."

"I'm sure the FBI has, as you say, more pressing matters."

"Public service and all. Good afternoon, Mr. Redfern. A pleasure."

Sydney walked out, frustrated with the turn of events. "That was a waste of time," she said when she and Griffin were in the car, driving back to ATLAS headquarters.

"Not totally. We now know that Senator Burgess is somehow connected to this firm. The question is how?"

"Maybe she's hoping to get hired on as a lobbyist once her term is over."

"If Redfern's firm is lobbying her about something, I'd like to know what it is."

"I did see a few file folders on his desk, unfortunately nothing that clued me in to what they were discussing, assuming any of those folders pertained to her visit. Being a glass half-full girl, I'd at least like to think that he'll take the steps to improve the living conditions in those apartments."

Griffin looked over at her, then back at the road. "Better take off those rose-colored spectacles next time you take a drink from that half-empty glass."

Twenty minutes later they were pulling into ATLAS. McNiel called both of them into his office the moment they arrived. "Have a seat," he said.

"Something wrong?" Griffin asked.

"That depends. What happened at the Redfern Group?"

"Following up a lead that ties Dorian Rose to some property managed by the firm. Ran into Senator Burgess walking out of there, so we had to scrap the Social Services guise. Why?"

"I just got off the phone with Pearson. *His* boss received a call from the White House. Andrew Charles, no less," he said, referring to the Senior Advisor. "He wants this investigation into this property and the Redfern Group to go away."

"That's a pretty quick conduit to the top."

"Redfern's a powerful lobbyist. Assuming he made the call and not Burgess—which we have to assume, since the call went to the FBI and didn't come here. Either way, you two need to officially back off from Redfern."

"Back off?" Sydney said. "His firm's just going to get away with—"

"Officially," McNiel repeated. "That, Ms. Fitzpatrick, is why you're on loan to this office, as opposed to Griffin going to yours. Translation: Don't leave a trail that's going to get us in trouble. If Redfern or one of his clients is involved in facilitating the movement of Yusuf or any other terrorists, knowingly or unknowingly, I don't give a rat's ass if the President himself were to walk in here and give us the order. I want Yusuf found before anyone gets killed."

Carillo's stomach rumbled, but hungry as he was, and even though the London safe house was fully stocked, he wasn't about to get up and chance that he'd miss a signal from Sheila's phone should it appear. What if it was in some spot between two buildings, then blinked out, like what happened to Eve's phone when Tex and Donovan had been tracking it? They'd lost it momentarily, but it had popped up again once she exited her hotel. Carillo had prayed for a similar case with Sheila's phone. On the one hand, knowing Sheila, she was tucked safely in some big hotel—and wouldn't that be just like her—where the signal wasn't getting through. On the other hand, her plan covered international service, so why the hell wasn't her cell blinking on the screen?

Tex finally called him on the house phone about an hour later. "We haven't found Trip's sister or niece. No sign of Sheila, either."

"Not the news I want to hear."

"On the bright side, the neighbor across the street says that she saw Marty's wife and kid drive off in their car a couple hours ago. Unfortunately we don't know where they went. At least we know they got out."

"Let's hope they weren't followed. What now?"

"Checking a couple other places, then heading back."

Carillo glanced at the clock. "Well, you know where I'll be."

"Nothing?"

"I'd swear the computer isn't working, but when I entered my phone number, it worked fine."

"She'll turn up."

In one piece, he hoped. "Do me a favor, when you guys come back? I'd love some food."

"Refrigerator's full."

"I'm afraid to leave the monitor."

"Turn the volume way up. If her number shows, it'll start beeping."

Carillo was still reluctant to step away, even for a moment, but when his hands started shaking due to lack of food, he turned the volume to maximum, then made a dash for the kitchen. He found a can of soda and the roast beef, was looking around for bread, when he heard it. *Beep . . . beep . . .*

He ran back and saw it. Bright red, flashing on the screen. Relief flooded through him with every blink of the cursor. He grabbed the phone, then hit Tex's number.

"She's here," he said, when Tex answered.

"Where?"

He used the track pad to zoom in, trying to read the small print on the GPS map. The moment he touched the device, the cursor stopped blinking. "What the— It's gone. I think I screwed up."

"The map still there?"

"Yeah. But when I zoomed in, it disappeared."

"Then she turned her phone off, or the signal was lost due to interference. Where was it coming from?"

"Just outside Paddington Station."

"We'll head over."

"I'm not that far away."

"I know. But if that signal pops up again, you need to be there."

He was right. But that didn't make it any easier.

On the off chance Marty had stashed the book at his flat, Trip made it his first stop. Judging from the mess, it was clear someone else had gotten there first. He searched in every cupboard, every drawer—not that there were that many places to look. There were only a few bits of furniture, Marty having taken just enough to get by when he'd separated from Trip's sister. Trip paced the floor, looking for a loose floorboard. Nothing. He searched the handful of science fiction paperbacks, even though he knew they weren't the right type of book. After a wasted hour he decided it was time to move on. Either someone had already been there and found it or it wasn't there to begin with.

He guessed the latter, since Marty wasn't about to entrust something that valuable to this neighborhood.

Trip's sister, Bea, however, lived in a much nicer house, and he had to admit the possibility that Marty might have hidden the book there. He watched Bea's house from down the street for several minutes to make sure it wasn't some sort of a setup, or better yet, that maybe his captor had lied about her and Emmie being kidnapped. But no, there appeared to be no one home, and he strolled in that direction, just a bloke out for a walk should anyone be looking.

And of course Mrs. Watson from across the street kept a close eye from her parlor window. He waved at her and she dropped the curtain, stepping out of sight. He supposed that was a vast improvement, considering that the entire six months he'd lived with his sister and Emmie after he was sacked, Mrs. Watson continually frowned at him as though he were a usurper for Bea's husband, Marty. What he didn't expect was for the white-haired woman to come out and talk to him. She never had before, and he half suspected she would inform him that she'd phoned the police.

"Beatrice isn't there," she called out.

He decided to ignore her, since really this was none of her business, and he knew where his sister hid the spare key. But then he realized what a good source she might be, living her life staring out that front window, so he crossed the street, asking, "Do you know where she is?"

"Not sure. A car came 'round for her and little Emmie late yesterday afternoon."

"What sort of car?"

Mrs. Watson's eyes brightened at the memory. "Posh. Waiting out front for her, they were. Two chaps in suits. Unfortunately, Beatrice and Emmie weren't home, so I walked over there and told them she'd already left."

He swallowed a sudden lump in his throat at the thought that Mrs. Watson had actually spoken to their kidnappers. "Already left? Did you tell them where she was going?"

"I have no idea where she was going. I say, you're looking a bit off-color."

He felt that way too, and tried to smile. "Something I ate, maybe. I'll just go in, have a kip, then. Cheerio, Mrs. Watson."

He started to walk off, and she said, "Will you be feeding Emmie's cat, then? Someone's got to feed it."

"I won't be staying that long, Mrs. Watson. Would you mind terribly? Until they get home?"

"Any idea how long that will be?"

"A few days at the most." He prayed that's all it was, and he returned to the house, fished the key out of the loose stone on the porch, then unlocked the door.

When he stepped inside, he froze at the sight in front of him. They'd already been here. He hoped Bea hadn't seen it, or Emmie. She would have been scared to death. Furniture was tossed, cupboards and drawers opened and emptied. There was a musty odor, as though milk had soured, and he roused himself, stepped over the broken china from the cabinet on his way to the kitchen. Sure enough, a bright pink plastic cup on the counter was the culprit, and he dumped the sour milk in the sink, then rinsed the cup out. Emmie's toys were scattered about the floor throughout the room, mixed in with the appliances and kitchen linens someone had pulled from the cupboard. Yesterday morning's newspaper was on the floor, and he picked it up, saw the article about Byron's so-called murder/suicide. A wave of nausea swept through him and he had to sit. This had all gone so horribly wrong.

Byron, Marty, and now Bea and Emmie . . .

What if those men had followed Bea? Somehow found her? The thought of his sister and niece being held somewhere was enough to get Trip to his feet once more. Searching this place wouldn't be so easy, but he knew he needed to be methodical, thorough, even if the first searchers hadn't been. Start with the attic, he thought. Work his way down. He was halfway through the house, his job mainly consisting of replacing things, since most of it had been pulled out, when it occurred to him what a monumental waste of time this was. They couldn't have found it here, because Marty would never have hidden it here to begin with. He didn't even live here anymore. And surely he wouldn't have put his wife and kid in danger that way?

Forget Marty's frame of mind, he told himself. Time was running out, and he returned downstairs, looking around at the overwhelming mess, wondering if he even dared leave without finishing the search. What if he was wrong? What if Marty had hidden it here and they just hadn't found it?

The doorbell rang, and he stilled, hoping whoever was

there would leave if they thought no one was home. The grandfather clock ticked away in the parlor, but other than that, the house was quiet. Not quiet enough, apparently. Whoever it was rang the bell again, then knocked sharply, calling out, "Trip? I know you're in there. Your neighbor told me."

It couldn't be . . .

He ran to the front room, looked out the peephole, opened the door and stared in disbelief.

Sheila stood on the porch, a suitcase in her hand, smiling. "Aren't you going to invite me in?"

31

"Good God, Sheila. What the bloody hell are you doing here?"

"I was worried about you. I didn't want you to be by yourself."

"Oh my God. You've got to leave."

"Fine. I'll leave."

She started to turn toward the door, and he grabbed her arm. "Are you crazy? What if they're out there? Oh my God. I can't believe this. Not now. I don't have time."

"Time for what? Is everything we had together a lie?"

He wasn't sure how to answer that. It was and it wasn't. He'd chosen her specifically because her husband was FBI, which he hoped would offer protection. And it had, until now.

"I never wanted to hurt you."

Her eyes welled up with tears. "It was a lie, wasn't it?"

"At first maybe . . . but I've grown very fond of you."

"Fond? I can't believe what an idiot I've been."

"It's not like that, Sheila. I'm in trouble. Big trouble. They killed Marty and they're going to kill my sister and my niece if I don't find this damned book they're after and I don't even know where to look."

"Then I'll help you." Hands on her hips, she surveyed the mess. It looked as though someone had stood in that same exact spot in front of the TV and knocked the shelf from the wall, sending Emmie's collection of children's DVDs flying. They covered the floor from the TV stand all the way into the kitchen. Sheila turned an accusing eye toward him. "Did you do this?"

"No. Someone else was here first."

"I'd ask you if they found it, but it looks like they were mad and just started throwing things around."

"They let me go to try to find it myself. That's how I found out they had Bea and Emmie."

"How do you know they *really* have them?"

"Because they told me."

"It's not like they're going to tell you the truth, is it?"

"No, but the neighbor saw a strange car here. I think they probably followed them. And if Bea and Emmie are not here, where are they?"

She couldn't even begin to answer, and moved into the room, started picking up the DVDs. "Your niece must own every Disney movie ever made."

"What are you doing?" he asked.

"Cleaning." She scooped a handful of DVDs from the floor, placing them in a neat stack on the TV. "You don't want them to have to come back to this mess, do you?"

"I don't think they're coming back."

"Trip . . ." She looked at him with such sadness and caring.

But when she tried to hug him, he said, "I need to find this book they're looking for. It's the only chance I have of surviving this."

"You need to call someone."

"I'm not calling the police."

"Then I'll call Tony," she said, taking out her cell phone.

He lunged for it, and she backed up, saying, "He's probably tracked my cell and is on his way here right now. God knows he'd never trust me to do anything by myself."

"Don't. Please . . ."

"You can't do this on your own."

"They'll kill them," he said, a last attempt to dissuade her from calling, because God help him, he didn't have the strength to stop her.

"They're going to kill them anyway, no matter what," she said, and he knew it was true. "If they have half a chance, Tony will know what to do. I promise you."

He sank to the floor, all energy and hope leaving him. He couldn't help the tears that came, and this time when Sheila started to dial, he didn't stop her.

When Carillo heard the beep, then heard his cell ring and saw Sheila's number show up on the caller ID, he nearly dropped his phone in his haste to connect. "Where the hell are you?" he asked.

"If you're going to swear at me, I'm hanging up."

"I'm not swearing."

"You are—"

"Sheila, this is important."

"I'm with Trip. We're okay. But he's scared. And I think we need help."

"You're damned straight—"

"Knock it off or I'm hanging up."

And she would. So he told himself to take a breath, calm down, and start over. "I've tried calling you. I was worried."

"I had my phone off. I forgot the charger at Sydney's, so I didn't want to waste my power."

That answered that question. "Do you know what the address is?"

"His sister's house."

He saw the cursor blinking on the monitor, the map show-ing it right where Tex and Donovan had been earlier in the afternoon. "Okay. Stay there, don't move. If something hap-pens, call 999."

"Why?"

"It's the British equivalent of 911."

"They should just keep them all the same."

God love her, he thought, because some days it was harder than others. "I'm sending Tex over."

"I gotta go. My phone's dying."

"See if Trip has a charger. And if you go anywhere or anything changes, *call*."

"I get it already."

He bit back his retort, because he sincerely doubted she got it at all, or she'd never have followed Trip out here. As soon as he disconnected, he called Tex from the landline, not wanting to tie up his phone in case she tried to call him again. "She just contacted me. They're at his sister's place."

"As in the place we were two hours ago?"

"The same."

"En route. Shouldn't take us longer than twenty minutes to get there."

Carillo hung up the phone, then stared at the computer screen, watching the cursor blink away. It seemed strong and steady, and as time passed he figured she must have found a charger. About ten minutes in, his phone beeped, and he saw a text message from her. As he opened it, the signal dropped off the screen. Probably her letting him know she was pow-ering down. He opened it and his heart seemed to skip then start up double time when he read: *Have to go. Someone at house. NOT Tex.*

"Christ . . ." He grabbed the landline phone, called Tex. "Something's wrong. Sheila says they had to go. Someone's in the house. At the house. "

"We're almost there. We'll call you back."

Five minutes later, Carillo pacing the entire time, he lost patience and called Tex. "What's happening?"

"Hold on, Carillo. Donnie boy's getting a report from one of the local bobbies on the house . . . Not sure what's going on . . ."

Carillo's gut twisted at the sound of the sirens he heard in the background. "Please quantify that statement with something that makes me think you're not talking about Sheila's safety."

"How's her signal coming in?"

"It's not. Why?"

"The house. It's on fire."

32

It took a couple phone calls, but Tex was finally able to get them past the perimeter that the local constabulary set up around the house while the firemen worked—once Alice Finch, their MI6 counterpart, arrived.

"I was in the middle of a lovely cup of tea when you rang," she told Tex. She glanced at Donovan. "Donnie. Good to see you again."

"You, too."

"We'd like to get into the house," Tex told her. "Meeting a bit of resistance from the bobbies."

"Let's at least wait until the fire's out, shall we?"

"Minor technicalities, Alice."

"Your accommodations are suitable? I sent someone over to air the place out before you got there."

"The safe house is fine," Tex said. "I need to get into *this* one."

"Shall I see if they can spray the water any faster, then?"

"If that's what it takes."

She walked off, and Donovan said, "She *used* to be fun, before her promotion turned her into Miss Stoic and Staid."

They watched as she approached a fireman, who then directed her to another. Eventually she returned, saying, "It shouldn't be long. The fire had been contained mostly in the kitchen. Apparently the neighbor across the street called when she saw the smoke."

Tex looked over. Saw the woman watching from her front yard. "Might as well have a chat."

"I'll go," Donovan said.

He walked off, and Alice said, "Not too keen on my company, is he?"

"Donovan? Itching at the bit to get this case wrapped up. So what's new with you these days?"

"I'm engaged. We—my fiancé and I—are having a baby." He looked down, saw she wasn't even showing yet. "Congratulations."

"Thank you." She smiled when she saw the fireman wave them over. "Looks like we can get in now."

"Hate to say it, Alice, but toxic smoke and babies, born or not, don't mix. Maybe wait out here."

"Good point."

Tex glanced back, saw Donovan talking to the neighbor. "Let Donnie know I've gone in, okay?"

He walked to the house. The front door was open and he entered, saw a red suitcase against the wall, and leaning over, saw Sheila's name on the luggage tag. Good sign, he figured, continuing in, the smell of smoke and wet burnt wood growing stronger as he walked down the entry hall to the front room. The damage was just as Alice said, mostly in the kitchen, and two firemen were still there, working. The place was a mess. Not from the fire, but as though someone had gone through and systematically dumped every drawer and cupboard in search of something, undoubtedly this elusive book.

"The whole house has been gone through," the fireman said, noticing him looking around.

"Anything besides the mess that, uh, isn't from a normal fire?"

"Not sure yet. Bloody hot, though. It started here in the kitchen. Fortunate that we were so close."

Tex thanked him, then continued his hunt for . . . what, he didn't know. He had to imagine that if Sheila or Trip were here, they'd have been found by the firemen. Still, there might be something that stood out, and he took it room by room. There were shelves filled with books, or rather, had been, as they were now all over the floor, and he kneeled, examined each one, hoping for a volume by Kipling. Most were paperbacks, a few hardcovers and a few children's books, not a Kipling among them. Even so, he flipped through several, but found nothing that stood out. Beside the bookcase was a small television on a stand, with a few DVDs stacked neatly atop the player. Disney animated movies. Tex let them be, instead walking up to the answering machine, wondering if there were any phone messages on it.

"Makes you wonder where the kid is," Donovan said, coming up behind him, picking up a couple of the movies. He set them on the kitchen counter, saying, "I'll look upstairs."

Tex noticed Alice hovering in the doorway.

"Ring me if you need anything else?" she said.

"I think we're good for now."

"I'm off, then."

"See ya, Alice." He returned to the living room, then eyed the telephone answering machine. There was no light blinking, but when he pressed the button, the automated voice said there were ten messages. He was beginning to wonder if there was any point as he fast-forwarded through the various dental, doctor, play dates messages, when he heard what sounded like a commotion upstairs. He left the machine, walked toward the stairs. "Donnie?"

Definitely some scuffling, he thought as the last message started playing.

"Bea, it's Marty . . ." Tex turned toward the machine, froze. "Something's come up. I—I'm in trouble. I think someone got to Byron and his family. They're dead . . . Oh, God. Bea. I need you to take Emmie to your mother's in Cornwall. Don't tell anyone. Stay there until you hear from me or the police. I'm sorry . . . I— Can you please tell Emmie that Daddy loves her? That I'll always love her?"

Tex was about to repeat it just to make sure he hadn't missed anything when he heard a bloodcurdling scream that echoed down the stairwell.

33

Tex ran up the stairs two at a time and found Dono-van struggling with a woman, who from the appearance of things had been hiding in a wardrobe.

"Sheila?"

She craned her neck so she could see him, then suddenly crumpled to the ground, and Donovan let her go. "Tex?" she said.

"It's okay. He's my partner. Donovan."

"She was hiding in the wardrobe. Scared the crap out of me."

"Who were you hiding from?" Tex asked.

"There were two men who came to the house. Trip saw them through the window and he told me to hide and not come out."

"Did you start the fire?" Tex asked, helping her from the ground.

"No!" Her eyes widened and her face turned red. "The frying pan? I forgot it. I was making lunch."

"Maybe it saved you when the fire department arrived."

"I heard the sirens but I was too afraid to look in case they were still inside."

"You're safe. Let's get you out of here."

"What about Trip?"

"You know where he is?"

She shook her head, and her eyes started to well up. "What if they got him?"

"Maybe they didn't. Those sirens were pretty loud." He glanced at Donovan, who was brushing dust off his knees. "You finish searching?"

"If he's hiding here, I don't know where. And the neighbor said only two men left in the same car seconds before the fire trucks got here."

"There you go," Tex said to Sheila. "In the wind. Again. Let's get out of here and call Carillo. He's going to want to know you're okay."

The three walked downstairs, and on an afterthought, Tex unplugged the answering machine and brought it with him. If Bea and the kid made it out of there, no sense letting it get out where they were.

Sheila grabbed her suitcase by the door, and he asked if she had a purse.

"In here," she said, patting the luggage.

Tex called Carillo. "We've got her. She's fine."

"Thank God."

"Now what?" Tex asked him.

"She and I are on the next flight out."

"What do you want us to do? Drive Sheila to Heathrow?"

"Heathrow?" Sheila said. "I am *so* not going home."

Carillo said, "Tell me I didn't hear what I thought I did."

"Afraid so, bud."

"Put her on the phone."

Tex held it out, saying, "Your husband wants to talk to you."

She raised her brows, planted one hand on her hip. "You

can tell my 'husband' that if he wants me to sign those divorce papers, then he better rethink his flight schedule. I've never been to England and I am *not* going home until I see something of it."

"You hear that?" Tex said into the phone.

"Loud and clear." He let out an exasperated sigh. "What do you think I should do?"

"I'm the last person to ask about marriage advice."

"Trust me. Advice on that, I don't need. About letting her stay? You think there's any danger?"

Tex glanced at Sheila, who was staring daggers at him, as though he were standing in the way of her world tour. He walked outside to get some privacy. "I guess it depends on how bad you want those papers signed."

"More than you can imagine. But not at the expense of my conscience if something happens to her."

"I sincerely doubt she's in any danger now that Trip's out of the picture. I don't think they were ever after her. Not good business sense to kill the wife of an FBI agent, unless you want the entire Bureau breathing down your neck."

"There is that."

"I'll skip the part about you purposefully flunking your psych to buy yourself a few days on the beach to come after her. So unless you've got anything better to do . . ."

"In other words, twiddle my thumbs here or at home."

"Show her a few sites. Maybe then she'll be buttered up enough to sign the papers."

"One can only hope. I'll look for a hotel."

Once Tex and Donovan had the Carillos bundled off safely in their hotel, they returned to the safe house, and Tex played the message on the answering machine again, hoping to locate where Bea and her daughter might have gone off to, assuming Bea heard the message before anyone got to her house.

"Cornwall," Tex said. "What is that? Four, five hours by train?"

"About that."

"Let's say Bea gets the phone message sometime between when Marty was shot and before Trip and Sheila get to the house."

"Except that the neighbor saw her and the kid drive off."

"But she also saw the other car show up later. I want to make sure they weren't followed."

"Maybe we should have Lisette stop in Cornwall on her way here. Double check," Donovan said as the landline to the safe house rang.

Donovan answered it.

"Since *when* do we involve ourselves in local crimes?" McNiel's voice was so loud, Tex could hear it from five feet away. Not waiting for an answer, McNiel asked, "Where's Tex?"

Donovan hit a button, saying, "Here. You're on speakerphone."

"Arthur Bingham from MI5 called me not ten minutes ago, because he's been on the phone with MI6, complaining about the bodies littering their streets after your visit. Murder-suicide? Orchestrated hit by the bridge? What the hell is going on there, and why isn't MI6 liaising for you?"

Tex glanced at Donovan, saying, "Slight snafu. We'll have it rectified before the night's out. Interesting development, though. Our contact said something about a book right before he was killed. A Kipling novel."

"Kipling?"

"That's all we know."

"Find out why the damned thing is so important."

"Any chance you can have Lisette stop in Cornwall first?" Donovan explained the necessity.

"Fine," McNiel replied. "I'll let her know. And if we're looking into the case, you might as well get a lead on who's running around killing these accountants. Can either of you identify anyone?"

Tex hesitated, then said, "Eve was there. She stole the man's briefcase—but she says she wasn't part of the hit."

They heard McNiel taking a deep breath, as though weighing all the information. "Any idea *what* was in this briefcase?"

"We have to assume the book in question."

"Find out what her agenda is. Find out what the hell is in that book. Keep me apprised of the details."

"Will do," Donovan said, then disconnected, dropping the phone into his pocket. He looked right at Tex. "Why do I get the feeling you didn't want to mention Eve's involvement?"

"I'm not sure. I think I should meet up with her like she asked."

"I and not we? You sure that's wise?"

"I'll make sure it's nice and public."

"Marty's meet was nice and public."

"I'll be fine."

"And if you're wrong?"

"Guess we'll find out in a few hours."

34

Once Micah's program ended at Claridge's, Eve excused herself to the washroom. She checked her reflection in the full-length mirror, deciding her champagne satin gown struck the right balance of demureness and sex appeal. The high neckline showed no cleavage. It wasn't needed. The soft drape of the fabric fell against her curves in such a way that sometimes it hinted at what lay beneath and at other times left no question.

The way the reporter, James Dalton, had been watching her, she knew without a doubt that this gown would intrigue him, leave him wanting more.

And right now she needed every weapon in her arsenal. It was bad enough he and his photographer showed up at the venue, but to find out that Marty Blanford had somehow been in touch with him? She'd been that close to recovering the book. She *saw* Marty guarding the briefcase. He must have hidden it. Unless somehow he'd gotten it to the reporter . . . ? Was that even possible?

It was the only explanation, she thought, applying her lipstick and noting the dark circles beneath her eyes. Sleep was almost nonexistent of late, and when she did manage to drift off, she often awoke from a nightmare that seemed to be recurring. Being sucked under in a riptide, struggling to swim to the surface, and then breaking through the churning white water, only to discover that no one could hear her scream as she was being pulled farther and farther from shore. And then, after waking, she lay there in the dark, waiting for her heart to stop racing, telling herself it was only a dream, all the while trying not to picture what seemed to be a warning. That if she wasn't careful, she was going to end up drowning, only to wash up on a stretch of shore where no one would find her, or even know that she was missing.

She didn't want to die.

Which was why she needed to handle this reporter very carefully. Right now it was all about recovering the book and doing damage control—something she was good at.

Especially when dressed like this.

After touching up her lipstick, she left the ladies' room, wading through the crowd of formally dressed attendees, politely extricating herself from those who wanted to chat. Finally she reached the curved grand staircase that descended to the ground floor, where the black and white checkerboard marble tiles gleamed like glass, reflecting the chandelier that crowned the spacious lobby. After retrieving her coat from a bellhop, she draped it over her arm and stepped outside. A line of black taxis stretched down the block, waiting in anticipation for the mass exodus of patrons, and she wondered if he had sent a car as she'd suggested, or if he came himself. She supposed it depended on how suspicious he was. Or how smart. Because who the hell would meet up with her after the mess Barclay's men made at the fund-raiser in D.C.? Someone with a death wish, or someone so blinded by the prize of a good story they failed to recognize the danger?

The crisp air felt exhilarating for a few seconds, until the cold became too much to bear, and she slipped her coat on, trying to maintain what little body warmth she could muster. When Micah and his latest followers offered her a ride back to their hotel in his limo, she declined. After ten minutes with no sign, she returned to the lobby, waited, greeted and said good-bye to a few scattered guests, then gave in, realizing James Dalton wasn't going to show.

The doorman hailed her a cab, and she slid in, telling the driver, "The Dorchester, please."

"Nice hotel," the driver said.

She didn't answer, having no wish to engage in conversation. What she needed to do was think about her next move with Mr. Dalton. But nothing came to her during the short drive. At the hotel, a liveried doorman assisted her from the cab, then walked her to the turnstile, saying, "Welcome back, Miss Sanders."

"Thank you."

If truth be told, she was glad James Dalton hadn't sent a car. What she really needed was rest, and she opened her beaded clutch, looking for her room key as she walked toward the elevator.

"Miss Sanders?"

She looked up, saw a bellhop walking around the counter toward her. She met him halfway.

"You have a visitor waiting for you at the Promenade Bar."

"Thank you."

"Would you like me to take your coat?"

As he helped her slip out of it, she glanced toward the bar. The Promenade opened off the lobby, an area that ran the length of the hotel, and she followed it to the lounge at the end, where she heard the soft strains of light jazz.

James Dalton sat on the far side of the oval bar, watching her as she entered. He didn't smile when he saw her, but lowered his glass, then allowed his gaze to roam appreciatively over her as she walked toward him. Definitely the right dress, she thought with some satisfaction.

"A drink, Miss Sanders?" he asked, standing.

"I'll have what you're having."

"Two more iced vodkas," he told the bartender. Once he had the drinks, he led her to a table well away from the bar and any patrons.

"You're not a reporter, are you, Mr. Dalton?"

The barest of hesitations, then, "Why? Because you went to the trouble of setting up a meeting for me this morning with Micah and I didn't show? As you've probably guessed, something came up."

Frankly, she'd forgotten about the meeting. Trying to follow Marty Blanford had understandably consumed her attention. "No, because here I am, and you haven't called the police."

"Perhaps I should clarify. I'm an *investigative* reporter. In my experience, the fastest way to kill a good story is to involve the police. *Especially* in a foreign country. They're more likely to lock me in a cell while they sort things out." He leaned forward, lowering his voice. "Being in custody makes it hard to get the facts for a good exposé. Something I fully intend to do, Miss Sanders."

"Exposé on what?"

"The embezzlement of your boss's money."

"I don't know how to make this any clearer, Mr. Dalton. What you're doing is dangerous. You have *no* idea what you're getting into."

"I find it exciting," Tex said. "Don't you?"

She exhaled, frustrated at trying to make him see reason. "Do you have any idea what they'll do to you and your friends if you continue this? If they find you with that book? They'll kill you."

"And what makes you think I have any book?"

"It wasn't in Marty's briefcase. It's why I was following him. It's—It's why I tried to contact Dorian the night they killed him."

"Then it wasn't suicide."

"I sincerely doubt it. And in case you're wondering, I didn't kill Dorian, either."

"With your track record? You care more about some *book* than a *life*. You *let* that man die right in front of me. Not a big stretch from there to think you might kill someone."

"Because of what happened today?" Eve said. "Without a trauma team, my staying there another few seconds was *not* going to save that man. He was already dead."

"And yet you had no problem stealing his briefcase and running off before the cops got there."

No wonder she dreamed about being sucked down into some swirling vortex. It was that feeling of desperation. The desolate realization that no matter what she did, what she said, *nothing* was changing . . . Then again, maybe she needed to drag him down with her. Scare him into cooperating. She picked up the chilled glass and took a long sip. It was a second before she could actually talk, the vodka seizing her throat with its burn, making her eyes water. "Did you read the paper about the murder suicide in Queen's Park?"

"What about it?"

"That was *them. They* were after Marty. *They're* who killed him. *Not* me." His expression never wavered, and she was lost. "How do I make you understand?"

"I guess you don't." He stood, and said, "Let me know when you want to talk about this book." And then he turned and walked off.

She stared at his departing figure as he continued past the piano, then on into the Promenade. She followed, increasing her stride to catch up. She had to get that book, find out where he was keeping it. But how?

The answer came to her the moment he walked out of the

hotel. She saw the doorman flagging a taxi, and she hurried after him, just as the vehicle pulled up. "At least give me the chance to explain," she called out.

"Explain what?"

She walked up to him, waved off the doorman, who backed away, apparently realizing she wished to speak privately. When the man was out of earshot, she said, "That if you don't turn over that book, more lives than just your own will be lost."

"Your concern is touching, Eve. But I think I'll pass."

"One block."

He looked at her in question.

"One circle around the block, and if I don't convince you, drop me off here, and you go on your way."

He glanced at the taxi, as though contemplating what the harm might be, then opened the back door for her, and she slid in. He closed the door, walked to the other side, and she took the moment to unlatch her purse, then reach in for her mirror, dropping the entire thing on the floorboard as he took a seat beside her, telling the driver to circle the block.

The purse contained nothing but her mirror, lipstick, room key, and cell phone, and she reached down to pick it up as he said, "Traffic's light, Miss Sanders. You might want to start talking."

"Good point. I can fix my lipstick later," she said, dumping everything in her lap, not even bothering to return it to her purse. "How to put this . . ." She scooted closer to him, lowering her voice. "The copy you have is rare. In the right hands, it could be *extremely* lucrative."

His brows rose slightly. "How lucrative?"

She leaned into him, put her hand on his shoulder and whispered, "More money than you could spend in a lifetime."

She stayed where she was, his face inches from hers. To her, their proximity was unnerving, perhaps because he seemed . . . so unmoved, and he asked, "Who would the buyer be?"

"Someone who wouldn't think twice about taking out the competition, as evidenced by what you saw this morning."

"Which would make someone in possession of it in a position to deal?"

"Exactly."

He stared at her for several seconds, and just when she began to think he was made of iron, his gaze dropped to her mouth and stayed there. She had him, she thought. And then he said, "Maybe you should've fixed that lipstick after all, Miss Sanders. Time's up."

It took her a moment to realize she was gaping at him in disbelief. Recovering, she slid back to her original seat as the taxi rounded the corner and pulled into the hotel. She gathered up her lipstick, mirror, and room key, returning the items to her purse. She started to slide out, hesitated, then looked right at him. "When you've come to your senses, give me a call."

He gave a sardonic tip of his fingers to his forehead, and she got out, ignored the greeting from the doorman, then stalked into the hotel.

Trying to keep her temper in check, she approached the front desk, saying, "I need to make an outside call."

The clerk directed her to the concierge station, which was unmanned at this hour. She picked up the phone, dialed the number, and listened to it ring. "Lou? Eve. How fast can you track my phone?"

"As soon as I move to my computer. Something wrong?"

"Couldn't be better. If all goes according to plan, we should find out where he's staying shortly. It's time to find out exactly what he knows."

35

The sound was so slight, Tex almost missed it. A
squeak of the floorboard, and then nothing. The total dark-
ness made it difficult to pinpoint the location. The unfamil-
iar surroundings were also a handicap. He tried to even his
breathing, tried to hear past the ambient noises of the house,
the street outside.

And there it was again. The floorboard outside the door.
The sound of a lock being picked . . .

He stilled.

The door opened just enough to let someone slide in, then
shut with a soft click. One person. That made it easy.

He waited . . . waited . . . and then he flicked on the light.

Eve stood not ten feet away, frozen against the wall,
dressed all in black, her auburn hair pulled back in a pony-
tail.

"If you're looking for your phone," he said, his weapon
pointed at her, "you left it in the taxi."

"How careless of me."

Her gaze flicked around the room, looking for an escape.
She took one step toward the door.

"I wouldn't if I were you."

"Since when do reporters carry guns? Who are you?"

"Better question. Who are you?"

She didn't answer, but he could see the sheen of sweat on her upper lip.

Donovan walked in the front door after her, locking it behind him, this time throwing the dead bolt. "She came alone."

"You were *waiting* for me?"

"Welcoming committee," Tex said. "Polite thing to do."

He holstered his weapon, then pulled a plastic tie from his pocket. She swallowed, tried to pull away as Tex cuffed her hands behind her back. "Why?"

"Precautions," he said, then gave her a thorough search before sitting her in a wooden chair facing them.

Her brow glistened and he saw her carotid beating fast. She was scared.

Good.

"Time to come clean, Miss Sanders. If that's your real name?"

She said nothing.

"Donnie?"

Donovan opened a drawer in the side table and pulled out a book, its paper cover showing it to be Kipling's selected works. A decoy. They had yet to find the real book, and this was the only plan they could come up with on such short notice. Her gaze locked onto it, a good sign, Tex thought, and he leaned toward her, so close he could smell the remnants of the perfume she'd been wearing earlier, her fear reviving it on her skin. A hint of jasmine filled his nostrils. "The book," Tex said. "You told me it could be lucrative?"

She looked at him and then Donovan. "So you *are* in it for the money? I told you, I have a buyer."

"What if we don't want to sell?"

"Then— Why not?"

"You said yourself it was too dangerous. I'm thinking we destroy it. Save a life."

Donovan pulled a lighter from his pocket, held it to the book.

She tried to stand, but Tex pushed her back into her seat.

She swallowed past a lump in her throat. "I'll do anything. Just let me have it."

"Tell us what it's for. Why is it so important?"

She took a deep breath, glanced at the book, licking her suddenly dry lips. "I don't exactly know."

"But people are dying?"

"Please . . ."

Tex took the book from Donovan. Held it in front of her. "Tell us or we burn it."

And Donovan flicked his thumb on the lighter, holding the flame so she could see it.

She eyed Donovan, then Tex, as though weighing her decision. It wasn't until Tex dropped the book into the wastebasket and Donovan rolled a piece of paper, then actually lit it, that she said, "Fine. I'll tell you."

A knock at the door caused her to jump. She looked in that direction, then screamed. Tex clamped his hand over her mouth. She twisted her head, bit him.

"Damn it," he said, pulling his hand away from her teeth, only to have her try to scream again. "You gonna get that?" he asked Donovan.

"If you manage to keep her quiet, yes." Donovan dropped the burning paper into the trash, and she struggled even more. Her eyes, wide with fright, locked on the book and the burning paper atop it as Donovan walked across the room, put his eye to the peephole.

"Finally," he said, unlocking and opening the door. "You were supposed to be here four hours ago."

"Sorry. Cornwall isn't exactly a Tube stop away, is it? And for your information, we found them. They're safe." Lisette

Perrault, their Paris-based agent, entered, then stopped short at the sight of Tex struggling with Eve.

"*Not* quite the welcome I was expecting," Lisette said to Tex, an amused expression on her face as she glanced at the woman, then did a double take. Her amusement turned to confusion. "Why do you have a CIA agent in custody?"

"CIA?" Tex said. "You're sure?"

"Very."

A whoosh from the trash caught everyone's attention as the flames engulfed the book.

Donovan grabbed a bottled water from the table, then dumped it on the trash can, dousing the flames. Tex was still trying to wrap his mind around Lisette's news, and Eve slumped back in her chair as though weak with relief.

"You *know* her?" Donovan asked Lisette.

"We worked an op in Berlin about eight months ago. Don't think she's changed that much. Genevieve Sanderson. CIA."

Tex stared at the woman, going over every contact with her, feeling as though now, finally, things were starting to make sense. She, however, was more concerned with the book. "Are you sure it's out?" she asked.

He kicked the trash can. "It was never in there."

She leaned forward, staring at the charred cover. "Then what's that?"

"Something we picked up at the bookstore," Tex said. "We never had it."

"What do you mean you never had it? Then who does?"

"How the hell should we know?" Tex said. "We're not the ones who stole the briefcase, are we?"

"Who *are* these people?" she asked Lisette.

"It's . . . complicated," Lisette told her. "For God's sake, Tex. Cut her loose and tell her what's going on."

Tex dug a knife from his pocket, flipped it open, and

sliced the plastic tie, saying, "We belong to a covert agency called ATLAS."

"Never heard of it."

"It wouldn't be very covert if you had, would it?"

Eve glared at him, then turned to Donovan, asking, "Assuming you're for real, ATLAS stands for what?"

"Alliance for Threat Level Assessment and Security."

"So you're in more than one country," she said, rubbing the circulation back into her wrists.

"Sorry about that," Tex said. "Precautions."

"So you said," Eve replied. "About the book . . ."

Donovan countered, "Why don't you start with you and your mission."

"You think I'm just going to sit down and talk because you throw some fancy acronym at me? I don't even know you."

Lisette drew a chair over and sat down next to her. "You can trust them."

"Sorry, Lisette," Eve said. "As much as I respect your word, until I get clearance, I can't talk."

"You want clearance?" Donovan said, taking out his phone. "Who would you like to receive that clearance from?"

"My handler, Lou. He's here in London."

"And his number would be . . . ?"

"If whoever you have on that end is anyone with connections, they shouldn't have a problem discovering his number. Have him call my cell phone."

"The cell phone you left in the taxi?" Tex said.

"They were kind enough to return it to me when I called and told them I *accidentally* left it in the cab."

Donovan explained the situation to McNiel, saying, "We've run into a slight . . . road bump. Micah's assistant is, according to Lisette, a CIA agent named Genevieve Sanderson, who refuses to talk until she receives clearance. She'd like her handler, Lou, to call her cell."

Lisette picked up her overnight bag, telling Tex, "As much as I'd love to be a part of this, I'm beat."

Tex stood. "I'll take you up."

Lisette started for the stairs. "I know the way. It looks like you'll be busy for a while sorting this out." She glanced at Eve. "Good to see you . . ."

"You, too, Lisette."

Tex returned to his seat, hoping it wouldn't take McNiel too long to get in touch with someone.

Apparently he needn't have worried, as Eve's phone rang about two minutes later. She answered it, listened, said, "Talk to you in the morning," then disconnected. She gave them a bland smile. "I guess you pull some pretty powerful strings in your organization."

They waited for her to explain.

"That was Lou. Apparently my clearance to talk to you comes straight from the director."

Tex asked, "Anything else you need before you tell us what's going on?"

"A tall beer might do it."

"About a year ago," Eve began, "a cache of weapons and U.S. currency was found in a remote village in Africa by some CIA agents who were following up on some intel about gun runners," which explained the photo of her and the gun dealers, Tex thought. "The money was being used to pay bribes to various officials to move certain individuals to the front of the refugee resettlement line. Because of the large amount of currency involved, they brought in the Secret Service to assist in the operation and to help with the documenting of serial numbers from the currency, which is when they found a couple bills with a 'Where's George?' stamp. Out of curiosity, they checked."

" 'Where's George?' " Tex asked.

"It's an educational Web site someone built that allows you to track the travels of paper money, as long as people are willing to enter the serial number and the location, then stamp it with the Where's George? Web site address. From there it's hit and miss that a bill will get located and tracked, more novelty than accurate reflection. Unless you get lucky. And in this case, we did. The bills in question came from an elementary school class that had collected pennies, converted it to paper currency, stamped it with Where's George? as part of their school project, then proudly donated the money to the different charities they'd picked at random from various Web sites. Two of those bills ended up in that weapons cache in Africa."

Tex thought about the odds. "Unusual, sure, but it could happen they'd end up together if donated together."

"You're right. Except that these kids only had one hundred dollars, and their donation consisted of a *single* ten-dollar bill to each separate charity. Ten charities. Ten bills. And two of them end up together in another country? That raises the odds considerably, don't you think?"

"I see your point," Donovan said. "So how did you make the connection to the charities?"

"Both charities are involved in the refugee resettlement program in some way. We couldn't find anything on the other eight."

"Are the charities real?" Tex asked.

"I think that depends on what you would consider an overhead cost," Eve told them. "When all is said and done, they're not charities, they're contractors. The U.S. essentially pays them an exorbitant fee to bring the refugees in, with what seems like little regard for what is actually being done with the money. If we're counting that they're supposed to be nonprofit but making an exorbitant profit, then no, they're not real charities. If you factor in that they're doing what we pay them to do, bring in refugees, then yes, they're real. We—or rather, the CIA and Secret Service—were less concerned with their overhead and more concerned with the how and why of the weapons and U.S. currency being found together, and what it was being used for. In other words, what was the end game?"

"And did you find that out?"

"We're talking a mixed bag. The Do Gooders, who believe wholeheartedly in the refugee program, and the piranhas and scavengers who have discovered exactly how profitable it really is. And since many of the refugees come from one of the black-list countries, which have no agreements to turn over bank records to ensure the money isn't being used for terrorism or criminal enterprises, where better to launder your ill-gotten funds?"

"A win-win for A.D.E.," Tex said.

"The thing is, we believe Vince—"

"Vince?" Donovan asked.

"An A.D.E. employee who recently was killed in a car accident, coincidentally or not, right after this book of his and Marty's came to light. He allegedly knew some of their funds were being diverted and were directly used to allow war criminals in through the refugee program. If that information got out, A.D.E. would be finished. No more Micah, no more profit."

Tex could well imagine. "Hence the hunt for the book."

"Exactly. But if the CIA found it first, we could find the link to at least *one* conduit that's allowing the criminals into the country. There's a list in there showing where they're coming from. At least we think so."

"So the CIA sent you after Micah and his Sticks to Bricks campaign?"

"Yes. We'd been tailing someone associated with the weapons cache and noticed his appearance at two of Micah's documentary showings. A couple of eavesdropped phone conversations confirmed they were trying to negotiate an offer for their accounting firm to assist him with his charity. So we came up with the cover of my being a college student looking to volunteer to be Micah's assistant free of charge as part of my marketing thesis, and began fielding the calls between him and A.D.E. in short order. It worked, since the A.D.E. contact—a man named Willis—was trying to convince Micah to work with them, and took me—the alleged college student—as an easier, more naive mark."

"A mark for what?" Donovan inquired.

"To not see how they were manipulating Micah and funneling the money he brought in."

"So how," Tex asked, "did you get in bed with A.D.E.?"

She narrowed her eyes at his choice of words. "Maybe because they discovered that my Eve Sanders identity has some relatives back in the U.S. who have less than stellar reputations, which they tried to hold over my head as a way of controlling me and thereby controlling Micah. I'm sure they never expected an impromptu visit from a couple of my *uncles,* who told them exactly what would happen if they harmed a hair on my head, but it had the desired effect and then some. They let me handle all matters with Micah, then started to include me in the business end."

"So you're in the perfect position."

"Too perfect. Micah's documentary film took off and they're raking in millions. My job now has become almost laughable, since my main goal in A.D.E.'s eyes as well as the CIA's eyes is to keep Micah happy and producing, while A.D.E. rakes it in and CIA follows the money. I am, for all intents and purposes, an executive assistant."

"Where would they be without you?"

"I'm not sure, but I have to wonder how many people have actually died *because* of me. And I'm helpless to stop it."

"It can't be your fault."

She gave a cynical laugh. "You've never been so wrong. I have to live with the guilt for the rest of my life, knowing that if I hadn't infiltrated A.D.E., found someone who was willing to look into a few things and document it for me, he'd still be alive."

"Dorian?"

"Vince. Here in London. A solo car accident that I'm sure was staged. He's the one who told me he was certain it was going on with a multitude of other charities, not only in the London office but the U.S. office where the charities are based. But he also said there was no way anyone at A.D.E. would ever be able to get out with the information. They're very strict. Women carry clear plastic purses, and the few men who do have briefcases have to submit to having them searched. They deal in a lot of cash, so they justify the over-the-top security to make sure cash isn't being smuggled out. If he was to document it, he'd have to find a way to do it so that he could smuggle it in and out without anyone knowing."

"The book?" Tex asked.

"The book. Vince managed to put the evidence in a book. Which, as you've probably guessed, is why I was so frantic when I thought you were burning it."

"And you don't know what it says?"

"Only the vague bits I've told you, and I don't even know that for certain. The morning Marty was killed, the way he held on to the briefcase, I would have sworn the book was in there. It wasn't."

"He mentioned something about a Kipling novel right before he died. He did not, however, say where it was."

She eyed the charred remains of the book in the trash can. "We need to find it before Trip does. It's bad enough that he'll probably resort to his old ways and try to extort money from Barclay. But it may very well tell us the route used to smuggle Yusuf out of Africa and into the U.S."

36

"How's Sheila?" Sydney asked when Carillo called her at Griffin's office that afternoon.

"Buying a guide book as we speak. I can't believe I let her talk me into staying."

"Maybe it'll be good for you. Relax a few days."

"I did mention that Sheila's with me, right?"

"Oh for God's sake. Play tourist for a couple days. When's the last time you've done that?"

"Never. How's it going there?"

Sydney informed him about the command from the top to stop the investigation into the Redfern Group's involvement with the refugees.

"If nothing else, it tells me you're on the right track."

"It'd be nice if I knew which direction that track was going."

"Ask Scotty."

"There's got to be an easier way."

"Hate to break it to you, kid, but your ex isn't known as Mr. Fast-track-to-the-top for nothing."

She sighed.

Carillo laughed. "What you need to do is find him another girl."

"You know any?"

"I'll check my little black book. Oh. Wait. Sheila burned it when we got married."

"Like you ever had one."

"Call him. If he doesn't have the answer, he'll know someone who does."

Even Griffin thought the idea held merit when she ran it by him.

Telephoning her ex-fiancé was not something she looked forward to. Scott Ryan was a nice enough guy who, unfortunately, seemed to think that any call from her was a sign that there was a chance for them to repair their relationship. He didn't seem to understand that they had grown worlds apart since those academy days when they first met. Whereas Sydney had no problem working out of the basement of Quantico, or even in some small field office away from the pomp and circumstance of the capital, Scotty thrived on it. He kept abreast of the political scene, knew every major politician on sight, whether he'd met the person or not, and if there was a function that could be attended involving said politicians, and a need for the FBI to be there, Scotty cleared his calendar.

She knew that Carillo was right, though. Scotty could at least point her in the right direction, so she called him.

"Sydney? How are you?"

"Great. Thanks."

"I heard you're going to be off for a couple weeks? Are you okay?"

Typical Scotty, knowing her schedule almost before she did. "I'm fine. But since I've got all this time, I thought maybe we could have drinks, catch up a bit? I was thinking of that grill we used to go to before I moved to San Francisco. On K Street."

"Sure."

"Say around five?"

"I'll see you there."

She hung up the phone. "This is not going to work out well."

"He's a big boy," Griffin said, walking into the office just then.

"Every time I think he's ready to move on, I find myself calling him to get something I need for a case. I'm starting to feel guilty."

"It's called networking."

"I'll tell myself that next time he calls asking me out again."

"Or just tell him no. Then again, maybe it's not Scotty who has the problem. Maybe you're sending the wrong signals."

She opened her mouth to protest, then stopped to wonder if she could really be guilty of that and not know it. "Definitely not. I think Carillo's right. I've got to find him someone." She looked at her watch. "So what are your plans for the night?"

"I've got a date with a pretty girl," Griffin said. "Why?"

"We're still on?"

"You're not getting out of it that easy, even if you are going out with your ex first."

Sydney made her way through the crowded bar, figuring Scotty would be somewhere he could look out, see who was coming in. He had always enjoyed the grill, due to the chance of seeing and being seen by those on the same fast track. There were plenty of political aides and Washington insiders who came there to unwind after a long day at the office, and Scotty knew how to move about a room to take advantage of it. He was handsome, personable, knowledgeable, and most importantly—in this circle—knew exactly what people wanted to hear.

As usual, it was crowded at this hour, and it was no surprise to Sydney that Scotty was already present when she arrived. She did not, however, approach, since he was deep in conversation with someone at the bar. Animated conversation. From past experience—and yet another example of why any relationship they'd had was doomed—he wasn't likely to notice her presence anytime soon.

She scanned the room, then saw Griffin at the other end of the bar. He turned, saw her, nodded. She walked over and he handed her a glass of red wine. "Hope I'm not being presumptuous. I recall you're not a white wine sort of person." He eyed Scotty, shaking hands with another man who walked up. "I should probably start making the rounds, see if I'm as good at networking as your ex."

She sipped the wine, pleased when she tasted cabernet, full-bodied and smooth against her tongue, with a slight pepper finish. She watched Scotty, saying, "Don't know about you, but I could never get used to this scene."

They heard a feminine laugh, then, "It's a love-hate thing."

Griffin and Sydney turned to see who had spoken. The woman stood about two inches shorter than Sydney, early twenties, blond hair, sparkling blue eyes. She held up a glass of white wine as a greeting, saying, "Sometimes I can't imagine working anywhere else, and sometimes I can't wait to get out of here."

Sydney empathized completely. "So are you a lobbyist? Politician?"

"Law student, actually."

"That would make this the place to network, then," Sydney said as Griffin left her to mix in with the crowd. Sydney glanced toward Scotty, thinking it was high time to interrupt him. Before she even had a chance to start in his direction, the woman stuck out her hand. "I'm Amanda."

"Nice to meet you," she said, trying to keep one eye on her ex in case he moved off.

"Sorry about being pushy. Our law professor makes us do that. He says we need to start building connections."

"Not a bad idea. Looking to go into political law?"

The woman laughed. "I know this is going to sound stupid, but I'm tempted to go into the FBI."

That put Sydney on guard. "FBI?"

"I know, crazy, right? But see that man over there? The cute guy in the dark suit at the end of the bar?" She lifted her wineglass and angled it in Scotty's direction. "He came to our school on government career day," she said, which immediately put Sydney at ease, now that there was a logical explanation. "I doubt I would have even thought about it until then. But every time I see him here, I start to wonder."

"It's a good career," Sydney replied.

"Of course my friends all think I'm nuts, since everyone *knows* the FBI doesn't pay shit compared to the big firms here on K Street, but I liked what he had to say. I even thought about asking him, you know, what it's like, but I get tongue-tied."

Sydney took a closer look at her. Pretty. Smart. No ring on her fingers . . . Maybe this was fate. "So you come here a lot?"

"When I'm in the area. I intern across the street two days a week. Or I did. Today was my last day."

"For what firm?"

"Tarlington, Wolfe and Rolland. Not the best, but at least it wasn't Wingman Squared, right?" Then, at Sydney's blank look, she said, "Wingman and Wingman . . . ? You're *definitely* not from around here, or you'd be nodding in sympathy. It's like the whole bar's talking about it." She leaned in, then lowered her voice, which in the crowded bar was something slightly less than shouting. "They're investigating one of the lobbyists at W2 for political corruption. Don't ask me the particulars. I have *no* idea."

"Did you say W2?"

"What insiders call the firm."

The folder on Redfern's desk. Not a tax file at all, she realized.

Amanda sipped her wine, then gave a deep sigh. "I waver, though. Law or FBI? I'd love to ask the guy, but he's surrounded. As usual. Besides, I don't have the guts to interrupt."

"Just so happens that I have an in," Sydney said. "You really think he's cute?"

Amanda turned an appreciative glance his way. "Are you kidding?"

"Perfect," Sydney said, taking her by the arm. "I'll introduce you."

"Time to go," Sydney said, dragging Griffin from the bar.

"Scotty?"

"Turns out that he doesn't know much about Redfern or his association with the refugee program. Besides, he's somewhat occupied."

Griffin looked over his shoulder at Scotty and the young woman Sydney had introduced him to. "You actually did it?"

"Yep. Killed two birds with one stone. She thinks he's cute. And he clearly thinks the same. Any luck and Scotty will be head over heels in love and I will have a personal life that doesn't include him checking up on my every move."

"That's only one bird," he said as his phone rang.

"I know." She looked over at him and smiled, very pleased with herself as she buttoned her coat against the frigid cold.

He answered his phone. "We're just walking out . . . I'll,

uh, ask," he said to the caller, then covered the phone with his hand. "McNiel. He wants an update and offered to buy dinner. I can tell him no . . ."

Not an auspicious start to their first official night out. However, it *was* his boss, so she gave a shrug, indicating she was fine either way.

"Sure," Griffin said into the phone. "There's a tapas restaurant about two blocks down." He disconnected, then dropped the phone into his pocket. "Sorry about that."

"Bosses . . ."

"Back to your big secret," he said to Sydney, guiding her in the direction of the restaurant.

"Have you heard of a law firm called Wingman and Wingman?"

He hesitated the barest instant, then said, "Wingman Squared. One of the top ten lobbyist firms the last several years running."

"How do you keep up with this stuff?"

"In my line of work, a necessity. What about them?"

"According to the girl I introduced Scotty to, one of their lobbyists is or is about to be investigated for political corruption. That may or may not be important. It is Washington, and since when is that news? What is, is that there was a file folder labeled W2 on Redfern's desk."

"End of the year. It could be taxes."

"Exactly what I thought, until I learned W2 is also the insider's nickname for Wingman Squared. Add to that, we have Senator Burgess leaving Redfern's office after at least a thirty-minute conversation with the W2 file on his desk at the same time? Coincidence? Or something more?"

"Not seeing a lot there."

She looked up at him, surprised. "You of all people I thought would get this. What about the call from Pearson, trying to put the kibosh on our investigation? Someone reached pretty far up the food chain to pull that off."

"Maybe we were asked to back off because of the investigation into Wingman's lobbyist."

"You don't think you would have heard about that investigation by now?"

"We'll run it by McNiel when we get to the restaurant. In the meantime, I have something for you." He reached into his pocket and pulled out a small white box, handing it to her. "It looks more expensive than it is. Was. I picked it up in Mexico."

She lifted the lid and saw an opal pendant set in silver. The stone sparkled orange and red beneath the streetlight. "It's beautiful."

"I might not have gotten your call at Christmas," he said, lifting the necklace from the cotton layer, "but I was thinking of you."

He draped the chain around her neck and fastened the clasp, then kissed her.

"Thank you."

"You're welcome," he said, taking her hand in his as they walked. And from that moment on, the investigation was the last thing on her mind.

37

If Sydney was disappointed that their first official date wasn't just the two of them, she hid it very well, Griffin thought, at least for the couple blocks it took to get to the restaurant. Like the grill they'd just left, the tapas restaurant bar was filled to capacity with those looking to take advantage of the after-hours networking and half-priced drinks. The restaurant area, however, was fairly quiet, it still being early hours for the dinner crowd. Griffin asked for a table in the far corner, well away from the noise of the bar, sitting with his back to the wall. McNiel walked in a few minutes after their arrival.

They ordered an assortment of tapas. A waiter served drinks, then left, and Griffin casually mentioned the rumor of a political corruption investigation at Wingman Squared, since he was sure that McNiel wouldn't want Sydney looking into it. The decades-old investigation was connected to Sydney's father and had far-reaching implications. It would not put Griffin, McNiel, and ATLAS in a good light. In other words, it definitely was not something he was about to discuss with Sydney even if he thought McNiel would allow it.

At least not here, not now, and he could hear Tex's *I told you so* ringing in his ears.

"Wingman Squared?" McNiel asked. "Where did you hear about this?"

And Sydney said, "At the bar."

McNiel eyed her. "What was said?"

"Just that everyone's talking about it, and that I must be new if I haven't heard of it. What made it interesting was that she called the firm W2."

"W2?" McNiel swirled the ice cubes in his drink, took a sip, then looked at Sydney. "I'm assuming this means something to you?"

Sydney described what she saw in Redfern's office. "Of course, he is a law firm, so maybe he's defending Wingman's lobbyist."

"I'll look into it," McNiel said. "Enough shop talk for the night. Here comes the waiter with our food." The conversation at that point turned to the mundane—weather, sports—and McNiel ordered more drinks, then leaned back in his chair. "So, tell me, Sydney. What does your family think about you being an FBI agent?"

"Depends on who you ask. My eleven-year-old sister is thrilled to no end, wanting to follow in my footsteps. My mother and stepfather . . . Let's just say they've come to accept the fact."

"So what'd you do before you came to the Bureau?" he asked, as though he hadn't read the same dossier as Griffin when they'd done a thorough background on her all those months ago when they asked for her help on another case.

Sydney apparently opted to pretend they knew nothing about her, and willingly talked about her family, spending the summers as a child on her uncle's farm and then her early years at the Sacramento PD before joining the Bureau. Hearing it in her words was a far cry from reading the dry report they pulled on her background, and Griffin found the time passing quickly as they laughed over some of her misadventures as a teen let loose on a farm. After which McNiel talked about his youth, growing up in California's Central Valley in an area not too unlike Sydney's uncle's town. Then, all too soon, McNiel was paying the tab, saying he needed to get home. "Finish your drinks," he said, signing the credit card receipt. "I've got an early morning meeting."

He left, and Sydney and Griffin followed a few minutes later, surprised to find the bar nearly empty and the downtown streets, normally thriving and bustling during the day, mostly deserted at that hour. When they walked out, Griffin said, "I was thinking maybe we could get dessert and coffee? Just the two of us?"

"Or we could skip the coffee and go straight to dessert?"

He looked over at her. "Are you suggesting what I think you're suggesting?"

She smiled but didn't answer, which was answer enough, and they walked down the street, arm in arm. After a while she said, "Dinner was nice. I like McNiel."

"He's a good guy to work for. Although I've heard rumors he's looking to get out. The sixteen-hour days are getting to him."

"What about you?"

"I've got a few good years left in me," he said as they strolled past an office building, the plate-glass panels reflecting the area around them. "Just hoping I won't have to test it out tonight."

"Quite the joker."

"Actually, my sense of humor is on the low side." He nodded toward the window to their right, and the reflection of the man he'd been watching across the street these past five minutes since they left the restaurant. "We're being followed."

38

Griffin put his hand on Sydney's back, urging her to walk faster. They were about a block from the parking garage. "He's been shadowing us since we left the restaurant."

"I was right about the whole W2 thing."

"I doubt it. But if you are, you can gloat later." Whoever it was had to have followed them from the grill to the restaurant. He wouldn't have noticed the tail as readily, given the number of pedestrians out at the time.

He quickened their pace, glanced into the reflection and noted the man was still paralleling them on the opposite side of the street. "He's either really bad at this or there's more than one and this guy's purpose is to draw our attention."

"I remember back when my life was so ordinary."

"Remember how much paperwork was involved with ordinary?"

"I'll take paper cuts over gunshots any day."

They entered the garage and stopped at the kiosk, where Griffin inserted his parking ticket, then paid with his credit card. The machine spat out the validated parking pass. From the corner of his eye he kept watch on the entrance. Though he didn't see anyone, he was fairly certain he heard the foot-fall of a person running across the street shortly after they entered. That meant the tail was probably waiting just out-side, undoubtedly knowing they'd have to stop to pay for their ticket. In other words, someone familiar with the area, someone who knew this was a self-service garage.

He took Sydney by the arm, leading her toward the first-level ramp. "When I let go of you, keep going like I'm still at your side." Their footsteps echoed in the deserted garage, and he noted the pattern, the cadence of their walk, one that was soon joined by a slight distortion as someone else en-tered the garage.

"Now," he whispered. He ducked behind a column and Sydney continued on. His back pressed to the cold cement, gun drawn, he listened, heard Sydney's footsteps growing softer, the other man's getting louder . . . When the man passed the column, Griffin reached out, grabbed him by the scruff of his coat collar, yanked back so the man fell against his chest.

"Who are you?" Griffin said, screwing his gun in the man's side, then realized the guy couldn't be older than maybe twenty-one or twenty-two. Probably still in college.

The kid's eyes widened, nostrils flared. "Don't shoot me. I'll give you my wallet. Whatever you want!"

"*Who* are you? And *why* are you following us?"

"T-Timothy Mad-Madison. Someone paid me. I swear. Don't hurt me."

Sydney rounded the corner, her gun held down at her side, and Griffin said, "Paid you for what?"

"He gave me a hundred bucks to follow you. He said he'd double it if I found out where you were parked, double that to tell him what car you were driving, and five hundred more if I g-got the license plate."

Griffin holstered his weapon while Sydney covered. "Why did he want it?"

Timothy, his gaze fixed on Sydney's gun, said, "He didn't say. I swear. He—He stopped me when I was going into the bar and asked if I'd keep an eye out for anyone who wasn't a regular and was asking questions."

"And how were you supposed to get this information to him?"

Timothy slipped his hand into his pants pocket and pulled out a slip of crumpled paper with a number written on it, which he gave to Griffin. "I—I wanted to get your license." He tried to laugh. "I needed the money."

"Let me see your phone."

He hesitated, looked from Griffin to Sydney, but then handed it over. Griffin pressed the recall button, saw the number there, the time showing just a few minutes before. "You *told* him we were here? In this garage?"

"Am I in trouble?"

"We might all be in trouble." He looked away for one instant, to motion Sydney over. Timothy dashed around the column, then fled toward the street. He was fast. Griffin chased after him, was just closing the distance as they reached the parking entrance. He heard the rev of an engine, then tires screeching a split second before he was blinded by headlights as the car raced toward them. He lunged forward, tried to grab the kid, to stop him.

Too late. The car hit Timothy as he burst onto the sidewalk. And then Griffin felt a rush of air as the fender clipped him, sending him flying like a rag doll.

39

Sydney's heart slammed into her ribs.

The acrid scent of burnt rubber assaulted her nostrils as she ran up, looked around for Griffin, panicking when she didn't see him at first. She turned in a circle, calling out his name, when she heard the sound of tires screeching across the blacktop as the sedan made a U-turn, its headlights outlining Griffin's still form in the gutter as it raced straight for him. For her. She aimed her gun, fired at the headlights over and over. The car veered, then fishtailed as it spun around, speeding off in the opposite direction.

"Griffin!"

She hurried toward him, kneeling, saw blood from a head wound, felt for a pulse.

"Griffin, talk to me. Please. Wake up . . ."

He stirred, and she holstered her gun, her hands shaking as she pulled her phone from her pocket, hit 911. She stood, surveyed the area as a crowd began to gather. When the dispatcher came on the line, she said, "FBI. Officer down. Two injured in a hit and run . . ."

"Location?"

"K Street. The parking garage across from the Wingman and Wingman building." Her gaze caught on Timothy, saw his crumpled form on the blacktop. "Oh my God, hurry."

Sydney pushed her way into the Emergency Room, flinging her credentials in the face of anyone who got in her way. Griffin was sitting up in the bed, alert, right cheek scraped, but otherwise looking good, and she breathed a sigh of relief. "That's one hell of a way to get out of a date. How are you?"

"I have a feeling I'm going to be sore tomorrow."

"I thought you were dead."

"Quiet. They're already talking about keeping me overnight for observation."

"And well they should."

"I don't like hospitals."

"Butch up, Griffin. You should be an old hand at this by now."

McNiel knocked on the wall, then entered. "Just got off the phone with the PD. They found the suspect vehicle about a block away, abandoned. Comes back stolen."

"Go figure," Sydney said.

"Looks like one of those dozen shots might have even hit the guy. Found some blood in the car, so at least we have that."

"You missed?" Griffin asked. "That many times?"

"Give me a break. I was blinded by the headlights."

He laid back on the pillow. "I've seen you shoot. Not worried."

McNiel eyed him, then slapped the end of the bed. "Looks like you'll be on desk duty for a while."

"I'll be fine. Give me a day."

"Desk duty or nothing."

"Desk duty," Griffin echoed, closing his eyes.

Sydney watched him for a moment, checking to make sure

his breathing wasn't changing. Ridiculous, she knew, but the image of him being hit by that car was still so frighteningly sharp in her mind.

McNiel motioned her to follow him out to the hallway, out of earshot. "Pearson's waiting for you in the lobby."

She nodded, then realized she hadn't inquired about the man who'd been following them. "Timothy. He was brought in the same time—"

"He didn't make it."

It was a second or two before she was able to process what he was saying.

"Go home, Sydney." When she looked back into Griffin's room, hesitant to leave, he said, "I'll stay. Get some rest. Busy day tomorrow."

"I—I have his gun."

"Tomorrow."

40

Clayton Barclay waited until he heard the door close and the sound of Eve's footsteps retreating down the hall before picking up the phone and pressing the recall button. "She just left," he said when the man on the other end answered. "How are the plans coming?"

"Everything's almost in place."

"Any word on Trip's progress?"

"Not yet."

"Let me know the moment you hear from him. And for God's sake, find his sister and niece. We can't very well kill Trip before we kill them, or someone's bound to question the order of things. Not if we're trying to paint him as a crazed gunman."

"Trip's not going anywhere, until we find them. Trust me."

"I do," he said, swiveling his chair around to glance out the window. Eve was hailing a taxi in front of the building. The woman was becoming bothersome. Always inserting herself into the business, because she knew that Micah would do what she wanted while disregarding everyone else. The man trusted her, and the money they were making off him had been worth the inconvenience of having to deal with his assistant . . .

"You hear me, boss?"

Barclay pulled his attention back to the phone. "What? No."

"What do you think of my idea about having Eve fly off to Africa with Micah in order to raise more awareness?"

"I'd have to wonder why anyone in their right mind would want to go there. It's not safe."

"That's my point exactly. Because who would question a photo op of Micah at some of the actual sites he's raising funds for? And the Kenya refugee camp is conveniently located a short drive from the Somalia border. The way I see it? It'd be a shame if something happened to Eve on the trip . . ."

"I do like the way your mind works, Willis." Barclay turned back to the window, watching Eve get into the taxi. "Be sure to book a first-class ticket for Miss Sanders. This is one photo op we don't want her to miss."

Micah stood when Tex and Donovan walked into the dining room of the hotel.

"Ah, the reporters from Washington," he said, shaking their hands. "Good to see you. Can I interest you in a late breakfast?"

"No thanks," Tex said. "We already ate. But I would like to get your views on how you think the refugee program is going. Are you happy with the way it's progressed? Any improvements on the way things are handled?"

"Couldn't be happier," Micah said, while Donovan snapped a few photos to make it look good. "In fact, I've just heard that the U.S. has earmarked even more money to be put into the refugee program. Wonderful news, since it will allow so many who are being persecuted in their own countries to be able to come to ours and have what we've always taken for granted. The American dream."

American pipe dream in a lot of cases, Tex thought, but he jotted Micah's statement into his notebook, trying to look interested as he added, "So what's next on your agenda?"

"You probably haven't heard, but we're going to Africa."

"Africa?" Tex saw the excitement on the man's face.

"To visit some of the actual refugee camps. Amazing that we're going to get to see it working from Ground Zero, so to speak."

"Ground Zero. Clever . . ." He closed his notebook and looked around. "So who all's going on this trip and when do you leave?"

"Eve and I leave this afternoon. Ah, there she is now," he said, nodding in the vicinity of the restaurant entrance.

"Very . . . exciting. I'll, uh, let my photographer get some shots of you while I interview Eve."

"Good. Good. Thanks for coming out."

"Any time."

Tex walked up to Eve, who had a very neutral look on her face, and he wondered what she was thinking about this latest development. She was dressed in a wine-colored business jacket and skirt, with black high heels. Very secretary looking, as opposed to the woman wearing all black who had broken into their safe house last night.

They shook hands, and he said, "Good to see you again."

"You, too. Did you get what you needed from Mr. Goodwin?"

"I did, but I was hoping for a different angle. Maybe from your point of view. Do you have a few minutes?"

"Of course. Why don't we sit in a quiet corner and let Micah finish his breakfast."

"Perfect."

They walked out into the Promenade lobby, taking a seat well away from anyone, and Tex asked, "What the hell?"

"Barclay informed me this morning that he wants Micah and me to head to Africa. I'm sure Micah told you all about it."

"Even odds," Tex said, "the closest he's ever been to one of those refugee camps is watching a National Geographic TV special from the safety of his own living room. Have you even seen his documentary? The one he shows at all his fund-raisers?"

"More times than I can count," Eve replied.

"The guy's a fraud."

"I'll admit there are . . . issues with his Sticks to Bricks. *He* means well," she countered.

"Bullshit. And you know it. The only thing he's doing is living the parasitic life of a celebrity and raking in money left and right for even bigger parasites like A.D.E. who have the art of exploitation down to a science. People are throwing money at this guy left and right with no clue as to how it's being spent, and he's just as clueless."

"Granted he has no real idea what these places are like, but he believes in what he's doing. We are not, however, going. I just finished talking to Lou, and after conferring with the powers that be at Langley, Micah and I will head to the airport, pretend we're en route, at which time I'll take ill and we'll get on a flight for the States instead."

"That's good, because I'm not about to let you go. Too dangerous."

Eve laughed. "Can you imagine if I came bursting in on one of *your* missions? Demanding that *you* stop because it's dangerous?"

"You already did," Tex replied. "When you called me yesterday afternoon, trying to convince me you weren't guilty of the hit on Marty."

"Touché, Mr. Dalton. Only I didn't know you were a covert agent, did I?"

"Tex."

"Well, then, *Tex.* Suffice it to say that all is well and you won't need to come charging in on your white steed. We've got things under control."

"Good, because I'm not very good on horseback."

She leaned back in her seat, glancing toward Micah as Donovan played photographer. "As much as I'm looking forward to getting back and putting this case to bed, I can't help wondering about this book. It would be nice to find it."

"Trust me. We looked. And unless it's in Marty's office—"

"It's not. Barclay had it searched top to bottom. Same with his house and apartment."

"—then I haven't a clue."

"What exactly did he say to you right before he was shot?"

"Promise to protect his wife and daughter. He handed me his briefcase, then unwound his scarf, saying something about hiding it in a Kipling novel."

"Rudyard Kipling. Why the hell Kipling?"

"Good writer?"

She took out her cell phone, opened up a Web browser, and moved her finger across the screen, searching for something. "I followed him from the Tube to where he got shot. He ducked into a restaurant for a few minutes, and Lou went back, searched the trash, so it's not there."

"What about a library? Or a bookstore? Could he have stopped and hidden it in plain sight?"

"Kipling, London books . . ." She read aloud what she typed on her virtual keyboard, then a moment later said, "Lots of copies out there." She turned her screen toward him, saying, "I don't suppose he gave you a specific title?"

"No."

"*Phantom Rickshaw? Gunga Din? Jungle Book? Just So—*"

"*Jungle Book?*"

"He said that?"

"No. But there were all these Disney DVDs at the house. Disney did *Jungle Book*, right?"

"Animated musical. You said he told you a novel."

"Give me a sec . . ." He pictured the moment, saw Marty removing his gloves, saying, *Just so you know. It's well hidden in that Kipling story.* Tex laughed. "He didn't say book. He said story."

"Story?"

"As in it *could* be a DVD. And last I heard, you could put several books on one of those."

Tex and Donovan left Eve at the hotel and drove straight for Marty's wife's house. The longest fifteen-minute drive of their lives. "You'd think," Donovan said as Tex turned down the neat little residential street, "that for a guy whose favorite movie is *Roger Rabbit,* you'd at least pay attention to other animated cartoons and the original stories they came from."

"Least thing you could have done was open it and make sure it's the real deal. You were holding them." Tex pulled up in front of the house. "Isn't that the nosy neighbor?"

"I'll have a proper British chat with her while you pick the lock."

"Good show, old boy."

While Donovan crossed the street, Tex walked up to the door. It took him less than a minute to bypass the lock and enter the residence, which smelled even more like a wet campfire now that it had been closed up all night. He saw the DVDs on the kitchen counter and scooped them up, relieved when he saw *The Jungle Book* among them. He opened it, saw a disc with the same name on the face of it, clearly the Disney copy, and he wanted to shout out his frustration, then hurl the thing across the room like a Frisbee. He started to close it, then realized there was a second DVD behind the first. He removed the top disc, saw one that was not a Disney imprint, closed the cover and walked out, pulling the door shut behind him.

"Everything looks good," he called out to Donovan, then waved to the neighbor, trying to keep it neutral enough to match whatever story Donovan might have spun for her.

Tex handed the case to him after he got into the car. "I think we have it."

"You didn't check it out?"

"Wasn't about to take a chance. We need to burn a copy and figure out what the hell's on it. Next stop. Safe house."

41

Tex slid the DVD into the drive as Donovan pulled up
a chair to take a seat beside him. When the icon appeared
on the computer monitor, Tex burned a copy, then set the
original aside before opening the files. "Here goes nothing."
He double-clicked on the copy DVD, and accessed a folder
containing files.

"You going to stare at them or open one?"

"You're like a kid at Christmas. Let's see what we have
under the tree first." What they had was a lot of photos,
dozens, and way down at the bottom of the list one very
large document file. He opened that first.

"What is it?" Donovan asked.

Tex scanned a few pages, clicking past each, trying to
make sense of it. "I'm looking . . ."

"Not fast enough." Donovan reached over, took the mouse
from Tex and scrolled down. "It's a refugee list."

"I'm not seeing that as earth shattering."

"Some of the names have an asterisk by them." He
scrolled down to the bottom. "It shows the office that issued
the name, because they had no ID." He scrolled even further.

"The names they had when they came in . . . don't match the names they ended up with." Donovan pointed to the other computer. "Access the No Fly list. I have a feeling . . ."

Tex did as he asked. Donovan read off the first name. Tex ran it. "Clear."

"What am I missing . . . ?"

"Criminal history?"

"Can we access this country?"

"Not from here. But we could get someone from MI6 who's already over there. If they have someone."

"Call."

Tex did. The only number he had was Alice's. "It's Tex."

"I guessed. How are things?"

"If this is what we think it is, we may have our first solid link on the first stop for the terrorists who are getting into the country."

She gave him the number of the agent in Kenya. He called and explained the situation once more, and was finally put in contact with an officer of the Kenyan police agency, a man named Jomo. Tex read off the first several names, along with their birth dates.

He heard the sound of a keyboard clicking in the background as the officer ran them. "They're all criminals," Jomo said, his voice deep, his accent distinct. "Every one of them. Their crimes range from minor theft to robbery, and one is for attempted murder. Where did you get these names?"

"From a contact here in England."

"Several of them have warrants for their arrest. Do you know where they are?"

"Not yet. But I'm beginning to think they're not where they're supposed to be."

"We have long believed that some of these offices that are opening to help these refugees are . . . how do you say it? Suspect."

"Suspect, how?"

"They receive grants of money from various charities to resettle these people in other countries. In theory, a good idea to help. In reality, when there is that much money changing hands, there is much graft and corruption, even within my own government, I'm sorry to say. The charities get paid by the body. No bodies, no money. To them, the background matters little. And for those eager to get out of a country that intends to prosecute, they are willing to pay even more. The icing on a cake, as you call it."

"Thank you. I appreciate your help."

"You are very welcome."

Tex ended the call and repeated the information.

Donovan showed him the photographs. "The offices where this information came from."

"That's where Eve was supposed to be going."

"Was."

"Almost too bad they're sending them home."

"We better call HQ."

Tex informed McNiel of what they found and what the Kenyan officer had told them.

"You're sure about the location of this office?"

"You mean where the one list of criminals was processed through under different names? Yes. There's even a photograph of the book sitting on the office desk. Whoever prepared this was very thorough. In fact, there's info on here that I'm not even sure what it belongs to. But it's got that evidentiary look to it. And that's not including the page with all the dollar signs on it. If I had to guess, there's a lot of money being laundered through a number of black-list countries. The tip of the iceberg. Just the little we were able to make of it tells me that A.D.E. would not want this out there."

"Send me what you have electronically. I want to know exactly what we're dealing with."

"I just sent an encrypted e-mail of what I have. I'll get MI6 to lock up the original. Since A.D.E. operates in both countries, I'm sure they're going to want in on the action."

McNiel called back in less than fifteen minutes. "Change of plans."

"Didn't know we had any plans," Tex told him.

"We didn't, the CIA did. And now we've made some of our own after receiving the latest intel that Yusuf may have gone through the refugee contractor office on your list."

"They're not still thinking he's in Africa, after all this time?"

"No. We're fairly certain he's here. But they *are* thinking that if you can find the office where he was issued his bogus ID, we may be able to figure out what name he came into this country with. If we can tie the evidence together to show the flaws in the system, we'll be able to shut down A.D.E., and any charity running under them. More importantly, we'll be able to stop at least that hole that is allowing the terrorists to enter the country through the refugee program. Which is why the CIA has changed their minds about calling Eve stateside. She's heading to the Dadaab refugee camp."

"That's insane. It's a friggin' war zone there."

"We're not about to walk away from a lead that might give us Yusuf and the criminal element used to facilitate his entry into the U.S. She's going. And since embedding journalists has become so common in this day and age, Donovan and Lisette are flying out with her as members of the press. Turns out the *International Journal for World Peace* is very interested in doing a feature article on Micah and his charity. I believe the editor will be calling his publicist with the good news as soon as the office opens. *You* get to tag along for good measure. We're hoping no one notices there's a third wheel."

"East Africa . . . Lovely time of year."

"Better than the rainy season."

"And what about Micah?"

"Find a good hotel in Nairobi where he can drink daiquiris until you're done. I have a feeling that once he gets his first glimpse of a real refugee camp, he won't object to the suggestion of being Photoshopped into the pictures."

42

The Greyhound to Washington, D.C., took slightly
less than three days. The bus, Yusuf found, was cleaner than
the one he took up to the Mexico border. He did not talk with
any of the passengers when they tried. His conversation with
the border patrol guard had spooked him enough to make
him realize there were nuances of speaking this American
language that one couldn't learn from watching old movies,
and he still worried about the police car that showed up at
the storage facility. If anyone put it together, they might
figure out what was going on, and the last thing he wanted
was to be memorable. When he started throwing up, spending more time in the bathroom than in his seat, few people
wanted to talk to him, so it really didn't matter. By the time
he arrived in Washington, D.C., the only one who paid him
any attention was a little old lady who had been seated on
the bus in the aisle across from him, until she finally moved
away on the last leg of the trip. As it was, his right hand felt
odd. He was weak, from vomiting and diarrhea, and had difficulty holding the backpack that contained his few clothes
and the capsule.

He did not like Washington. Far too cold. Even the leather jacket he had purchased in Mexico was not warm enough. He waited outside the bus station for the man who was supposed to pick him up, but his fingers hurt from the cold and he was shivering. Eventually he had to return to the terminal to wait. Not too long, though, before the car described to him in the phone call—a green Chevy Impala—stopped in front of the terminal.

He walked out, saw the Kenyan flag decal in the window—they'd decided it was safer to fly a Kenyan flag instead of Somalian—then opened the vehicle door. The driver, a dark-skinned man with short black hair stared at him a second, saying, "You have come a long way."

"For God's work."

"Good, good. Hurry, then. It's cold out there."

Yusuf got in, closed the door, and immediately felt the heat from the car blasting against him.

They drove for several minutes in silence, both of them instructed not to discuss the other's business. The man stopped in front of a brick apartment building. Yusuf exited the vehicle and then the man drove off.

Yusuf looked around him, feeling very much like he'd been dropped on some other planet. The air was cold, crisp, and his nose was running like a faucet as he hurried across the street, nearly slipping on a patch of ice as he stepped onto the sidewalk. He entered the building, which stank worse than the refugee camp in Dadaab, eventually found apartment 203 on the second floor and knocked.

The door opened slightly, a chain barring the way. "Who are you?"

"I am here from home. I have come a long way."

The man lowered the chain and opened the door wide. "Come in."

Yusuf entered. The apartment was sparse, the carpet threadbare, the walls a dingy gray from about waist-level

down. Four men sat around the table, eyeing him as he eyed
them. He heard the door closing behind him, turned to look,
and the man who had let him in indicated he should join the
others at the table. He did, grateful to notice that the smell
inside this apartment was not as bad as outside.

"How was your trip?"

"Long."

"Did you have any trouble getting into the country?"

He'd been told that if there was any indication that anything had gone amiss, they would be scrapping the plans.
Too much rode on the success, and they would far prefer
waiting, replanning, and he thought about the incident at the
border. If they were looking for anyone, it would be a student at UCLA. No one would think to look for him here in
Washington. "None. Everything went smooth."

The man nodded. No one there used their real names. He
didn't know them, and they didn't know his. Just as well.
"Do you have the item?" the old man asked.

He nodded, then took the heavy capsule out of his backpack, handing it over.

"Did you make the calls when you arrived?" he asked
Yusuf.

"Yes. San Francisco, Los Angeles, New York, and Washington, D.C."

The old man nodded and the others smiled. The four targets would be hit simultaneously, the venues chosen due to
the heavily populated areas. Only theirs would have the capsule. But theirs was the most important, with its proximity
to the White House, and it would instill the right amount of
panic in the entire country.

"We should get started," one of the men said.

"Patience," the old man replied.

Patience? Yusuf had no time for patience. He seemed to
be getting sicker each day. If they waited too long, he intended to strike out on his own.

43

Sydney's ex, Scotty, was hovering outside Pearson's office in the morning when she arrived to give her statement of the accident and shooting.

"I just heard," Scotty said. "My God, why didn't you call?"

"I didn't think about it. It all happened so fast."

"Are you okay? You're not hurt?"

"I'm fine," she said.

"To think I was there last night. I—" He cocked his head, saying, "I never did find out why you wanted to meet?"

She glanced toward Pearson's office, then drew Scotty away. "Have you heard anything about an investigation into Wingman Squared?"

This time it was Scotty who looked around to make sure they weren't overheard. "What do you know about that?"

"Nothing. The girl I introduced you to last night mentioned that everyone in the bar was talking about a political corruption case involving them."

"Political corruption?" He took a deep breath, the whole time looking at her as if coming to a weighty decision. "See me when you get done with Pearson. And do me a favor. Don't mention Wingman Squared to him. Not if you know what's good for you."

"Why?"

"Can you please just trust me on this? For once?"

"Fitzpatrick?"

Sydney turned at the sound of Pearson's voice. He stood in the doorway, watching them. "Coming." She looked back at Scotty. It wasn't that she didn't trust him, more that she wondered what his agenda was. "How about coffee later?"

"Sure."

She left him, walked into Pearson's office, closing the door behind her.

"How are you this morning?"

"Not bad, considering."

"So what happened?"

She thought about what Scotty had said, not mentioning Wingman Squared. It seemed counterintuitive, since Pearson was aware she and Griffin were working an investigation outside of the FBI's influence. A quick decision, and she decided to start the story where they were being followed. "Griffin and I were walking back from the restaurant after having dinner with McNiel, and he caught some college student following us. The kid said someone paid him, and the next thing I knew a car was coming out of nowhere and plowing them down. When it came back around for a second try, I shot at it."

"Did you see anyone? A description? Anything?"

"No. The headlights were on."

"Any ideas as to why they singled you out?"

Trust me, Scotty had said, and it seemed she could feel the staccato beat of her pulse in the space of her hesitation. "No."

He held her gaze far longer than she felt comfortable under, and it was everything she could do to maintain her cool. After all, it wasn't really a lie. She had no idea who was behind the wheel. Her speculation was just that. Finally he said, "You're still okay working with McNiel?"

"So far."

Someone knocked on his door, then opened it. His secretary. "Sorry to disturb you, sir, but the deputy director called down."

"Thanks." He looked at Sydney. "Written report to me, as soon as you get a chance."

"Of course." She stood. When it seemed he had nothing else to say, she left and called Scotty. "Where are you?"

"My office. But let's go somewhere. I'd rather not talk about this here."

"Java Stop?"

"Meet you there in about fifteen."

She was curious, and had concocted a number of implausible scenarios as to why she shouldn't discuss Wingman Squared with Pearson. Pearson dealt with politicians on a daily basis. This was Washington, after all, and if the case had to do with political corruption, she supposed that made a certain sort of sense. But surely he wasn't trying to say that Pearson was involved?

No. She'd worked with Pearson before on another ATLAS case. In fact, the last time she'd been to the Java Stop, she met Tex after Griffin had gone missing, and Pearson gave his blessing, such as it was, when she'd been enlisted to help. So if Pearson wasn't involved in the corruption, then who? Her head was spinning by the time she arrived at the coffee shop. Scotty was already there, had her coffee waiting, and she sat, grateful for the caffeine after her restless night. She wanted to get to the hospital, find out how Griffin was doing, but hadn't yet had a chance after getting through all the red tape of a shooting. And now this. She only hoped that whatever he had to say wasn't a waste of her time. Some agenda of Scotty's that she hadn't been able to foresee.

And sure enough, before she could get a couple words in edgewise, he asked, "I was wondering what you were doing this coming weekend?"

She hoped for a date with Griffin, but knew better than to count on anything in their line of work. Nor was she about to throw it in Scotty's face, so said simply, "I have plans."

He slid an envelope toward her. "I got an invitation to the Vista View's Rooftop grand opening."

"Scotty—"

"Look, I know we're not a thing anymore, but anyone who is anyone will be there, and you know it looks better if you have a date at these things. This is the hot political event of the year. A couple former congressmen bought the place and renovated it. To even get an invitation . . . This is big."

Scotty was all about the movers and shakers, and she knew it meant a lot to him. It was not, however, the world she liked to frequent. "What about that girl you met last night?"

"Amanda?"

"Yeah."

"I don't know, Syd. It's not like I know her."

"You could *get* to know her. She seemed competent. A law student, after all."

He hesitated. "What if she can't go?"

"Then call me. I'll see what I can swing. Now about this Wingman Squared thing?" she asked, imagining any number of possible reasons he might give for making this into something it wasn't. "Why shouldn't I mention it to Pearson?"

"If Pearson even knew you were looking in that direction, he'd assign you to some obscure little corner of the country as far from here as possible."

"Why?"

He looked from side to side, then leaned forward, whispering, "Because they were involved in the BICTT scandal."

There had to be some mistake.

When she didn't respond, he said, "The bank the CIA was laundering money through?"

But she knew exactly which bank he was referring to. She just couldn't believe it. BICTT had been closed down for the last couple of decades at least, and she was trying to wrap her head around the implications of what he was saying. Wingman and Wingman tied into BICTT? Scotty knew nothing about that envelope Carillo had given her—the numbers from BICTT she'd locked in her desk file—and it wasn't like she could come out and announce it, or ask anyone else. Yet if it was true, that Wingman Squared was connected to CIA, surely Griffin and McNiel knew that? So why the hell hadn't they told her when she'd mentioned Wingman Squared last night?

Sydney pushed her chair back and stood. "I've got to go."

"What's wrong?" Scotty asked. "Look, if it's about this thing with Pearson, I just think—"

"Don't worry. He won't hear it from me. Not anytime soon, at least. I'm not about to open that can of worms."

He nodded, and when it was clear she was insistent on going, said, "At least take your coffee."

"Thanks."

She grabbed the cup and walked out, hurrying across the parking lot to her car. When she got in and started it, she sat there for a few moments, staring out the windshield, trying to remember her conversation last night with Griffin and McNiel when she'd mentioned Wingman Squared. It wasn't that they'd come out and denied knowing about it, more that they hadn't really offered information on it. Griffin knew the company, and McNiel said he'd look into it.

The W2 file on Redfern's desk . . . Like it wasn't that big a deal.

She drove straight to the hospital, figuring that if anyone owed her an explanation, Griffin did. When she inquired as to which room he was in, she was told he'd checked out.

"When?"

"Early this morning."

"I was informed last night that he was being kept for observation."

"I'm sorry, ma'am. All I can tell you is that he is no longer in this hospital."

"Thank you."

She wasn't sure why the news bothered her, except for the events of the night before. The fact he hadn't been honest with her.

And that made her laugh. Cynically, of course, because when had he ever been honest with her?

She drove to ATLAS, almost expecting to be stopped on the way in, feeling like she was the only one who didn't know what was going on. But no one stopped her and she was able to access the upper floors without issue. Griffin wasn't in his office, neither was McNiel; and she wasn't sure what she was supposed to do without them.

She sat at Griffin's desk, staring at his computer.

Wingman Squared.

She moved the mouse and the monitor lit up. Password protected. Not that she expected to see anything less on a government computer. Her gut, however, told her that if a file on Wingman and Wingman was to be found, Griffin would have it there.

Unfortunately, she'd never paid attention when he entered his password, because quite simply, she'd never thought that she would need to get into his files.

She'd pulled the keyboard forward and placed her hands on the keys when McNiel walked past the door, then stopped on seeing her.

"Sydney. I wasn't expecting you."

"I dropped by the hospital. Griffin wasn't there."

"He's at home. Apparently he knows better than the doctors."

"Why am I not surprised?"

He walked in, looked at the computer screen. "Is there something you were looking for?"

After Scotty warned her off, she wanted to see McNiel's reaction. "Information on Wingman and Wingman."

"Because you saw the file on Redfern's desk?"

"Yes. And because someone tried to kill Griffin last night after I was asking about it in the bar."

"What do you think you know?"

Besides having an envelope filled with numbers that were somehow related? How she wished she could ask him about that. The cursor blinked on the computer screen, and she realized she had about two seconds to come up with something plausible, a semblance of the truth. She'd been a fool to even mention it to him, since he and Pearson were practically joined at the hip. She couldn't let them know about that envelope, but if she denied any knowledge, he'd be suspicious. "They have a connection to the CIA and possibly BICTT."

"You've done a bit of homework since last night."

"A bit. I was worried about who was going after Griffin."

"Can I give you some advice? Let it go. Wingman Squared and BICTT have nothing to do with this case. Nothing to do with what happened to Griffin last night."

"But—"

"We handle a lot of cases here, Sydney. And sometimes they overlap. Your case—the one you were specifically brought here for—has everything to do with a terrorist that may be trying to get into this country, may already be here, and has nothing to do with the files you saw on Redfern's desk with a W2 label. Do I make myself clear?"

"Very."

He looked at the monitor again and said, "The number you want is two four."

"Two four?"

"The extension to IT. You'll need computer access if you're going to help find this bastard."

And then he left, and she was sitting there alone at Griffin's desk, trying to figure out what the hell it all meant. If the cases weren't related, then who had tried to kill Griffin and why? Did she trust McNiel that this W2 business had nothing to do with last night? That her seeing the file on Redfern's desk was merely happenstance?

She had to trust him. McNiel undoubtedly had every reason to keep secrets from her, but she sincerely doubted he'd risk Griffin's or even her life in the name of national security. So it was that she mentally put it aside, called IT to get her computer access, and started looking up the things related to the case in question. The problem was, she wasn't even sure what she was supposed to be looking up, and she kept drifting back to the moment in the parking garage when she saw Griffin hit by the car.

Someone had gone to a lot of trouble to follow them. What didn't make sense was sending an innocent kid to spy on them. Unless that was a distraction? Something to slow them down, allow the car to take them out when they stopped to investigate.

Griffin was too aware of his surroundings, and perhaps whoever had been following them knew this.

But how would they have known to follow them to the bar if it had nothing to do with Wingman Squared across the street? She'd picked it because it was close to Redfern's office, and unless someone had her cell phone or Griffin's office phone bugged, they would have had to follow her from the subway and then a taxi, which she doubted, or followed Griffin's vehicle, which seemed more likely.

And Griffin had left from the ATLAS building.

Just as they had the night the gunmen took them by surprise at the From Sticks to Bricks fund-raiser . . .

She pushed back from the chair, walked to the window,

and looked out. As busy a street as it was out front, someone
could have easily followed them from here to the hotel that
night. It wasn't a secret where they were coming from. Tex
had handed out *Washington Recorder* cards with the address
on it. Sure they'd gotten away that night, but how hard would
it be to park at one of those outlying corners and wait for a
van to drive out, or follow Griffin to a bar after he got into
the SUV he was driving, then wait for them to come walking
back after a night of drinking, sending a naive college kid to
distract them . . .

Since she knew that McNiel wouldn't endanger his own
men by leading her astray from the W2 angle, then whoever
came after Griffin probably followed him from the paper to
the bar. And since that was the second time someone came
after him after leaving the building—meaning someone followed him while he was in the guise of a reporter—she'd
have to say that put the suspect squarely in the A.D.E. court.

They clearly didn't want reporters snooping around.

The question was, why?

44

While Sydney waited for IT to send down a password to access the computer, she checked her work voice mail, receiving a call from Scotty, who complained that she wasn't answering her cell phone—hard to do when no signal came into or out of the ATLAS building—then one from Pearson, reminding her to finish her report. The third call was from Lieutenant Sanchez at the PD. "Hate to bother you," he said, "but I had a shooting last night, and your name came up—which it seems to do a lot of late. Give me a call when you get a chance."

She telephoned the number he left, wondering if it was about the man she shot at as he tried to run down Griffin.

"Sanchez."

"Sydney Fitzpatrick."

"Hey, thanks for calling back so quick. Any chance you can meet me at the hospital?"

"You're on day shift now?"

"First day on, so you can imagine my surprise to be fielding a call and hearing your name once again. And no, not the shooting you were involved in last night. This one was a robbery maybe an hour before. Some guy chased his victims into a building, then shot at them through the door. Hit a nine-year-old kid."

Definitely not her case from last night. "Do you need a suspect sketch?"

"Actually, we got the guy. Hoping the kid makes it. It's just that, like I said, your name came up from a friend of the family. I know the Bureau doesn't typically involve themselves in your basic robbery, but, if you'll pardon the expression, you sort of owe me one—and I'm not even counting last night's shooting on K Street. I'm talking about the suicide undercover FBI thing you threw on me."

"Extenuating circumstances."

"Tell you what. If you can get this guy off my back, I'll call us even, because right now, he is making my life a living hell."

"I'm on my way."

"Meet me in the lobby."

Lieutenant Sanchez was actually waiting for her in the front of the hospital. "Thanks. I hope you don't mind if I talk and walk at the same time? I have a Kiwanis meeting I need to get out to."

"Talk away."

"You remember a man named Ito Abasi?"

She looked over at him, surprised. "On-site manager at one of the slums out near the naval yard?"

"The same. He's the one who dropped your name. Here's the thing." Sanchez stopped, shoved his hands in the pockets of his uniform jacket. "The guy is probably calling us fifty times a day to report stuff we can't possibly get to. If we lived in Mayberry, sure, but this is D.C., and when it comes to rats and plumbing, and the crap he has to deal with, all we can do is refer him to the proper housing authorities and call it a day."

She well-remembered the stench. "The place needs to be razed."

"I feel for the guy, I do, but the few times we've actually been able to get someone to answer the phone in whatever department handles his type of calls, we get the same answer. Budget cuts. No manpower. They'll get to it when they get to it," he said, his tone telling her exactly what he thought of that excuse. "And so he calls again, because we're the only ones who answer the phone. Then, out of the blue last night, in the middle of this shooting investigation, he drops your card on my officer and says you're working a case and that we should contact you."

"A case?"

"Quote, unquote."

"Did he say *what* case?"

"Not exactly. He mentioned the suicide, but my officer assured him the kid's shooting last night wasn't related."

"Knowing what little you know about the, er, suicide, do you think it's related?" she asked, wondering why the man would insist she be contacted.

"There is no way on God's green earth the two cases are related. The guy robbed a couple out in front of the Target store about an hour before, which is where this family was shopping. He followed them from the Target to the apartment building. A dirtbag who saw an opportunity and took it. His girlfriend, who wasn't present at the second robbery, confirmed his story. Apparently he's done this before, and so left his itinerary with her. The robbery part. The shooting, unfortunately, is a new facet to his criminal history. He tripped on a torn piece of carpet in the hallway and the gun went off. And a witness in the hallway confirmed it."

"Bottom line, Lieutenant Sanchez. Why am I here?"

"Frankly, I don't know. Mr. Abasi is desperate that someone sit up and take notice. You and I both know last night wouldn't have happened if my dirtbag hadn't committed a robbery. But Mr. Abasi thinks it wouldn't have happened had there been proper lighting, a security lock on the door that led to the building, a floor with a carpet that wasn't so shredded people tripped on it every time they ran, which, when holding a loaded firearm, can have deadly consequences. And the sad thing is, he's right. There's a boy fighting for his life upstairs in that hospital because some landlord's too greedy to do what needs to be done. The kid's entire life, he's probably never been in a room as nice as that one, and he has to get shot to get there."

"I'm not sure I can do anything more than you've done."

He looked beaten, and Sydney felt for him as he turned toward the hospital, then took a ragged breath. "I know. But I've exhausted every available government agency trying to help them, and I guess when I heard your name, I thought, why not?"

Why not? Because her one attempt to look into the Redfern Group ended up with her being ordered off any possible investigation. Still, she empathized with Sanchez's plight. "Where is Mr. Abasi?"

"Upstairs with the boy's parents."

"I'll go talk to him."

"That's all I can ask."

Ito Abasi was in the room, sitting next to a man and woman she presumed were the boy's parents. The boy was in a room with a breathing apparatus and monitors beeping in the background. Mr. Abasi looked up, saw her, and excused himself to join her.

"Thank you so much for coming," he said, clasping her hand in both of his. "I know this has nothing to do with your case, and that you hope to find Dorian's killer, but I do not know where else to turn. These people, they need your help, Ms. Fitzpatrick. Please . . ."

"They caught the man who did this."

"Yes, but at what point do we say enough is enough? Their older daughter was raped and killed in Dadaab, when she left to gather firewood. And then they come here and now their son is nearly killed by more violence. You have seen how they must live, and no matter who I talk to, no one will help. Only Lieutenant Sanchez ever returns my calls, and even he is powerless. We are set to receive another family in the next two days," he said, then waved toward the hospital room, the boy lying so helpless in his bed. "How is this any better than where they come from when they have nowhere to go? Please help us. Please."

She looked into the room, saw the father, his arm around his wife's shoulder and she brushing the tears from her face. How was it better? Sydney had no idea if it was or it wasn't, but she recognized injustice when she saw it.

"I don't know what I can do. But I can try."

"Thank you. Thank you," he said as she left, feeling guilty because his appreciation seemed so sincere. Lieutenant Sanchez was no slacker, and if he failed, then how could she possibly make a difference? He, at least, had the inside connection to all the departments in the city. She had a desk in the Quantico basement without a clue on where to turn next.

Then again, there was always Doc. If anyone could find the sliver of a chance in a hopeless case, he was the man.

She called him from the car and told him about the robbery and Mr. Abasi's plea for help. "I don't suppose you have anything in that bag of tricks you keep handy? Not only that, but if Redfern is somehow involved in this mess that put Griffin in the hospital, then anything I can do to take him down a notch is worth it."

"Even if Redfern knows who tried to take out Griffin, the attorney-client privilege means that you're not going to find out, unless he decides his practice is worth sacrificing."

"What would you do?"

"Regarding the thing with Griffin, or the slumlord angle?

If the former, question the guy, rattle his cage enough so he passes on the info and forces someone to make a move."

"Except the FBI has been ordered off his case."

"How long have you and Carillo been working together?"

"Good point. So if I really wanted a creative way to rattle his cage *and* get him or his clients to take some action on bringing these apartments up to living standards . . . ?"

"Get out the phone book and get every single government agency involved in housing codes and violations and sic 'em on him. In other words, tie his ass up in housing court. And while he's busy fending them off, you make sure he's aware of a nice little law that says in nonpayment cases a tenant could file a countersuit for three years of back rent if the conditions violated the DC Housing Code. I'm guessing there are a lot of violations that would qualify."

"Doesn't seem like a lot."

"It is if the majority of those tenants joins in."

"I can't see every one of them joining in. They're scared refugees who have no way to fend for themselves, especially if they find themselves suddenly evicted."

"They would if you had the right person on board. I'm e-mailing the information to you now. Linwood Tillett. It'll be cheaper for them to raze the buildings and start over than fight this guy."

"And what happens if they do raze it? Where does everyone go?"

"They'll have to front big bucks to put the displaced refugees up somewhere."

"I'm not sure it's about money," she said. "What if there's something else going on? Some other reason they don't care that there are so many refugees having to live this way?"

"First and foremost, Sydney, it's *always* about money. But let's say you're right, that for whatever reason, money's no object. The last landlord Tillett sued was able to get the judge to sentence the owner to live for several days in his rat-infested property so he'd remember not to let it happen again. I'm going to guess that Redfern and any clients Redfern has are not going to want that to happen."

She checked the e-mail he sent over on her phone's screen, then drove to the attorney's office, immediately dismayed by what she saw. It was not in some fancy downtown high-rise, like the Redfern Group. It wasn't even in some posh older location. If anything, it was in a very nondescript office building as far from the movers and shakers as one could get. She called Doc, questioning his judgment. "You sure this Linwood Tillett can take on the Washington bigwigs? Redfern's got a direct pipeline to the upper-echelon politicians."

"Trust me. I don't care how many senators Redfern has in his pocket. When he sees Tillett walking into the room, he's going to have an epiphany. Almost makes me wish I was there to see it."

Sydney still had her doubts about the effectiveness of Linwood Tillett, but at this point it was the only tool she had in a very empty toolbox. And even though she had been technically ordered to back off Redfern's case, the memory of those apartments and the sight of that little boy in the hospital was enough to justify the black mark on her record or even a suspension should Redfern decide to complain again.

Now all she had to do was call him and get him in for an interview. For that, she was going to need Lieutenant Sanchez's help, and she left a message for him detailing her plan, and for him to call her once he got out of his Kiwanis Club meeting.

"I've never heard of this attorney," he said when he phoned about an hour later.

"Neither have I, but my associate assured me he's the one to champion our cause. I can, however, use some finagling on your part. I need Larry Redfern to come down to the PD for an interview. And he can't know I'm involved, or some-one's likely to stop it before our plan gets off the ground."

"Connected?"

"Very."

"Let me see what I can dig up."

He called back about twenty minutes later. "Turns out Mr. Redfern has a couple parking tickets he neglected to pay. They were in Virginia, but seeing as how they're our good neighbors, I think we're going to have to tow his car."

"Can you get to it?"

"As a matter of fact, I've got a tow truck hooked up to it as we speak. We're leaving a courtesy notice that he can come down and complain to me personally if he has issues, and if he's as much of a prima donna as you say, I'm guessing he's going to have plenty of issues."

"Thanks."

"If this does the trick, it'll be worth it."

45

"So how're you liking working the eight-to-five shift?"

Lieutenant Thomas Sanchez looked up from the shift summary he was reading to see Sergeant Ennis in the doorway, holding a report. "I'll be liking it a lot better in about two hours when I get off for the day. If someone could disconnect the phone, it would be perfect. What's up?"

"Just wondering where to forward this," Ennis said, walking into the office and taking a seat in one of two chairs facing the desk. "A suspicious circumstances report that came in last night. One of those odd ones that you wonder is it legit or another crackpot."

"Is there a day that goes by we don't get one of those calls?"

"Uh, not like this. Got a little old lady on the bus from San Diego to here saying she was riding next to a terrorist with radiation sickness. She's pretty sure he was carrying a nuclear warhead."

"Nuclear warhead? Carrying it where? On the top of the bus?"

"In his pocket. Apparently they've improved them since

World War Two. She saw it when he was sleeping. *And* she says it made her sick, too, but she wanted to report it to us before she saw her doctor this morning." Ennis walked over, handed him the report. "The way I see it, this is *way* too important to entrust to a lowly sergeant. I'm thinking, you know, definitely Watch Commander territory."

Sanchez took the paper from him. "Welcome to day shift, right?"

"Hey, I'm doing my fiduciary duty, reporting it to my boss."

He left, and Sanchez sat there with the report, wondering who the hell he reported it to. This wasn't one of those things they put in the policy and procedures manual, primarily because there wasn't one that covered nuclear warheads, even the miniaturized fictional versions. He read it and sighed. The woman came across as a nut. Unfortunately, after 9/11, the FBI wanted all the reports from all the nuts—just in case.

He was about to fax it over to the Joint Terrorism Task Force when he realized he could simply give it to Sydney Fitzpatrick. As soon as she got out of her interview with Redfern, *she* could walk it over to JTTF. Right up her alley, since she seemed to be dealing with any number of nuts at any given time these days.

He looked at the schedule, three more months of day shift. And here he'd been looking forward to normal police work. The sort that didn't involve the FBI or nuts on a bus.

46

Larry Redfern tapped a cadence on the faux wood-grain tabletop, as though keeping beat to some unheard tune in his head. The moment he saw Sydney walk into the room, he stood, nearly knocking the chair over in his haste. "When I'm through with you, you'll be lucky to have a job. You'll wish you never met me."

"I already wish that, Mr. Redfern. Please, have a seat. I'm still waiting for someone to get here. Traffic's such a bear this time of day." She smiled at him, then looked toward the door, hoping like hell Doc had the right of it. "Ah, here he is now," she said when Linwood Tillett walked in. His suit was not Brooks Brothers, in fact the jacket, brown tweed, seemed at odds with the navy slacks. He was a short man, pudgy, balding with gray hair and a close-cropped gray beard, with blue eyes that peered up at her over his wire-rimmed spectacles. He seemed so harmless, it was hard to believe he wielded any clout in this arena. Or any arena, for that matter.

She glanced over at Redfern to gauge his reaction and was pleased to see him pale at the sight of the old man.

"I don't know what it is you think I've done," Redfern said, "but this is blackmail."

"Blackmail?" Linwood Tillett replied. "That's a pretty strong statement, considering I haven't done or said a thing. Yet. And when you think about it, all we're asking you to do is follow the law. How many apartment buildings do you own?"

Redfern swallowed, then glanced toward Sydney, standing in the back of the room, then back at Mr. Tillett. "Ten. Or so."

"Are they all Section 8 subsidized housing?"

"I'm not sure."

"Are they all used to house refugees?"

"I don't know."

"What do you know about them?"

"That I had a manager who took care of most of that end of my business, but he died. Dorian Rose."

"Who was, coincidentally, employed by A.D.E., a government contractor who considers themselves a charity to resettle refugees?"

"If you say so."

"For an attorney, Mr. Redfern, you seem to be slightly disorganized."

"I assure you, Mr. Tillett, I'm very organized."

"Oh, good. Then you'll have no problem producing all the records I intend to subpoena regarding your relationship with any charity and the profit you are making off of the refugees." He adjusted his glasses, wrote some notes on a yellow legal tablet before proceeding. "One thing that concerns me. You say you were not aware of the condition of those buildings? The condition your tenants were forced to live in?"

"I own the properties. I hire people to run them for me. Apparently my trust was misplaced. When they're less than honest, there isn't much I can do but try to make amends after the fact."

"How is it that you are housing nothing but refugees in your buildings?"

Redfern hesitated, glanced at Sydney, then back, and Sydney noticed a slight trembling in his hands as he clasped them in his lap. "I have an arrangement with a charitable organization to house them at a discount."

"And the name of this organization?"

"A.D.E."

Tillett jotted more notes, then tapped the pen on the tab before looking up. "Here's what's going to happen, Mr. Redfern. When this lovely FBI agent gets done questioning you, and you cooperate in every way, you will start on the first building. You will move your tenants, every one of them, into a hotel or motel by this evening. It doesn't have to be the Hilton, just one that you would feel comfortable sleeping in yourself."

Redfern's jaw dropped. "Do you know how much that'll cost?"

"In fact, yes. I've done this before, as I'm sure you're aware." He looked at his watch, then stood, with an exaggerated sigh. "Unfortunately I don't have time to linger, because I'm due in housing court and you know how testy those judges get when you're late. Now where was I . . . Of course. Move them into a motel, *fix* the building so that it is livable—"

"And if it isn't?"

"Direct them to a new home that *you* would be comfortable living in, and then start in on the next building. Is there any part of that you don't understand? The last building owner I took to court seemed to have difficulty with that part. The place-being-livable part."

"I understand," Redfern said, a much more subdued person.

"Good. Because you are now on my radar, and every one of your tenants is now my client. Do I make myself clear?"

Redfern nodded.

Tillett stood, slid a card onto the table toward Redfern, then said, "Feel free to call if you have any questions." He turned to Sydney, held out his hand, his eyes crinkling over his spectacles. "Thank you so much for the client referral."

"A real pleasure." He left, and Sydney took his seat, smiling at Redfern. "Such a nice little man, isn't he?"

"Darling."

"Now, let's see . . . Dorian. Your poor former employee. How is it you came to hire him?"

"A.D.E. recommended him to me."

"Convenient."

"Look, Ms. Fitzpatrick—"

"That's Special Agent Fitzpatrick."

"I might be guilty of a few housing violations."

"A few?"

"Times ten buildings, fine, I concede the issues, but in all fairness, I'm not the only landlord who is making money from the government's oversight."

"Baby steps, Mr. Redfern."

"As I was saying, the apartments aside, this all occurred *after* I had contacted a contractor about tearing the buildings down. A.D.E. approached me because they needed immediate housing and we thought we could buy a few months, and one thing turned into another. It's not an excuse, but that's the truth. There's no government conspiracy. Not on my part at least. I don't know anything about A.D.E., their operations, or the program they're involved with."

"And Senator Burgess's involvement with this?"

"None. That I know of anyway. She's a proponent of the refugee program is all. Her visit to my office was of a different nature."

"Something to do with Wingman Squared?"

He opened his mouth, closed it again, stared at her for a solid second, then asked, "Why would you say that?"

"I saw the file on your desk."

"That file is confidential and covered by attorney-client privilege."

"Any connection as to why someone tried to run down me and my friend the other night?"

"And your friend would be?"

"Zachary Griffin. The man who was in your office with me the other day."

"No, Ms.—Special Agent Fitzpatrick. Without saying anything further, I seriously doubt anyone from that file is involved in what you're involved in."

"Let's try this, then. Why would someone from A.D.E. try to run us over?"

"Far easier, since they're not my client. Ignoring my small slice of the pie renting apartments, being a government contractor in the refugee program is like hitting the mother lode."

"Because they get money to run the programs. I get it."

"Because they get a *lot* of money to run the program. Put it this way. If I told you that I could turn your two hundred dollars cash into twenty-two hundred cash, courtesy of the U.S. government, and all you needed to do was a little creative accounting by collecting a thousand dollars in donated clothes, furniture, even your junker car—running or not—you'd be opening an investigation on me for running a pyramid scheme. And yet that's exactly how the federal government is funding these private charities. Don't even get me started on the private funds *above* two hundred dollars. Why do you think they're hunting for buildings like mine to house the refugees in? Because the less they have to pay from their private donors and from the money the government is giving them to bring in, house, clothe, and feed the refugees, the more they get to stick in their pockets." He leaned forward. "We're talking a multimillion-dollar business courtesy of Uncle Sam. The sooner they get them on welfare, boot them out of my apartments, the sooner they can bring in new refugees and creatively earmark funds for them."

"How many refugees does this involve?"

"Countless. It's a revolving door, and the name of the game is money, and everyone is playing. Some of them are better at it. And you can damned well guarantee that the charities are paying big bucks to lobbyists to keep that door spinning. Because the moment the government decides to stop bringing in refugees, their golden wells dry up."

"Like A.D.E.?"

"Exactly. They have their fingers on the pulse of Washington, and Great Britain. And here you are, bringing unwanted attention that is likely to cost them millions upon millions of dollars."

It certainly explained why someone had targeted Griffin outside the parking garage. People had been killed for less.

She stood. "Am I going to be expecting any more calls from high-ranking officials to back off?"

"Now that I know what it is you're looking into, no."

"You thought I was looking into W Squared?"

"Weren't you?"

"Until I saw the file on your desk, I wasn't even aware they existed."

"My mistake, then."

She wanted to ask him more, but knew she couldn't without drawing undue attention. Especially knowing he had that direct pipeline to the top of the government.

He left, and she walked out after him, stopping as she passed the Watch Commander's office, when Sanchez called out to her.

"I don't suppose you're going by the field office?" he asked.

"I could be. Why?"

"I have a suspicious report that needs to be dropped off at

the JTTF," he said. "Some lady said a guy on the bus was carrying a nuclear warhead."

"A nuclear warhead? On a bus?"

"Pocket-sized, in case you're wondering how it fit. Apparently he spent most of the bus ride in the restroom throwing up, so she figured it was radiation poisoning. Probably nothing but an overactive imagination, but these days . . ."

"I'll swing by and make sure it gets to the rocket scientist squad."

"You have one?"

"Someone has to deal with these sorts of calls." She eyed the report, thinking that these were the reports she'd always enjoyed back when she was a cop. The sort that broke up the monotony of police work, usually narrated by someone who'd gone off their meds, or someone who needed to be on them to begin with.

What she read, however, was anything but funny.

In fact, it scared the living daylights out of her.

She prayed that what the woman had seen in the man's pocket—the small metallic canister about the size of a billiard ball—was anything but what she thought it was.

47

"What are you doing?"

Sydney's voice sounded a million miles away, and Griffin turned his cell phone the right way when he realized he was holding it upside down. "Sleeping. Why?"

"Yusuf's here. In D.C. At least I think it could be him."

"How do you know?"

She told him about the police report. "Only no one believed the woman, probably because she was calling this metal cylinder in his pocket a nuclear warhead."

"A . . . what?" He sat up, feeling out of it. "Back up. I missed something."

"The stolen cesium 137 from the storage facility in southern California."

He was wide-awake now. "The witness saw it?"

"She described the capsule perfectly. And his symptoms, at least the way she told it, definitely match radiation poisoning."

Griffin got out of bed, walking to the bathroom. "I'll meet you at the office."

"About that. I think someone followed you from your office last night. Otherwise, how would they know we were at the bar?"

She heard him taking a deep breath. "I was watching for a tail, but that doesn't mean there wasn't one. It makes sense," he said. "Do you remember the back way in?"

It was a somewhat convoluted route that ran below the streets in a tunnel and ended up in a warehouse a couple blocks away. "Not well enough to do it myself."

"Your pass card and fingerprint on the biometric lock will get you in. But if you want to wait for me, I'll be there in about twenty. Do me a favor, though. Call McNiel, let him know about the police report and your theory on being followed."

"Are you sure McNiel won't have a problem with you coming in? You just got out of the hospital."

"A bump on the head. The CAT scan came back clean."

"Then why were you sleeping if you're fine?"

"Damned nurses came in and woke me all night long. See you in a few."

He showered and dressed, then met Sydney at the garage warehouse, the two of them parking their cars inside. He entered a code, pressed his finger to the reader, and the metal door clicked open. The ATLAS building was accessed via an underground passage that ran parallel to the Metro subway system. They descended the stairs, then entered the brick-lined passageway, their footsteps echoing as they walked.

The same security measures were used to access the entrance to the elevator, which took them up to the fifth floor. McNiel was waiting for them in his office.

Sydney gave him the report she'd picked up from the police, and even though she'd briefed him on the phone, he took the time to read it. When he finished, he set it on his desk, asking her, "You actually talked to the witness?"

"Right before I called Griffin. I wanted to see if there was any validity to it."

"And what was your take?"

"Put it this way. If we hadn't known about the cesium 137 capsule being stolen from San Diego, I would have written her off the moment I heard the words 'nuclear warhead.' But this thing she saw in his pocket? It fits the description."

McNiel glanced at the report again. "The two of you hit the Greyhound station. See if they have any surveillance equipment on the premises. If it is him, this could be the break we're looking for. I'll notify someone to look into possible contamination in the building. I want you two to find out where that bus is so we can check it as well. Last thing we need is to spread radiation across the continent via Greyhound."

Griffin stood. "Sydney told you her theory about someone watching our building?"

"She did. I've assigned Henderson to look into it. Until we know one way or another, continue using the back entrance. If it turns out she's right, Henderson will call you when he's ready to throw you out there as bait."

The glass-fronted Greyhound terminal was crowded with passengers, some with luggage, some without, and it was fairly noisy, the acoustics causing voices to carry in the large building. Griffin and Sydney found the security office and talked to the officer in charge, Sydney's FBI credentials gaining them instant cooperation. The first thing they did was order the bus that drove in from San Diego to be stopped. It was apparently heading back. They did not inform the security officer why, nor did they mention the possibility of contamination. No sense in instilling panic, since everyone who'd been on the bus for any length of time would have to be tracked down. That, however, would be handled by others.

The officer took them into a small room where the video surveillance was located, and after finding the right time period, allowed them to watch the passengers who departed from the bus, then entered the terminal.

A man matching Yusuf's description entered the terminal, made a call from a cell phone, then waited inside for at least twenty minutes, using the bathroom a couple times before departing out the front doors, and Griffin was just able to make out the taillights of a car as he walked out. "Do you have any video of the passenger loading zone?"

"Yes. It's nighttime, though, so I don't know how good it'll be."

He found that camera zone, played it, and they saw a small sedan waiting out front as the man exited the station. He walked over, got in the car, and it drove off.

"Not very clear," Sydney said, leaning over, trying to make out the license number. "We could see if it can be enhanced."

"Can you make copies of both videos?" Griffin asked.

"Sure." The security officer took a blank DVD from a case and inserted it into the computer. When it was finished, Griffin and Sydney left to drive the DVD to the FBI lab where a tech would attempt to enhance it.

Pearson met them at the lab to view the video. "Do you think it's Yusuf?" he asked Griffin, while Jim, the tech, played the DVD on his computer.

"We definitely can't eliminate him based on what we see."

Sydney added, "Had there not been several hundred people traipsing in and out of that building since the time of the video, maybe we could have tried for fingerprints."

Pearson watched up until the vehicle drove off, then told the tech, "Call me the moment you get a plate number. I want to get it to the task force."

"Pretty grainy stuff," Jim said, moving some controls on the screen with his mouse. "Shouldn't take too long . . ."

They left him to his work. In the hallway, Pearson asked Sydney if she'd spoken with Carillo.

"Not today."

"Then you'll be glad to hear that he found his wife."

He left, walking in the opposite direction, and she turned to Griffin, asking, "How is it that Pearson's always one up on us?"

"He and McNiel. Thick as thieves, those two."

He was just about to ask if she wanted to get some coffee when Jim called out to them. "Got a partial plate you might be able to work with. It's the best I can do." He handed Sydney a printout of the photo. "Unfortunately, with the angle of the car, that first number and first letter are hard to make out. But judging from the style of Impala, it looks like the year might be mid-2000s, 2005, maybe? That should at least narrow your plate down at the DMV, if it was an original license. And not stolen."

"Better than what we had," Griffin said. "Thanks."

"We can run the partial plate number," Sydney told him, then asked the tech if she could borrow a computer to log into.

"Patrick's not here. Use his."

She entered her password into the computer, then brought up the program to run the partial. It returned several possible hits, and she scanned the vehicle makes, eliminating anything that wasn't a Chevrolet. That left two. One ended up showing the title salvaged to a junkyard—which didn't necessarily rule it out. The second vehicle belonged to a woman named Mary Smith. The third was registered to a man named Salim.

A name, however, meant little. They'd need to verify beyond that to confirm anything. A little checking, however, and they had the information: a traffic ticket issued to Salim, showing that the car was indeed the same color as the one they were looking for. It raised the possibility that Salim was the driver.

"I think we have him," Griffin said.

"I'll call Pearson."

48

Tex attempted to stretch out in the cramped airline
seat, well into the flight to Kenya, wishing his cover as a
reporter allowed him to sit in first class, which happened
to be full. Not that he was complaining. The much smaller
commuter plane they'd have to take to get from Nairobi to
Garissa wouldn't be nearly as accommodating to someone
his size. And here at least he had an empty seat to his right.
He was hoping to catch a nap now that they'd passed the area
of turbulence, but saw Eve walking in his direction from
first class.

"All the way in the back?" she said, sitting next to him.

"Not like there was a lot of choice. There was this or the
bulkhead. More leg room there, but this one puts me about
fifteen rows from Mother Goose."

She glanced in that direction, saw a woman standing,
trying to calm her infant and quiet a toddler at the same
time. "I'll take the baby over Micah at the moment. He
snores. Loudly."

"He's actually asleep?"

"He doesn't like flying. One sleeping pill and two drinks, he was out before we took off."

"Nice."

"At least it gives us a moment to talk," Eve said. "I'm getting a bad feeling about this whole trip."

"Ya think? They're sending you into a friggin' war zone."

"Refugee camp."

"Same thing, these days," Tex said. "What with the insurgents raiding and pillaging anything that's not tied down. Every dime that boss of yours is giving to his charity is probably being used to buy arms."

"I know you're probably right, but Micah means well."

"Throwing money at organizations who can't control it is as irresponsible as letting the people they're alleging to help starve to death. It's like throwing water on an oil fire."

"We're going to have to agree to disagree. As much as I know that A.D.E. has their fingers in a few pies—"

"A few?" Tex thought of the facts and figures he'd seen in the DVD. If they somehow managed to find the books in Dadaab that linked the A.D.E. funds to the issuing of false identification—and aiding the influx of war criminals and terrorists into the country as a result—it was still just a small part of the problem. "What about all the money being laundered by these so-called charities?"

"Very big pies, then. Pies they shouldn't be involved with. Even so, *some* of that money *is* going to the sources it's supposed to go to."

"Let's pretend that A.D.E. is doing what they claim to be doing, and all that money of Micah's *is* going to the charities in question. Do you have any idea what those organizations are doing with that money?"

"Bringing refugees to America. Trust me. He and I have walked through the areas where they're living."

"See, that's where all the bleeding hearts get it wrong," Tex said. "That money the U.S. is allegedly granting to

A.D.E. lines the pockets of politicians and warlords who use
it to keep the civil unrest going as they fight over controlling interests in drug and human trafficking, as well as guns
and weapons smuggling. And that's not even counting the
money that's laundered. Like your marked bills that ended
up with that weapons cache. I'll lay even odds Micah's
money is right there in the thick of things."

"At least some of it makes its way to the people."

"For Micah's sake, I hope you're right," he said, and decided to leave it at that. CIA or not, it was clear she had
no idea the true extent of the corruption and chaos the civil
unrest had caused, and it was getting worse every day.

Not that he needed to convince her. In a few hours she was
going to see it firsthand.

When their commuter plane landed at Garissa the following morning, Tex, Eve, Donovan, and Lisette stepped onto
the tarmac into sweltering heat and were met by the guide
that A.D.E. had hired. Hussein, a tall black man wearing a
blue plaid shirt and khaki pants, smiled at Micah, holding
out his hand. "Welcome, Mr. Micah. We are very glad to
have you here."

"Thank you. It's very exciting to see where our efforts are
actually having an impact."

Tex refrained from rolling his eyes, and wondered how
Eve was able to maintain her upbeat persona whenever she
was around the guy.

"And you must be the beautiful Eve Sanders," Hussein
said, smiling. "But who are these other people with you?"

"Reporters."

"So many of you?" he said. "No matter. You should know
that the roads are closed. Too many bandits. Not safe. We'll
be flying over."

And so he hustled them into a waiting plane. When they

arrived at the Dadaab airstrip, Hussein walked them over to the waiting SUV to drive the remainder of the way to Dadaab.

The driver, however, seemed to question the number of passengers. "My itinerary shows four. Miss Sanders, Mr. Micah, and two reporters from the *International Journal for World Peace*. Mr. Archer and Ms. Perrault. No third reporter."

Tex leaned forward, read the clipboard. "They made a mistake."

The man looked at him, his gaze narrowing. "We'll have to come back for you three. Miss Sanders and Mr. Micah will be with me."

When one of the guides started to reach for Donovan's bags, he stopped him. "Cameras," he said. "I need them."

He shrugged, then grabbed the other bags. Once the vehicle was loaded, Tex followed Eve and Micah.

The man blocked his way. "Reporters in next trip."

Tex dug into his pocket and pulled out a wad of cash. "Make an exception?"

"You may ride in the backseat with Miss Sanders."

"Perfect."

Eve walked up to Tex once the driver turned toward the vehicle. "Why'd you do that?"

"Call it intuition, but I'm not liking the odds. Anyone that hung up on seating for such a short trek makes me nervous."

The dirt road seemed to stretch endlessly into the desert, its surface marred with potholes and loose gravel, but it wasn't altogether too bad, thanks to the four-wheel-drive vehicle.

The photographs Tex had seen in preparation for the mission didn't do justice to the reality. Though the civil war raged on the other side of the Somali Kenyan border, the road they traveled on held a feeling of utter desolation. A vast wasteland dotted with carcasses of cattle with bleached white leather stretched over bare bones amidst the gray shrubs and the skeleton limbs of trees stabbing at the sky beneath a relentless sun. And all around them the wind stirred up the red dirt until it swirled in the air like smoke from a bomb.

Nearing the camp, the horizon seemed to be a moving mass of color as refugees on the outskirts, mostly women and children, gravitated toward some central location.

"New refugees arriving to get registered," Hussein told them. "They walk through the desert, their children dying from malnutrition, those that they haven't buried on the side of the road on their journey here. They come, thinking they will get help, and yet there are children dying of malnutrition right inside the very camp that is supposed to help them."

They drove past fresh mounds in the dirt. Graves, Tex realized, on seeing a group of women and children standing around one that had not been filled in. A gaunt man kneeled in the fresh-turned earth, crying atop a very small shrouded body. Too small, and Tex put his arm around Eve as she caught her breath, turning her head into his shoulder, not wanting to look as the man lowered his child into the grave.

They drove on for minutes, and Tex started to realize that the sheer size of the camps was greater than he'd imagined. He had grown up in a town of fifty thousand and an area that covered about the same square miles as the refugee camps. Except here the tents were packed so close together, it held close to a half million people. As they approached in their vehicle, he saw that wire fencing separated the camps from the outside world. On the inside, children played soccer, seemingly oblivious to the armed uniformed guards who patrolled the scrubland on the perimeter beneath a brutal sun.

The compound where the UN workers and other NGO volunteers were housed was a short drive from the main camps, surrounded by a triple razor wire fence. A fleet of white UN vehicles were parked beyond a gate that was opened by an armed guard. Brick huts topped with corrugated iron roofs filled the compound, where very few people currently resided. Many of the nonessential personnel had been pulled out due to the rising hostilities of the sleeper al-Shabab terrorists inside and outside the camps. Hussein walked them to the office, then said he'd be sending a car in the morning to pick them up and drive them to the camps. He left, and they stepped from blazing heat to blissful semicool air-conditioning, where they were assigned a "movement pass"—a badge worn on their clothes that let the guards know they were allowed to move throughout the compound.

Micah was eager to get started. "We should film the grave of the child," he said. "Very moving."

The grave was too fresh in Tex's mind, and he bit back a reply, as Eve mentioned that perhaps they should meet some of the residents and talk to them first.

Tex looked at his watch, worried about the separation. He didn't like that Donovan and Lisette were left behind. In fact, he had a very bad feeling about the way the entire trip had been set up. Something was wrong, but he couldn't quite put his finger on it.

49

Donovan admitted to being surprised when the ve-hicle actually returned for them. He and Lisette had discussed the possibility that Eve and Micah's employer had some ulterior motive. But then the car came along and transported them to Dadaab without mishap, and he put the feeling aside. The following morning, once they checked in at the office using their guise as reporters, they entered the reception tent where incoming refugees were being screened. He found it hard to stand meekly by as women who were nothing more than skin and bones carried in skeletal children with large eyes and distended stomachs. The walking dead, Donovan thought. Eerily quiet, whether because strangers had entered or because the children lacked even the strength to cry, he didn't know. He looked around, saw a man wearing a UN shirt walking toward them, his attention fixed on a clipboard. Donovan hoped the man spoke English, and asked where those who hoped to resettle in America would register.

The man stared at him for several seconds, and Donovan

repeated the question in French, hoping he might understand that language.

"I understood you the first time. And the second," he responded in English. "I am just trying to decide the best way to answer a question that hardly has an answer, unless one is willing to pay."

"How much?" Donovan asked, reaching into his pocket.

The doctor laughed. "Not you. The person seeking resettlement. Unless the refugee is lucky enough to fall into the class that the United States and other countries have granted asylum—such as the Bantu, for instance—then one might live his whole life in this camp. We are on our third generation in the twenty-some-odd years the camp has been here. They come in, more than a thousand a day. They are essentially a people without a country, because once they are here, they are not allowed to leave. Like the movie your Tom Hanks made based on the Iranian refugee who lived in the Paris airport for seventeen years. Mehran Nasseri. *This* is their airport."

Lisette took another look around, asking, "You said something about people willing to pay?"

"I did. There are those who have managed to earn or steal or be given money who will circumvent the system in place, moving to the head of the line, as you would say. That would not be here. I have heard rumors only of where it might be, where one could obtain legitimate identification. There is a thriving black market within the confines of one of the other camps. I could direct you there, but I wouldn't recommend it, as it isn't safe. Especially for a woman."

"Where would that be?" Donovan asked.

He gave them directions. "But the camps are very large and the distance between them vast. You would need to drive."

"Could one hire a driver?"

"If you have money, yes. But it is, as I said, dangerous."

He spoke in sharp guttural tones to a boy of about ten who was sitting on a bench near the tent's entrance. The boy nodded and ran out. "He will fetch Ali. You can trust him."

"Thank you."

"I'm not sure you will think so once you get there."

Donovan and Lisette walked out, moving off to one side, away from the long line of mostly women and children who waited their turns to be seen by the doctors. Many sat in the dirt, their clothes and skin coated with red dust.

Donovan and Lisette informed Tex of where they were going. By the time they returned, the boy who had left was bringing with him a man dressed in gray pants and an orange shirt, his feet and plastic sandals the same color as the dirt.

The man, Ali, smiled at them and said in broken English, "You hire my truck?"

"Yes."

He nodded. "You pay?"

Donovan held up several bills and the man's eyes widened. "This way. This way."

They followed Ali past one of the few brick buildings, to where a rusted white pickup was parked. A late-model Datsun, which put it circa 1980s.

It was as the doctor said, a long drive through the camp past corrugated shanties and tents that lined either side of the dirt roads. The driver was an expert at dodging pedestrians or navigating obstacles, honking every few seconds at a goat herder urging his livestock across an intersection or women rolling jerry cans filled with water through the dust as chickens scurried past. Then they arrived at what looked like a marketplace, where a group of men sat around on logs chewing what Donovan assumed was khat.

"There," Ali said. A few cinder-block buildings with tin roofs came into view and he slowed the vehicle, pointing. "There. The place you ask for is the second one. You be careful."

Donovan saw several men milling about the front of the buildings. They looked up, their dark gazes watching the trio. "You'll wait?" Donovan asked.

The man seemed to think about it.

"I'll double the pay."

"If you hurry. Dangerous."

Donovan and Lisette exited the vehicle, walked toward the building and the men who seemed to be following their every move.

"Maybe this wasn't a good idea," she said.

"Probably not. But apparently the evidence we need to shut down A.D.E. is here."

They walked into the building, stepping past several men who stared at them as they entered. The structure was stuffy and dim. A man in a blue plaid shirt and gray slacks sat at a desk. He looked up, said something in Somali.

"Do you speak English?" Donovan asked.

He pursed his lips as though thinking about it, got up, opened a door and called out to someone. An older man walked in, a white skull cap covering his gray hair, his beard dyed red with henna. He wore all white with no trace of red dust, as though he never stepped foot outside. Donovan asked him if he spoke English.

He nodded but didn't answer.

"We're looking for a book of names."

The man's gaze flicked to the desk toward a ledger, then back, as he said, "No books. No names."

"We'll pay."

"No books. No names." He turned and left, closing the door behind him.

Donovan glanced at Lisette, who raised her brows, whispering, "Money talks."

Donovan reserved enough cash to pay their driver, and held up several bills. The man at the desk glanced back at the door his partner had left through, then handed the ledger to Donovan. He opened it, saw names and dates, realizing what he needed was in the middle of the book. The time period between when Yusuf had escaped from prison and when he was suspected of leaving the country. Four pages. Donovan tore them from the book, handed it back to the man along with the money. He folded the pages, stuffed them in his boot and said, "Almost too easy. Let's go."

They stepped out the door, only to find their driver and the white truck gone and the three men who'd been loitering out front all holding very large knives as though Donovan and Lisette were turkeys to be carved.

Had that been all there was, Donovan wouldn't have worried.

It was the other ten men, also armed, suddenly stepping out from between the buildings, that set the hairs prickling on the back of his neck.

And then Lisette, saying, "I think the proper term is, 'Oh shit.' "

50

Donovan held his hand up and out about waist high,
thinking he might have a chance of taking out three or four,
assuming he could get to his gun before they threw their
knives. "You want money?" he asked.

One of them yelled at him, pointing to the ground. He
didn't know Somali or Swahili, but knew enough Arabic to
ask once again if they wanted his money. The men raised
their knives higher.

The sound of a revving engine caught their attention, and
as one every person there turned to look. The little white
pickup sped toward them, a large cloud of dirt flying out
behind it like a demon from hell. The pirates stared momentarily, then scattered as they realized the truck was aiming
straight for them. As Ali hit the brakes, the back end fishtailed out, spraying the men with gravel. Donovan grabbed
Lisette's hand, pulled her onto the tailgate and into the back
as Ali hit the gas, racing out of there, honking every few
feet until he was a safe distance away. He slowed then and
looked back through the window, saying, "Like NASCAR!"

"You, my friend, have earned a very, very large tip."

"No tip! Money, yes?"

"Lots of money," Donovan said as Ali sped out of there.

When they reached safety, Donovan paid Ali, and then he and Lisette joined the others at the compound restaurant for a meal of goat and rice. Micah decided it was not one he was about to try again soon. "I don't know how people live on this," he said.

"I'm not sure there's much choice," Eve said.

"It's too damned hot to eat." Micah pushed his plate away. "I think I need a nap."

"I'll walk you to your room," Eve offered.

Donovan drank from a bottle of Tusker beer, grateful to have it after the hellish adventure he and Lisette had been through. Though from what Tex had told them, his might have been a close second, having to follow a clueless Micah around while he played UN ambassador. Sure, the guy was right in that there wasn't enough attention on the plight of the refugees, but offering the pipe dream to resettle the entire camp to America was doing no one any good. Plus, letting in the crooks and terrorists with them was even less incentive. Once Eve left with Micah, Donovan brought out the logbook pages. Lisette photographed them with her cell phone as he called McNiel to tell him what they'd found.

"Nice work," McNiel said. "But is there any way to connect the names to photos?"

"We could run them against the records at reception," Donovan said. "They have photographs of every person who's come in."

"Sounds good," McNiel said. "We also need to connect the names each of these men came into the camp with, and the names they left with. The more info we have, the better."

"We'll get on it," Donovan said, then repeated McNiel's request as Eve returned and took a seat.

"The repatriation records," she suggested. "Someone

there might be able to run it for us. We can check that, while you and Lisette check the other."

"But would they do it," Lisette asked, "knowing what we're looking for? Especially if one of them is guilty of assisting getting these illegals into the U.S.?"

Tex said, "I'm going to guess that the corrupt individuals won't be stepping forward. There was, however, a lovely young woman who was infatuated with Micah, and thinks what he is doing is nothing short of a miracle."

"Slow down," Donovan said as Tex reached for the documents. "Let Lisette get confirmation that McNiel received her photos of the things before we go waving them around anywhere. We almost got mugged getting it. Don't want to get mugged trying to figure out what's on it."

Once Lisette received word, Eve and Tex walked out to get a ride back to the camp to find the woman they hoped would help them. Donovan thought about ordering another beer, but as they sat there in the shade of the gazebo, he noticed Hussein, the man who had driven them from the airstrip, talking to another man who seemed sketchy. An exchange of money went down, he was sure of it, then the pair left, walking after Tex and Eve.

"Something's up," Donovan said, sliding his chair back. "I don't like the way that looks."

When they got to the compound gate, Donovan saw Tex and Eve getting into a vehicle—not with the driver who had brought them here, but with the man he seemed to be paying off.

"Is it just me," Lisette said, "or does Hussein seem a bit too eager to leave?"

"Exactly what I thought," Donovan replied, and quickened his pace. He caught up with Hussein. "Hey!" he said as the man opened the door of another car.

Hussein looked back at him and practically jumped into the vehicle.

Donovan ran up, grabbed the door before he could close it. "What's going on?"

"What do you mean?"

"I saw you paying that man."

"Because your friend wanted a ride, nothing more."

"Good. Then give us a ride to where they're going."

"I have someplace I need to be."

"Change your plans."

He looked from Donovan to Lisette. "As you wish."

"Take the front," Donovan told Lisette as he climbed into the backseat, to keep a better eye on the road and Hussein, who started the car, then pulled out. Donovan was alarmed to see how much farther the other car had driven. "Faster."

"Too dusty. It is not safe," Hussein replied, slowing even more, and hell if he didn't look a little nervous. No, not nervous. Scared to death. Like it really wasn't safe. But not because of any dust. More because of what was happening on the other side of the vast brown cloud. And then, surprising Donovan even more, Hussein abruptly stopped the vehicle, saying, "Something's wrong with the car. The gas. I'll check."

He reached down, pulled the hood release, popping it open, then got out of the car and walked toward the front end.

Donovan casually reached into his camera bag and drew a pistol that had been hidden near the top. He passed it to Lisette, then jumped out of the Jeep.

"What's going on?"

"Fuel line leak."

"Bullshit." He walked up. "You're stalling so we don't meet up with the others. Why?"

Hussein lunged at Donovan, fist first. Donovan tried to sidestep, but the blow glanced off his chin. He threw a punch in the man's gut, his breath coming out in a loud gasp as Hussein fell forward into him. Donovan grabbed him by his arms, swung him around, then threw him against the side of the Jeep, bringing his arm up in a twist lock, forcing his face down until it was mere inches from the hot engine. "Listen very carefully. Where are they taking them?"

"Please. They'll kill me."

"I'll kill you, and I'm a helluva lot closer. Now what the hell is going on?"

He refused to talk.

With one hand still holding Hussein in a wrist lock, Donovan reached up with the other, grasped his head and pressed it down toward the engine, feeling the heat singeing his fingers. Hussein screamed.

"Talk."

"Please!"

Donovan lifted him up just enough to keep from burning.

"Kidnappers!" Hussein said. "They're going to hold them for ransom. They won't hurt the man. He is very famous. Valuable."

Except they had the wrong man. Micah might be valuable, but what would happen when they discovered Tex instead? He looked at Lisette before asking, "*Where* are they taking them?"

"I don't know."

He shoved the man's face toward the engine again.

"A village near the Somalian border."

"Which village?"

"Liboi."

51

The SUV kicked up a mass of dust behind it. Tex glanced behind him, thinking they were heading in the wrong direction, but with three massive camps covering so much ground, he wasn't sure. "Isn't the camp we want the other way?"

"No, no. This way. Shortcut."

Another vehicle was heading in their direction. White. Probably another UN worker. But when the two vehicles met up, stopped, the man who got out was not wearing the insignia of a UN worker. He did, however, have the universal sign of a pirate: an assault weapon pointed right at them.

They were ordered out at gunpoint, and Tex looked around, hoping someone might notice, maybe a patrol in the area. No one. Next thing he knew, he and Eve were cuffed with plastic ties behind their backs and escorted into the other vehicle, placed in the backseat and ordered to lie down.

He understood very little of the language, Somali, but it didn't really matter. He knew what was going on. They were going to be held for ransom. The only problem was that the track record of Somali kidnappers letting their victims go alive was about nil.

Donovan steered the Jeep he'd commandeered from Hussein down the two-lane road that cut through the sand and scrub stretching as far as the eye could see, while Lisette studied the satellite map in comparison to the coordinates sent to them. "How far?" he asked.

She shuffled through some papers. "Maybe thirty-forty kilometers to go."

"Does that match where the phone signal was coming from?"

"About."

The signal had stopped about thirty minutes before, and they figured someone must have discovered the phones and removed the batteries. Donovan looked at the gas gauge. If Hussein was telling the truth, and that was where they had taken them, they should have enough fuel to get there.

McNiel called a few minutes later with an update. "Marco should be landing at Garissa any moment. He'll extract Micah from Dadaab, get him on a plane back, then meet up with you if you haven't secured Liboi. Have you met up with the Kenyan military?"

"Not yet. We're still several miles out. Tell me the list we sent is worth this."

"Griffin's working on it."

"Get the bastard. I don't want this to be for nothing."

Overhead, scattered cirrus clouds slipped across a cerulean sky, where just visible behind the trees of the dusty village, the setting sun tinged the horizon a burnt orange. It would be a while yet before they'd switch over to night vision, and Donovan adjusted the focus of his binoculars until he was able to see clearly, then scanned the area of the desert village that lay about eighteen kilometers west of the border of Somalia. Intel passed on to one of the Kenyan troops stationed in the area brought them to the outskirts of the town, such as it was, very close to the border, which was closed and guarded by troops. Stopping them before they got across was their only hope, and Donovan prayed they hadn't been led astray. He was sprawled on the ground with the scrub and trees for cover, Lisette next to him. They'd been there for the last thirty minutes, sweating in the heat and dust, watching for some sign, while their Kenyan contact was off trying to get further information.

"How I spent my Christmas vacation," Lisette said. "Do you realize that Marco and I had actually planned a ski trip?"

"You two are back together?" he asked.

"Why? You can't get a date for the prom?"

He laughed. "Just glad to hear it. He sure was pissy while you two were broken up."

She lowered her camera, glanced over at him with a wry look. "Much like you were on our last assignment after *you* got dumped?"

"That was different."

"Could have fooled me," she said, returning her attention to the village in front of them to snap a few photos.

"Can't help it if I wear my heart on my sleeve."

"You're a good catch, Donnie boy. Don't let anyone tell you different."

He swung his binoculars to the left, scanning that area, then stopped when a man stepped out of one of the buildings, an automatic rifle slung over his shoulder. "Pretty heavy firepower for someone guarding a tin-roofed shack."

"Where?"

"About ten o'clock."

She aimed her camera and he heard the snap of the lens

as she shot. "That's got to be where they're holding them."

There was a rustle in the brush behind them. Donovan glanced over his shoulder and saw Robert Odoyo, the Kenyan military officer dressed in camouflage fatigues, crawling toward them. "What have you found?"

Donovan pointed.

"I would call in more troops, but we need to tread carefully," Robert said. "They will not hesitate to kill them outright if they feel there is no escape."

"I'm all for small-scale operations—especially when we're outgunned."

"Good, because that may be our only hope. If we fail and they get them over the border to Somalia . . ."

"That's not gonna happen."

Two women in colorful flowing skirts and head scarves walked past the front of the pirate house, carrying heavy pails of water from the well that was about a quarter of a mile away. Another woman in a drab gray gown with a niqab covering her face and head walked in the opposite direction, her bucket empty.

Lisette, who seemed to be following the woman's movements with the lens of her camera, snapped a photo, then showed the digital screen to Donovan. "That, my friend, is how we get closer."

"Not bad, Lisette. Not bad at all."

The clothing they eventually found smelled of the desert air, having been lifted from lines in the yards of some of the unfortunate Liboi households who had not yet brought in their laundry after washing. Donovan left ten times the value in money in its place.

52

The stifling heat even in the blacked-out room sapped all Tex's strength, and several times he almost nodded off. His shoulders and neck were stiff, his gut sore from a kick, and his knees bruised when he was forced to the ground, but other than that he felt fortunate. He'd been in worse scrapes, and apparently their kidnappers were in a big hurry to hide them away, due to the troops guarding the roads. They'd be waiting for nightfall, undoubtedly, assuming they were going to attempt to get them across the Somalia border. And that, in Tex's mind, beat the alternative, which was to simply kill them.

Eve stirred beside him. They were propped up against the mud wall, their hands tied behind them. He wasn't sure if she'd been napping, but neither of them had spoken while their captors were in the room, their one attempt resulting in the kick to Tex's gut. Nor had they said a thing for several minutes after being left alone, out of worry that the man might return. The voices in the next room were loud as someone laughed, and then, eventually, all was quiet. He hoped that meant they'd left.

Tex eyed their smashed cell phones, just visible in the dim light that filtered in through boards over what constituted windows on the exterior corrugated tin wall. The phones had at least survived until their arrival here, the kidnappers not bothering to look for them before tossing them into this room. He knew that Donovan would have tracked their cells the moment he noticed they were missing.

Assuming he'd noticed in time, before the phones were smashed.

It wasn't like they'd discussed when they were to return. After all, the camps were large, and getting from one to the other was not the shortest of trips. Who knew how long it would take before Donovan or Lisette started to wonder what was going on.

But with the fading light also went any hope of rescue. If their kidnappers managed to get them across the border, their chance of being rescued alive diminished considerably. That thought sent him back to the task of trying to loosen up the plastic ties at his wrists. Eve was apparently doing the same.

"Any luck?" he finally whispered, when it seemed he was making no progress.

"Not yet." She gave a quiet, almost heartbreaking laugh. "Funny, but I didn't think my career was going to end this way, never mind my life."

"Gotta remember the rules. First one, don't give up."

"What's the second one?"

"Don't ever forget the first one."

"When you wrangled your way up to that stage when Barclay's gunmen came after you? I thought, my God, you're crazy. The guy's got a gun and you're running up onto the stage?"

"Seemed like the thing to do."

"No stage to run up on here."

"Night's not over, darlin'."

She gave a quiet, "Hm." Then, after a moment, "When we get out of here, you want to go out? There's this great little bar at this refugee camp down the road . . ."

He looked over at her, certain she was merely bolstering her spirits. Girls like her didn't date guys like him. Not with any success, at least, something he well knew from the experiences of every agent he worked with. Griffin, Marco, Donovan . . . But even though he knew it was just small talk, he said, "We get out of here, I'll take you to any bar you want."

"*Any* bar?"

"Any."

"You're on." She started scooting away from him.

"Change your mind already?"

"Are you kidding? Any bar? I know exactly where I want to go, and now that I have incentive to get out of here, I thought I'd do something about it. There was a little light coming in from that wall earlier. Made of metal, maybe it'll cut through the ties."

He watched as Eve shifted closer to the outer wall and felt around with her fingers. But then she said, "No edge to the metal. It's bending out, not in."

"It was worth a try."

She sat there for a moment, and he could tell from the slump of her shoulders she was disappointed. But then she shook her head. "No way. You are *not* getting off that easy. I was thinking of a bar in Paris. You realize I've never been?"

"Paris? A little pricey for a first date."

"You know what else I'm thinking? There is *no way* whoever built this *crappy* little shack did a good enough job not to have a nail or piece of tin or *something* sticking out that we couldn't use."

"They probably don't get the Do It Yourself channel out here."

"Exactly, right? So get your ass up and help me look."

He smiled. They might die trying, but at least they *were*

trying. He rolled to his side, then stood, moving against the metal wall, feeling the day's heat still radiating from it. And as he slid against the warm corrugated siding, he felt a seam catch against his sleeve. Too high, but that at least told him she was on to something. If one was there, surely another seam lower down might be used to slice the ties?

The door to the other room suddenly opened, the guard stopping in surprise at the sight of Tex on his feet. "What are you doing?"

"Scratching my back."

"Get down."

Eve dropped to the ground. Tex tried, but that metal snagged his shirt. The guard apparently took his hesitation as a sign of disrespect. He crossed the dirt floor, grabbed Tex by his shoulders, and slammed him against the wall. The corrugated metal seemed to spring him back into the man's arms, which only made him madder.

"You pig!" He threw Tex again with the full force of his weight, the metal rumbling like a clap of thunder as his head, shoulder, and hip hit it full force, before he slid to the ground, a second before the man kicked him in his ribs, the blow glancing off, most of the force hitting the side of the building. He lay there stunned for several seconds, hearing nothing but the damned metal wall ringing in his ear while he tried to catch his breath. The guard stormed from the room, and Tex felt a brush of air as the door slammed shut.

Only the air didn't come from that side of the room.

It came from the wall behind him. Hot air with the scent of the bush.

He shifted, felt some pain in his side, figured he was bruised.

"Tex?"

He didn't answer. He didn't want it to be his imagination. Not the breeze at all. Just him feeling light-headed from the blow to his ribs, or something.

"Tex? Are you okay?"

He felt it then. For real that time. He opened his eyes, looked at Eve. "You feel that?"

"Feel what?"

"The air moving. From the outdoors in. I think the bastard who tried to crack my ribs may have actually cracked open the seam in the wall."

53

Moving the metal siding out wasn't as easy as they'd
thought. Eve wasn't even sure if Tex could hold it for her,
since it wanted to spring back. They couldn't get it wider, not
without making so much noise that it would alert the guard
in the other room. Not wide enough for Tex to get through.
But it turned out he could hold it for her by pressing with his
feet while she slid through between his legs and the sandy
floor. Even then she was hesitant.

"I can't leave you."

"You will. You'll get out, get help somehow. You'll hide
until daylight if necessary. You just get out."

"My hands."

"You'll find a way to cut the ties."

And still she wasn't sure if it was a good idea. Granted,
staying wasn't a good idea, but leaving without him? And
where could she go where she wouldn't stick out like a sore
thumb? Had they been at the refugee camp, she could pass
as a volunteer worker. Here in this small village, where she
didn't know a word of the local language and doubted that
any of the residents knew hers?

"Go."

"Remember," she said. "Paris."

"You better not stand me up."

She eyed the hole in the siding. "I'm thinking I might be due for a tetanus shot, so try not to let it snap shut on me."

"Quit stalling and get your ass out there."

"Maybe—"

"Go!"

She dropped to her side, scooting along the ground on her back until her head was positioned at the opening. She could see the night sky, the endless stars just above the ragged edge of the metal, reminding her that she didn't want her face anywhere near that should Tex lose his precarious hold on it with his boots. Like an upside-down inch worm, she used her feet to scoot out, feeling the metal edge scraping against her left hip, then catching tight. She tried again. Couldn't move.

"I'm stuck."

She felt him shifting as he tried to move the metal out farther. It creaked loudly. Her heart skipped a beat at the sound, and she swung her hips up, felt the material tear, but she was free. She slid all the way out, then lay there a full second, breathing in the hot night air, staring at the stars in the black sky.

Move. She twisted to her side, sat up, then eyed the metal sticking out. She shuffled back toward it, using the sharp edge to cut the wrist ties, the adrenaline working to get her past the pain of the metal slicing her skin. When her hands were free, she kneeled at the opening. "Maybe I can lift it high enough."

She grasped the edges and pulled. The nails or screws held it too tight. "I need to find something for leverage," she whispered. "I'll be back."

"Be careful, Eve."

She looked around the yard, such as it was, an area of sand

and low scrub, surrounded by a crude fence of sticks along one side and bushes on the other. She decided on the bushes, since they led away from the front of the house. At a crouch, she hurried in that direction, then startled as a dark wraith-like figure came at her from the side of the house. Before she could turn and run, it grabbed her, clamped a hand over her mouth, then dragged her into the night.

Eve was not going down without a fight. She tried biting at the hand, thrashing, kicking, but the blows she expected never came, and when she looked into her captor's eyes she was surprised to see a finger at his—her?—mouth, signaling for quiet. She stared at the wraith, her heart racing as she tried to hear past the pulse pounding in her ears.

"Eve. Quiet," came the whisper.

She stilled, looked past the head coverings to the eyes that watched her. "Lisette?"

"Yes."

Eve would have collapsed had she not been on the ground. "Thank God. Tex is still in there. He's hurt."

"How bad?"

"Ribs, I think."

"Can he walk?"

"I think so. You have a plan?"

"Not yet. But we're working on it. According to our source, we have about five minutes to get Tex out of there before their reinforcements get here to whisk you two over the border." She helped Eve to her feet, then took her hand, leading her away from the house. "This way."

Eve glanced back, saw the tiny opening she'd escaped from. "We can get him out. Between the two of us—"

"You were lucky. A guard walks around the yard every few minutes. How you missed him, I don't know."

And as if to prove her words, they heard the scrape of

the guard's feet on the grit of dirt. The two women stilled, waited for him to pass, and Eve was grateful his attention seemed less on the building itself or even his surroundings and more on where he was walking. When he disappeared around the front, they continued on, meeting with Donovan and an army officer, holed up behind a cover of thick brush, watching the place with night vision goggles.

"Nice of you to join us, Eve," Donovan said.

"Would have been here sooner if I'd known you were waiting."

"This is Robert." She shook hands with him as Donovan explained, saying, "Apparently this group isn't known for reasoning or fair play. The moment they suspect they're being set upon, they kill their hostages. So you can understand why we didn't send the cavalry in."

She felt a knot in the pit of her stomach at the thought of Tex lying in that dark room. Alone. Hurt. "Tell me what I need to do."

"Sort of playing this one by ear, but after watching you slip out of there, I'm thinking that will also be Tex's only hope."

"I tried lifting it by myself."

"I'm sure between me, Robert, and Tex, we can do it. Only we're going to need a very big distraction out front. Something big enough that all hands on deck go running."

Eve examined the robes and niqab that Lisette wore. "If you can find another set like that for me, and a couple jerry cans, I have an idea."

The robes were stifling, and Eve couldn't imagine having to wear something like that day in and day out in the heat or not. She was already sweating and sticky before putting the robes on. It was worse now, and she had to make a mental effort to get past it as she and Lisette each carried a heavy jerry can filled with sloshing liquid toward the terrorist house. No one bothered them, not that there was anyone out at this hour. This part of the town was fairly deserted, perhaps because the inhabitants knew their neighbors were dangerous.

When they rounded the corner of the path that would take them to the house, they lowered their cans to the ground, then rolled them across the sand with their feet, like they saw the women doing back at the refugee camp. As they approached the house, Eve kept watch from the corner of her eye. No one confronted them.

The guard who walked the grounds eventually made his way to the front, saw them, and yelled something. She had no idea of the meaning, and she called out, *"Nini? Nini?"*

It was the only thing she knew to say. She'd heard the women yelling it at the camp, then the echo of whatever had been spoken to them, so figured it meant *What?*

He yelled again, this time taking a step toward them.

"Here goes," Eve said. She shoved her can as hard as she could, watched it roll toward the front of the house. The man stopped it with his foot, shouting at them. A moment later the front door opened and two more men looked out. The guard turned toward the house, talking rapid fire, undoubtedly explaining what he'd seen, his foot still on the water jug.

Eve stepped in front of Lisette, blocking the guard's view while Lisette bent over, pulled off the top of her jug, stuffed a rag inside it, then lit the thing on fire.

The guard swung his gun in their direction, and Lisette pulled Eve away, dropped the jug on its side, and kicked it straight toward the house.

The three men stared in disbelief, not moving.

The two women picked up their robes, turned and ran,

Eve looking back over her shoulder in time to see the guard diving away and the men jumping back inside the house, shouting something. A loud explosion shook the air, and she felt the heat of it as the flames jumped up. It did not blow up the house, and the two men inside looked out, yelling, and she heard them running in their direction.

She only hoped they didn't catch her and Lisette before they reached safety.

54

Tex wasn't sure how long he'd been in that room, how long it had been since Eve escaped. He hoped she'd made it, hoped Donovan was out there somewhere. And if truth be told, he hoped like hell he'd make it out, because he wanted that date in Paris. Maybe she'd stand him up, change her mind once the light of day came, but he wanted that chance.

He tried once again to lift the metal, but it held fast, and the loud creaking noise made him worry they might overhear, then discover that Eve was missing before she had an opportunity to get away. He shifted around so he could look out the hole at the stars. Damned lot of them out here in the middle of nowhere, he thought, a moment before the world around him shook. The explosion seemed to echo off the walls, blowing them apart. The door burst open and he saw one of the kidnappers standing there, a wild look on his face. The man pointed his gun at him, and Tex felt a rush of air as shots were fired and someone yanked him head first through the hole.

Gunfire cracked through the metal as someone returned

fire, and then he was free and Donovan and a uniformed army officer were pulling him to his feet, dragging him across the barren yard to the cover of the bushes. Someone sliced his hands free, and he ran with the men, ignoring the sharp pain in his side from his bruised ribs. And just as he and the others cleared the house, several uniformed troops ran past them, apparently to clean up the mess, now that the hostages were free.

"You okay?" Donovan asked him, as they neared a Jeep parked next to a military truck. And standing between both vehicles were Lisette and Eve, a sight for sore eyes, even if they were both dressed in drab head-to-toe robes.

Eve ran up, hugged him. "You're okay?"

"Ouch . . ."

She backed off. "Sorry."

"I'm fine. Been through worse."

Lisette gave him a gentler hug. "Good to have you back."

"Any chance we can get the hell out of this godforsaken desert?"

Donovan smiled. "Can't be too injured. You're just as cranky as ever. But I'm with you. Let's get the hell out of here. Marco's waiting for us in Garissa. A little perturbed that he missed the fun."

"What's he doing there?"

"Babysitting Micah." He turned to the army officer. "I think we're ready to head back, Robert. Thank you for your assistance."

"Just to make sure you don't lose your way again, we'll escort you to the airstrip."

"An offer we're not about to refuse."

Every bump in the road, such as it was, was like a stab to his bruised side, but anything was better than being in that dark shack alone, and Tex wasn't about to complain. A small plane took them from the Liboi airstrip to Garissa. Once they were in the air on their way to the Nairobi airport, he relaxed.

Micah, seated next to Eve, and behind him on the too small plane, felt it necessary to give a dissertation of his trip at the camp. "I'm not sure I'll go back anytime soon. Mind you, I'm glad I did," he said, "but the accommodations there are atrocious."

So much for the philanthropist, Tex thought as Marco, seated next to him, did his best to feign politeness. Once they landed, Tex grabbed Marco's arm, saying, "Please tell me I'm not sitting anywhere near that guy? I'll take a screaming baby over him any day."

"Tough break, *amico mio*. The ATLAS jet awaits and we have to stop off in London first. How are you?"

"Bruised is all."

Marco grinned. "Don't want to ride back to the States with him, then? If not you, who's going to make sure he arrives safe and sound?"

"You. I'll trade you the next two ops if you go. I'd have a hard time knowing that he's gonna go on with his fund-raising."

"His, how do you say it? *Gig* is legitimate. It's the government contractor A.D.E. taking his money who is not. At least according to the CIA. I have a feeling that once he gets back and sits down with them to sort it all out, his future fund-raising efforts might be curtailed for a bit."

Tex stood. "Let's get this show on the road. Eve and I have a bone to pick with her ex-boss at A.D.E."

55

Joint Terrorism Task Force Briefing
FBI Headquarters

Sydney stood at the back of the crowded room next to Griffin, watching Pearson and the unit chief at the front. Every chair was filled with FBI agents and DC Metro officers, all waiting to be briefed on the upcoming operation. There wasn't a uniform or identifying insignia in sight, since the entire op would be handled undercover.

"Listen up," Bill Barry, head of the Terrorism Section, said, then waited for everyone to quit talking. "We have a report from a credible source that Yusuf has definitely entered the country and has activated a cell in our area. More importantly we believe he has the means to construct a small radioactive device. *If* any of you come in contact with anything that looks remotely like what you see on the second page of the op plan, do not touch it, pick it up, examine it, and most of all don't breathe near it unless your life insurance policy is paid up to date. The powder is extremely radioactive and it won't take much to kill you. Any questions so far?"

No one had any.

"Turn to page three." The sound of rustling paper filled the room for several seconds before he continued. "On this page you'll see a screen shot of the vehicle we believe was used to pick up Yusuf from the Greyhound bus station. The man you see getting into the vehicle is, we believe, Yusuf. The driver is unknown, but the registered owner is Salim Sharif."

An agent in the front raised his hand, saying, "And if we find him or his vehicle?"

"Because of the threat of the possible nuclear substance, do not enter the vehicle. Assume the car is contaminated, assume any subjects in the car are contaminated. NEST will take over from there to handle the vehicle, subjects, and anything else found from that point on," he said, referring to the Nuclear Emergency Support Team deployed to the area.

He continued with the remainder of the op plan, then went through the assigned teams. "Any questions?"

There were a few, quickly answered, and they started filing out.

Griffin, Sydney, McNiel, and Pearson remained behind while the room cleared. Technically, they wouldn't be joining in the actual hunt for Sharif, or even Yusuf. They'd been following up on the names from the Dadaab list, hoping it would lead to the other cells. Right now their job was intel and support, something Sydney gathered that Griffin wasn't used to. But after seeing him nearly killed in front of her eyes, his hovering behind the scenes away from the action suited her just fine. "Have you had breakfast yet?" she asked him as they followed McNiel and Pearson.

"A piece of toast on the way out the door."

"That's breakfast?"

He gave her a sideways glance. "What'd you have?"

"Pop tart. Unfrosted. Toasted just long enough to get the corners dark brown."

Pearson looked over his shoulder at the two of them. "We're going out for an omelet. If you two gourmets can pull yourselves away from such an enticing culinary discussion, you're welcome to join us. It'll take the task force a while to set up and get out there. And who knows when we'll get to eat again."

His words turned out to be true. And yet, with all the FBI agents in the field, it was the police department that found the vehicle in question, with Salim Sharif behind the wheel. At a gas station two blocks from the omelet house.

So much for breakfast.

"McNiel volunteered you for the sketch," Griffin told Sydney once they cleared the scene and returned to the office. "I'll drive you over."

"I thought we had a photo of Yusuf?"

"We do. Just not a current one. Hard to say how much he's changed sitting in some jail cell. More importantly, we still don't know if that's who Sharif picked up from the bus station, since the surveillance photos aren't clear." They took the elevator down. "The PD has Sharif in an interview room. He's cooperative and comes up clean as far as any radiation."

"And if he hadn't?"

"Guess you'd be doing it in a space suit."

They set up in an interview room at the station. Griffin stood outside the room, watching behind the one-way glass while Sydney conducted the interview and started the sketch. The detective who was assisting with the investigation walked up beside Griffin, saying, "Not sure if your office is interested, but we found a phone in his car. He says it's not his."

"Anyone run anything on it?"

"No. In light of what's going on, we figured it was best to keep it intact. Not exactly our expertise. And, while we'd normally book the thing in our evidence locker, it made the radiation detector go beep-beep-beep. Since the only place anyone here wants to hear that noise is on a video game, we're letting you keep it."

Griffin signed the evidence sheet for the phone, then stepped down the hall to call McNiel. "We have a cell phone that may belong to the man he picked up from the bus stop."

"Anyone look at it yet?"

"No. There may be a slight contamination issue."

"I'll send someone from NEST to collect it. Keep your fingers crossed that we get lucky."

Griffin returned to the interview room, watching as Sydney questioned the man, a technique with which he was becoming all too familiar. Basic description, face shape, eyes, nose, mouth, what would you change, then minutes upon minutes while she shaded in the face and the hair for the final reveal. Even though he'd seen the process several times and knew how good she was, the finished result still surprised him.

And this time was no different.

She held up the sketch for Salim to view, and Griffin got his first glimpse of the face.

He took out his phone, called McNiel once more. "It's definitely Yusuf."

Back at the ATLAS office, the phone had been cloned. Griffin was in McNiel's office reading the preliminary report when Jones from tech walked in. "Got those numbers triangulated. Your informant's story matches up. His cell phone's on here. We're putting a locate on the other numbers as we speak. So far we have one in San Francisco, L.A., and New York. They're the only numbers that come up. He called them once, less than a minute each, and that's it. But we've actually matched a couple names on the Dadaab list to those locales."

He handed the updated report to McNiel, who walked over to a wall map of the U.S. "How close can you get me to where those numbers are?"

"Very," Jones said. "Smartphones. Makes our job a lot easier."

"And the apartment where he dropped Yusuf off? Was there a landline number?"

"Nothing. So it must have been a prearranged drop."

"Contact the carriers on those four cell numbers. I want ears and eyes on everything that goes in and out. I don't care if it's a call, text, or goddamned smoke signal, I want to know what's being said and I want it in real time."

"Yes, sir."

He left and McNiel studied the map, telling Griffin, "I'll call Pearson. We need a team sitting on each of the corresponding numbers. The intel states he was to activate sleeper cells. It looks like he's done that."

"What about the apartment here?" Griffin asked, picking up the photo of the place as Sydney walked in.

"No specific number, just the building. And the question is how to handle it. If they're in the middle of putting together a radioactive explosive device, I'm not sure I want to risk storming it. Not without knowing exactly which apartment we're dealing with."

Sydney took the photo from Griffin's hand. "That looks like the place we were in the other day. The one owned by the Redfern Group."

"Same street, as it turns out. Different building."

"He, or his so-called client," she said, "owns the whole block and the one behind it. And if you were a terrorist, where best to hide than among legal refugees from your own country?"

"What we need," McNiel said, "is a plan to get in, low-key, get eyes on the inside. Can Redfern get us in without any fanfare?"

"Hardly," Sydney said. "He's as likely to get killed from the residents as he is from the terrorist. That being said, if it is one of his buildings, I have an idea that may just work."

56

The old man walked into the apartment, his face
looking troubled. Yusuf was on the couch, napping, still
feeling sick. In the kitchen, one of the four men sat at the
table hammering at the lead casing to remove the cesium
137. "They've arrested Salim," the old man said.

"Salim?" Yusuf asked.

"The man who drove you here the first night."

"For what?" the old man's son asked.

"We don't know," he said. "But we must be very careful."

The knot in Yusuf's stomach grew tighter. He didn't know
if it was from the sickness or the thought that he'd lost his
cell phone. "Should we leave?" he asked.

"Salim knows nothing. Not your name. Not even our
apartment number. We stay. For now."

Relieved, Yusuf felt his empty pocket. Perhaps he should
have mentioned that the phone was missing, or pretend he
only just discovered it . . . It was so hard to think these days,
almost as if he lived in a fog. He hadn't used it since arriving
in Washington at the bus station. He'd pulled the phone out,
made the calls to each of the sleeper cells, called for his ride,

then slipped the phone in the pocket of his new leather coat.

But there was a hole in the pocket. A cheap Tijuana coat, the leather too thin, the workmanship shoddy. A slight possibility existed that the phone had been lost at the bus station. He'd gone there to look for it, had actually walked into the place to ask, but stopped when he'd seen a man and woman at the counter, one of them showing a badge. At the time, he found it merely coincidental, but decided not to mention it to the old man, for fear he'd shut down the planning. But when nothing more happened, no sudden knock at the door, Yusuf decided their presence at the bus station was coincidental. But now? He found the timing suspicious, even more so with the arrest of Salim.

He needed that phone to set the chain of events into motion. Four cities with explosions, but only one would be dirty. The discovery of radiation in that one would set panic in the locales where the other three were set to detonate.

But with no phone, there would be no call. And no call, they would not set off the bombs. Only one man knew the numbers of the different cells, for their own protection. And that man, who had entrusted the phone to Yusuf, was in Somalia. That worried feeling in his stomach grew stronger, twisting and gnawing at him. What if he'd lost the phone in Salim's car that night? If the authorities found it, would they be able to discern anything?

He decided not. The other cells didn't matter. So what if their bombs were not placed and detonated? The only one that mattered was this one in the capital. Everyone in America would be watching. Their leaders would be threatened, many would become sick and die.

He listened to the old man going over final details with his son, watched as the younger man carefully poured the bluish dust into the plastic zip-top bag, then placed it carefully into the backpack, using duct tape to secure it to the pipe bombs.

Say something, now, before it is too late.

But he was not that brave, perhaps because he was feeling so sick. They were all feeling that way now. The old man advised Yusuf to stay away from the dust, as he would need his strength to commit the final act.

Yusuf gathered the will to get off the couch and stand. He felt better when he was outside in the fresh air. The cold seemed to revive him. "I'm going for a walk," he told them.

"Be careful," the old man said. "We're depending on you."

They were depending on *him*.

That thought echoed in his head as he descended the stairs, hearing a commotion down the hall toward the front entrance, someone knocking on a door, then a woman's voice calling out that she was from the Department of Social Services. They were always in the building, helping the refugees with their food stamps and welfare.

He pulled the hood of his Giants shirt up over his head, shoved his hands in the pockets of his leather coat, then walked down the hall, careful to keep his head down when he saw the manager standing with a man and woman who seemed familiar to him. As he passed, the man and woman entered the apartment, and the manager turned to Yusuf, asking him in Somali if he had received word of the building renovation, then handed him a paper with printing on it.

Yusuf took the paper and hurried past. He saw the top word: NOTICE.

He didn't bother to read the rest, which would have been a struggle, since he was not schooled in written English. He'd heard from the old man that the building's owner was being forced to renovate every building on the block and temporarily move everyone out.

He didn't care.

When he stepped outside, the crisp, cold air cleared his head, helped him think. He crumpled up the paper, then realized why the man and woman seemed familiar. He'd seen them before. At the bus station asking questions.

She was the woman with the badge.

Somehow they'd found him.

There was a back entrance. He could slip upstairs before they even knew he was there. He'd come too far to quit now, even without the phone. And without the other cells, maybe it was not as big as they'd originally planned, but the old man didn't need to know.

After all, when it was over, none of them would be alive to find out . . .

57

Sydney, Griffin, and Ito Abasi, the apartment man-
ager, were nearly finished with the ground floor of the
second building, and Sydney was amazed that she was able
to stand the smell for as long as she did. Mr. Abasi, being
fluent in a number of languages, having been a university
professor in Somalia before fleeing the country twenty years
ago, translated as Sydney knocked on each door.

"Department of Social Services," she called out. If no one
answered, Griffin palmed a small wand, which he lowered
to the threshold to at least get a reading of the entryway as
he slipped a notice of inspection beneath the door. If it was
opened, Mr. Abasi stated they were there to do a home inspection for the renovation of the building, and Sydney and
Griffin walked in, Sydney with a clipboard, pretending to
inspect, Griffin with the equipment, taking a surreptitious
reading of the premises.

And so it went. They finished the first floor and were getting ready to start on the second when Sydney checked her
clipboard. "I think we underestimated the number of flyers
we'd need."

"There're more in the car," Griffin said. In fact, they'd made up enough to search several buildings, not having a clear idea from Salim exactly which complex his passenger entered, only which one he dropped him off in front of.

They walked out to the car, a borrowed sedan with a Department of Social Services decal on the back of the window.

While Griffin retrieved the flyers, Mr. Abasi and Sydney stood outside, Sydney grateful to be breathing in the fresh air. The break was far too short and they returned inside, climbed the stairs, then knocked on the first door. The woman who answered was given a flyer, as Mr. Abasi translated the notice. When the woman closed the door, he told Sydney, "She says that she is surprised that Mr. Redfern has agreed to the renovations of this building so soon when the first one has not yet been started."

"Probably not as surprised as Mr. Redfern will be," Sydney replied, then knocked on the next door. "Department of Social Services."

Mr. Abasi laughed, a deep rich sound. "I like your style, Miss Fitzpatrick."

All laughter faded when, as Griffin reached down to slip the flyer beneath the door, the radiation detector alerted them with a steady *tick, tick, tick.*

"They've arrested four people in the cell from that apartment," McNiel said, approaching Griffin at the NEST command center that was set up down the street. The entire road was closed off, and now, with the very real threat of a radioactive substance, they were in the process of going door to door searching, and evacuating. "Yusuf wasn't there."

The entire team that had searched for Salim was now searching for Yusuf. FBI agents in the vicinity were patrolling the streets, and news vans were starting to arrive on the perimeter, as they investigated what was being reported as a hazmat of a dangerous chemical.

It was, in fact, amazing how fast the incident took place. Once they'd found the apartment with the radiation source, they backed off to let the entry team take over and to get the building cleared. Now it was damage control and the hunt for Yusuf before he had a chance to activate the device, should he have it with him.

"Have we gotten any intel yet?" Griffin asked.

"On Yusuf?" McNiel clarified. "A neighbor said she saw him leave a few minutes before you arrived. The occupants of the apartment deny that he, or anyone else there, is involved in any terrorist activities. They don't know why or how the apartment became contaminated with radiation, and the wires and bits of equipment are from a hobby."

"Then the source is no longer in the apartment?"

"It looks that way, unfortunately. They're going over it now. I'll let you know if they find anything."

Sydney walked up with two cups of coffee, handing one to Griffin. "Looked like you could use a cup."

"What I can use is a break. They arrested the cell. Yusuf wasn't there."

"We'll find him."

"Of that I don't doubt. I only hope we do so before it's too late."

58

Carillo read the text from Tex.

Arrived at Heathrow last night. Going to take down
A.D.E. Can use help. You in? Call.

Sheila, oblivious to the case going on around her, opened
her guidebook, then held it up to show Carillo the picture.
"That's where I want to go. The ship."

"A ship? They've got one of those in San Francisco. Only
bigger," he said, looking up Tex's number. At the moment,
they were walking from their hotel, then on to Connaught
Street. Sheila had picked the route because she wanted to
see where one of the former prime ministers lived.

"That must be it," she whispered as they neared a cof-
feehouse. He looked up from his phone, saw two uniformed
police officers holding submachine guns at the entrance to
an alleyway between two rows of houses. Considering that
the standard force in London didn't carry weapons at all,
that was some pretty heavy firepower. The guards gave them

a quick once-over as they walked by, and Carillo glanced past them, saw it was a dead-end street.

Definitely some pricey real estate, he thought, pressing Send to call Tex. They rounded the corner onto Connaught Square, to see two more armed guards standing at the steps in front of the house, and even though Sheila wanted to walk past, Carillo decided to guide her across the street, worried that she might try to engage them in conversation. "Better view," he whispered to her as Tex finally answered the phone. "Have a good time?" Carillo asked.

"Not a place I hope to visit again soon. We did, however, find pages in a book used to document the buying and selling of fake identification. Turns out that A.D.E. knew some of the refugees coming in had no ID and facilitated the purchase of said documents to supplement their program. How about you? Heard from Trip since we left?"

"Not a peep."

"It'd be nice to round him up, too. He's involved in this more than he's letting on."

Sheila, having lost interest in the former prime minister's residence, stopped at the next corner to consult her guidebook, while Carillo and Tex talked about what time to meet later that afternoon. She waved at Carillo to catch his attention. "The London Eye. It's like a big Ferris wheel, and you can see the entire city."

"You did notice the patchy fog?" he said, covering up the phone.

"Maybe it's not foggy all over."

"Lotta money to pay to only see part of the city."

"Well, what do you want to do, Tony? It's our last day."

He heard Tex laughing on the other end. "Not at all funny, Tex. But yeah," Carillo said into the phone. "I'm in."

"I'll call you when we get it set. Maybe try to be back around two."

"Perfect." Saved him from hours of shopping, and he

looked over at Sheila as he pocketed his phone, saying, "How about we just walk? Maybe take in a museum. You ever see the Rosetta Stone?"

"Museums are so stuffy, with paintings and dusty relics no one but collectors want to look at."

"Right. Wouldn't want to waste your time on that." He shoved his hands in his coat pockets. Spending their last day in England on a giant Ferris wheel, looking at the fog, was fine by him, now that he actually had something better to do before they left tomorrow. "Lead away, Sheila. You want to go up in the London Eye, I'll go with you. But I get to pick lunch. Pub food. Shepherd's pie, stew, fish and chips, and peas."

For someone who had spent the last couple days eating at fancy tourist establishments that served things like "high tea," she agreed surprisingly easily, and even asked for a recommendation from a local about where to eat not too far from the London Eye.

The food was more than decent, and Carillo finished the last few peas on his plate, then looked at his watch. "Time to hit your Ferris wheel, Sheila."

She sighed as she pushed her plate away. "You've been very sweet to follow me around the city."

Not that he had a choice. "That's what friends are for."

"It's nice to hear you say that."

"Up and at 'em, Sheila. Sights to see, before we head back for the day. I promised Tex I'd meet up with him by two."

They walked along the River Thames, then crossed the Golden Jubilee Bridge, where vendors had small arts and crafts for sale.

The line for the London Eye was long, even with the low clouds, and Sheila changed her mind. With only an hour left before they had to head back, she decided she'd rather visit Big Ben and Westminster Abbey, now that they were here.

Sheila went inside the adjacent County Hall building to

use the restroom. He stood outside, not taking any chances that she might walk away on her own and get into more trouble, even though she hadn't given him any signs that she was trying to take off.

Now that he thought about it, when all was said and done, the last couple days hadn't been that much of a strain. By tomorrow they'd be on the plane, en route to San Francisco, and he hoped that once they got there, they could put this whole business with Trip behind them. In fact, surprisingly, Sheila hadn't mentioned him once. Knock on wood, he thought. Maybe that meant she'd finally grown up, realized that Trip was trouble.

Carillo strolled across to the wall opposite the ladies' room, where he could watch the doorway. She exited a few minutes later, phone in hand, her face pale, her blue eyes looking frantic as she searched for him.

"Sheila? Over here."

When she located him, the relief he expected to see wasn't there. Great. He knew exactly what it meant. Goddamned Trip. "What's wrong?"

"I'm sorry, Tony. I'm so, so sorry. Please don't hate me."

"What the hell?"

"Trip. He told them we had it."

Carillo was getting a very bad feeling about this. "Had *what*?"

"Whatever this thing is they were looking for."

"The book on the DVD? Tex already found it."

"But they don't know that. Neither does Trip. They still think it's out there."

"Jesus. What the hell are you saying?"

"That Trip was trying to save his sister and his niece, so he told them that we had it."

"We, as in you and I?"

She nodded.

Carillo stared in disbelief. "Why the hell would he do that? His sister and niece are at a safe house!"

"He doesn't know that!"

"Didn't you tell him?"

Sheila started crying. "I—I only just talked to him this morning. You told me not to."

"Why the hell didn't you tell me he called?"

"Because I knew you'd be mad. I didn't know he'd . . . He was so nice to me, and—and I thought he was good . . ." She handed Carillo her cell phone, opened her purse and started digging through it, pausing to wipe her eyes with her sleeve. "I never thought he'd do something like this. I swear, Tony."

Carillo looked around them. Suddenly every man and woman in the vicinity became suspect as he wondered if they'd been followed.

"First off, I'm not mad. I'm . . . worried. Okay? Call him back."

She tried. "He's not answering."

Carillo ran his fingers through his hair, taking a deep breath as he scanned the area once again, trying to think what to do. First thing, get them the hell out of anyplace they might become a target. Trip's brother-in-law had been shot out in the open like this, back when they thought *he* had the thing.

Carillo grabbed her hand, pulling her toward Westminster Bridge, crowded with far more tourists and cars than the pedestrian bridge they'd crossed—the better to get lost in. If they were surrounded by a lot of people, they were harder targets. "Tell me exactly what you told him," he said, taking out his cell phone to call Tex.

"I can't walk this fast and talk."

"You remember the woman at Trip's house in San Mateo?" he said, not stopping. "She killed your maid and stole her cleaning supplies so that she could kill Trip. That's the kind of people who are after us. So start talking. Everything you told Trip about where we are, what we're doing."

"I—I told him what hotel we were at, and that we were leaving tomorrow morning."

"When?"

"This morning. That's when he told me I should visit the London Eye. But if he meant for us to be killed, he wouldn't have called me just now, right? And it is his sister and niece. And he knows you're an FBI agent and you can protect us."

"Give him a goddamned Brownie point for effort," he said, leading her up the steps to the street, "and pray to God I don't see him. Ever." Carillo called Tex. No answer. He looked left, then right, deciding they'd start across Westminster Bridge. Carillo stopped next to a cart that sold chestnuts, looking around for signs of a tail as he dug out a couple bills to pay for some.

"Why are we buying chestnuts?" Sheila asked as he drew her to the far side of the cart.

"Because I need a moment to think," he said. And to see if they were being followed. No sense in scaring her any more than she was already scared.

If they were going to get out of this, he was going to have to be extremely careful. *If* they were being followed, these men were armed and had already killed. Unlike back home, he had no weapon. And neither did the police, so he wasn't about to flag one down, thereby endangering a law officer in the mix, never mind any citizen who got in the way of a stray bullet.

Then again, he wasn't about to sacrifice himself as a target. He handed the paper cone filled with chestnuts to Sheila, then called Tex again as he took in their surroundings, trying to come up with anything that resembled a plan.

"I don't like these," Sheila said.

"You've never had them, so how do you know?"

"I have, too, at the Dickens festival."

"I just spent two pounds on the things. Pretend to like them, okay?"

"Okay, don't be so crabby."

Carillo eyed the walkway they'd just left, saw two men, one in a black leather coat, the other a gray jacket, rushing up the steps toward Westminster Bridge. They seemed to be walking with a purpose, and every instinct told Carillo these were the men.

Answer the phone, Tex. But as before, the call went straight to Tex's voice mail. Carillo turned away so Sheila couldn't hear. "We've got a problem. Trip told Barclay that Sheila and I have the DVD. Possibly two on our tail. On the east side of Westminster Bridge."

As he disconnected, he noticed a group of camera-wielding tourists approaching from the parkway, climbing the steps in front of the two men, then turning right onto Westminster Bridge. Just as they reached the chestnut cart, Carillo drew Sheila into the mix, staying close to the front of the group. They were about halfway across the bridge when everyone stopped to look out across the water as the London Eye started turning. Out came the cameras. Carillo stopped with them, had Sheila stand against the guardrail, posing for a picture with the London Eye in the background. The two men stopped suddenly, leaned over the water, watching the current as though they found it extremely fascinating. Carillo pretended to aim his cell phone at Sheila, but snapped a photo of the men, and sent it to Tex.

"Time to go," he said, taking her hand, then continuing in the direction of Westminster Abbey and Big Ben. A lot of sightseers on that side to get lost in, but unfortunately both were on the opposite bank *and* across the street. He was just hoping to make it to the other side of the bridge, and made a show of looking at his watch, then quickening his pace as though they were late for an appointment, not worried about someone following them.

"Do we really need to walk this fast?" Sheila asked. "One minute you're all, hurry up, the next it's, let's stop to take a picture."

"I just want to get to the other side."

"There's ice cream up there," she said, pointing to a concession stand at the end of the bridge, just beyond the stairs that led down to the riverbank. "I'd rather have that than chestnuts."

Tex finally called back. "You okay?"

"So far."

"Still on you?"

"Yeah. Just crossing Westminster Bridge."

"We're at the safe house," Tex said. "Too far to get to you in time. There's a subway entrance on the corner. Turn right. Take the Circle Line to Edgeware or the Jubilee to Baker. Text me with which train you get on."

"Will do."

Carillo let Sheila lead him in the direction of the concession stands on the corner, where a tall sculpture of some women in a horse chariot towered over a souvenir stand. The perfect place to survey the area, and he told Sheila he wanted to look at postcards, pulling one out, noticing the two men were still on the bridge but approaching fast.

He replaced the postcard, stepped around the corner, saw the Westminster Station Underground sign.

"Sheila, look at this," he said, making a point to hold up a large picture from one of the racks, hoping their tail had no clue they'd been made.

She came closer, and he shoved the photo back in the rack, then pulled her around the corner, out of view. Time to clue her in. "We're being followed."

She didn't argue as he led her to the Underground entrance, down the stairs into the subway tunnel. He dug out his wallet, hit it against the reader, and pushed her through the gate. Tex said something about the Jubilee line, but he wasn't about to risk the insanely long escalator ride into the deep subway. An announcement sounded throughout the platform that a train was leaving. He didn't care which one it was. He guided Sheila on board, stepped on after her, and prayed the doors closed in time.

When he looked back, he saw the two men running across the platform as the final announcement was made. The men split up, each running to a different door, and in a split second as the portals slid shut, they hopped on board.

59

It was the longest nine minutes of Carillo's life. The two men pushed their way through the crowded cars of the Tube, working their way toward him, only to be stopped at the door that separated them. The man put his hand on the door, watched Carillo, then pointed up as he lifted his jacket slightly. Posted above the secured door was a sign that read DANGER OF DEATH, warning passengers that if they forced the door open, they might die.

Great. A smartass thug.

If there was a saving grace, it was that the thugs weren't making any further moves toward them, even when the train stopped. They stayed in their car, Carillo in his. Maybe that meant they thought he and Sheila were going to lead them to this DVD. He hoped.

He texted a message to Tex, hoping it would get through: *Circle Line, still being followed.*

And then he scanned the posted chart of the stops. He knew that if the pair managed to get close to him and Sheila, she would be a liability, since she'd have no clue how to handle herself in this situation. He studied the chart, trying to decide if he wanted to chance riding to Edgeware where Tex was hopefully waiting. Paddington was the stop just prior to Edgeware, likely to take longer, since it was a major terminal. Good crowd to get lost in, but maybe too big to navigate.

He glanced over, saw the thugs watching him, probably trying to anticipate his move. "Take the seat by the door, Sheila. And don't get up until I tell you."

The men moved by their door. Carillo realized it didn't matter. Whether he and Sheila stayed on or got off, they'd do the same.

Carillo kept his attention focused on the thugs as a pleasant but impersonal computerized voice announced, "Bayswater."

"What's going on, Tony?"

"We'll be fine, Sheila. Just do as I say."

As the train slowed, about a couple of dozen people began crowding toward the door, early commuters on their way home. Maybe he wouldn't wait. When the elderly woman next to Sheila got up, Carillo sat on the edge of the seat, holding tight to Sheila's hand. He glanced over, realized the crowd shielded the two of them from view, and he leaned toward his wife. "When that door opens, we're going to stay low and slip into the middle of the crowd. When I tell you to run, run."

She nodded.

The doors opened and the crowd stepped off in a fairly orderly manner. He pushed Sheila into the exiting commuters, and she slipped off the train just in front of him. He glanced back, saw the men watching the tops of the heads. Carillo swiftly followed Sheila, grabbing her hand. "Run!"

They flew toward the exit, and he looked back, saw the men had waited a few seconds too long and were now trying to wade through the people who were pouring onto the train. The departing passengers crowded onto the escalator. He pushed past several, saying, "Excuse me. Wife needs

a doctor. Excuse me." They moved to one side as he and
Sheila raced up the moving stairs, then out. As soon as they
reached street level, Carillo looked around.

They needed transportation. He saw a taxi dropping off
a couple at the curb up ahead, the driver reaching into the
backseat to take out the suitcases.

"This way," Carillo said. The driver was carrying the bags
to the sidewalk as he and Sheila approached, and Carillo
asked, "Can you take us to Shepherd's Bush?"

"Hop in. Be right with you," he said.

While he was accepting his fare, then advising his former
passengers on where to find the best pub in the neighborhood, Carillo opened the back door for Sheila. He glanced
at the Tube entrance, saw the two thugs scanning the street,
then one of them pointed. They ran toward the taxi.

Carillo eyed the cabbie, who was waiting patiently while
the passenger counted out coins. Carillo hurried around,
opened the driver's door, got in and took off.

"Hey!" the cabbie yelled. "Stop, you sodding tosser!"

"Buckle up, Sheila."

"What are you doing?"

"Getting us the hell out of here." He checked the rearview
mirror, glimpsed the man in the black coat drawing a gun
on the driver of a blue BMW just pulling up to the curb in
front of the station.

Carillo hit the gas, thanking God it was a one-way street.
He dug his cell phone out and tossed it back to Sheila. "Hit
Send, ask for Tex, and tell him what's going on."

"You drove through a lighted zebra crossing!"

"What the hell are you talking about?"

"The crosswalk!"

"It was either that or risk getting shot, now make the call
and put it on speakerphone."

"Oh my God . . . You could have hit that mother and her
baby in the pram!"

"Do it, Sheila."

"I am, for God's sake. It's ringing."

Carillo honked his horn, then found himself forced to make a right turn by a sudden large NO ENTRY notice painted in the intersection.

Another one-way street. Luck was with them.

Tex came on the line. "Carillo?"

"Here. We, uh, borrowed a taxi."

"Where are you?"

"Just got off the Tube at Bayswater. Heading for . . ." He looked up for a sign. "Hell. I don't know where."

"No GPS in the car?"

Carillo checked the dash. "No. And we're being chased by a—looks like a blue BMW. Outcarred and outgunned."

Sheila held up her phone. "I have GPS."

"Turn it on," Tex said.

"We're on Inverness Terrace, headed toward Bayswater," she said.

"Any chance you can lose your tail?" Tex asked.

"Damned road's too narrow," Carillo said. "But at least there's not much traffic." He floored the throttle. Just when he thought he was losing them, the street divided inexplicably with rows of cars parked down the center. As the BMW started gaining ground, a caterer's van pulled out from one of the many small hotels lining the avenue.

When he reached Bayswater Road, Carillo had to remember not to cross over to make his left-hand turn. Driving on the wrong side of the road was unnerving enough *without* being chased.

"Update?" Tex asked.

And Sheila said, "We're on Bayswater Road. Heading toward Marble Arch."

"Still on you?" Tex asked.

"Working on it," Carillo said, honking, then pulling around a red double-decker bus that was slowing in front of him. He slammed on his brakes as a small gold car darted out from in front of the bus. Cursing at the sudden diversion of traffic, Carillo turned into Lancaster Terrace and then found himself in a maze of small streets winding around central gardens. The BMW was still close behind them.

"Look!" Sheila cried. "The Victoria Pub! We're close to our hotel. They wouldn't follow us there, would they?"

Carillo glanced in his rearview mirror, the BMW getting closer. "Yes. What I wouldn't give for good old-fashioned American cops with guns right now."

"Too bad the prime minister's security service isn't for rent."

Carillo braked hard, then made the first turn. "That, Sheila, is the most intelligent thing you've said all day."

"It is?"

He slowed for another turn, hoping he'd remember the way they'd walked this morning. Connaught Street . . . Yes, definitely it. He hoped the armed officers were currently present, not just when the former P.M. was in residence, because right now he could use a break. He slowed at the alley, not seeing the officers beneath the archway, then drove past and turned into the garden square, hoping the two would be standing out front, hot on the job.

He drove around the park, slowed, saw the suspects still on his tail as he turned, followed the square around, drawing up in front of the former prime minister's home. The two officers eyed him suspiciously. He pulled out his credentials, held them up as he opened the car door, saying, "FBI. I need help."

The officer swung his submachine gun at Carillo as the suspect vehicle careened around the corner toward them.

A deafening crack of gunfire echoed through the square, followed by an eerie silence, then the sound of Sheila screaming.

60

Tex drove to Connaught Square, his heart racing as fast as the car's engine, while Eve tried to get an update on the shooting. "They're checking," she said, covering the receiver of her cell phone.

"Come on, come on," he said as a bus slowed in the lane ahead of him.

"Yes. I'm here . . ." Eve listened, then, "Oh my God. Are you sure? Do *not* let him die. We need him."

Tex whipped around the bus, too impatient to wait. "What happened?" he asked, glancing over at her, then back at the road.

"I'm still trying to figure it out. Just get us there."

"I'm trying." He turned off of the Edgeware Road, hoping to avoid the traffic, instead turning onto Kendal, a much quieter street, before making a left on Portsea Place. But when he reached Connaught, he saw that the police had the square cordoned off and were redirecting all traffic away from the area. When Tex reached the blockade, he rolled down his window as an ambulance, its siren blaring, came in from the other side. The officer waved it through, then turned to Tex. "You'll have to turn back around, sir."

"One of our agents was involved in the shooting."

"Do you have some identification, then?"

He did not, and just when he wondered how they were going to get past the blockade, the officer answered to someone on the radio. "Apparently they know you," he said, then waved Tex through.

He pulled up behind the ambulance, leaving plenty of space for them to work. When they got out, Eve saw the car riddled with bullet holes. "Jesus."

He looked around, saw Sheila talking to an officer, clearly shaken.

"About time you two got here."

Tex spun around, saw Carillo beside the ambulance. "You *stole* a taxi?"

"Stole is kinda a harsh word."

"I'm sure everyone at Scotland Yard will agree. What happened?"

"The passenger pulled a gun as they came around the corner. I think the officers took offense." Carillo looked back to where the medics were covering a body with a blanket to shield it from view.

"That him?"

"Yep. The driver got lucky. Took a couple in the arm."

"He say anything?"

"Can't shut him up. Almost like his life flashed before his eyes. The way I see it, when MI5, then MI6 gets done debriefing him, you two are going to be very, very busy."

"That almost sounds like you're not planning on sticking around."

"Soon as we clear up the little misunderstanding about the taxi, we're outta here. Maybe even a real vacation. The kind that consists of a six-pack of beer and my couch."

"You sure? We could use you."

Carillo nodded in Sheila's direction. "I need to get her back before she completely loses it. But do me a favor? When you get that little weasel Trip in your clutches?"

"Done."

Tex and Eve walked into the conference room at New Scotland Yard to meet with Detective Inspector Whitmore of the City of London Police, who was assigned to the murder of Marty Blanford, and Detective Inspector Talbott of the Metropolitan Police, who was handling the shooting at Connaught Square. Because the cases were related, they were now combining forces, and the two DCIs had just returned from interviewing their suspect at the hospital, who confirmed that the weapon found at the scene of the shooting in front of the prime minister's residence was the same weapon used to kill Marty out at Blackfriars Bridge.

"Actually the news gets even better," Talbott informed them. "This Trip you've been searching for? According to our suspect—a man named Willis—Trip is sitting in some locked room trying to save his hide with this Barclay fellow, by sending him here and there for this missing book that is likely to shut down Barclay's entire operation. They don't seem to realize you've recovered it already."

"Maybe," Tex said, "we can use that to our advantage."

"How so?" DCI Talbott asked.

"Somehow get word to Barclay about the location of that DVD. See if he takes the bait. Comes after it."

"Brilliant," Talbott said. "If we could come up with a workable plan."

"Trip's sister," Tex said.

To which Eve replied, "Trip is slimy, but he's not that slimy."

"He did, however, throw Sheila out there as bait . . ." They exchanged glances, and Tex smiled as he took out his phone. "Gentlemen, I think we have a plan."

Carillo's emphatic no echoed in Tex's ear.

"C'mon. It's not like she has to be here. You can even have her call from your hotel room."

"You really think he's going to believe anything Sheila tells him?"

"Yeah, I do. Because he's desperate."

"So what's this great plan of yours?"

"She tells him that she's going to have you find it for him. After all, you've saved the day for them how many times? Is there really anything you *can't* do?"

"Regular Superman."

"Exactly. All Sheila needs to do is play the concerned girlfriend, doing the thing she does best—"

"Getting me to do her dirty work."

"Bingo."

"And then she calls him to say you've figured out where it is. Only one problem with that, Sherlock. Sheila's not that good an actress."

"You telling me you can't get her to believe that you'd actually do this for her?"

"I'm pretty sure I'm not that good of a liar."

"C'mon, Carillo . . ."

Tex heard him take a deep breath, then, "Where's the setup going to take place?"

"I think the sister's house."

"Fine. I'll figure a way. Let me know when you want her to make the call."

"Trip? It's Sheila."

"Sheila, love, you're okay?"

"Yes." She glanced at Carillo, who nodded, and then she leaned over the cell phone, talking just above a whisper, something Carillo decided would be best to hide any inconsistencies that Trip might hear in her voice. "I—I needed to talk to you."

"Is something wrong? You sound funny."

"I don't want Tony to hear. He's in the other room. But I heard him talking about this . . . this book you're looking for?"

"What about it?"

When she didn't respond, Carillo slid the paper closer to her. He'd written a script of sorts, and she glanced at it, then shook her head, tears slipping down her cheeks.

Great. He reached over, ended the call.

"I can't do this," she said. "I loved him. He loves me. Or he did."

"The only person Trip loves is Trip."

"I just think he's confused—"

God help him, because the only one confused in this room was her, and when her cell rang and he saw Trip's number there, he realized he had just a few seconds to straighten her out. "Sheila. He *never* loved you." Her lower lip trembled as he said the words. "I may not like you at times, and God knows you don't like me, but I'd *die* before I ever let Trip or any other bastard hurt you. *That*, Sheila, is love."

He slid the ringing cell phone toward her.

She took a deep breath, sat up straight, and he saw a spark of anger, whether directed at him or not, he didn't know. But she answered the call. "Hello?"

"Sheila? Why'd you hang up?"

"Tony walked into the room. I didn't want him to hear."

"Smart thinking. You said he was talking about the book?"

Carillo saw her hesitation, and he nudged the script closer, but she shook her head, saying into the phone, "Yeah. They were talking about what Marty said right before— Right before he was shot. He told them he'd hidden it in a Kipling story."

"Kipling?"

"Yes. So they went back to the house, looking for books by Rudyard Kipling."

"Did they find it?"

"No. But don't you get it?"

"Get what?"

"He never said a *book*. He said *story*."

"I don't get it, Sheila."

"Kipling wrote *The Jungle Book*."

"So?"

She leaned closer to the phone, then lowered her voice in a conspiratorial whisper. "There was a *Jungle Book* DVD case at your sister's house. I saw it. What if he copied it to a DVD and *that's* where he hid it?"

There was a stretch of silence on the other end, then, "My God, Sheila. That's brilliant. I can't believe I didn't think of that. I say, you haven't told Tony about this, have you?"

She looked at Carillo. When he shook his head, she answered, "No. Should I?"

"No. No. I'll have a look first. What if it's nothing? I do have to get going, love. If I find anything, I'll ring you up."

When Sheila heard the beep, signifying the call had disconnected, she held up her middle finger toward the phone, saying, "Ring this up, you bastard." Then, to Carillo, she said, "I can't believe how blind I was."

"Sheila, you did great. Amazing, even."

"Really?"

"Really," he said, taking out his phone to call Tex. When he answered, Carillo said, "It's done."

"We're setting up on the place now. Can't wait to nail the little weasel."

Eve heard the click of the lock, then a faint squeak as the front door opened. Tex tapped her shoulder, pointed, then moved toward the light switch, ready to turn it on when the time was right. They were in the far corner of the darkened kitchen that stank of charred wood and smoke, the damage mostly confined to the stove area. A swath of moonlight fell across the carpet from the window near the TV stand. Sitting right on top was the case to Disney's *The Jungle Book*. There were a few other children's movies on the kitchen counter. Eve heard some static coming from her earpiece, but the radio seemed to be cutting out. There were two officers in the house across the street, watching from the neighbor's front window, as well as two agents parked down the block in a van. She assumed someone was trying to radio them that Trip was on his way in, and she glanced toward Tex. He didn't seem concerned, so she assumed it was only her radio that wasn't working.

A floorboard creaked in the front hall, and then a figure stepped into the living room, seemingly unaware that they were watching from the kitchen. More static. And this time she saw Tex adjusting his earpiece. A moment later he gave her a thumbs-up and flicked on the light.

Trip, the DVD case in his hand, turned toward them, his eyes going wide. "Eve?"

She gave the DVD a pointed look. "*The Jungle Book*? Seems a little juvenile. Even for you."

"This? It's, uh, for Emmie."

"You've found her, then?"

"No. But when she returns. You know, give her something to do."

"He's quite the devoted uncle," Tex said.

"Isn't he?" Eve replied. "So what's on the DVD, then, Trip? What's so important you'd risk coming out in public, especially after having the nerve to sic Barclay's thugs on Sheila and her husband?"

"That?" He laughed, taking a step toward the door. "That was a misunderstanding. And I did call to warn them."

"Or call to see if they'd been killed yet?"

"You've got it all wrong."

Eve stepped forward, eyeing the DVD. "Aren't you going to look at it?"

He snapped open the case and his face drained of color when he found it empty. "Where is it?"

"Ah, geez," Tex said. "Did Sheila forget to mention that we found it the afternoon you left her to burn all alone upstairs? All that evidence against Barclay and A.D.E. scanned onto one disc. Amazing how much stuff you can fit on those things."

"And it's worth millions," Trip said. "Barclay will do anything to get it back."

"Is that all it was to you, Trip?" Eve asked. "A bargaining tool to extort money?"

"Not at first. But there's still a chance we can get something."

"You're an idiot, Trip," Eve told him. "It's too late. We've turned it in."

His face drained of color. "It's not here? Do you realize what you've done? Barclay's going to kill me."

To which Tex said, "Only if he can get a gun into prison, since that's where you're both going."

"Eve," Trip said, taking a step toward her. "You said you'd help me."

"I did help you. You were tied up in that warehouse and I cut you loose."

More static in her earpiece, followed by the sound of the front door opening and closing.

She turned to see who had come in, expecting one of the officers from across the street.

Barclay stood just inside the door, a look of surprise flashing across his face when he saw Eve.

Apparently he wasn't expecting to see her alive—and she might have relished the moment, had he not been pointing a gun at her.

61

"My sources told me you were dead."

The voice came from down the hallway, and Tex, still in the kitchen, couldn't see who it was. Even so, he held his gun at a low ready position, and with his other hand keyed his radio, then tapped at his earpiece. Where the hell was their backup? Something had gone wrong, because he'd heard nothing but static since they'd gotten here.

"Sorry to disappoint you, Mr. Barclay," Eve said, slowly lifting her hands, undoubtedly to warn him, without giving away his presence, that not only was her boss from A.D.E. there, but he was armed. "They probably lied to you so they'd get paid. It seems your little kidnap plot on the Somalian border didn't quite go off as planned."

Trip stepped to the side, away from her.

"Don't move," Barclay ordered. "Either of you."

Tex edged his way toward the living room, then stopped when he realized he could see the hallway and Barclay's reflection in the window. Barclay's gun was pointed toward Eve and Trip, and he raised it, asking, "Where's the DVD, Trip? You promised me it was here."

"I—I thought it was."

Tex knew he either needed to get Eve out of the line of fire or get Barclay into it. He looked around, saw one of the kid's DVDs on the counter, and an idea struck. "I have it," he called out, walking over to the counter, grabbing the DVD, then moving back to where he could see Barclay's reflection. "Do you hear me?"

A burst of static on the radio sounded in his ear, and he realized the backup team could hear him. They must have realized there was a problem with the communication and were letting him know. To be sure, he said, "You do hear me, right?"

A second burst of static came through and he hoped it was a confirmation.

Trip, apparently thinking Tex was talking to them, nodded, pointing in Tex's direction, probably eager to shift attention away from his sorry ass. "He told me he'd found it when I got here."

"Who are you pointing to?" Barclay asked. "Who's talking over there?"

Eve, holding very still, said, "A friend of mine."

Tex unsnapped the case, removing the DVD with one hand, then holding it up, shiny side out. "Look in the window to the right of the television, Barclay." Tex angled the disk back and forth several times. "You see it?" He heard a double click of static on the radio.

"Who are you?" Barclay demanded.

"Eve hired me. To help her find this," he said, moving the DVD back and forth. "Heard it's worth something to you."

"It is."

"Good. Because if anything happens to Eve, I'm gonna make a million copies of it. Front page news."

"And you think you'll get out of here?"

"Yeah, I do. Like you, I've got a gun. And a side door for a quick getaway. So here's how it's going to work. Eve is going to walk over here, get the DVD, toss it to Trip, and then she and I are going to leave out the side door. Agreed?"

"Agreed," Barclay said.

Trip turned a frantic eye toward Eve as she stepped toward the kitchen. "You're not going to leave me here, are you?"

If Trip suspected the DVD was fake, he could ruin it for them. Tex pointed his gun at him. "Zip it, Trip."

As Eve cleared the hallway, Tex, knowing that Barclay could see them, held out the DVD. He waited until Eve was close enough to reach it. But instead of letting her take it, he threw it toward Trip, grabbed Eve's arm, then pulled her behind him.

"It's fake!" Trip cried.

Barclay aimed his gun toward Trip.

A loud explosion sounded and the front and side doors burst open. Tex and Eve were pushed out of the way as uniformed officers carrying shields ran past them, storming the room.

Tex caught a glimpse of Trip diving to the floor, covering his head with his hands, and then Barclay being pushed to the ground as an officer screwed a gun in his ear, ordering him not to move.

He looked at Eve. "You okay?"

"I am now."

Alice walked in, eyed the two of them. "Sorry about that bit of a radio problem."

"Bit? Huge."

"You managed to get past it, and in the end that is what counts, right?" She smiled, then stepped past them to where Barclay lay prone on the floor. "Bring the two of them out to the car. I believe MPS wants to interrogate Mr. Barclay about the spate of shootings in the area."

One of the officers lifted Barclay to his feet, then walked him outside, another following with Trip.

Tex and Eve waited until they cleared before walking out

to join Alice as they proceeded to advise both men of their rights.

"Quite the operation," Alice said. "They're serving search warrants on Barclay's offices here, and I understand they are concurrently being served in the U.S."

Barclay apparently heard, and he halted in his tracks, refusing to get into the police car, so that he could face them. "Serving a search warrant? On my offices? For what? Because a few people get hurt? That happens all over the world. It's collateral damage. What we're doing is for the greater good."

"And what?" Tex said. "You're so blinded by your goodness that you send hit men out to kill anyone who gets in your way?"

"As I said, the greater good."

"Well, greater good this, asshole," Tex said, helping him into the back of the police car. "Don't sleep *too* soundly at night. Wouldn't want to find yourself being dragged out of your cell to be resettled in another country that has the death penalty."

"You can't extradite me."

"Not legally," Tex said, slamming the car door shut.

"You realize," Alice said to Tex, "that they're like ants, these bad charities that are using the refugees for profit. We've stomped on this bunch, but who knows how many more will move in and take up the slack?"

"Maybe so. But no sense rolling out the red carpet for them when they move in."

Eve walked up, placed her hand on Tex's shoulder. "I don't know about you, but I'm ready for a break."

They started to walk away, but he stopped, looked back at Alice. "Thanks for your help."

"Any time, Tex."

"I forgot to ask. Girl or boy?"

"Boy."

He nodded, then grinned. "You could name him after me."

"Recalcitrant is rather a long name for a child, don't you think?"

"Cal for short."

She smiled. "Have a good flight home, Tex."

"Home?" He linked his arm through Eve's. "Not yet. Got a dinner date at the Eiffel Tower."

62

Sydney and Griffin sat at their respective comput-ers, poring over the digital photographs taken by the team that had entered the apartment allegedly used by Yusuf and the others to make a dirty bomb.

Normally Griffin would have been in there searching it himself, but the cesium 137 contamination necessitated the hands-off approach. Though he hadn't yet seen the report from NEST and the bomb squad, the photographic evidence was clear: pipes, caps, wires, glass jars, nails, detonators, and two empty digital watch boxes on the floor. It was essentially everything they needed to make a couple of bombs.

That and the now empty capsule that had at one time contained the cesium 137 was disconcerting, to say the least. The highest reading came from the kitchen tabletop, a smaller amount on the floor. Most of the highly radioactive substance was still missing, and the only logical assumption was that they had managed to complete at least one bomb, but evidence showed they could have made two.

It was exactly what they'd feared. And though every law

enforcement agency was on high alert, unless they came across something that told them where Yusuf might be heading, the odds of finding him in time were dwindling with each passing second.

"There's nothing here," Sydney said, rubbing her neck. "I've been over every scrap they photographed."

"Keep looking. It's clear we interrupted them in the middle of this thing. If we're lucky, they dropped something, made a mistake."

Sydney leaned back in her chair, then switched the mouse to the other hand, probably to give it a rest. "If they left—"

She stopped when the phone rang.

Griffin answered, and the secretary said, "There's a Mr. Abasi on line two."

"Thank you."

He picked up the second line. "Mr. Abasi, what can I do for you?"

"I have been thinking about the man who was walking by right before we ran out of the flyers. He took one and crumpled it, shoving it in his pocket as though he did not care."

"What about him?"

"I've seen him upstairs in the vicinity of the apartment where you found the radiation. According to the neighbor, he is a visitor who arrived on the very night you indicated. There is no other apartment he could have belonged to, and the fact he did not care . . . Who living there doesn't care?"

"Your point, Mr. Abasi?"

"My point, Mr. Griffin, is that I recalled what he was wearing, which may help you find him. A black leather jacket, and a black hooded sweatshirt beneath the jacket, because he had the hood on. I saw him earlier in the day when his jacket was not zipped. The sweatshirt beneath had a San Francisco Giants logo on it."

"Thank you, Mr. Abasi. That does help."

"One more thing, Mr. Griffin. The boy across the street?

He said that the man was carrying a large blue backpack when he left, and a smaller black bag."

Griffin thanked him once more, then, just to be sure that the subject Abasi saw was not one of the men already in custody, he called the team that had made the arrest. "The suspects you picked up from the apartment. Any of them wearing a black hooded San Francisco Giants sweatshirt or black leather jacket?"

"Not a one," the agent said.

"Thanks."

He hung up, then called McNiel. "We need to get a clothing description added to the bulletin." He gave him Mr. Abasi's description.

"I'll get it out at once. We've got officers canvassing the neighborhood now. If we're lucky, we'll find someone who saw something."

Their luck changed an hour later. McNiel phoned Griffin with the intel. "We have a video siting of him at a convenience store a couple blocks from the apartments. The police have already been by and are following it up. But I want you two over there to see if there's anything they might have overlooked."

"We're on it."

Apparently the clerk had seen the news report on TV of the suspected terrorist but hadn't made a connection until the police walked in with the new bulletin and a clothing description. "It was the Giants logo on his sweatshirt that caught my eye," the clerk told Griffin. "You could just make it out in the vee of his coat? So first thing I said was, 'You from California?' And he's like, not hearing me, and then some customers came in to pay for gas. Next thing I know, he's gone."

"Can you run the video for us?" Griffin asked.

"Sure."

He took them in the back office, brought it up on the computer monitor, pointing to the screen as a man matching Yusuf's description entered the store with a heavily weighted backpack on his shoulder. He walked to the back, took a bottle of water from the refrigerated cooler, then strode up to the counter, where he had to wait while another customer paid for a purchase. They saw the moment where the clerk tried to engage him in conversation.

As stated, he seemed not to be listening, his attention apparently fixed on a small-screen television mounted on the wall behind the cash register. Several customers walked in and up to the counter, and then suddenly he turned to leave, pausing near a rack at the door. It looked as if he picked something up, but his back was to the camera and they couldn't see.

"What's on that rack?" Griffin asked.

"Tourist stuff. Maps and postcards."

Sydney asked for a copy of the video, and waited while the clerk made one for her. In the meantime, Griffin retraced Yusuf's path through the store, trying to see what he saw.

The main body of the store yielded nothing, and he returned to the counter, stood there, eyed the TV and the commercial currently playing, advertising toothpaste. He didn't see anything else of interest, then moved to the rack where the maps and postcards were displayed. There were at least a dozen various photos of Washington, D.C., landmarks but nothing that stood out. Besides, a terrorist would have a hard time getting to any of the monuments or museums with that backpack.

The maps, however, seemed a more likely prospect. Especially for someone who knew where he wanted to go but didn't know how to get there.

But where was it he wanted to go?

The billion-dollar question.

Griffin went back over the video in his mind, a thought forming as he walked the route again, past the refrigerator. This time, like Yusuf, he grabbed a bottle, walked up to the counter to pay. There had been a customer in front of Yusuf, and Griffin recalled from the video that Yusuf had turned his attention to the TV while he waited . . .

And then left without his water.

Something on TV caught his attention, made him forget his purchase.

Griffin returned to the back office. "Play the video again."

The clerk ran it a second time.

Yusuf walking in, grabbing the water, counter, waiting, TV . . .

"Stop it there."

He leaned forward, tried to see what was on the television but couldn't quite make it out. "Do you remember what channel was playing?" he asked the clerk.

"The same one that's on now. The afternoon news show. Channel 3."

Sydney took out her phone. "I'll find out what was airing."

"I can tell you," the clerk said. "They were showing that party at that new power hot spot, according to the newscaster."

"What party?" Griffin asked.

"At that rooftop restaurant that just opened up near the White House? Invitation only for the grand opening, so they're covering all the celebrities and politicians who are there. Like anybody even cares. C'mon. It's Washington, right?"

Griffin thought of one person who might care. "Is the DVD finished?"

The clerk ejected it from the computer and handed it over.

In the car, Sydney said, "Definite confirmation from the news station. They have cameras in the restaurant as we speak."

"Call McNiel and Pearson. They need to notify the White House and Secret Service. Tell them we're on our way."

"Oh my God. Scotty's there."

"You're sure?"

"Definitely. He asked me to go with him."

63

Yusuf stood across the street, looking up at the top of the hotel he'd seen on the news. The restaurant was ten stories up, and as soon as he'd heard them mentioning the guests, the political leaders and movie stars, he knew that was exactly where he needed to be.

It no longer mattered that their original target, the Metro subway, was probably now crawling with police all on the lookout for him.

This was by far a better choice.

There were already news cameras, which meant the world would see the explosion live. His name would be remembered, and he almost wished he would be around to see the news footage that would flood the airwaves.

He crossed the street toward the hotel, noticing people at the glass doors, checking the IDs of everyone who entered. The news reporter had said it was an invitation only event, the hotel and restaurant closed to the public.

Yusuf continued past the front, then on around the block until he came to the rear of the hotel. There was a truck backed up to a loading dock, and two men were unloading boxes from it. One man wore blue coveralls, the other a white uniform, the sort a restaurant worker might wear.

Yusuf walked closer, saying, "I'm supposed to start working here today. Is this where I enter?"

The man in white nodded toward a door near the dock that stood propped open with a brick. "Through there."

He entered, wandering down a long hallway, not sure where to go when he reached the end that branched off in a tee. A man stepped around the corner, then stopped short on seeing him. "Are you the busboy the temp agency sent over?"

He had no idea what a busboy or temp agency was. "Yes."

"I needed five. Not one." He gave an exasperated sigh. "Better hurry on up, then. They need you."

Yusuf nodded, and when the man raised his brows, as though expecting some sort of action, Yusuf started past him.

"Hey! What do you think you're doing?"

Yusuf stopped, his heart starting to thud.

"Gotta have a uniform. This way," the man said, leading him in the opposite direction, then stopping by a door. He opened it, pointing to stacks of white shirts and pants. "Find your size, get dressed, and then take the service elevator up."

"Service elevator?"

"Right over there." He pointed down the hall. "Tenth floor. When you get up there, take a left to the kitchen. They'll show you what to do."

64

Pick up, Scotty, pick up . . .

Sydney received Scotty's voice mail, again, and disconnected.

Griffin was driving hell-bent toward the hotel. He glanced over at her. "Maybe Scotty decided not to go."

"Oh, trust me. This is right up his alley," she said, trying his number again, this time unblocking hers so he could see it on the screen. "No way would he miss it."

He answered, and she heard music and talking in the background. "Scotty, thank God."

"Sydney? I can barely hear you. What's wrong?"

"Are you at that party? The rooftop thing?"

"What? Yes. I told you I was going."

"I'm on my way there. The terrorist they're looking for—"

"Hold on. Can't hear a word," he said loudly. A few moments later, the music greatly muted, the voices not as loud, he came back on, saying, "You're coming here?"

"Yes, I—"

"You told me you didn't want to go. I brought Amanda."

"For God's sake, Scotty, will you shut up for a second? I'm talking about the terrorist. We think he may be on his way to your location with a dirty bomb."

". . . Here? Why?"

"He saw it on the news. With all the coverage, it's a very convenient high-profile target. One he actually has a chance of getting into."

"Security's pretty tight. He can't get in without an invitation."

"Let's hope not. But he had an hour head start. He could already be there."

"Has someone called Secret Service?"

"Yes."

"How long until you're here?"

"We're just a couple minutes away."

Scotty and the head of hotel security were waiting for them when they pulled up in front of the hotel. Griffin double-parked, and Sydney grabbed the folder with photos of Yusuf as she got out.

"How sure are you about this?" Scotty asked Sydney.

"We're not sure about anything yet, but are you willing to take a chance?"

"Me? No. I already sent Amanda home in a cab. But there are about a half-dozen senators upstairs who are going to be very upset if you yank the rug out from under their feet for a false alarm."

"Have you told them?"

"You obviously haven't been up there yet. They wouldn't be able to hear me if I shouted it from a loudspeaker. It's over capacity as it is."

Griffin was watching the front entrance of the hotel, and she asked, "What are you thinking?"

"That he wouldn't have come in this way." Griffin turned to the security head; Mason, according to his name tag. "If you were trying to sneak in, how would you do it?"

"The only possible way is the back. We've got deliveries going all day, stocking up for the week's grand opening events once it opens to the public. There's a security guard out there who's supposed to be checking every person who comes in."

"How many people in the hotel?"

"In the rooms? None. The renovation's not finished yet. And the construction workers have the day off so there wouldn't be any noise during the party. The only people in the building are staff on the first floor and the top floor in the restaurant. They can't even access the other floors unless they use the stairs."

"Okay," Griffin said. "Scotty, I could use your help in clearing the building."

"I'm in."

"Syd?"

"I'll go with Mason to see if anyone matching that description came through."

Griffin and Scotty briefed the hotel manager, then headed in the opposite direction to the main elevator. Sydney left with Mason through the lobby.

"This way," Mason said, leading her down a hall, the dark carpet soaking up most of the light. Eventually they reached another door, which he opened, allowing her to enter first. The passage continued, but unlike the area they'd just left, the floor here was an industrial off-white linoleum, reflecting the fluorescent lighting overhead. They continued on, made a right turn, and eventually came to the loading dock, where a security guard stood watch as a truck backed down the ramp and a worker guided the driver.

When the guard noticed Mason, he stood a bit straighter. Sydney opened her folder, showing him Yusuf's photo, and Mason asked, "Have you seen anyone who looks like him?"

The guard shook his head, but then called out, "Hey, Zeke. C'mere a sec."

The man held up his hand, indicating the truck driver should stop, and he walked over. "Yeah?"

Sydney showed him the photo. "Have you seen him?"

"He one of the temp workers?"

She looked at Mason, who said, "We hired extra workers from an agency to cover the party." To Zeke, he said, "You saw someone who looked like him?"

"Boy . . . We had, what? Maybe five or six come through. But he reminds me of the last one."

"How long ago was that?" Sydney asked.

"Fifteen, twenty minutes, I guess."

Mason then instructed Zeke to turn away the driver and shut down the deliveries. The security guard was told that no one goes in, only out. "Tell all employees to meet in front of the Treasury Building. We're clearing the premises."

"For what?" Zeke asked.

Mason looked to Sydney for an answer, and she said, "Gas leak. Danger of explosion." Far less panic that way. She hoped.

Zeke, however, didn't seem to be buying the explanation. At least not all of it. "Why the photo? I mean, he have something to do with it?"

"We're not sure," was all she said. "But if you see him, call 911."

He nodded, undoubtedly making his own assumptions, and left to inform the truck driver of the delay, while she and Mason returned inside. "Where would he have gone if he was pretending to be a worker?" she asked.

"He'd need a uniform. Down here." Mason led her back through the hallway into what appeared to be a large linen supply room, where uniforms and towels were folded on shelves. "He would have changed in the men's locker room, however." That was two doors down, and he knocked on the door before opening it for her. She placed her hand on her gun, moving from the edge of the door only after she could see inside. It was simply a large room with lockers around the perimeter.

Several didn't have locks, and she started opening them. The fourth one contained khaki pants, a black leather jacket and, on top of them, a Giants sweatshirt. She closed the door quickly. "This room needs to be secured. It could be contaminated."

They backed out. "Now what?"

"Now we go upstairs and get everyone the hell out of here."

Mason's hand shook as he turned the key in the lock. The threat hadn't been real until then, and she figured that confronting a terrorist with a dirty bomb was not something he'd ever anticipated running into in the hotel security business.

"What's the fastest way to the rooftop?" Sydney asked.

"The service elevator. It's probably how he got to the kitchen from here."

He led her to it, then hit the button. When it opened, several men and women—kitchen workers, judging from the food stains on their white uniforms—stepped off, and Sydney looked at each face, but didn't see her suspect. No fear, only confusion, and she took that as a good sign. One woman saw Mason, telling him, "We were told we had to leave the building. What's going on?"

"We think there's a gas leak. Nothing to worry about. Meet at the Treasury Building."

And when he would have followed Sydney, she said, "I think it might be wiser for you to stay down here. Guide everyone who's leaving the party through the lobby out the doors."

"Of course," he said, looking vastly relieved. She pressed the Up button, and as the doors closed, he said, "Be careful."

It was a quick ride to the top. The elevator opened in a nearly deserted kitchen, a few workers waiting to descend. Sydney searched the faces, immediately discounting the women, ruling out the men who didn't fit the profile.

Her weapon drawn, she opened the first door she came to, and found a room filled with large bins of dirty towels, aprons, and uniforms, waiting to be taken to the laundry. She was just about to step in when a noise caught her attention and she looked up. She saw a woman in a black and white uniform backing slowly from the main kitchen, her attention fixed on the double doors that led out, probably to the dining area.

The girl turned, clearly frightened, even more so when she saw Sydney's gun.

"FBI," Sydney told her in a low voice, eyeing the name tag on her shirt. "Carla. What's going on out there?"

"A man's got a bomb. He put it on a table and he's going to set it off."

"Any more workers?"

Carla shook her head.

"Take the elevator down. When you get off, press the Up button for me."

"Okay."

When she looked ready to bolt, Sydney put her finger to her lips. "Slowly, quietly."

She nodded, then left, and Sydney moved to the kitchen doors, grateful that the kitchen was closed off from the main dining area. Though a small window would have been nice, working with what she had, she pressed slightly, opening the door just enough to see out. On the right, tables and chairs were arranged next to floor-to-ceiling windows that gave an impressive and commanding view of the capital skyline with the Washington Monument in the distance. At the moment, every table was empty, including those outside on the terrace.

She hoped that meant the restaurant was also empty, but the look on that girl's face as she'd turned around told her otherwise, and she edged the door open wider.

A man dressed like a restaurant worker, his back to her, stood in the middle of the room, addressing a group of people standing in a knot by the bar, Griffin and Scotty included. Yusuf. He raised one hand, held up a cell phone, his thumb poised over the keypad. With his other hand, he pointed at something, and she glanced in that direction, saw several PVC pipes bound together with tape and wire on a table near the door that led out to the lobby. "No one else move," he said. "No one leaves. No one goes near that door to try to escape, or I blow it up and everyone in here dies."

A clear indication to shoot if she ever saw one. And she might have, had not Griffin and Scotty stood directly behind him.

Right in the line of fire.

65

The movement of the kitchen door caught Griffin's attention, and he saw Sydney through the crack, her gun pointed in their direction.

He wanted to tell her to leave, not to risk her life, and he willed the information to her, wishing for once she'd do the right thing.

Instead she opened the door more, and he knew that if she was going to be successful, they needed a distraction.

He didn't expect that it would come from Yusuf himself. The man apparently recognized Senator Burgess and pointed to her. "I saw you on TV," Yusuf said. "Move over here with the others."

Senator Burgess looked at the group, then at Griffin, her gaze narrowing.

"Now!" Yusuf said. "Or everyone dies."

She didn't move.

"Now!"

From the corner of his eye Griffin saw Sydney slip into the room, heard Scotty whispering, "Jesus," and knew exactly what she was doing.

Time to help. "Senator. He's not joking. Do as he says."

Sydney took a tentative step forward, and Yusuf, his attention still fixed on the senator, said, "Yes! I am not joking!" then held his phone higher. And with every step the senator took, Sydney edged from the kitchen door, clearing the way for a shot.

In the distance, Griffin heard the sound of a helicopter, undoubtedly coming from the White House. Whether to move the President from the grounds or from the Secret Service to get eyes on the interior of the restaurant, he didn't know. Right now their best chance was with a lone FBI agent who stood behind a wooden door, about twenty feet behind Yusuf.

One more step and he thought she'd have it, but then the rotors of the helicopter were suddenly visible as it rose in front of the windows, the glass shuddering with the spinning blades. Yusuf, startled by the sound, turned in that direction.

Sydney pushed out, to the side, gaining the angle, firing twice.

The bullets pierced through his body. The phone flew from his hand.

The bomb detonated.

66

The blast knocked Griffin back. His head hit the bar behind him.

He sat there, stunned for several seconds, his ears ringing. He looked around for Sydney, saw her moving toward Yusuf, who was sprawled on the carpet a few feet away. She pointed her gun at the man's chest, said, "Is he dead?"

Griffin shook himself, got up, checked Yusuf's carotid. "Yes."

"You okay?" she asked, holstering her weapon.

"Fine." He looked around at the others, several dozen men and women, some on the floor, others standing, many with shrapnel cuts. They'd survived. He wasn't sure about the man and woman nearest the door, lying there, not moving. A strange silence pervaded the room, and then a murmur of low, panicked voices grew as they started to rouse themselves, take in the situation.

A woman started crying, and someone said, "Oh my God!"

"Scotty," Griffin said. "I need you and Sydney to get everyone out. Now. And no cell phones."

Scotty nodded and he and Sydney started helping others to their feet, then guiding them to the lobby, Sydney directing them to the stairs, not the elevator. Senator Burgess, her face pale, her hands shaking, probably from being singled out, did not exit with the others. Instead, she moved toward the injured couple near the door, kneeling down beside them. When Scotty returned, he reached for the senator's hand to help her up but she shook her head no. "I used to be a nurse. I'm not leaving until these people get help." She took the woman's arm, placed her fingers on her wrist, feeling for a pulse. Her gaze, however, landed on Yusuf. "Who is that?" she asked Griffin. "And why did he target us?"

"A loophole in your refugee program."

"I don't understand."

"And I don't have time to go into it right now," he said, then regretted his sharp tone. She was only trying to help. "How are they?"

"Alive." She turned her attention back to the woman. "I'll stay with them until the EMTs arrive."

"We can't let anyone up here," he replied. "There may be a secondary device."

The senator looked up sharply. "Another bomb?"

"The first was probably a distraction," Griffin replied as Scotty and Sydney walked in from the lobby. "Why else make it so obvious? There were two empty watch boxes in that apartment, which means two timers."

"Jesus," Scotty said. "What do you want us to do?"

Griffin eyed the couple on the floor by the senator, the man trying to sit up, the woman just beginning to stir. "Get those two out of here. Scotty? Do you think you and the senator can handle that, while Sydney and I search?"

"Sure."

Scotty moved to the senator's side, and together, they tried to assist the man to his feet. It was clear he was going to have trouble, probably due to the blow on the head. He was a big man, too big for the senator to help, and Griffin doubted she'd be able to carry the woman on her own. Scotty would have to drag them out.

So be it, he thought, motioning Sydney away, out of the senator's hearing. "I don't suppose you saw his backpack on your way up? I'm guessing it contains the bomb with the cesium 137."

"Just his clothes downstairs. I made a cursory search in the kitchen, but there's a dozen places he could have stashed it." She angled her head toward the windows. "That helicopter spooked him when the glass started rattling."

Griffin looked in that direction. "Enough to think it might have been the second bomb going off?"

"Definitely."

"It makes sense. Yusuf would want to take out as many people as he could. Where better than the dining area?"

"And he wanted everyone away from the door."

"Let's start at the windows and move in."

Sydney took the end closest to the bar, and Griffin started near the kitchen. He saw several tray stands against the wall, each draped with a red cloth to cover the aluminum legs and wheels. He pulled up the first one, found nothing. Repeated it with each. All empty. Griffin started looking around the room, realized just how many there were. Yusuf would have seen the same. He would have picked one centrally located.

Before Griffin finished the thought, Sydney called out.

"It's here!"

The tray stand draped with red cloth was next to the bar, covered with glasses and plates from the revelers. Not even noticeable, until Sydney held up the red draping. He saw the dark blue backpack sitting in a gray dish tray beneath it.

"I'd feel a lot better about this if you weren't here," he said.

"What about you?" Sydney asked.

"Unless you know something about defusing bombs, I'm all that's left."

"And you're going to need help until the bomb squad arrives."

"Assuming we even have that much time. Go see where Scotty and the senator are."

Sydney moved toward the door, glanced out. "They've got them by the stairwell."

Griffin lifted the red cloth that draped the tray, noting there was nothing around it. No wires, just a backpack sitting upright in the plastic bin. He slid the knife from his boot, inserted the tip of the blade and sliced slowly up through the canvas, careful to keep his knife from touching anything inside. He cut across as well, until he could peel back the sides of the backpack, revealing the bomb beneath.

"Oh, shit."

"Oh, shit?" She returned to his side. "That phrase does *not* go good with bombs."

He pointed. "Photoelectric switch. It started the timer once the light hit it." He tried to think what he'd need to work in this area. "Bring me one of those big laundry hampers filled with very wet towels. Roll it out here, then empty half of the towels out."

She ran toward the kitchen. A moment later he heard water running, and was glad she was out of the room in case this thing went off unexpectedly. The bomb seemed fairly simple. Several pipes taped together; wires leading to the zippered opening, which would have set it off had he tried to unzip it; and wires to the photoelectric cell and also to another cell phone. Had Sydney not killed Yusuf after he set off the first bomb, he would have undoubtedly set off the second one as they tried to move away from the first explosion. She'd bought them some much needed time, and he used his knife to tilt the digital watch to see exactly how long.

Four minutes, twenty-nine seconds and counting down fast.

That, however, was not what set his heart racing. There at the bottom, a clear plastic zip-top bag containing the bluish white powder.

The good news was that if it blew before he could take action, he wasn't likely to suffer a slow radiation death. Sydney, however, wouldn't be so lucky, since the powder would spread with the blast. Gray duct tape was used to secure the bag of powder to the bomb, and he used his knife to slice down the right side of the tape, careful not to pierce the bag or touch the pipes. He cut slowly.

The kitchen doors clattered open as Sydney pushed the cart through. Heavy with wet towels, she had to lean into it as she wheeled it toward him, then started pulling the sloshing towels onto the floor as he sliced into the tape.

He stopped. His heart thudded at the near fatal mistake.

He gently slid the knife out.

This was *not* going to end well.

Scotty showed up in the doorway. "We need help. The man can't walk on his own. He's too big for the senator, and she can't carry the woman, who's still mostly out of it."

Sydney didn't move.

"Go!" Griffin ordered. Syd hesitated, clearly not wanting to leave him. He looked up at her. "There's less than three minutes for me to try to contain the bomb. I can't worry about you. Not while I'm trying to do this."

He could see the indecision in her eyes. "Okay," she said, then turned and ran after Scotty.

The second she cleared the restaurant doors, he lifted the plastic tray, backpack and all, setting it inside the large hamper. He gathered the wet towels, laid them on top, his eye catching on the timer as he covered the backpack. One minute fifteen seconds. He tried not to think about her as he examined the bomb, the tape across the powder, and the wire hidden behind the tape. If only he had more time. If only he had a way to get the powder from the device.

This thing was going to explode and there was *nothing* he could do about it.

All he knew was that when this thing blew, he didn't want it anywhere near Sydney and that stairwell.

67

The sound of heavy booted feet echoed up the stairs
as Sydney and the senator carried the woman down, Scotty
and the injured man following behind them. It was slow
going. The woman was near dead weight, and the senator
felt the need to query Scotty about Yusuf and this loophole
Griffin had mentioned.

"Not the right time, Senator," Scotty said.

"I intend to fix it. This loophole," she said. "Or try."

"That's all we can ask."

They'd just reached the second landing down, nearly running head on into three men in black gear, armed, helmeted,
gloved, and wearing gas masks. Undoubtedly members
from the NEST team.

The first man took the woman from them, hefted her into
his arms, then turned back, headed down.

The second and third officers stepped up to assist Scotty,
when the bomb exploded.

The stairwell shook. It felt like an earthquake rocked the
building, and Sydney balanced herself against the side, her
heart racing as she looked toward the top of the stairs. The

whole world seemed to stop in that one moment. No one moved. Suddenly her heart started thudding as she realized what had happened. "Griffin!"

Scotty grabbed her around the middle, and her knees started to give out.

She gripped the banister. "He's in there."

"We'll find him. I promise." He pulled her hand free from the banister, guided her forward.

The next few seconds and minutes blurred together. She had no idea how she got down the next eight flights of stairs and out to the street. The whole time, Scotty held her tight, refusing to let her back into the building.

"He did it," Scotty said. "He saved everyone."

Only then was she aware of the chaos around her. The police cars cordoning off the block, the sound of sirens as fire trucks rushed to the area. And then Scotty was leading her across the street to the back of a white utility truck, where uniformed personnel were removing equipment. One turned around and ran a radiation detector up and down the length of her.

"She's clean."

He moved off to check someone else, and Sydney turned, looked over at the hotel, her gaze moving up the stories to the top, toward the restaurant she couldn't quite see from this angle. She had no idea what sort of damage was done, if it had been survivable. She couldn't see smoke or signs of a fire, and she prayed that was a good sign.

"I think we should have EMS look you over," Scotty said, taking her hand once more.

"I'm fine," she told him. "I need to find Griffin."

"They're not letting anyone in there."

He was right about that. They had stationed uniformed officers around the entrances of the hotel to keep everyone out as NEST prepared to enter.

"Besides, Sydney, there's something I wanted to talk to you about."

"Not now, Scotty. Please."

"The Wingman Squared case."

She looked at him, and it took a moment for her to gather her thoughts. "Why would you bring that up now?"

"Because you left the coffee shop before I could finish telling you, and it's not like I can talk about this in the office. I know you think you know everything about BICTT and your father's case, but . . . well, when this is all cleared up out here, when you want to come by, I—I have a file you might be interested in."

"A file . . . ?"

Someone shouted, and several people started running in that direction. She turned, tried to figure out what was going on. And then she saw him. A half block away, coming from the side of the hotel.

"Oh my God. Griffin . . ."

She started toward him, and Scotty caught her hand, stopping her. "Sydney?"

She looked at Scotty, realizing he was expecting some sort of answer, putting his job on the line by letting her see a file she shouldn't see. "Can we talk about this later? Tomorrow."

He hesitated and she had the distinct feeling that he didn't want to let her go. He looked past her toward Griffin, then finally dropped her hand. "Sure. Tomorrow."

She turned, ran across the street, but the men with the radiation detectors swooped down on him before she could reach his side, taking readings, then, finding residue on his hands, hustling him off to a station for decontamination. She wasn't allowed in shouting distance, and when they finished that, the EMTs cut her off as they helped Griffin toward the ambulance. He was limping and it grew more pronounced the longer he walked. They had him take a seat on the back bumper of the ambulance while they looked at his leg.

"Doesn't seem to be broken," one of the EMTs said. "But we should probably take you to the hospital, have it looked over."

"Twisted my ankle. It'll be fine."

When he stood, she hesitated the barest of seconds, then threw herself into his arms. He kissed her, holding her tight, and when he finally pulled back, he simply looked at her.

"What?" she said.

"Nothing," he replied, digging his keys from his pocket and handing them to her. "Just glad to see you, that's all."

They started toward the car, Griffin limping beside her. "So . . ." she started, not even sure what to say at first, then decided on the obvious. "How'd you get hurt?"

"The usual. Jumping down the stairwell after I rolled the bomb into the walk-in freezer."

She looked up at him and smiled. "Just another day at the office, Griffin?"

"Yep." He put his arm around her, then leaned in close, whispering, "Makes me look forward to quitting time."

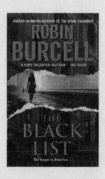